OXFORI

EAR

WOME… WRITING

PAUL SALZMAN is a senior lecturer in the School of English, La Trobe University, Melbourne, Australia. He is the author of *English Prose Fiction 1558–1700: A Critical History* (Oxford, 1985) and has published and edited extensively in the areas of sixteenth- and seventeenth-century prose fiction and women's writing.

OXFORD WORLD'S CLASSICS

For over 100 years Oxford World's Classics have brought readers closer to the world's great literature. Now with over 700 titles—from the 4,000-year-old myths of Mesopotamia to the twentieth century's greatest novels—the series makes available lesser-known as well as celebrated writing.

The pocket-sized hardbacks of the early years contained introductions by Virginia Woolf, T. S. Eliot, Graham Greene, and other literary figures which enriched the experience of reading. Today the series is recognized for its fine scholarship and reliability in texts that span world literature, drama and poetry, religion, philosophy and politics. Each edition includes perceptive commentary and essential background information to meet the changing needs of readers.

OXFORD WORLD'S CLASSICS

Early Modern Women's Writing

An Anthology, 1560–1700

Edited with an Introduction and Notes by

PAUL SALZMAN

OXFORD
UNIVERSITY PRESS

Great Clarendon Street, Oxford OX2 6DP

Oxford University Press is a department of the University of Oxford.
It furthers the University's objective of excellence in research, scholarship,
and education by publishing worldwide in

Oxford New York

Athens Auckland Bangkok Bogotá Buenos Aires Calcutta
Cape Town Chennai Dar es Salaam Delhi Florence Hong Kong Istanbul
Karachi Kuala Lumpur Madrid Melbourne Mexico City Mumbai
Nairobi Paris São Paulo Singapore Taipei Tokyo Toronto Warsaw

with associated companies in Berlin Ibadan

Oxford is a registered trade mark of Oxford University Press
in the UK and in certain other countries

Published in the United States
by Oxford University Press Inc., New York

First published as an Oxford World's Classics paperback 2000
Reissued 2008

British Library Cataloguing in Publication Data

Data available

Library of Congress Cataloging in Publication Data

Data available

ISBN 978-0-19-954967-2

13

Typeset in Ehrhardt
by RefineCatch Limited, Bungay, Suffolk
Printed in Great Britain by
Clays Ltd, Elcograf S.p.A.

CONTENTS

ACKNOWLEDGEMENTS

This edition was completed with the assistance of an Australian Research Council Small Grant and grants from the La Trobe University Faculty of Humanities and Social Sciences. Colleagues in the School of English have, as always, been extremely supportive. The scholars who work on women writers of the sixteenth and seventeenth centuries are particularly generous with advice and assistance and I owe a great deal to their collective and individual encouragement. I particularly wish to thank Elaine Hobby for many invaluable suggestions; Marion Wynne-Davies for her generous assistance with *Love's Victory*; Mihoko Suzuki; Jo Wallwork; James Fitzmaurice; Kate Lilley; and members of the Margaret Cavendish discussion list, in particular Elizabeth Hageman, Anne Shaver, Susanne Woods, Alexandra Bennett, Deborah Taylor-Pearce, Jeffrey Masten, Jennifer Rowsell, Anna Battigelli, and Deborah Burks.

Thanks as usual go to Susan Bye for her patience and critical assistance and to Imogen, Joseph, and Charles for cheering me up.

Use of the Huntington Library manuscript of *Love's Victory* (HM 600) is made with the kind permission of the Huntington Library, San Marino, California.

Material from the Portland Papers is included by permission of the Marquess of Bath, Longleat House, Warminster, Wiltshire, Great Britain.

ABBREVIATIONS

ELH	*English Literary History*
ELN	*English Language Notes*
ELR	*English Literary Renaissance*
HLQ	*Huntington Library Quarterly*
MLQ	*Modern Language Quarterly*
MLR	*Modern Language Review*
NM	*Neuphilologische Mitteilungen*
PQ	*Philological Quarterly*
SEL	*Studies in English Literature 1500–1900*

INTRODUCTION

In a famous passage in *A Room of One's Own*, Virginia Woolf asked 'why women did not write poetry in the Elizabethan age'.[1] She went on to speculate about an imaginary Judith Shakespeare, who might have been destined for a career as illustrious as that of her brother William, except that she had none of his chances and, in Woolf's vision, committed suicide. The truth is that many women wrote during the sixteenth and seventeenth centuries, though their writing careers were certainly more obscure than that of Shakespeare. This collection should serve to introduce modern readers to the full variety of women's writing from the late sixteenth century until the end of the seventeenth century. During that time quite a number of Judith Shakespeares did indeed write plays; they also wrote poems, prose fiction, diaries, prophecies, letters, tracts, philosophy—any genre that men wrote in attracted at least some women writers.

This collection begins with the poetry of Isabella Whitney, published in the late 1560s and early 1570s, and it ends with a selection of the varied output of the first English woman writer who could be described as professional: Aphra Behn, whose work began to appear in the 1670s and continued to be published until nearly the end of the seventeenth century. The 'early modern' in the title of this anthology points to the development of women's writing during the late-sixteenth and seventeenth centuries, part of the period labelled 'early modern' by historians because they have seen it as transitional between medieval and modern. The twelve women whose work is collected here represent a sample of a considerable body of writing by women during this period. Until recently it was thought, following on from Virginia Woolf, that early modern women writers were extremely scarce. It has now become evident, as manuscript sources as well as printed books are uncovered, that while far fewer women wrote than men (it has been estimated that an average of 1 per cent of all published writing in the seventeenth century was produced by women), a bibliography of published and unpublished writing from Whitney to Behn would still run to thousands of items.

[1] Virginia Woolf, *A Room of One's Own* (1928, rpt. Harmondsworth, 1972), 47.

In the late sixteenth and early seventeenth centuries, many women writers came from an aristocratic background (Mary Wroth, for example, was a member of the influential Sidney family), but women from much more humble (though not uneducated) backgrounds also wrote: Isabella Whitney, for example, had to earn her keep through service in a gentlewoman's household in London. During the course of the seventeenth century, under the influence of the social upheaval that was part of the English Civil War, less privileged women wrote an increasing number of works, particularly in religious genres (examples here are Hester Biddle, Priscilla Cotton, and Mary Cole). English society changed dramatically during the early modern period. Isabella Whitney wrote during the early part of Elizabeth I's reign; between Whitney and Aphra Behn, who lived to see the arrival of William and Mary in 1688, England had four further monarchs (James I, Charles I, Charles II, and James II), a commonwealth, and a protectorate. While it is hard to generalize, a number of significant changes in the nature of women's writing occurred during this period (just as writing in general underwent a dramatic change). Writers such as Whitney, Aemilia Lanyer, and Mary Wroth belong to a quite different world from writers at the end of the seventeenth century such as Behn and Philips. By the end of the seventeenth century there was at least some elementary sense of a tradition (or traditions) of women's writing, so that, for example, the death of both Behn and Philips saw eulogies from other writers (male and female). On the other hand, both Aphra Behn at the end, and Mary Wroth at the beginning of the seventeenth century attracted fierce condemnations for daring to write secular literature—a preserve supposedly best left to men. While some women offered mutual support, others saw publication (if not writing itself) as demeaning; for example, the brilliant letter writer Dorothy Osborne, who was writing for her lover's eyes only, could mock Margaret Cavendish for being so foolish as to write and publish poetry.

While we have some sense now of how many women wrote, it is very difficult to determine who read them and in what quantities their works were distributed. This is partly because (as this collection is intended to illustrate) women wrote in such a wide variety of modes and genres. By the end of the period under consideration here, Aphra Behn stands as one of the most successful playwrights of the Restoration, whose work was watched and read by large numbers of people. In comparison, Isabella Whitney's two volumes were published once each and it is impossible to determine how many copies were sold and who might have read her poems. In the time between these two examples, individual cases vary enormously. Aemilia Lanyer published a book in a clear bid for patronage (it was prefaced by addresses to numerous powerful women starting with the queen), though once again we cannot determine how successful the publication was. Unpublished work is more complicated, because work in manuscript is not necessarily intended to remain uncirculated (a familiar example being Donne's poems which circulated extensively in manuscript). Anne Clifford's diary was a 'private' piece of writing only in so far as it was clearly intended to be read within her family, but it is certainly directed towards a reader or readers. Writers who imagine a circumscribed audience, such as Clifford or Dorothy Osborne, can be contrasted to those who clearly envisaged themselves as writers with a public (real or projected), the best example being Margaret Cavendish, who published a huge volume of writing grand in both content and appearance. One can compare the high social position of Cavendish (who was married to the Duke of Newcastle) with women from humble backgrounds who nevertheless also projected an audience. This is most evident in the religious writing of the Civil War period, where, for example, Quakers such as Priscilla Cotton and Mary Cole addressed the entire country, as well as their fellow believers.

This anthology offers the reader both the possibility of tracing certain patterns in the works collected here and also some sense of the historical shifts and changes that occurred between Whitney and Behn. The collection begins with Whitney in part because of the startlingly modern tone of voice in her poetry. Paradoxically, the writer most removed from us in time is the one who perhaps speaks to us most directly. The three plays that are included are intended to demonstrate just how differently such a form could work for different women at different times in the seventeenth century: Mary Wroth's *Love's Victory* circulated in manuscript and was clearly intended for private performance; the ambitious Margaret Cavendish, writing *Bell in Campo* at a time when the theatres were closed during the Civil War, published the play in her usual elaborate fashion and certainly imagined public performance; Aphra Behn's *The City Heiress* is the production of a professional playwright in complete control of her medium. The context and techniques of these three plays could not be more different, but they share an interest in what we would now call sexual politics.

The religious writing included here also points to the diversity of style, background, and approach in an area that accounts for the great bulk of writing by women (and men) in the seventeenth century. Aemilia Lanyer's religious poem, *Salve Deus Rex Judaeorum*, is in contrast with the prophecies of Eleanor Davies and the Quaker polemic of Priscilla Cotton and Mary Cole and Hester Biddle. As well as religious writing, less obviously literary categories are represented by Anne Clifford's diary, Dorothy Osborne's letters, and some brief philosophical/scientific writing by Margaret Cavendish. But these examples hardly serve to represent the large amount of work done by women in the area of conduct books, medical treatises, philosophical discussion, and so on.[2] However, while the emphasis here is on writing of some literary interest, its political implications are also highlighted, from Clifford's account of her resistance to the rough persuasions of King James over her claims to her family estate to Aphra Behn's Tory engagement with the Popish Plot in *The City Heiress*.

Isabella Whitney (fl. 1567–1578)

We know very little about Isabella Whitney, apart from some information provided in her poetry. She was born in Cheshire and came from a gentry family which included her brother Geoffrey Whitney, who published *A Choice of Emblems* (1586). She entered into some sort of service in London, perhaps as an attendant to a gentlewoman there, but was apparently (if we believe her statements in her poetry) forced to leave London, poor and no longer in service. In 1567 she published *The Copy of a Letter, lately written in metre by a young gentlewoman to her unconstant lover.* This brief volume contains two poems by Whitney about the unfaithfulness of men and answers to her poems from two male writers, W.G. and R.W. The result is a kind of dialogue between the sexes over the nature of love and its

[2] A good thematic example of such an anthology is Charlotte F. Otten (ed.), *English Women's Voices*, 1540–1700 (Miami, 1992); for autobiographical writing, Elspeth Graham *et al.*, *Her Own Life* (London, 1989), is invaluable.

effects. Whitney seems to have been the only non-aristocratic woman poet in the Elizabethan period (certainly she was the only one published), and her literary poise is remarkable.

The first poem from *The Copy of a Letter*, the powerful 'I.W. To Her Unconstant Lover', is something of a literary *tour de force*. Whitney uses a form popular with male writers in the 1560s influenced by 'the newly fashionable mode of Ovid's *Heroides*, in which the Roman poet represented attempts by seduced and abandoned heroines to reclaim the men who betrayed them'.[3] While male writers often wrote poems that used a female voice, Whitney's poem is far more immediate and part of its fascination is the shift from aggression at the beginning to a style of cool wit, as she both puts her old love in his place and reassesses the pantheon of classical male heroes. While we cannot know the exact circumstances surrounding Whitney's decision to publish her poetry, it is clear from the nature of the volume and the poems that she had considerable literary ambitions.

This ambition is even more evident in Whitney's second publication: *A Sweet Nosegay or a Pleasant Posy* (1573). This much larger collection begins with a versification of Hugh Plat's *Flowers of Philosophy* (1572) and then turns to a selection of poems to Whitney's friends and family. The volume concludes with a 'Will and Testament', Whitney's most substantial poem, which extends her range considerably. The 'Will and Testament' is a complex interweaving of two modes which at the time prevailed against female power, but which Whitney is able to renegotiate, at least at a literary level: the blazon (the itemized description of the female body) and the will, a contested genre for women in so far as their property rights were uncertain.[4] Whitney wraps the city of London within the blazon form, and uses the fictional will, both to mourn the necessity for her to leave the city through her poverty, and to exact a revenge through a satirical social description of it. Whitney works through the paradox that this testament to her poverty and exile from a harsh city offers up to the reader a singularly powerful poetic voice.

[3] Ann Rosalind Jones, *The Currency of Eros* (Bloomington, Ind., 1990), 43.
[4] See Wendy Wall, 'Isabella Whitney and the Female Legacy', *ELH* 58 (1991); see also her book *The Imprint of Gender* (Ithaca, NY, 1993).

Aemilia Lanyer (1569–1645)

Writing a generation later than Whitney, Aemilia Lanyer offers the reader an equally powerful poetic voice. Perhaps the most striking aspect of Lanyer's volume of poetry, *Salve Deus Rex Judaeorum*, published in 1611, is the elaborate manipulation of the customary printed dedication to a potential patron. Lanyer wrote dedications to nine prominent women (as well as two general prefaces), including Queen Anne and Anne and James's daughter, Princess Elizabeth. (All the dedications are included in this anthology.) The dedications appear in different combinations in surviving copies of *Salve Deus*; taken together they create at least the impression of a community of powerful women who are enlisted by Lanyer to support, as she notes in the dedication to the queen, 'a woman's writing of divinest things'. Women's religious writing was the most sanctioned form of literary activity they could undertake, the most prominent example being the Countess of Pembroke's translations of the Psalms, cited by Lanyer as something of a precedent. However, Lanyer's account of the Passion in particular offers a striking vindication of women (as opposed to men).[5] Lanyer is therefore able to turn the 'respectable' mode of religious poetry into a mode which counters the often misogynistic attitudes sanctioned by the Church.

Lanyer was born in 1569, and was the daughter of a court musician called Baptist Bassano and Margaret Johnson.[6] As her dedications indicate, Lanyer seems to have spent some time in the service of Susan Bertie, Countess of Kent. By 1587, when her mother died, Lanyer had become the mistress of Henry Cary, Lord Hunsdon. When she became pregnant in 1592, she was married to Alphonso Lanyer, a court musician like her father. Her son, born in 1593, was named Henry (a clear indication of the identity of his natural father). In 1598 she gave birth to a daughter, named Odillya, who died nine months later. During the early years of the seventeenth century Lanyer spent some time at the estate of Cookham with Margaret and Anne Clifford, an occasion which gave rise to the country house poem, 'The Description of Cookham'. *Salve Deus*

[5] See Catherine Keohane, '"That Blindest Weakenesse Be Not Over-Bold": Aemilia Lanyer's Radical Unfolding of the Passion', *ELH* 64 (1997), *passim*.

[6] Biographical information from Susanne Woods (ed.), *The Poems of Aemilia Lanyer* (New York, 1993).

was registered for publication late in 1610; its success is difficult to estimate, but Lanyer did not publish anything further and no manuscript versions of her writing have been discovered. After her husband's death in 1613 she was involved in constant legal battles to retain his hay and grain patent. Lanyer founded a school in 1617, but abandoned this in 1619. Lanyer outlived her son by twelve years, dying in 1645.

As a volume, *Salve Deus* falls into three parts: the series of dedications, the poem that gives the volume its title, which runs to some 1,800 lines, and 'The Description of Cookham'. (This anthology includes all the dedications, about one-sixth of 'Salve Deus', and the whole of 'Cookham'.) While quite disparate in terms of genre, the volume is united through its projection of 'an enduring female community'.[7] However, there has been some debate over Lanyer's representation of her relationship to that community. In 'The Description of Cookham', in particular, Lanyer laments her exile from both the Clifford household and the estate which provided her with some security; indeed, the poem has been described as 'an elegy for Lanyer herself'.[8] From this perspective, the dedicatory poems to the volume are a complex negotiation of Lanyer's position as a figure on the margins of court society who is now attempting to reinsert herself into a specifically female nexus of aristocratic power. The attempt failed, but the poetry remains a powerful testament to Lanyer's frustration with the narratives into which early modern women were so often inserted. This includes the 'narrative' of religion, which Lanyer challenges in particular through her reclamation of Eve in the section from *Salve Deus* included here.

Anne Clifford (1590–1676)

Lanyer wrote 'The Description of Cookham' just before Anne Clifford married Richard Sackville, Earl of Dorset. Lanyer may well have felt a special affinity for Clifford, who was a remarkable example of an aristocratic woman who, under duress, clung to a family identity which bypassed accepted patriarchal convention. Clifford was

[7] Barbara Lewalski, *Writing Women in Jacobean England* (Cambridge, Mass., 1993), 241.

[8] Lisa Schnell, '"So Great a Difference Is There in Degree": Aemilia Lanyer and the Aims of Feminist Criticism', *MLQ* 57 (1996), 32.

the daughter of George Clifford, Earl of Cumberland, and Margaret Russell.[9] Her father lived apart from her mother for much of their marriage, though they were reconciled on her father's deathbed. Anne Clifford was born in 1590 and was their sole surviving child. She was, therefore, able to inherit a number of estates and titles, including the office of sheriff of Westmorland, under a special entail which did not discriminate between male and female heirs. George Clifford did not break the entail, but he willed all these estates to his brother (who inherited his earldom), providing Anne with a sum of money instead and the reversion of the estates only if his brother had no male heirs. Under her mother's guardianship, Anne contested the will, but the judges ruled against her. Nevertheless, her mother remained in residence in Westmorland until her death in 1616. In the meantime, Anne was married to Richard Sackville in 1609. As the section of Anne's diary excerpted here shows, Sackville placed her under enormous pressure to concede to the terms of her father's will in return for an increased cash settlement. She resolutely refused to accede to this, even under threat from the king himself. Sackville continued a series of attempts to force Clifford to renounce her claim until his death in 1624.

Clifford bore five children during her marriage: three sons who died as infants and two daughters: Margaret, born in 1614, is the child referred to frequently in the diary extract; Isabella was born in 1622. In 1630, Clifford married Philip Herbert, Earl of Pembroke. She lived largely apart from him after two years of marriage. In 1643, following the death of both her uncle and his son, she finally inherited her estates and moved to take up residence in Westmorland (she had five castles, all of which she restored), running her estates until her death in 1676 (her daughter Margaret died the same year).

Anne Clifford wrote a large amount of what might be called personal material, although it is important to note that none of this writing is 'private' in the way that a modern diary might be considered to be private. Rather, Clifford writes something that might be called family testimony, presumably initially as a record of how she held out as heir, and later as a record of how she managed her

[9] Biographical information from Richard T. Spence, *Lady Anne Clifford* (Stroud, 1997), and Lewalski, *Writing Women*.

inheritance. She also has an acute sense of how she and her family fit into Jacobean public life—even when she is immured at Knole (the Sackville estate in Kent) 'like an owl in the desert'. That part of her writing that is presently known consists of a detailed diary for the years 1616, 1617, and 1619; a series of 'great books' containing genealogical material and miscellaneous information; and a running diary from 1650 to Clifford's death.[10]

This anthology includes one year of the early diary, from January 1616 to January 1617.[11] This was a time when Clifford was perhaps under greatest pressure, and includes the death of her mother and the difficult confrontation with the king. Her resilience is evident everywhere, from her resistance to all the pressure placed upon her (including a long counselling session from the Archbishop of Canterbury) to the (implied) defiance with which she chooses her clothes. Yet this part of the diary also underlines how complex Clifford's response to her situation was: she retains (or at least expresses) considerable loyalty to, even some sort of devotion for, her husband, despite his treatment of her. Barbara Lewalski suggests that the diary gives us access to 'a self in process'.[12] But this is a self quite unlike a modern self, and the introspection we demand from diary and autobiography has to be read into the compressed images and events recounted by Clifford; nothing is offered up to us as already analysed by the writer. Clifford does insistently underline the relationship between her situation and the great events of court life, but this is done in an enumerative, rather than analytical, manner. Only momentarily do we gain a flash of something more revelatory: the vivid glimpses we receive of Clifford's relationship with her daughter, or the intriguing asides about her reading.[13]

[10] All of this material is readily accessible in D. J. H. Clifford (ed.), *The Diaries of Lady Anne Clifford* (Stroud, 1992); for the 1616–19 diaries the best source is Katherine O. Acheson (ed.), *The Diary of Anne Clifford 1616–1619: A Critical Edition* (New York, 1995).

[11] It should be noted that this diary no longer exists in its original form, but in two later transcripts (which differ from each other): the probably 19th-century Knole MS, and the 18th-century Portland MS.

[12] Lewalski, *Writing Women*, 150.

[13] Mary Ellen Lamb offers an interesting interpretation of Clifford as a reader in 'The Agency of the Split Subject: Lady Anne Clifford and the Uses of Reading', *ELR* 22 (1992).

Mary Wroth (c.1587–c.1653)

The most prolific aristocratic woman writer in the seventeenth century is undoubtedly Mary Wroth. Wroth came from a pre-eminently literary family: her uncle was the renowned Elizabethan writer Philip Sidney and her aunt, Mary Sidney, Countess of Pembroke, was famous as a translator of the Psalms and of Robert Garnier's *Tragedy of Antony*, as well as being a notable patron.[14] Wroth was the oldest daughter of Robert Sidney and Barbara Gamage, and is thought to have been born in 1587. During much of her childhood her father was governor of Flushing in the Netherlands and Wroth spent some time there, but mainly lived at the Sidney estate of Penshurst in Kent. During her time at Penshurst Wroth evidently formed a close attachment to her first cousin William Herbert, which may have precipitated moves to marry the cousins to other people: Mary to Robert Wroth, in 1604, and Herbert four months later to Mary Talbot.[15] Mary's husband, Robert Wroth, seems clearly to have been unappealing and rumours of their unhappy marriage were soon in circulation. Robert Wroth was something of a favourite with King James, who visited his estate at Loughton Hall and appointed him riding forester (someone who leads the king's hunting expeditions)—his rural interests and pursuits are significant, given Mary Wroth's negative depiction of the character named Rustic in *Love's Victory*. While Robert Wroth was hailed by Ben Jonson as one who 'canst love the country', Mary took a prominent part in court activities, dancing in Jonson's *Masque of Blackness* in 1605. Mary Wroth, like her father, attached herself to Queen Anne's court circle (her father was Anne's lord chamberlain), rather than the king's. Her first son James was born in 1614, the year of her husband's death, but died in 1616. After Robert Wroth died Mary

[14] For biographical information about Wroth, see in particular the introductions to Josephine Roberts (ed.), *The Poems of Lady Mary Wroth* (Baton Rouge, La., 1983) and *The First Part of the Countess of Montgomery's Urania* (Binghampton, NY, 1995); for Wroth in her family context see Gary Waller, *The Sidney Family Romanc*e (Detroit, 1993).

[15] Josephine Roberts speculates that the cousins may have contracted a *de praesenti* marriage (i.e. a kind of oral pledge), though Roberts points out that this cannot be known for certain but must rather be deduced from Wroth's fictional treatment of such a situation in her prose romance *Urania*; see Josephine Roberts, '"The Knott Never to Bee Untide": The Controversy Regarding Marriage in Mary Wroth's *Urania*', in Naomi Miller and Gary Waller (eds.), *Reading Mary Wroth* (Knoxville, Tenn., 1991).

either resumed or continued her relationship with William Herbert, and bore two children by him: William and Katherine.

Perhaps because of her association with William Herbert, Mary Wroth took a less active role in court activities after her husband's death.[16] Her literary endeavours may well have started earlier, though it is difficult to date much of her work. She wrote a sonnet sequence modelled to some degree on Philip Sidney's *Astrophil and Stella*: Wroth's 'Pamphilia to Amphilanthus' exists in manuscript, but was also included with her immense prose romance, *The Countess of Montgomery's Urania*, part of which she published in 1621. *Urania* is a complex, multifaceted narrative, part of which involves the disguised representation of a series of events involving Wroth's contemporaries (including accounts of her own marriage). One such depiction provoked the ire of Edward Denny, who responded fiercely to a story in *Urania* which involved scandal surrounding the marriage of his daughter. The resultant furore led Wroth to write to King James's favourite the Duke of Buckingham, offering to withdraw the book, and she never published the lengthy manuscript continuation. Little is known about Wroth's activities from this time until her death in the early 1650s.

While *Urania* is Wroth's major literary achievement, it does not lend itself to excerpts, and so she is represented here by her pastoral drama, *Love's Victory*.[17] *Love's Victory* was probably written some time between 1620 and 1622 (though it cannot be dated with any real accuracy). It exists in two manuscripts, suggesting some circulation, if only within Wroth's family, and may well have had some kind of private performance. *Love's Victory* is an extremely skilful example of a dramatic form which may, at first, seem highly artificial to a modern reader. Wroth projects (as she does in *Urania*) allusively sketched figures from her own life into the pastoral setting, most particularly a depiction of herself as Musella, William Herbert as Philisses, and Robert Wroth as Rustic. The pastoral drama imagines a happier ending for the cousins' relationship, with their supposed death causing Rustic to renounce his

[16] Though Lewalski notes that she was by no means excluded from them and was scarcely exiled for her affair; see Lewalski, *Writing Women*, 148.

[17] I have included Book I of *Urania* in my *Anthology of Seventeenth-Century Fiction* (Oxford, 1991); one can only hope that Roberts's fine edition of *Urania* will bring it many new readers.

claim on Musella, whereupon they promptly revive and prepare to marry.

Love's Victory examines female friendships and female community. However, it also places great stress on a favourite theme of Wroth: the power of desire, specifically female desire. In *Love's Victory*, Venus and Cupid preside over human affairs, but Venus's victory ensures that, to at least some degree, desire is satisfied once it is honoured.

Wroth's poetry evokes a much more disturbing sense of desire as a dangerous force, not just within a patriarchal world, but within a poetic genre shaped by considerable misogyny. The five sonnets included here from the 'Pamphilia to Amphilanthus' sequence offer only a taste of Wroth's considerable poetic accomplishment. They are excellent examples of her complex, often even tangled syntax, which reflects her favourite image of desire as a labyrinth out of which subjectivity needs to be disentangled. Recent critics of the poetry have stressed the often contradictory nature of the subjectivity explored in the poems.[18] From those included here, one might in particular note the complex examination of the solitary woman standing back from court activity in Sonnet 23 ('When everyone to pleasing pastime hies'). Here is a figure who, rather than hunt, hawk, play music, or 'discourse' with others, communes with herself: 'I with my spirit talk and cry'.

Eleanor Davies (1590–1652)

From Wroth we move to another aristocratic writer, but one working in a very different genre (and one who found her inspiration by speaking quite literally with a spirit). Eleanor Touchett was born in 1590 to George Touchett, Baron Audley, and Lucy Mervin.[19] In 1609 she married Sir John Davies, the author of *Orchestra* and a lawyer (for a time the king's attorney in Ireland). In 1625, Eleanor Davies heard the voice of the prophet Daniel

[18] See in particular, Naomi J. Miller, *Changing the Subject: Mary Wroth and Figurations of Gender in Early Modern England* (Lexington, Ky., 1996); Heather Dubrow, *Echoes of Desire: English Petrarchism and Its Counterdiscourses* (Ithaca, NY, 1995).

[19] Biographical information from Esther S. Cope, *Handmaid of the Holy Spirit: Dame Eleanor Davies, Never Soe Mad a Ladie* (Ann Arbor, 1992).

warning her that the day of judgement was nineteen and a half years away and that she was to be a prophet. From that time on, Davies devoted herself to publishing prophecies, beginning with the tract she immediately wrote outlining her experience, which she presented to the Archbishop of Canterbury, George Abbot. Until her death, in 1652, Davies produced a large number of works, virtually all of them published without official permission. Her career can be divided into three periods. From 1625 to 1633 she focused her attention on the court in an attempt to persuade Charles to fight against popery. During this period she accurately predicted the death of her husband and of the Duke of Buckingham; she then married Sir Archibald Douglas and, when he opposed her prophesying, predicted his decline. From 1633 to 1640 she was increasingly subject to persecution. Following her opposition to Archbishop Laud, he ordered her books burned and had her imprisoned for two and a half years; she then spent a further two years in the Tower. From 1640 to 1652 the course taken by the Civil War seemed to confirm her prophecies (particularly the deaths of Laud and King Charles) and she published a very large number of works during this period.

Two of Davies's briefer works are included here, both written in this third period of her career. They provide good examples of the kind of writing characteristic of Davies: densely allusive; full of cryptic references to public events entangled with her own life; punning and poetic; apocalyptic; full of visions. Davies's early work precedes the outpouring of women's prophetic writing that formed an important part of the religious ferment of the Civil War. She was then joined by women from a variety of sects, the length of whose work has prevented the inclusion of more than a brief sample here. The prophecies of the remarkable Fifth Monarchist Anna Trapnel would make an interesting comparison. Davies is a particularly idiosyncratic writer, often extremely difficult to decipher. However, recent criticism has offered insights into how to understand and sympathize with 'unruly' women's texts.[20]

[20] See, for example, Richard Pickard, 'Anagrams etc.: The Interpretive Dilemmas of Lady Eleanor Douglas', *Renaissance and Reformation*, 20 (1996); Teresa Feroli, 'The Sexual Politics of Mourning in the Prophecies of Eleanor Davies', *Criticism*, 36 (1994); Megan Matchinske, 'Holy Hatred: Formations of the Gendered Subject in English Apocalyptic Writing, 1625–1651', *ELH* 60 (1993).

Priscilla Cotton and Mary Cole (fl. 1650s/1660s)

Davies was unusual in being an aristocratic woman who prophesied. But considerable numbers of women made themselves heard as part of the radical religious sects that flourished during the period of the Civil War. Out of the very large number of works available, two tracts by Quaker women are included here, simply because that sect provided the largest number of women religious writers in the seventeenth century. Priscilla Cotton and Mary Cole wrote *To the Priests and People of England* in 1655 while imprisoned in Exeter Jail. No detailed biographical information about these two women is available; both of them published other tracts individually. *To the Priests and People of England* forms part of a continuing debate, not only amongst Quakers, on the position of women within religious discourse. The debate over women's right to preach and take part in Church governance was evident throughout this period; many tracts attacked the women who, during the Civil War in particular, both preached and argued in favour of being allowed to do so.

The most famous of the defences of women's right to preach is the Quaker Margaret Fell's *Women's Speaking Justified* (1666). But Cotton and Cole not only predate Fell, they offer, in a comparatively brief polemic, a particularly lively, indeed audacious, argument. They 'engage in an intellectual play which simultaneously displays their own familiarity with the Bible, and parodies the use made of it by the learned'.[21] Their witty defence of women involves 'a riotous game of paradox and irony', particularly evident in their use of Paul's comment in 1 Corinthians that a woman may not prophesy with her head uncovered.[22]

In an extremely detailed and multifaceted reading of Cotton and Cole's tract, Hilary Hinds draws attention to the text's 'concern with the instability and precariousness of silence', given that it interrelates the admonitions against women speaking and the general Quaker interest in silence as a necessary context for communication with God.[23] Cotton and Cole intend to 'silence' the priests who

[21] Elaine Hobby, 'Handmaids of the Lord and Mothers in Israel: Early Vindications of Quaker Women's Prophecy', in Thomas Corns and David Loewenstein (eds.), *The Emergence of Quaker Writing* (London, 1995), 93.

[22] Ibid.

[23] See Hilary Hinds, *God's Englishwomen: Seventeenth-Century Radical Sectarian Writing and Feminist Criticism* (Manchester, 1996), ch. 7.

oppose the speech of women, partly by putting them through a kind of gender reversal: 'Indeed, you yourselves are the women.'[24] In Cotton and Cole's argument, the category 'woman' stands for weakness, stands, indeed, for those not entitled to speak. On the other side of this category stand certain actual women who are justified (spiritually) in speaking and who thus move into the category of the empowered (traditionally rendered as male, but here translated away from embodied sexual difference).

Hester Biddle (c.1629–1696)

Hester Biddle was a more prominent Quaker writer and activist than Cotton and Cole.[25] She was born around 1629 and died in 1696. After she became a Quaker, like a number of other women, she travelled quite extensively to spread the word: she visited Amsterdam, Newfoundland, and Barbados, and, during a trip to France, met Louis XIV.[26] Biddle's work is much more fiercely apocalyptic than Cotton and Cole's tract. In 1655 Biddle published the twin tracts *Woe to Thee, City of Oxford* and *Woe to Thee, City of Cambridge*, which denounced those centres of learning as 'smothered in filth', and called them to repentance.[27] *The Trumpet of the Lord* is once again a tract written from prison (Newgate) and, like Biddle's earlier writing, it is a powerful call to repentance, directed at a series of targets, beginning with the city of London. (It is therefore something of a parallel to the much shorter Cambridge and Oxford tracts, taking in England's greatest city.)

Biddle offers 'a word of wholesome counsel and advice unto thy kings, rulers, judges, bishops and priests', warning of the forthcoming day of judgement, which is very near at hand. At the same time, Biddle offers a defence of the Quakers against their persecutors. She includes an autobiographical passage tracing her conversion at a

[24] Ibid., 187.

[25] Biographical information is taken from Elaine Hobby, '"Oh Oxford Thou Art Full of Filth": The Prophetical Writings of Hester Biddle', in Susan Sellers (ed.), *Feminist Criticism: Theory and Practice* (Hemel Hempstead, 1991).

[26] For two other examples of the writings of Quaker women who travelled extensively, see extracts from the work of Katherine Evans and Sarah Cheevers and Joan Vokins in *Her Own Life*, ed. Elspeth Graham *et al.* (London, 1989).

[27] Hobby includes the full text of *Woe to Thee, City of Oxford* in her article cited in n. 25.

Quaker meeting and her passionate conviction that her old religion is vain and profitless. Her polemic is designed simultaneously to strengthen the conviction of her fellow Quakers and to induce others to see the light and follow her. As a piece of writing, *The Trumpet of the Lord* is extraordinarily polished; Biddle's prophecy relies upon transparent argument, in contrast to Eleanor Davies's conundrums. Biddle shifts tone from denunciation to admonition to cajoling and concludes with a poem.

Margaret Cavendish (1623–1673)

Of all the writers in this anthology, Margaret Cavendish was the most ambitious to carve out a space for herself as a thinker and writer: 'I am not covetous, but as ambitious as ever any of my sex was, is or can be', she wrote in the preface to her utopian fiction *The Blazing World*. Cavendish produced a large body of writing in every imaginable genre: poems, plays, stories, autobiography, biography, philosophical and scientific treatises, familiar letters, orations, literary criticism. Margaret Lucas was born *c.*1623 to a wealthy family near Colchester. Although she describes herself as a painfully shy child, with the onset of the Civil War and the removal of the court to Oxford (where the Lucas family also moved after their estate was looted), Margaret decided to become a Maid of Honour to Queen Henrietta Maria. In 1644 she accompanied the queen into exile in France, where she became William Cavendish's second wife. During the 1640s Margaret and William lived in exile, first in Paris, then in Antwerp.

During this time Margaret began to produce her early work: the poetry and philosophy that was published as *Poems and Fancies* and *Philosophical Fancies* in 1653. Three poems are included from this period of her writing—a typical philosophical poem expounding some of Cavendish's atomist views and two of her animal poems, the best known of which is the extraordinarily powerful 'The Hunting of the Hare'—and a cautionary tale, 'The Matrimonial Agreement', which offers a typically sharp, not to say cynical, view of marriage, however much Margaret's own marriage might have been a happy one.

Margaret returned to England without William in 1652 in an attempt to negotiate an income from her husband's sequestered estates. She prepared her volumes for publication (as handsome folios) during her stay in England and returned to Antwerp after a year and a half. She returned to her writing, gathering together a series of essays as *The World's Olio* (1655), an olio being a stew. A very brief example is included here, which offers a sharp vignette of the social consequences of civil war. At this period she also began writing plays, partly inspired by a travelling group of actors who performed in Antwerp (and who included female actors in their troupe), which were sent to be published in England, but the manuscript had to be recopied after the ship carrying it to England sank. The volume was eventually published in 1662.

Recently, critics have moved away from seeing Cavendish's plays as simply undisciplined and have instead placed them in the context of the 'closet' drama of the period. But however much Cavendish may have produced plays that seemed then (and to many seem now) unactable within the context of a professional theatre, she had an acute sense of a theatrical context for her plays and certainly envisaged them as 'staged'.[28] One has only to look at the careful description of set-piece actions in *Bell in Campo* to see this theatrical imagination at work. Cavendish's plays are especially interested in the idea of performance in relation to female identity. This is particularly evident in *Bell in Campo*, which specifically examines the possibility of women entering the male world of heroic action. But there are, one must note, two sides to Cavendish's female characterization: the play constantly shifts between the heroic Lady Victoria, who is more formidable than any of the male combatants in the play, and the dutiful wife Madam Jantil, whose set pieces mourning her husband parallel Lady Victoria's martial speeches.[29] Both figures are, in their contrasting ways, heroic, and both project a powerful self-image which reflects the author's own overcoming of her shyness through her ambitious publication and self-publicizing.

Bell in Campo is also a clear reflection of the Civil War and its

[28] Many 'closet dramas' were adapted or used as sources in the Restoration by professional playwrights, a good example being Aphra Behn's use of Thomas Killigrew's *Thomaso* for *The Rover*. Some of William Cavendish's plays were revised for the Restoration stage; indeed Pepys, among others, thought that the Dryden-revised *Humorous Lovers* was Margaret's play, rather than William's—Pepys described it as 'the most ridiculous thing that ever was wrote', 11 Apr. 1667.

[29] Appropriately in this portrait of a devoted marriage, William supplied a number of speeches for Madam Jantil.

effects, both on those who actually participate in the battle that Cavendish portrays as being between 'Reformation' and 'Faction', and on those such as Madam Jantil and Madam Passionate who remain at home. It imagines a society which, after the great achievement of Lady Victoria and her 'heroickesses', will alter the order of merit within current levels of status to acknowledge the way female bravery might lead to advancement. While this is part of what might be called the utopian side of the play, it is admixed with some very sharp social criticism. *Bell in Campo* provides an interesting transition point between the clearly 'private' drama of *Love's Victory* and the involvement of a number of women, the most prominent being Aphra Behn, with the public theatre after the Restoration.

Before her death in 1673, Cavendish went on to publish further scientific writing, including what is currently her best-known work, *The Blazing World*, in *Observations Upon Experimental Philosophy* (1666); her biography of William in 1667; a second volume of plays in 1668; and revised editions of her earlier work. In recent years she has finally begun to receive the serious attention which she so craved.

Dorothy Osborne (1627–1695)

Dorothy Osborne presents the strongest of contrasts to Margaret Cavendish, something underlined by her disdain for Cavendish's self-presentation as a writer: 'Sure the poor woman is a little distracted, she could never be so ridiculous else as to venture at writing books, and in verse too!' (pp. 256–7). Yet even though Osborne wrote for an audience of only one, she was a highly self-conscious and skilled writer whose letters are immediately appealing. Osborne was born in 1627; her father, Sir Peter Osborne, was Lieutenant-Governor of Guernsey, which held out against the forces of Parliament in the early 1640s, though Sir Peter resigned his command and went to St Malo in 1646. While stopping at the Isle of Wight *en route* to join her father, Dorothy Osborne met William Temple, who joined her on her journey. During this time the two fell in love, but were immediately separated when Temple went on to Paris in 1648. He remained in Paris until 1650. Upon his return to London, he and Dorothy Osborne resumed their meetings, but both families opposed the idea of their marrying: Temple's father sent him to the Netherlands and Osborne went to live at the family estate of Chicksands where her brother Henry attempted to persuade her to marry a number of 'good prospects'. Opposition to the relationship continued until, after the death of Osborne's father, they eventually married in 1654.

The seventy-seven surviving letters written by Osborne to Temple not only chart the progress of their relationship in face of family opposition (a relationship that Osborne offers to relinquish a number of times), but they are a strong expression of a determined personality—one no less determined than Margaret Cavendish, however much Osborne may have shrunk from public display. And the letters are clearly designed to impress the recipient with their author's wit, verve, and integrity. Osborne writes with an acute sense of the literary nature of many of her themes, particularly of love and fidelity, casting her eye especially upon the French romance for models of behaviour. The letters therefore construct the kind of relationship Osborne seeks in marriage. Along the way, the confident character description and acute eye for social nuance turn the letters into narrative set pieces.

Upon their marriage, Dorothy and William led a fairly retired life in Ireland, but the Restoration saw William an MP and later a diplomat. Dorothy died in 1695; her letters were carefully preserved by William, although he apparently destroyed his own letters to her.

Katherine Philips (1632–1664)

Like Margaret Cavendish, Katherine Philips had a clear sense of her destiny as a writer, but her self-presentation was more subtle and, at least as far as her contemporaries were concerned, successful.[30] Katherine Fowler was born in 1632. A precocious child, she attended a girls' boarding-school in Hackney where she met a number of the friends who formed part of her literary circle. In 1648 she married Colonel James Philips, who was thirty-eight years her senior. He was a leading Parliamentarian in Wales, while Katherine

[30] In offering this view of Philips as being far from the self-effacing female poet of conventional literary history, I am following the opinion of Elaine Hobby in *Virtue of Necessity* (London, 1988), 128–42.

had Royalist sympathies and Royalist friends. Her first published poem appeared in 1651 amongst the fifty-four dedicatory poems to William Cartwright's posthumous collected works, thus making clear her political sympathies, as Cartwright was being turned into a Cavalier literary icon at this time. From this period on, Philips began to establish her literary coterie, giving her friends Romance names (she was Orinda) and promoting the idea of something like a salon on paper, to make up for her physical isolation in Wales.

Philips often discussed an ideal, Platonic friendship in her poems and her correspondence. While this friendship is certainly a philosophical frame in Philips's thought, she wrote many love poems that express what can now be characterized as lesbian desire.[31] Much of this passion was directed towards Anne Owen, who joined Philips's circle in 1651 and was given the name Lucasia (a character in one of Cartwright's plays). Owen inspired a whole series of powerful love poems from Philips, each one a poised example of her lyric skill. The selection in this anthology emphasizes this side of Philips's writing, though she also wrote in other poetic genres, including an interesting series of philosophical poems. Upon the Restoration, she was able to save her husband from persecution through her Royalist connections, and perhaps also through a judicious series of poems addressed to Charles and his household.

The relationship with Lucasia broke down when the widowed Anne Owen insisted on marrying her choice, Marcus Trevor, rather than Philips's choice for her, Charles Cotterell. Philips accompanied Lucasia to her new home in Ireland, and while in Dublin in 1662 she was encouraged by Roger Boyle, Earl of Orrery, to complete a translation of Corneille's *La Mort de Pompée*. This was performed in Dublin in 1663 and was a great success. At the time of her sudden death from smallpox, in 1664, Philips had achieved a significant literary reputation.

In style, Philips's lyrics are similar to the easy Cavalier mode of writers such as Carew, Suckling, Lovelace, and Cartwright. As Elaine

[31] For this approach see especially Elaine Hobby, 'Katherine Philips: Seventeenth-Century Lesbian Poet', in Elaine Hobby and Chris White, *What Lesbians Do in Books* (London, 1991); Germaine Greer, *Slip-Shod Sibyls* (London, 1995), ch. 5, and Arlene Stiebel, 'Not since Sappho: The Erotic in Poems of Katherine Philips and Aphra Behn', in Claude J. Summers (ed.), *Homosexuality in Renaissance and Enlightenment England: Literary Representations in Historical Context* (New York, 1992).

Hobby has pointed out, her love poetry combines what she characterizes as an encoded Royalism with lesbian desire.[32] The Cavalier heritage is evident in both these aspects of Philips's verse, in so far as the Cavalier love lyric was translated into an allowable expression of lesbian desire by way of Philips's theme of 'friendship'. This is perhaps most evident in the powerful poem written on the subject of Lucasia's parting from Orinda: 'Adieu, dear object of my love's excess' (p. 279). Also included here are Philips's two moving elegies on the death of her son Hector, to show her skill in a quite different mode.

Aphra Behn (c.1640–1689)

The last writer in this collection has the highest profile of all seventeenth-century women writers, given the reappearance of her plays on the public stage. Many of the details of Aphra Behn's life remain obscure, despite the efforts of no less than four modern biographers. There has been some evidence which relates Behn to a family named Johnson in Kent, and she was probably born around 1640. It now seems clear that Behn spent some time in Surinam in the early 1660s, which formed the basis for her most well-known non-dramatic work, *Oroonoko* (1688). After her return to London, when she apparently married a Mr Behn (about whom once again almost nothing is known), she went on a spying mission to the Netherlands. She returned to London in debt in 1667. There she began her literary career. Her first play, *The Forced Marriage*, was performed in 1670. Over the next decade, she produced on average a play a year, writing nineteen altogether. During the 1670s she was successful as well as prominent, particularly after the great popularity of *The Rover*, staged in 1677. During this time Behn also wrote a large amount of poetry, which she collected in *Poems Upon Several Occasions* (1684).

Behn may not exactly have earned her entire living by her pen, but she was part of the 'professional' literary scene and made a significant contribution to it.[33] By the early 1680s she had added a series of

[32] See Hobby, 'Katherine Philips'; for a complex and important argument about the combination of politics and desire in Philips, see Carol Barash, *English Women's Poetry, 1649–1714* (Oxford, 1996).

[33] The reference to Behn making money by her pen is from *A Room of One's Own*, 82.

translations to her *œuvre*, including a number of French works, though she also (without knowing Latin) was involved in translations from Ovid and Cowley. At this time the amalgamation of the two London theatre companies limited the opportunities for making money from plays. She began writing prose fiction with *Love Letters Between a Nobleman and His Sister* (1684), a thinly disguised account of a contemporary scandal. Its success led her to produce two sequels, and perhaps at this time she began writing more fiction: *The Fair Jilt* and *Oroonoko* both appeared in 1688. At this late stage of her career, Behn seems to have been constantly in debt, as well as ailing; she died on 16 April, 1689.

Drawing from Behn's prodigious dramatic output, this collection includes a late play that represents her skills in political propaganda, as well as comedy. *The City Heiress* was performed in April 1682. It is one of a group of plays commenting on the aftermath of the Popish Plot, a supposed Catholic conspiracy promulgated by Titus Oates and seized upon by Whigs opposed to the Catholic James II's succession to the throne. The play pours scorn upon the Whigs, particularly through the character of Sir Timothy Treat-all, whose Whig aspirations are opposed to his nephew Tom Wilding's Tory allegiances. Wilding is the rake-hero of the play and he follows in the footsteps of similar Behn characters, notably Willmore in *The Rover*. But, as critics have pointed out, Wilding is a particularly tarnished rake and the play takes a fairly cynical attitude towards him. Behn also offers a complex portrait of Lady Galliard, seduced by Wilding but ultimately abandoned by him in favour of Charlotte, the heiress. Charlotte, Lady Galliard, and Wilding's mistress Diana are all finely drawn female characters and the play is both witty and scathingly satirical. It also demonstrates the dramatic poise of a highly skilled, professional playwright, and merits revival as much as any of Behn's plays currently being performed.

From Behn's substantial amount of poetry a small selection has been chosen that concentrates on her multifaceted analysis of sexual desire, from her wry poem about impotence, 'The Disappointment', to her complex exploration of a form of lesbian desire in 'To the Fair Clarinda'. Behn's lyrics about desire offer a sophisticated response to the misogyny of the Restoration poetry written by wits such as Rochester. Behn matched the male poets' sexual frankness, but she offered a sharp critique of masculine values, particularly in poems such as the two which counter the views of the unknown 'Alexis'.

While Behn's prose fiction is most notable for her three long works, *Love Letters*, *Oroonoko*, and *The Fair Jilt*, she was an accomplished short-story writer in a number of modes. *The Wandering Beauty* represents the lighter side of this output. *The Wandering Beauty* is a kind of fairy tale which also pays considerable attention to landscape and addresses the issue of enforced marriage with a light touch. It presents a convincing image of female rebellion in Arabella, a character strong willed enough to run away from her parents and their proposed marriage for her.

By the time *The Wandering Beauty* was published (in 1698, nine years after Behn's death), something that might be called a tradition of women's writing had been established, and while it has been common to contrast the 'virtuous' Katherine Philips with the morally suspect Aphra Behn, Behn in particular demonstrated that it was possible for a woman to sustain a career within the masculine world of letters. Taken as a whole, this collection of early modern women's writing should offer an unquestionably affirmative answer to Woolf's question about Judith Shakespeare.

NOTE ON THE TEXTS

All the items included here have been edited afresh from the original sources. Source texts have been collated with early and modern editions, but individual copies have only been collated on a limited basis. All the texts have been modernized on fairly conservative principles: the spelling has been modernized, but I have tried to leave the punctuation unchanged except where doing so would confuse a modern reader. In prose works I have often added paragraphs; in plays characters' names have been standardized as has the way that speeches are assigned to them.

Full textual details for each item will be found in the textual notes, which also include a list of significant variants.

SELECT BIBLIOGRAPHY

Anthologies/Editions

Suzanne Trill, Kate Chedgzoy, and Melanie Osborne, *Lay By Your Needles, Ladies, Take the Pen: Writing Women in England 1500–1700* (London, 1997); James Fitzmaurice *et al.*, *Major Women Writers of Seventeenth-Century England* (Ann Arbor, 1997); Germaine Greer *et al.*, *Kissing the Rod: An Anthology of 17th Century Women's Verse* (London, 1988); Louise Schleiner, *Tudor and Stuart Women Writers* (Bloomington, Ind., 1994); Mary Garman *et al.*, *Hidden in Plain Sight: Quaker Women's Writings 1650–1700* (Wallingford, Pa., 1996); Charlotte F. Otten, *English Women's Voices*, 1540–1700 (Miami, 1992); Elspeth Graham *et al.*, *Her Own Life* (London, 1989); Katharina M. Wilson and Frank J. Warnke, *Women Writers of the Seventeenth Century* (Athens, Ga., 1989); N. H. Keeble, *The Cultural Identity of Seventeenth Century Woman: A Reader* (New York, 1994); Randall Martin, *Women Writers in Renaissance England* (London, 1997).

General Critical Studies

Hilda Smith, *Reason's Disciples: Seventeenth-Century English Feminists* (Urbana, Ill., 1982); Jonathan Goldberg, *Desiring Women Writing: English Renaissance Examples* (Stanford, Calif., 1997); Carol Barash, *English Women's Poetry, 1649–1714* (Oxford, 1996); Sara Heller Mendelson, *The Mental World of Stuart Women* (Amherst, Mass., 1987); Kim Walker, *Women Writers of the English Renaissance* (New York, 1996); Margaret Patterson Hannay, (ed.), *Silent but for the Word: Tudor Women as Patrons, Translators, and Writers of Religious Works* (Kent, Oh., 1985); Tina Krontiris, *Oppositional Voices: Women as Writers and Translators of Literature in the English Renaissance* (London, 1992); Margaret Ezell, *Writing Women's Literary History* (Baltimore, 1993); Elaine Hobby, *Virtue of Necessity: English Women's Writing 1649–88* (London, 1988); Barbara Lewalski, *Writing Women in Jacobean England* (Cambridge, Mass., 1993); Elaine Beilin, *Redeeming Eve: Women Writers of the English Renaissance* (Princeton, 1987); Margaret Ferguson *et al.* (eds.), *Rewriting the Renaissance* (Chicago, 1986); Kate Chedgzoy *et al.* (eds.), *Voicing Women* (Keele, 1996); Clare Brant and Diane Purkiss (eds.), *Women, Texts, Histories 1575–1760* (London, 1992); Isobel Grundy and Susan Wiseman (eds.), *Women, Writing, History, 1640–1740* (London, 1992); Helen Wilcox (ed.), *Women and Literature in Britain 1500–1700* (Cambridge, 1996); Betty

Travitsky and Adele Seeff (eds.), *Attending to Women in Early Modern England* (Newark, NJ, 1994).

Isabella Whitney

Isabella Whitney, *A Sweet Nosegay and The Copy of a Letter*, ed. Richard Panofsky (facsimile, New York, 1982); Betty Travitsky, 'The "Wyll and Testament" of Isabella Whitney', *ELR* 10 (1980); Wendy Wall, 'Isabella Whitney and the Female Legacy', *ELH* 58 (1991); Paul Marquis, 'Oppositional Ideologies of Gender in Isabella Whitney's Copy of a Letter', *MLR* 90 (1995); Krontiris, *Oppositional Voices*, ch. 2; Beilin, *Redeeming Eve*, ch. 4; Ann Rosalind Jones, *The Currency of Eros: Women's Love Lyric in Europe 1540–1620* (Bloomington, Ind., 1990), ch. 2; Ann Rosalind Jones, 'Nets and Bridles: Early Modern Conduct Books and Sixteenth-Century Women's Lyrics', in Nancy Armstrong and Leonard Tennenhouse (eds.), *The Ideology of Conduct: Essays on Literature and the History of Sexuality* (New York, 1987), 39–72; Betty Travitsky, 'The Lady Doth Protest', *ELR* 14 (1984).

Aemilia Lanyer

Susanne Woods (ed.), *The Poems of Aemilia Lanyer* (New York, 1993); Diane Purkiss (ed.), *Renaissance Women: The Plays of Elizabeth Cary/The Poems of Aemilia Lanyer* (London, 1994); A. L. Rowse (ed.), *The Poems of Shakespeare's Dark Lady* (London, 1978); Lewalski, *Writing Women*, ch. 8; Krontiris, *Oppositional Voices*, ch. 4; Beilin, *Redeeming Eve*, ch. 7.; Lisa Schnell, '"So Great a Diffrence Is There in Degree": Aemilia Lanyer and the Aims of Feminist Criticism', *MLQ* 57 (1996); Janel Mueller, 'The Feminist Poetics of Aemilia Lanyer's Salve Deus Rex Judaeorum', in Lynn Keller and Christanne Miller (eds.), *Feminist Measures: Soundings in Poetry and Theory* (Ann Arbor, 1994); Jacqueline Pearson 'Women Writers and Women Readers: The Case of Aemelia Lanier', in Kate Chedgzoy *et al.* (eds.), *Voicing Women: Gender and Sexuality in Early Writing* (London, 1997); Catherine Keohane, '"That Blindest Weakenesse Be Not Over-Bold": Aemilia Lanyer's Radical Unfolding of the Passion', *ELH* 64 (1997); Wendy Wall, 'Our Bodies/Our Texts? Renaissance Women and the Trials of Authorship', in Carol Singley and Susan Sweeney (eds.), *Anxious Power: Reading, Writing, and Ambivalence in Narrative by Women* (Albany, NY, 1993); Lorna Hutson, 'Why the Lady's Eyes Are Nothing Like the Sun', in Isobel Armstrong (ed.), *New Feminist Discourses: Critical Essays on Theories and Texts* (London, 1992); Lynette McGrath, 'Let Us Have Our Libertie Againe': Amelia Lanier's 17th-Century Feminist Voice', *Women's Studies*, 20 (1992).

Anne Clifford

Katherine O. Acheson (ed.), *The Diary of Anne Clifford 1616–1619: A Critical Edition* (New York, 1995); D. J. H. Clifford (ed.), *The Diaries of Lady Anne Clifford* (Phoenix Mill, 1992); Lewalski, *Writing Women*, ch. 5; Mary Ellen Lamb, 'The Agency of the Split Subject: Lady Anne Clifford and the Uses of Reading', *ELR* 22 (1992); Richard T. Spence, *Lady Anne Clifford* (Stroud, 1997).

Mary Wroth

Josephine A. Roberts (ed.), *The Poems of Lady Mary Wroth* (Baton Rouge, La., 1983); Mary Wroth, *Love's Victory*, ed. Michael Brennan (London, 1988); S. P. Cerasano and Marion Wynne-Davies (eds.), *Renaissance Drama By Women* (London, 1996), contains modernized text of *Love's Victory*; Mary Wroth, *Poems*, ed. R. E. Pritchard (Keele, 1996); Elizabeth Hanson, 'Boredom and Whoredom: Reading Renaissance Women's Sonnet Sequences', *Yale Journal of Criticism*, 10 (1997); Josephine A. Roberts, 'Deciphering Women's Pastoral: Coded Language in Wroth's *Love's Victory*', in Claude Summers and Ted-Larry Pebworth (eds.), *Representing Women in Renaissance England* (New York, 1997); Naomi J. Miller, *Changing the Subject: Mary Wroth and Figurations of Gender in Early Modern England* (Lexington, Ky., 1996); Heather Dubrow, *Echoes of Desire: English Petrarchism and Its Counterdiscourses* (Ithaca, NY, 1995); Gary Waller, *The Sidney Family Romance: Mary Wroth, William Herbert, and the Early Modern Construction of Gender* (Detroit, 1993); Naomi J. Miller and Gary Waller (eds.), *Reading Mary Wroth: Representing Alternatives in Early Modern England* (Knoxville, Tenn., 1991), esp. essays by Nona Fienberg, Ann Rosalind Jones, and Jeff Masten on the poems, and by Barbara Lewalski on *Love's Victory*; Mary Ellen Lamb, *Gender and Authorship in the Sidney Circle* (Madison, 1990); Naomi J. Miller, 'Rewriting Lyric Fictions: The Role of the Lady in Lady Mary Wroth's Pamphilia to Amphilanthus', in Anne M. Haselkorn and Betty Travitsky (eds.), *The Renaissance Englishwoman in Print: Counterbalancing the Canon* (Amherst, Mass., 1990); Margaret Anne McLaren, 'An Unknown Continent: Lady Mary Wroth's Forgotten Pastoral Drama "Loves Victorie"', in Haselkorn and Travitsky, *The Renaissance Englishwoman in Print*; Carolyn Ruth Swift, 'Feminine Self-Definition in Lady Mary Wroth's Love's Victorie (c. 1621)', *ELR* 19 (1989); Josephine A. Roberts, 'The Huntington Manuscript of Lady Mary Wroth's Play, Loves Victorie', *HLQ*, 46 (1983); Josephine A. Roberts, 'The Biographical Problem of Pamphilia to Amphilanthus', *Tulsa Studies in Women's Literature*, 1 (1982); May Nelson Paulissen, *The Love Sonnets of Lady*

Mary Wroth: A Critical Introduction (Salzburg, 1982); chapter in Lewalski, *Writing Women*; chapter in Beilin, *Redeeming Eve*.

Eleanor Davies

Esther S. Cope (ed.), *Prophetic Writings of Lady Eleanor Davies* (New York, 1995); Esther S. Cope, *Handmaid of the Holy Spirit: Dame Eleanor Davies, Never Soe Mad a Ladie* (Ann Arbor, 1992); Richard Pickard, 'Anagrams etc.: The Interpretive Dilemmas of Lady Eleanor Douglas', *Renaissance and Reformation*, 20 (1996); Teresa Feroli, 'The Sexual Politics of Mourning in the Prophecies of Eleanor Davies', *Criticism*, 36 (1994); Megan Matchinske, 'Holy Hatred: Formations of the Gendered Subject in English Apocalyptic Writing, 1625–1651', *ELH* 60 (1993).

Priscilla Cotton and Mary Cole/Hester Biddle

Hilary Hinds, *God's Englishwomen: Seventeenth-Century Radical Sectarian Writing and Feminist Criticism* (Manchester, 1996); Phyllis Mack, *Visionary Women: Ecstatic Prophecy in Seventeenth-Century England* (Berkeley, 1992); Margaret Ezell, *Writing Women's Literary History* (Baltimore, 1993), ch. 5; Elaine Hobby, '"Oh Oxford Thou Art Full of Filth": The Prophetical Writings of Hester Biddle', in Susan Sellers (ed.), *Feminist Criticism: Theory and Practice* (Hemel Hempstead, 1991); Elaine Hobby, 'Handmaids of the Lord and Mothers in Israel: Early Vindications of Quaker Women's Prophecy', in Thomas Corns and David Loewenstein (eds.), *The Emergence of Quaker Writing* (London, 1995); Elaine Hobby, 'The Politics of Women's Prophecy in the English Revolution', in Helen Wilcox *et al.* (eds.), *Sacred and Profane* (Amsterdam, 1996).

Margaret Cavendish

Anna Battigelli, *Margaret Cavendish and the Exiles of the Mind* (Lexington, Ky., 1998); Kathleen Jones, *A Glorious Fame: The Life of Margaret Cavendish, Duchess of Newcastle* (London, 1988); Victoria Kahn, 'Margaret Cavendish and the Romance of Contract', *Renaissance Quarterly*, 50 (1997); Bronwen Price, 'Feminine Modes of Knowing and Scientific Enquiry: Margaret Cavendish's Poetry as a Case Study,' in Helen Wilcox (ed.), *Women and Literature in Britain* 1500–1700 (Cambridge, 1996); Dale B. J. Randall, *Winter Fruit: English Drama, 1642–1660* (Lexington, Ky., 1995); Paul Salzman, 'Shakespeare and Margaret Cavendish: The Crisis in Editing and Early Modern Women's Writing', *Meridian: The La Trobe University English Review*, 16 (1997); Mihoko Suzuki, 'Margaret Cavendish and the Female Satirist', *SEL* 37 (1997); *Women's Writing*, special Margaret Cavendish issue, vol. 4 (1997); Sylvia Bowerbank, 'The Spider's Delight: Margaret Cavendish and the Female Imagination', *ELR* 14 (1984); Linda R. Payne, 'Dramatic Dreamscape: Women's Dreams and Utopian Vision in the Works of Margaret Cavendish, Duchess of Newcastle', in Mary Anne Schofield and Cecilia Macheski (eds.), *Curtain Calls: British and American Women and the Theater, 1660–1830* (Athens, Oh., 1991); Laura Rosenthal, *Playwrights and Plagiarists in Early Modern England: Gender, Authorship, Literary Property* (Ithaca, NY, 1966); Sophie Tomlinson, '"My Brain the Stage": Margaret Cavendish and the Fantasy of Female Performance', in Clare Brant and Diane Purkiss (eds.), *Women, Texts & Histories 1575–1760* (London, 1992); Susan Wiseman, 'Gender and Status in Dramatic Discourse: Margaret Cavendish, Duchess of Newcastle' in her *Politics and Drama in the English Civil War* (Cambridge, 1998).

Dorothy Osborne

The Letters of Dorothy Osborne to William Temple, ed. G. C. Moore Smith (Oxford, 1928); Dorothy Osborne, *Letters to Sir William Temple*, ed. Kenneth Parker (Harmondsworth, 1987); James Fitzmaurice and Martine Rey, 'Letters by Women in England, the French Romance, and Dorothy Osborne', in Jean Brink *et al.*, *The Politics of Gender in Early Modern Europe* (Kirksville, Mo., 1989).

Katherine Philips

The Collected Works of Katherine Philips, i. *The Poems*, ed. Patrick Thomas (Stump Cross, Essex, 1990); George Saintsbury (ed.), *Minor Poets of the Caroline Period*, i (Oxford, 1905); Lydia Hamessley 'Henry Lawes's Setting of Katherine Philips's Friendship Poetry in His Second Book of Ayres and Dialogues, 1655: A Musical Misreading?', in Philip Brett and Elizabeth Wood (eds.), *Queering the Pitch: The New Gay and Lesbian Musicology* (New York, 1994); Claudia A. Limbert, 'The Unison of Well-Tun'd Hearts': Katherine Philips' Friendships with Male Writers', *ELN* 29 (1991); Arlene Stiebel, 'Not Since Sappho: The Erotic in Poems of Katherine Philips and Aphra Behn', in Claude J. Summers (ed.), *Homosexuality in Renaissance and Enlightenment England: Literary Representations in Historical Context* (New York, 1992); Dorothy Mermin, 'Women Becoming Poets: Katherine Philips, Aphra Behn, Anne Finch', *ELH* 57 (1990); Celia Easton, 'Excusing the Breach of Nature's Laws: The Discourse of Denial and Disguise in Katherine Philips' Friendship Poetry', *Restoration*, 14 (1990); Patrick Thomas, *Katherine Philips* (Cardiff, 1988); Ellen Moody, 'Orinda, Rosania, Lucasia et aliae: Towards a New Edition of the Works of Katherine Philips', *PQ* 66 (1987); Elaine Hobby, 'Katherine Philips: Seventeenth-Century Lesbian Poet', in Elaine Hobby and Chris White, *What Lesbians Do in Books* (London, 1991); Germaine Greer, *Slip-Shod Sibyls* (London, 1995), ch. 5.

Aphra Behn

The Works of Aphra Behn, ed. Janet Todd, 7 vols. (London, 1992–6); Janet Todd, *The Secret Life of Aphra Behn* (London, 1996); Janet Todd (ed.), *Aphra Behn Studies* (Cambridge, 1996); Heidi Hutner (ed.), *Rereading Aphra Behn* (Charlottesville, SC, 1993); Robert Markley, '"Be Impudent, Be Saucy, Forward, Bold, Touzing, and Leud": The Politics of Masculine Sexuality and Feminine Desire in Behn's Tory Comedies', in Douglas Canfield and Deborah Payne (eds.), *Cultural Readings of Restoration and Eighteenth-Century English Theater* (Athens, Ga., 1995); Arlen Feldwick, 'Wits, Whigs, and Women: Domestic Politics as Anti-Whig Rhetoric in Aphra Behn's Town Comedies', in Carole Levin and Patricia Sullivan (eds.), *Political Rhetoric, Power, and Renaissance Women* (Albany, NY, 1995); Susan Owen, '"Suspect My Loyalty When I Lose My Virtue": Sexual Politics and Party in Aphra Behn's Plays of the Exclusion Crisis, 1678–83' *Restoration*, 18 (1994); S. J. Wiseman, *Aphra Behn* (Plymouth, 1994); Angeline Goreau, *Reconstructing Aphra: A Social Biography of Aphra Behn* (New York, 1980); Jacqueline Pearson, *The Prostituted Muse* (London, 1988); Frederick M. Link, *Aphra Behn* (New York, 1968).

Further Reading in Oxford World's Classics

An Anthology of Elizabethan Prose Fiction, ed. Paul Salzman.
An Anthology of Seventeenth-Century Fiction, ed. Paul Salzman.
Aphra Behn, *Oroonoko and Other Writings*, ed. Paul Salzman.
—— *The Rover and Other Plays*, ed. Jane Spencer.

CHRONOLOGY

1558 Elizabeth I crowned.

1567 Isabella Whitney, *Copy of a Letter*.

1569 Aemelia Lanyer born.

1573 Isabella Whitney, *A Sweet Nosegay*.

*c.*1587 Mary Wroth born.

1590 Eleanor Davies born. Anne Clifford born.

1595 Shakespeare, *Romeo and Juliet*.

1603 Death of Elizabeth. James I crowned.

1611 Aemelia Lanyer, *Salve Deus Rex Judaeorum*. Shakespeare, *The Tempest*.

1613 Princess Elizabeth (daughter of James I and Anne) marries Frederick, Elector Palatine. Elizabeth Cary, *The Tragedy of Mariam*.

1618 Thirty Years' War begins when Frederick accepts the crown of Bohemia, precipitating conflict between Catholic and Protestant Europe.

1621 Mary Wroth, *Urania*.

1623 Margaret Cavendish born.

1625 James I dies. Charles I crowned.

1627 Dorothy Osborne born.

*c.*1629 Hester Biddle born.

1628 Duke of Buckingham killed. Charles I begins his 11 years' 'personal rule' (without calling a parliament).

1632 Katherine Philips born.

*c.*1640 Aphra Behn born.

1642 Civil War begins.

1645 Aemilia Lanyer dies.

1649 Charles I executed. Eleanor Davies, *Revelations*.

1651 Eleanor Davies, *The Benediction*.

1652 Eleanor Davies dies.

*c.*1653 Mary Wroth dies.

1653 Beginning of the Protectorate under Cromwell. Margaret Cavendish, *Poems and Fancies*; *Philosophical Fancies*.

1654 Anna Trapnel, *The Cry of a Stone*. Dorothy Osborne marries William Temple.

1655 Priscilla Cotton and Mary Cole, *To the Priests and People of England*. Margaret Cavendish, *The World's Olio*.

1656 Margaret Cavendish, *Nature's Pictures Drawn by Fancy's Pencil*.

1660 Restoration: Charles II crowned.

1662 Margaret Cavendish, *Plays*.

1663 Katherine Philips's translation of Corneille's *Pompey* performed in Dublin.

1664 Katherine Philips dies. Katherine Philips, *Poems*.

1666 Margaret Cavendish, *Observations Upon Experimental Philosophy*. Margaret Fell, *Women's Speaking Justified*.

1669 Frances Boothby's play *Marcelia* performed in London.

1670 Aphra Behn's first play, *The Forced Marriage*, performed in London.

1673 Margaret Cavendish dies.

1676 Anne Clifford dies.

1677 Aphra Behn, *The Rover*.

1682 Aphra Behn, *The City Heiress*.

1684 Aphra Behn, *Poems Upon Several Occasions*.

1685 Charles II dies. James II crowned.

1688 Glorious Revolution: James II goes into exile, William and Mary succeed him.

1689 Aphra Behn dies.

1695 Dorothy Osborne dies.

1696 Hester Biddle dies.

1698 Aphra Behn, *The Wandering Beauty*.

EARLY MODERN WOMEN'S WRITING

ISABELLA WHITNEY
(fl. 1567–1578)

From *The Copy of a Letter, lately written in metre by a young gentlewoman to her unconstant lover. With an admonition to all young gentlewomen, and to all other maids in general, to beware of men's flattery. By Is. W. Newly joined to a love-letter sent by a bachelor (a most faithful lover) to an unconstant and faithless maiden.* (*c.*1567)

'I.W. To Her Unconstant Lover'*

As close as you your wedding kept
  yet now the truth I hear:
Which you (yet now) might me have told
  what need you nay to swear?

You know I always wished you well
  so will I during life:
But sith you shall a husband be
  God send you a good wife.

And this (where so you shall become)
  full boldly may you boast:
That once you had as true a love,
  as dwelt in any coast.

Whose constantness had never quailed
  if you had not begun:
And yet it is not so far past,
  but might again be won —

If you so would: yea and not change
  so long as life should last:
But if that needs you marry must
  then farewell, hope is past,

And if you cannot be content
  to lead a single life,

(Although the same right quiet be)
then take me to your wife.

So shall the promises be kept,
that you so firmly made:
Now choose whether ye will be true,
or be of Sinon's trade.*

Whose trade if that you long shall use,
it shall your kindred stain:
Example take by many a one
whose falsehood now is plain.

As by Aeneas* first of all,
who did poor Dido leave,
Causing the Queen by his untruth
with sword her heart to cleave,

Also I find that Theseus* did,
his faithful love forsake:
Stealing away within the night,
before she did awake.

Jason* that came of noble race,
two ladies did beguile:
I muse how he durst show his face,
to them that knew his wile.

For when he by Medea's art,
had got the fleece of gold
And also had of her, that time,
all kind of things he would,

He took his ship and fled away
regarding not the vows
That he did make so faithfully,
unto his loving spouse.

How durst he trust the surging seas
knowing himself forsworn;
Why did he 'scape safe to the land,
before the ship was torn?

I think king Aeolus* staid the winds
and Neptune ruled the sea:

Then might he boldly pass the waves
no perils could him slay.

But if his falsehood had to them,
been manifest before:
They would have rent the ship as soon
as he had gone from shore.

Now may you hear how falseness is
made manifest in time:
Although they that commit the same,
think it a venial crime.

For they, for their unfaithfulness,
did get perpetual fame:
Fame? Wherefore did I term it so:
I should have called it shame.

Let Theseus be, let Jason pass,
let Paris* also 'scape:
That brought destruction unto Troy
all through the Grecian rape.

And unto me a Troilus* be,
if not you may compare:
With any of these persons that
above expressed are.

But if I cannot please your mind
for wants that rest in me:
Wed whom you list, I am content,
your refuse for to be.

It shall suffice me simple soul,
of thee to be forsaken:
And it may chance although not yet
you wish you had me taken.

But rather than you should have cause
to wish this through your wife:
I wish to her, ere you her have,
no more but love of life.

For she that shall so happy be,
of thee to be elect:

I wish her virtues to be such,
she need not be suspect.

I rather wish her Helen's face,
than one of Helen's trade:
With chasteness of Penelope*
the which did never fade.

A Lucrece* for her constancy,
and Thisby* for her truth:
If such thou have, then Peto* be
not Paris, that were ruth.

Perchance, ye will think this thing rare,
in on[e] woman to find:
Save Helen's beauty, all the rest
the Gods have me assigned.

These words I do not speak, thinking
from thy new love to turn thee:
Thou knowest by proof what I deserve
I need not to inform thee.

But let that pass: would God I had
Cassandra's* gift me lent:
Then either thy ill chance or mine
my foresight might prevent.

But all in vain for this I seek,
wishes may not attain it
Therefore may hap to me what shall,
and I cannot refrain it.

Wherefore I pray God be my guide
and also thee defend:
No worser than I wish myself
until thy life shall end.

Which life I pray God, may again,
King Nestor's* life renew:
And after that your soul may rest
amongst the heavenly crew.

Thereto I wish King Xerxes'* wealth,
or else King Cressus' gold:*

With as much rest and quietness
 as man may have on mould.*
And when you shall this letter have
 let it be kept in store,
For she that sent the same hath sworn
 as yet to send no more.
And now farewell, for why at large
 my mind is here expressed?
The which you may perceive, if that
 you do peruse the rest.

FINIS. Is. W.

'The Admonition by the Author,
to all young gentlewomen:
And to all other Maids being in love.'

Ye Virgins ye from Cupid's tents
 do bear away the foil,
Whose hearts as yet with raging love
 most painfully do boil.
To you I speak: for you be they,
 that good advice do lack:
Oh, if I could good counsel give
 my tongue should not be slack.
But such as I can give, I will
 here in few words express:
Which if you do observe, it will
 some of your care redress.
Beware of fair and painted talk,
 beware of flattering tongues:
The mermaids do pretend no good
 for all their pleasant songs.
Some use the tears of crocodiles,
 contrary to their heart:
And if they cannot always weep,
 they wet their cheeks by art.

Ovid, within his *Art of Love*,*
doth teach them this same knack
To wet their hand, and touch their eyes:
so oft as tears they lack.

Why have ye such deceit in store?
have you such crafty wile?
Less craft than this god knows would soon
us simple souls beguile,

And will ye not leave off, but still
delude us in this wise?
Sith it is so, we trust we shall,
take heed to fained lies.

Trust not a man at the first sight,
but try him well before:
I wish all maids within their breasts
to keep this thing in store.

For trial shall declare his truth,
and show what he doth think:
Whether he be a lover true,
or do intend to shrink.

If Scilla* had not trust too much
before that she did try:
She could not have been clean forsake
when she for help did cry.

Or if she had had good advice
Nisus had lived long:
How durst she trust a stranger, and
do her dear father wrong.

King Nisus had a hair by fate
which hair while he did keep:
He never should be overcome
neither on land nor deep.

The stranger that ye daughter loved
did war against the King
And always sought how it he might
them in subjection bring.

This Scilla stole away the hair,
  for to obtain her will:
And gave it to the stranger that,
  did straight her father kill.

Then she, who thought herself most sure
  to have her whole desire:
Was clean reject, and left behind
  when he did whom* retire.

Or if such falsehood had been once,
  unto Oenone* known:
About the fields of Ida wood,
  Paris had walked alone.

Or if Demophoon's deceit,*
  to Phillis had been told:
She had not been transformed so,
  as poets tell of old.

Hero* did try Leander's truth,
  before that she did trust:
Therefore she found him unto her
  both constant, true, and just.

For he always did swim the sea,
  when stars in sky did glide:
Till he was drowned by the way
  near hand unto the side.

She scrat* her face, she tear her hair
  (it grieveth me to tell)
When she did know the end of him,
  that she did love so well.

But like Leander there be few,
  therefore in time take heed:
And always try before ye trust,
  so shall you better speed.

The little fish that careless is,
  within the water clear:
How glad is he, when he doth see,
  a bait for to appear.

He thinks his hap right good to be,
  that he the same could spy:
And so the simple fool doth trust
  too much before he try.

O little fish what hap hadst thou?
  to have such spiteful fate:
To come into one's cruel hands,
  out of so happy state?

Thou didst suspect no harm, when thou
  upon the bait didst look:
O that thou hadst had Lynceus' eyes*
  for to have seen the hook.

Then hadst thou with thy pretty mates
  been playing in the streams
Whereas sir Phoebus daily doth,
  show forth his golden beams.

But sith thy fortune is so ill
  to end thy life on shore:
Of this thy most unhappy end,
  I mind to speak no more.

But of thy fellow's chance that late
  such pretty shift did make:
That he from fisher's hook did sprit*
  before he could him take.

And now he pries on every bait,
  suspecting still that prick:
For to lie hid in every thing
  wherewith the fishers strick.

And since the fish that reason lacks
  once warned doth beware:
Why should not we take heed to that
  that turneth us to care.

And I who was deceived late,
  by one's unfaithful tears:
Trust now for to beware, if that
  I live this hundreth years.

FINIS. Is. W.

From *A Sweet Nosegay or a Pleasant Posy* (1573)

'The Author (though loath to leave the city) upon her friend's procurement, is constrained to depart: wherefore (she feigneth as she would die) and maketh her Will and Testament, as followeth: With large legacies of such goods and riches which she most abundantly hath left behind her: and thereof maketh London sole executor to see her legacies performed.'

A communication which the Author had to London, before she made her Will.

The time is come I must depart,
  from thee, ah famous city:
I never yet to rue my smart,
  did find that thou hadst pity.
Wherefore small cause there is, that I
  should grieve from thee go:
But many women foolishly,
  like me, and other moe,
Do such a fixed fancy set,
  on those which least deserve,
That long it is ere wit we get,
  away from them to swerve.
But time with pity oft will tell
  to those that will her try:
Whether it best be more to mell,*
  or utterly defy.
And now hath time me put in mind,
  of thy great cruelness:
That never once a help would find,
  to ease me in distress.
Thou never yet, wouldst credit give
  to board me for a year:
Nor with apparel me relieve
  except thou payed were.
No, no, thou never didst me good,
  nor ever wilt I know:

Yet am I in no angry mood,
  but will, or ere I go
In perfect love and charity
  my testament here write:
And leave to thee such Treasury,
  as I in it recite.
Now stand aside and give me leave
  to write my latest will:
And see that none you do deceive,
  of that I leave them till.

The manner of her Will, and what she left to London: and to all those in it: at her departing.

I whole in body, and in mind,
  but very weak in purse:
Do make, and write my testament
  for fear it will be worse.
And first I wholly do commend,
  my soul and body eke:
To God the Father and the Son,
  so long as I can speak.
And after speech: my soul to him,
  and body to the grave:
Till time that all shall rise again,
  their judgment for to have.
And then I hope they both shall meet
  to dwell for aye in joy:
Whereas I trust to see my friends
  released, from all annoy.
Thus have you heard touching my soul,
  and body what I mean:
I trust you all will witness bear,
  I have a steadfast brain.
And now let me dispose such things,
  as I shall leave behind:
That those which shall receive the same,
  may know my willing mind.

I first of all to London leave
  because I there was bred:
Brave buildings rare, of churches store,
  and Paul's* to the head.
Between the same: fair streets there be,
  and people goodly store:
Because their keeping craveth cost,
  I yet will leave him more.
First for their food, I butchers leave,
  that every day shall kill:
By Thames you shall have brewers store,
  and bakers at your will.
And such as orders do observe,
  and eat fish thrice a week:
I leave two streets, full fraught therewith,
  they need not far to seek.
Watling Street, and Canwick Street,*
  I full of woollen leave:
And linen store in Friday Street,
  if they me not deceive.
And those which are of calling such,
  that costlier they require:
I m[e]rcers leave, with silk so rich,
  as any would desire.
In Cheap* of them, they store shall find
  and likewise in that street:
I goldsmiths leave, with jewels such,
  as are for ladies meet.
And plate to furnish cupboards with,
  full brave there shall you find:
With pearl of silver and of gold,
  to satisfy your mind.
With hoods, bongraces,* hats or caps,
  such store are in that street:
As if on th'one side you should miss
  the other serves you for't.
For nets of every kind of sort,
  I leave within the pawn:
French ruffs, high pearls, gorgets* and sleeves

of any kind of lawn.
For purse or knives, for comb or glass,
or any needful knack
I by the stocks have left a boy,
will ask you what you lack.
I hose do leave in Burchin Lane,
of any kind of size:
For women stitched, for men both trunks*
and those of Gascoyne guise.*
Boots, shoes or pantables* good store,
Saint Martin's hath for you:
In Cornwall, there I leave you beds,
and all that 'longs thereto.
For women shall you tailors have,
by Bow, the chiefest dwell:
In every lane you some shall find,
can do indifferent well.
And for the men, few streets or lanes,
but bodymakers be:
And such as make the sweeping cloaks,
with guards beneath the knee.
Artillery at Temple Bar,
and dags* at Tower Hill:
Swords and bucklers of the best,
are nigh the Fleet until.
Now when thy folk are fed and clad
with such as I have named:
For dainty mouths, and stomachs weak
some junkets must be framed.
Wherefore I 'pothecaries* leave,
with banquets in their shop:
Physicians also for the sick,
diseases for to stop.
Some roisters* still, must 'bide in thee.
and such as cut it out:*
That with the guiltless quarrel will,
to let their blood about.
For them I cunning surgeons leave,
some plasters to apply.

That ruffians may not still be hanged,
  nor quiet persons die.
For salt, oatmeal, candles, soap,
  or what you else do want:
In many places, shops are full,
  I left you nothing scant.
If they that keep what I you leave,
  ask money: when they sell it:
At Mint, there is such store, it is
  impossible to tell it.
At Steelyard* store of wines there be,
  your dulled minds to glad:
And handsome men, that must not wed
  except they leave their trade.
They oft shall seek for proper girls,
  and some perhaps shall find:
(That need compels, or lucre lures)
  to satisfy their mind.
And near the same, I houses leave,
  for people to repair:
To bathe themselves, so to prevent
  infection of the air.
On Saturdays I wish that those,
  which all the week do drug:*
Shall thither trudge, to trim them up
  on Sundays to look smug.
If any other thing be lacked
  in thee, I wish them look:
For there it is: I little brought
  but nothing from thee took.
Now for the people in thee left,
  I have done as I may:
And that the poor, when I am gone,
  have cause for me to pray,
I will to prisons portions leave,
  what though but very small:
Yet that they may remember me,
  occasion be it shall:
And first the Counter* they shall have,

lest they should go to wrack:
Some coggers,* and some honest men,
that sergeants draw a back.
And such as friends will not them bail,
whose coin is very thin:
For them I leave a certain hole,*
and little ease within.
The Newgate* once a month shall have
a sessions for his share:
Lest being heaped, infection might
procure a further care.
And at those sessions some shall 'scape,
with burning near the thumb:
And afterward to beg their fees,
till they have got the sum.
And such whose deeds deserveth death,
and twelve have found the same:
They shall be drawn up Holborn Hill,*
to come to further shame:
Well, yet to such I leave a nag
shall soon their sorrows cease:
For he shall either break their necks
or gallop from the press.
The Fleet,* not in their circuit is,
yet if I give him naught:
It might procure his curse, ere I
unto the ground be brought.
Wherefore I leave some Papist old
to under prop his roof:
And to the poor within the same,
a box for their behoof.
What makes you standers by to smile.
and laugh so in your sleeve:
I think it is, because that I
to Ludgate* nothing give.
I am not now in case to lie,
here is no place of jest:
I did reserve, that for myself,
if I my health possessed.

And ever came in credit so
  a debtor for to be.
When days of payment did approach,
  I thither meant to flee,
To shroud myself amongst the rest,
  that choose to die in debt:
Rather than any creditor,
  should money from them get.
Yet 'cause I feel myself so weak
  that none me credit dare:
I here revoke: and do it leave,
  some bankrupts to his share.
To all the bookbinders by Paul's
  because I like their art:
They every week shall money have,
  when they from books depart.
Amongst them all, my printer must,
  have somewhat to his share:
I will my friends these books to buy
  of him, with other ware.
For maidens poor, I widowers rich
  do leave, that oft shall dote:
And by that means shall marry them,
  to set the girls afloat.
And wealthy widows will I leave,
  to help young gentlemen:
Which when you have in any case
  be courteous to them then:
And see their plate and jewels eke
  may not be marred with rust.
Nor let their bags too long be full,
  for fear that they do burst.
To every gate under the walls,
  that compass thee about:
I fruit wives leave to entertain
  such as come in and out.
To Smithfield* I must something leave
  my parents there did dwell:
So careless for to be of it,

none would accompt it well.
Wherefore it thrice a week shall have,
of horse and neat* good store,
And in his 'Spital,* blind and lame,
to dwell for evermore.
And Bedlam* must not be forgot,
for that was oft my walk:
I people there too many leave,
that out of tune do talk.
At Bridewell* there shall beadles be,
and matrons that shall still
See chalk well chopped, and spinning plied,
and turning of the mill.
For such as cannot quiet be,
but strive for house or land:
At th'Inns of Court,* I lawyers leave
to take their cause in hand.
And also leave I at each Inn
of Court, or Chancery:
Of gentlemen, a youthful rout,
full of activity:
For whom I store of books have left,
at each bookbinder's stall:
And part of all that London hath
to furnish them withal.
And when they are with study cloyed:
to recreate their mind:
Of tennis courts, of dancing schools,
and fence they store shall find.
And every Sunday at the least,
I leave to make them sport
In diverse places players, that
of wonders shall report.
Now London have I (for thy sake)
within thee, and without:
As comes into my memory,
dispersed round about
Such needful things, as they should have
here left now unto thee:

When I am gone, with conscience
  let them dispersed be.
And though I nothing named have,
  to bury me withal:
Consider that above the ground,
  annoyance be I shall.
And let me have a shrouding sheet
  to cover me from shame:
And in oblivion bury me
  and never more me name.
Ringings* nor other ceremonies,
  use you not for cost:
Nor at my burial, make no feast,
  your money were but lost.
Rejoice in God that I am gone,
  out of this vale so vile.
And that of each thing, left such store,
  as may your wants exile.
I make thee sole executor, because
  I loved thee best.
And thee I put in trust, to give
  the goods unto the rest.
Because thou shalt a helper need,
  In this so great a charge,
I wish good fortune, be thy guide, lest
  thou shouldst run at large.
The happy days and quiet times,
  they both her servants be.
Which well will serve to fetch and bring,
  such things as need to thee.
Wherefore (good London) not refuse,
  for helper her to take:
Thus being weak, and weary both
  an end here will I make.
To all that ask what end I made,
  and how I went away:
Thou answer may'st like those which here,
  no longer tarry may.
And unto all that wish me well,

or rue that I am gone:
Do me commend, and bid them cease
my absence for to moan.
And tell them further, if they would,
my presence still have had:
They should have sought to mend my luck;
which ever was too bad.
So fare thou well a thousand times,
God shield thee from thy foe:
And still make thee victorious,
of those that seek thy woe.
And (though I am persuade) that I
shall never more thee see:
Yet to the last, I shall not cease
to wish much good to thee.
This, 20 of October I,
in Anno Domini:
A thousand five hundred seventy three
as almanacs descry,
Did write this will, with mine own hand
and it to London gave:
In witness of the standers by,
whose names if you will have
Paper, Pen and Standish* were:
at that same present by:
With Time, who promised to reveal,
so fast as she could hie
The same: lest of my nearer kin,
for anything should vary:
So finally I make an end
no longer can I tarry.

FINIS. by IS. W.

AEMILIA LANYER
(1569–1645)

*Salve Deus Rex Judaeorum**
Containing

1. The Passion of Christ
2. Eve's Apology in defence of Women
3. The tears of the daughters of Jerusalem
4. The salutation and sorrow of the Virgin Mary.

With diverse other things not unfit to be read.
Written by Mistress Aemilia Lanyer, wife to Captain Alfonso Lanyer, servant to the King's Majesty. (1611)

'To the Queen's* most Excellent Majesty'

Renowned Empress, and great Britain's Queen,
Most gracious mother of succeeding kings;
Vouchsafe to view that which is seldom seen,
A woman's writing of divinest things:
    Read it fair Queen, though it defective be,
    Your excellence can grace both it and me.

For you have rifled nature of her store,
And all the goddesses have dispossessed
Of those rich gifts which they enjoyed before,
But now great Queen, in you they all do rest.
    If now they strived for the golden ball,
    Paris* would give it you before them all.

From Juno you have state and dignities,
From warlike Pallas, wisdom, fortitude;
And from fair Venus all her excellencies,
With their best parts your Highness is endued:
    How much are we to honour those that springs
    From such rare beauty, in the blood of kings?

The Muses do attend upon your throne,
With all the artists at your beck and call;
The sylvan gods and satyrs every one
Before your fair, triumphant chariot fall:
    And shining Cynthia* with her nymphs attend
    To honour you, whose honour hath no end.

From your bright sphere of greatness where you sit,
Reflecting light to all those glorious stars
That wait upon your throne; to virtue yet
Vouchsafe that splendour which my meanness bars:
    Be like fair Phoebe,* who doth love to grace
    The darkest night with her most beauteous face.

Apollo's beams* do comfort every creature
And shines upon the meanest things that be,
Since in estate and virtue none is greater
I humbly wish that yours may light on me:
    That so these rude, unpolished lines of mine,
    Graced by you, may seem the more divine.

Look in this mirror of a worthy mind
Where some of your fair virtues will appear,
Though all it is impossible to find,
Unless my glass were crystal, or more clear:
    Which is dim steel, yet full of spotless truth,
    And for one look from your fair eyes it sueth.

Here may your sacred Majesty behold
That mighty monarch both of Heaven and earth,
He that all nations of the world controlled,
Yet took our flesh in base and meanest birth:
    Whose days were spent in poverty and sorrow,
    And yet all kings their wealth of him do borrow.

For he is crown and crowner of all kings,
The hopeful haven of the meaner sort,
It's he that all our joyful tidings brings
Of happy reign within his royal court:
    It's he that in extremity can give
    Comfort to them that have no time to live.

And since my wealth within his region stands
And that his cross my chiefest comfort is
Yea in his kingdom only rests my lands,
Of honour there I hope I shall not miss:
    Though I on earth do live unfortunate,
    Yet there I may attain a better state.

In the meantime, accept most gracious Queen
This holy work, virtue presents to you,
In poor apparel, shaming to be seen,
Or once t'appear in your judicial view:
    But that fair virtue, though in mean attire,
    All princes of the world do most desire.

And sith* all royal virtues are in you,
The natural, the moral, and divine,
I hope how plain soever, being true,
You will accept even of the meanest line
    Fair virtue yields; by whose rare gifts you are
    So highly graced, t'exceed the fairest fair.

Behold, great Queen, fair Eve's apology,
Which I have writ in honour of your sex,
And do refer unto your Majesty,
To judge if it agree not with the text:
    And if it do, why are poor women blamed,
    Or by more faulty men so much defamed?

And this great lady I have here attired,
In all her richest ornaments of honour,
That you, fair Queen, of all the world admired,
May take the more delight to look upon her:
    For she must entertain you to this feast,
    To which your Highness is the welcom'st guest.

For here I have prepared my paschal lamb,*
The figure of that living sacrifice;
Who dying, all th'infernal powers orecame,
That we with him t'eternity might rise:
    This precious Passover feed upon, O Queen,
    Let your fair virtues in my glass be seen.

The lady Elizabeth's grace.

And she* that is the pattern of all beauty,
The very model of your Majesty,
Whose rarest parts enforceth love and duty,
The perfect pattern of all piety:
O let my book by her fair eyes be blest,
In whose pure thoughts all innocency rests.

Then shall I think my glass a glorious sky,
When two such glittering suns at once appear;
The one replete with sovereign majesty,
Both shining brighter than the clearest clear:
And both reflecting comfort to my spirits,
To find their grace so much above my merits

Whose untuned voice the doleful notes doth sing
Of sad affliction in an humble strain;
Much like unto a bird that wants a wing
And cannot fly, but warbles forth her pain:
Or he that, barred from the sun's bright light,
Wanting day's comfort, doth commend the night.

So I that live closed up in sorrow's cell,
Since great Eliza's* favour blest my youth;
And in the confines of all cares do dwell,
Whose grieved eyes no pleasure ever vieweth:
But in Christ's sufferings, such sweet taste they have,
As makes me praise pale sorrow and the grave.

And this great lady whom I love and honour,
And from my very tender years have known,
This holy habit still to take upon her,
Still to remain the same, and still her own:
And what our fortunes do enforce us to,
She of devotion and mere zeal doth do.

Which makes me think our heavy burden light,
When such a one as she will help to bear it:
Treading the paths that make our way go right,
What garment is so faire but she may wear it;
Especially for her that entertains
A glorious queen, in whom all worth remains.

Whose power may raise my sad dejected Muse,
From this low mansion of a troubled mind;
Whose princely favour may such grace infuse,
That I may spread her virtues in like kind:
  But in this trial of my slender skill,
  I wanted knowledge to perform my will.

For even as they that do behold the stars,
Not with the eye of learning, but of sight,
To find their motions, want of knowledge bars
Although they see them in their brightest light:
  So, though I see the glory of her State,
  It's she that must instruct and elevate.

My weak distempered brain and feeble spirits,
Which all unlearned have adventured this:
To write of Christ, and of his sacred merits,
Desiring that this book her hands may kiss:
  And though I be unworthy of that grace,
  Yet let her blessed thoughts this book embrace.

And pardon me (fair Queen) though I presume,
To do that which so many better can;
Not that I learning to myself assume,
Or that I would compare with any man:
  But as they are scholars, and by art do write,
  So nature yields my soul a sad delight.

And since all arts at first from nature came,
That goodly creature, mother of perfection,
Whom Jove's almighty hand at first did frame,
Taking both her and hers in his protection:
  Why should not she now grace my barren muse,
  And in a woman all defects excuse.

So peerless princess, humbly I desire,
That your great wisdom would vouchsafe t'omit
All faults; and pardon if my spirits retire,
Leaving to aim at what they cannot hit:
  To write your worth, which no pen can express,
  Were but t'eclipse your fame, and make it less.

'To the Lady Elizabeth's Grace'*

Most gracious lady, fair ELIZABETH,
Whose name and virtues puts us still in mind,
Of her,* of whom we are deprived by death;
The phoenix of her age, whose worth did bind
All worthy minds so long as they have breath,
    In links of admiration, love and zeal,
    To that dear mother of our common-weal.

Even you, fair princess, next our famous queen,
I do invite unto this wholesome feast,
Whose goodly wisdom, though your years be green,
By such good works may daily be increased,
Though your fair eyes far better books have seen;
    Yet being the first fruits of a woman's wit,
    Vouchsafe you favour in accepting it.

'To All Virtuous Ladies in General'

Each blessed lady that in virtue spends
Your precious time to beautify your souls;
Come wait on her whom winged fame attends
And in her hand the book where she enrols
Those high deserts that majesty commends:
    Let this fair queen not unattended be,
    When in my glass she deigns herself to see.

Put on your wedding garments everyone,
The bridegroom* stays to entertain you all;
Let virtue be your guide, for she alone
Can lead you right that you can never fall;
And make no stay for fear he should be gone:
    But fill your lamps with oil of burning zeal,
    That to your faith he may his truth reveal.

Let all your robes be purple, scarlet, white,
Those perfect colours purest virtue wore,
Come decked with lilies that did so delight
To be preferred in beauty, far before
Wise Solomon* in all his glory dight:*

The robes that Christ wore before his death.

Whose royal robes did no such pleasure yield,
As did the beauteous lily of the field.

Adorn your temples with fair Daphne's crown* *In token of constancy*
The never changing laurel, always green;
Let constant hope all worldly pleasures drown,
In wise Minerva's* paths be always seen;
Or with bright Cynthia, though fair Venus frown:
With Aesop cross the posts of every door,
Where sin would riot, making virtue poor.

And let the muses your companions be,
Those sacred sisters that on Pallas* wait;
Whose virtues with the purest minds agree,
Whose godly labours do avoid the bait
Of worldly pleasures, living always free
From sword, from violence, and from ill report,
To these nine worthies* all fair minds resort.

Anoint your hair with Aaron's precious oil,*
And bring your palms of victory in your hands,
To overcome all thoughts that would defile
The earthly circuit of your soul's fair lands;
Let no dim shadows your clear eyes beguile:
Sweet odours, myrrh, gum, aloes, frankincense,
Present that king who died for your offence.

Behold, bright Titan's shining chariot* stays,
All decked with flowers of the freshest hue,
Attended on by age, hours, nights and days,
Which alters not your beauty, but gives you
Much more, and crowns you with eternal praise;
This golden chariot wherein you must ride,
Let simple doves and subtle serpents guide.

Come swifter than the motion of the sun,
To be transfigured with our loving Lord,
Lest glory end what grace in you begun,
Of heavenly riches make your greatest hoard,
In Christ all honour, wealth and beauty's won:
By whose perfections you appear more fair
Than Phoebus,* if he seven times brighter were.

God's holy angels will direct your doves,
And bring your serpents to the fields of rest,
Where he doth stay that purchased all your loves
In bloody torments, when he died oppressed,
There shall you find him in those pleasant groves
    Of sweet elysium,* by the well of life,
    Whose crystal springs do purge from worldly strife.

There may you fly from dull and sensual earth,
Whereof at first your bodies formed were,
That new regenerate in a second birth,
Your blessed souls may live without all fear,
Being immortal, subject to no death:
    But in the eye of heaven so highly placed,
    That others by your virtues may be graced.

Where worthy ladies I will leave you all,
Desiring you to grace this little book;
Yet some of you methinks I hear to call
Me by my name, and bid me better look,
Lest unawares I in an error fall:
    In general terms, to place you with the rest,
    Whom fame commends to be the very best.

'Tis true, I must confess (O noble fame)
There are a number honoured by thee,
Of which, some few thou didst recite by name,
And willed my muse they should remembered be;
Wishing some would their glorious trophies frame:
    Which if I should presume to undertake,
    My tired hand for very fear would quake.

Only by name I will bid some of those,
That in true honour's seat have long been placed,
Yea even such as thou hast chiefly chose,
By whom my muse may be the better graced;
Therefore, unwilling longer time to lose,
    I will invite some ladies that I know,
    But chiefly those as thou hast graced so.

'To the Lady Arabella'*

Great learned lady, whom I long have known,
And yet not known so much as I desired:
Rare Phoenix, whose fair feathers are your own,
With which you fly, and are so much admired:
True honour whom true fame hath so attired,
In glittering raiment shining much more bright,
Than silver stars in the most frosty night.

Come like the morning sun new out of bed,
And cast your eyes upon this little book,
Although you be so well accompanied
With Pallas, and the muses, spare one look
Upon this humbled king, who all forsook,
That in his dying arms he might embrace
Your beauteous soul, and fill it with his grace.

'To the Lady Susan,* Countess Dowager of Kent, and Daughter to the Duchess of Suffolk'

Come you that were the mistress of my youth,
The noble guide of my ungoverned days;
Come you that have delighted in God's truth,
Help now your handmaid to sound forth his praise:
You that are pleased in his pure excellency,
Vouchsafe to grace this holy feast, and me.

And as your rare perfections showed the glass*
Wherein I saw each wrinkle of a fault;
You the sun's virtue, I that fair green grass,
That flourished fresh by your clear virtues taught:
For you possessed those gifts that grace the mind,
Restraining youth whom error oft doth blind.

In you these noble virtues did I note,
First, love and fear of God, of prince, of laws,
Rare patience with a mind so far remote
From worldly pleasures, free from giving cause
Of least suspect to the most envious eye,
That in fair virtue's storehouse sought to pry.

Whose faith did undertake in infancy,
All dangerous travels by devouring seas
To fly to Christ from vain idolatry,
Not seeking there this worthless world to please,
  By your most famous mother so directed,
  That noble Duchess, who lived unsubjected.

From Rome's ridiculous Prior and tyranny,
That mighty monarchs kept in aweful fear;
Leaving here her lands, her state, dignity;
Nay more, vouchsafed disguised weeds to wear:
  When with Christ Jesus she did mean to go,
  From sweet delights to taste part of his woe.

Come you that ever since hath followed her,
In these sweet paths of faire humility;
Condemning pride, pure virtue to prefer,
Not yielding to base imbecility,
  Nor to those weak enticements of the world,
  That have so many thousand souls ensnarled.

Receive your love* whom you have sought so far
Which here presents himself within your view;
Behold this bright and all-directing star,
Light of your soul that doth all grace renew:
  And in his humble paths since you do tread,
  Take this faire bridegroom in your soul's pure bed.

And since no former gain hath made me write,
Nor my desertless service could have won,
Only your noble virtues do incite
My pen, they are the ground I write upon;
  Nor any future profit is expected,
  Then how can these poor lines go unrespected?

'The Author's Dream to the Lady Mary,* the Countess Dowager of Pembroke'

Methought I passed through th' Idalian groves,*
And asked the Graces,* if they could direct
Me to a lady whom Minerva* chose,
To live with her in hight of all respect.

Yet looking back into my thoughts again,
The eye of reason did behold her there
Fast tied unto them in a golden chain,*
They stood, but she was set in Honour's chair.

And nine fair virgins* sat upon the ground,
With harps and viols in their lily hands;
Whose harmony had all my senses drowned,
But that before mine eyes an object stands,

Whose beauty shined like Titan's* clearest rays,
She blew a brazen trumpet, which did sound
Through all the world that worthy ladies praise,
And by eternal fame I saw her crowned.

Yet studying, if I were awake, or no,
God Morphy* came and took me by the hand,
And willed me not from slumber's bower to go,
Till I the sum of all did understand.

The God of dreams

When presently the welkin* that before
Looked bright and clear, me thought, was overcast,
And dusky clouds, with boist'rous wind's great store,
Foretold of violent storms which could not last.

And gazing up into the troubled sky,
Methought a chariot did from thence descend,
Where one did sit replete with majesty,
Drawn by four fiery dragons, which did bend

Their course where this most noble lady sat,
Whom all these virgins with due reverence
Did entertain, according to that state
Which did belong unto her excellence.

When bright Bellona, so they did her call,
Whom these faire nymphs so humbly did receive,
A manly maid which was both fair and tall,
Her borrowed chariot by a spring did leave.

Goddess of war and wisdom

With spear, and shield, and currat* on her breast,
And on her head a helmet wondrous bright,
With myrtle bays, and olive branches dressed,
Wherein me thought I took no small delight.

To see how all the Graces sought grace here,
And in what meek, yet princely sort she came;
How this most noble lady did embrace her,
And all humours unto hers did frame.

Now faire Dictina by the break of day, *The moon*
With all her damsels round about her came,
Ranging the woods to hunt, yet made a stay,
When harkening to the pleasing sound of fame;

Her ivory bow and silver shafts she gave
Unto the fairest nymph of all her train;
And wondering who it was that in so grave,
Yet gallant fashion did her beauty stain:

She decked herself with all the borrowed light
That Phoebus would afford from his fair face,
And made her virgins to appear so bright,
That all the hills and vales received grace.

Then pressing where this beauteous troop did stand,
They all received her most willingly,
And unto her the lady gave her hand,
That she should keep with them continually.

Aurora, rising from her rosy bed, *The morning*
First blushed, then wept, to see faire Phoebe graced,
And unto Lady May these words she said,
'Come, let us go, we will not be out-faced.

I will unto Apollo's wagoner,
A bid* him bring his master presently,
That his bright beams may all her beauty mar,
Gracing us with the lustre of his eye.

Come, come, sweet May, and fill their laps with flowers,
And I will give a greater light than she:
So all these ladies' favours shall be ours,
None shall be more esteemed than we shall be.'

Thus did Aurora dim fair Phoebus' light,
And was received in bright Cynthia's place,
While Flora all with fragrant flowers dight,*
Pressed to show the beauty of her face.

Though these, me thought, were very pleasing sights,
Yet now these worthies did agree to go,
Unto a place full of all rare delights,
A place that yet Minerva did not know.

That sacred spring where art and nature strived
Which should remain as sovereign of the place;
Whose ancient quarrel being new revived,
Added fresh beauty, gave far greater grace.

To which as umpires now these ladies go,
Judging with pleasure their delightful case;
Whose ravished senses made them quickly know,
T'would be offensive either to displace.

And therefore willed they should for ever dwell,
In perfect unity by this matchless spring:
Since 'twas impossible either should excel,
Or her fair fellow in subjection bring.

But here in equal sovereignty to live,
Equal in state, equal in dignity,
That unto others they might comfort give,
Rejoicing all with their sweet unity.

And now, me thought, I long to hear her name,
Whom wise Minerva honoured so much,
She whom I saw was crowned by noble fame,
Whom envy sought to sting, yet could not touch.

Me thought the meager elf* did seek by ways
To come unto her, but it would not be;
Her venom purified by virtue's rays,
She pined and starved like an anatomy:*

While beauteous Pallas with this lady fair,
Attended by these nymphs of noble fame,
Beheld those woods, those groves, those bowers rare,
By which Pergusa,* for so hight the name

Of that fair spring, his dwelling place and ground;
And through those fields with sundry flowers clad,
Of several colours, to adorn the ground,
And please the senses even of the most sad:

He trailed along the woods in wanton wise,
With sweet delight to entertain them all;
Inviting them to sit and to devise
On holy hymns; at last to mind they call

Those rare, sweet songs* which Israel's king did frame
Unto the Father of eternity;
Before his holy wisdom took the name
Of great Messias, Lord of unity.

Those holy sonnets they did all agree,
With this most lovely lady here to sing;
That by her noble breast's sweet harmony,
Their music might in ears of angels ring.

*The psalms written newly by the Countess Dowager of Pembroke**

While saints like swans about this silver brook
Should Hallelujah sing continually,
Writing her praises in th'eternal book
Of endless honour, true fame's memory.

Thus I in sleep the heavenliest music heard,
That ever earthly ears did entertain;
And durst not wake, for fear to be debarred
Of what my senses sought still to retain.

Yet sleeping, prayed dull slumber to unfold
Her noble name, who was of all admired;
When presently in drowsy terms he told
Not only that, but more than I desired.

'This nymph,' quoth he, 'great Pembroke hight by name,
Sister to valiant Sidney, whose clear light
Gives light to all that tread true paths of fame,
Who in the globe of heaven doth shine so bright;

That being dead, his fame doth him survive,
Still living in the hearts of worthy men;
Pale death is dead, but he remains alive,
Whose dying wounds restored him life again.

And this fair earthly goddess which you see,
Bellona* and her virgins do attend;
In virtuous studies of divinity,
Her precious time continually doth spend.

So that a sister well she may be deemed,
To him that lived and died so nobly;
And far before him is to be esteemed
For virtue, wisdom, learning, dignity.

Whose beauteous soul hath gained a double life,
Both here on earth, and in the heavens above,
Till dissolution end all worldly strife:
Her blessed spirit remains, of holy love,

Directing all by her immortal light,
In this huge sea of sorrows, griefs, and fears;
With contemplation of God's powerful might,
She fills the eyes, the hearts, the tongues, the ears

Of after-coming ages, which shall read
Her love, her zeal, her faith, and piety;
The fair impression of whose worthy deed,
Seals her pure soul unto the deity.

That both in heaven and earth it may remain,
Crowned with her maker's glory and his love;'
And this did Father Slumber tell with pain,
Whose dullness scarce could suffer him to move.

When I awaking left him and his bower,
Much grieved that I could no longer stay;
Senseless was sleep, not to admit me power,
As I had spent the night to spend the day:

Then had God Morphy showed the end of all,
And what my heart desired, mine eyes had seen;
For as I waked me thought I heard one call
For that bright chariot lent by Jove's fair queen.

But thou, base cunning thief, that robs our spirits *To sleep*
Of half that span of life which years doth give;
And yet no praise unto thy self it merits,
To make a seeming death in those that live.

Yea wickedly thou dost consent to death,
Within thy restful bed to rob our souls;
In slumber's bower thou steal'st away our breath,
Yet none there is that thy base stealths controls.

If poor and sickly creatures would embrace thee,
Or they to whom thou givest a taste of pleasure,
Thou fliest as if Actaeon's hounds* did chase thee,
Or that to stay with them thou hadst no leisure.

But though thou hast deprived me of delight,
By stealing from me ere I was aware;
I know I shall enjoy the self same sight,
Thou hast no power my waking sprites* to bar.

For to this lady now I will repair,
Presenting her the fruits of idle hours;
Though many books* she writes that are more rare,
Yet there is honey in the meanest flowers:

Which is both wholesome, and delights the taste:
Though sugar be more finer, higher prized,
Yet is the painful bee no whit disgraced,
Nor her fair wax, or honey more despised.

And though that learned damsel and the rest,
Have in a higher style her trophy framed;
Yet these unlearned lines being my best,
Of her great wisdom can no whit be blamed.

And therefore, first I here present my dream,
And next, invite her honour to my feast,
For my clear reason sees her by that stream,
Where her rare virtues daily are increased.

So craving pardon for this bold attempt,
I here present my mirror to her view,
Whose noble virtues cannot be exempt,
My glass* being steel, declares them to be true.

And Madam, if you will vouchsafe that grace,
To grace those flowers that springs from virtue's ground;
Though your fair mind on worthier works is placed,
On works that are more deep, and more profound,

Yet is it no disparagement to you,
To see your Saviour in a shepherd's weed,
Unworthily presented in your view,
Whose worthiness will grace each line you read.

Receive him here by my unworthy hand,
And read his paths of fair humility;
Who though our sins in number pass the sand,
They all are purged by his divinity.

'To the Lady Lucy, Countess of Bedford'*

Methinks I see fair virtue ready stand,
T'unlock the closet of your lovely breast,
Holding the key of knowledge in her hand,
Key of that cabin where your self doth rest,
To let him* in, by whom her youth was blest
  The true-love of your soul, your heart's delight,
  Fairer than all the world in your clear sight.

He that descended from celestial glory,
To taste of our infirmities and sorrows,
Whose heavenly wisdom read the earthly story
Of frail humanity, which his godhead borrows;
Lo here he comes all stuck with pale death's arrows:
  In whose most precious wounds your soul may read
  Salvation, while he (dying Lord) doth bleed.

You whose clear judgement far exceeds my skill,
Vouchsafe to entertain this dying lover,
The ocean of true grace, whose streams do fill
All those with joy, that can his love recover;
About this blessed ark bright angels hover:
  Where your fair soul may sure and safely rest,
  When he is sweetly seated in your breast.

There may your thoughts as servants to your heart,
Give true attendance on this lovely guest,
While he doth to that blessed bower impart
Flowers of fresh comforts, deck that bed of rest,
With such rich beauties as may make it blest:
  And you in whom all rarity is found,
  May be with his eternal glory crowned.

'To the Lady Margaret Countess Dowager of Cumberland'*

Right honourable and excellent lady, I may say with Saint Peter, 'silver nor gold have I none, but such as I have, that give I you':* for having neither rich pearls of India, nor fine gold of Arabia, nor diamonds of inestimable value; neither those rich treasures, aromatical gums, incense, and sweet odours, which were presented by those kingly philosophers to the babe Jesus, I present unto you even our Lord Jesus himself, whose infinite value is not to be comprehended within the weak imagination or wit of man: and as Saint Peter gave health to the body, so I deliver you the health of the soul; which is this most precious pearl of all perfection, this rich diamond of devotion, this perfect gold growing in the veins of that excellent earth of the most blessed paradise, wherein our second Adam had his restless habitation. The sweet incense, balsams, odours, and gums that flows from that beautiful tree of life, sprung from the root of Jesse, which is so super-excellent, that it giveth grace to the meanest and most unworthy hand that will undertake to write thereof; neither can it receive any blemish thereby: for as a right diamond can lose no whit of his beauty by the black foil underneath it, neither by being placed in the dark, but retains his natural beauty and brightness shining in greater perfection than before; so this most precious diamond, for beauty and riches exceeding all the most precious diamonds and rich jewels of the world, can receive no blemish, nor impeachment, by my unworthy hand writing, but will with the sun retain his own brightness and most glorious lustre, though never so many blind eyes look upon him. Therefore, good Madam, to the most perfect eyes of your understanding, I deliver the inestimable treasure of all elected souls, to be perused at convenient times; as also, the mirror of your most worthy mind, which may remain in the world many years longer than your Honour, or myself can live, to be a light unto those that come after, desiring to tread in the narrow path of virtue, that leads the way to heaven. In which way, I pray God send your Honour long to continue, that your light may so shine before men, that they may glorify your Father which is in Heaven: and that I and many others may follow you in the same track. So wishing you in this world all increase of health and honour, and in the world to come life everlasting, I rest.

'To the Lady Katherine, Countess of Suffolk'*

Although, great lady, it may seem right strange,
That I a stranger should presume thus far
To write to you; yet as the times do change,
So are we subject to that fatal star,
  Under the which we were produced to breathe,
  That star that guides us even until our death.

And guided me to frame this work of grace,
Not of itself, but by celestial powers,
To which, both that and we must needs give place,
Since what we have, we cannot count it ours:
  For health, wealth, honour, sickness, death and all,
  Is in God's power, which makes us rise and fall.

And since his power hath given me power to write,
A subject fit for you to look upon,
Wherein your soul may take no small delight,
When her bright eyes beholds that holy one:
  By whose great wisdom, love, and special grace,
  She was created to behold his face.

Vouchsafe, sweet lady, to accept these lines,
Writ by a hand that doth desire to do
All services to you whose worth combines
The worthiest minds to love and honour you:
  Whose beauty, wisdom, children, high estate,
  Do all concur to make you fortunate.

But chiefly your most honourable lord,*
Whose noble virtues fame can ne're forget:
His hand being always ready to afford
Help to the weak, to the unfortunate:
  All which begets more honour and respect,
  Than Croesus' wealth, or Caesar's stern aspect.

And rightly showeth that he is descended
Of honourable Howard's ancient house,
Whose noble deeds by former times commended,
Do now remain in your most loyal spouse,
  On whom God pours all blessings from above,
  Wealth, honour, children and a worthy love;

Which is more dear to him than all the rest,
You being the loving hind and pleasant roe,*
Wife of his youth, in whom his soul is blest,
Fountain from whence his chief delights do flow.
    Fair tree from which the fruit of honour springs,
    Here I present to you the king of kings:

Desiring you to take a perfect view,
Of those great torments patience did endure;
And reap those comforts that belongs to you,
Which his most painful death did then assure:
    Writing the covenant with his precious blood,
    That your fair soul might bathe her in that flood.

And let your noble daughters likewise read
This little book that I present to you;
On heavenly food let them vouchsafe to feed;
Here they may see a lover much more true
    Than ever was since first the world began,
    This poor rich king that died both God and man.

Yea, let those ladies which do represent
All beauty, wisdom, zeal, and love,
Receive this jewel from Jehovah sent,
This spotless lamb, this perfect patient dove:
    Of whom fair Gabriel, God's bright Mercury,
    Brought down a message from the deity.

Here may they see him in a flood of tears,
Crowned with thorns, and bathing in his blood;
Here may they see his fears exceed all fears,
When Heaven in justice flat against him stood:
    And loathsome death with grim and ghastly look,
    Presented him that black infernal book,

Wherein the sins of all the world were writ,
In deep characters of due punishment;
And naught but dying breath could cancel it:
Shame, death, and hell must make the atonement:
    Showing their evidence, seizing wrongful right,
    Placing heaven's beauty in death's darkest night.

Yet through the sable clouds of shame and death,
His beauty shows more clearer than before;
Death lost his strength when he did lose his breath:
As fire suppressed doth shine and flame the more,
  So in death's ashy, pale discoloured face,
  Fresh beauty shined, yielding far greater grace.

No dove, no swan, nor ivory could compare
With this fair corpse, when 'twas by death embraced;
No rose, nor no vermilion half so fair
As was that precious blood that interlaced
  His body, which bright angels did attend,
  Waiting on him that must to Heaven ascend.

In whom is all that ladies can desire;
If beauty, who hath been more fair than he?
If wisdom, doth not all the world admire
The depth of his, that cannot searched be?
  If wealth, if honour, fame, or kingdom's store,
  Who ever lived that was possessed of more?

If zeal, if grace, if love, if piety,
If constancy, if faith, if fair obedience,
If valour, patience, or sobriety;
If chaste behaviour, meekness, continence,
  If justice, mercy, bounty, charity,
  Who can compare with his divinity?

Whose virtues more than thoughts can apprehend,
I leave to their more clear imagination,
That will vouchsafe their borrowed time to spend
In meditating, and in contemplation
  Of his rare parts, true honour's fair prospect,
  The perfect line that goodness doth direct.

And unto you I wish those sweet desires,
That from your perfect thoughts do daily spring,
Increasing still pure, bright, and holy fires,
Which sparks of precious grace, by faith do spring:
  Mounting your soul unto eternal rest,
  There to live happily among the best.

'To the Lady Anne, Countess of Dorset'*

To you I dedicate this work of grace,
This frame of glory which I have erected,
For your fair mind I hold the fittest place,
Where virtue should be settled and protected;
If highest thoughts true honour do embrace,
And holy wisdom is of them respected:
    Then in this mirror let your fair eyes look,
    To view your virtues in this blessed book.

Blessed by our Saviour's merits, not my skill,
Which I acknowledge to be very small;
Yet if the least part of his blessed will
I have performed, I count I have done all:
One spark of grace sufficient is to fill
Our lamps with oil, ready when he doth call
    To enter with the bridegroom to the feast,
    Where he that is the greatest may be least.

Greatness is no sure frame to build upon,
No worldly treasure can assure that place;
God makes both even, the cottage with the throne,
All worldly honours there are counted base;
Those he holds dear, and reckoneth as his own,
Whose virtuous deeds by his especially grace
    Have gained his love, his kingdom, and his crown,
    Whom in the book of life he hath set down.

Titles of honour which the world bestows,
To none but to the virtuous doth belong;
As beauteous bowers where true worth should repose,
And where his dwellings should be built most strong:
But when they are bestowed upon her foes,
Poor virtue's friends endure the greatest wrong:
    For they must suffer all indignity,
    Until in heaven they better graced be.

What difference was there when the world began,
Was it not virtue that distinguished all?
All sprang but from one woman and one man,
Then how doth gentry come to rise and fall?

Or who is he that very rightly can
Distinguish of his birth, or tell at all,
In what mean state his ancestors have been,
Before some one of worth did honour win?

Whose successors, although they bear his name,
Possessing not the riches of his mind,
How do we know they spring out of the same
True stock of honour, being not of that kind?
It is fair virtue gets immortal fame,
'Tis that doth all love and duty bind:
If he that much enjoys, doth little good,
We may suppose he comes not of that blood.

Nor is he fit for honour, or command,
If base affections over-rules his mind;
Or that self-will doth carry such a hand,
As worldly pleasures have the power to blind
So as he cannot see, nor understand
How to discharge that place to him assigned:
God's stewards must for all the poor provide,
If in God's house they purpose to abide.

To you, as to God's steward I do write,
In whom the seeds of virtue have been sown,
By your most worthy mother, in whose right,
All her fair parts you challenge as your own;
If you, sweet lady, will appear as bright
As ever creature did that time hath known,
Then wear this diadem I present to thee,
Which I have framed for her eternity.

You are the heir apparent* of this crown
Of goodness, bounty, grace, love, piety,
By birth it's yours, then keep it as your own,
Defend it from all base indignity;
The right your mother hath to it, is known
Best unto you, who reaped such fruit thereby:
This monument of her fair worth retain
In your pure mind, and keep it from all stain.

And as your ancestors at first possessed
Their honours, for their honourable deeds,
Let their fair virtues never be transgressed,
Bind up the broken, stop the wounds that bleeds,
Succour the poor, comfort the comfortless,
Cherish fair plants, suppress unwholesome weeds;
    Although base pelf* do chance to come in place,
    Yet let true worth receive your greatest grace.

So shall you show from whence you are descended,
And leave to all posterities your fame,
So will your virtues always be commended,
And everyone will reverence your name;
So this poor work of mine shall be defended
From any scandal that the world can frame:
    And you a glorious actor will appear
    Lovely to all, but unto God most dear.

I know right well these are but needless lines,
To you, that are so perfect in your part,
Whose birth and education both combines;
Nay more than both, a pure and godly heart,
So well instructed to such fair designs,
By your dear mother, that there needs no art:
    Your ripe discretion in your tender years,
    By all your actions to the world appears.

I do but set a candle in the sun,
And add one drop of water to the sea,
Virtue and beauty both together run,
When you were born, within your breast to stay;
Their quarrel ceased, which long before begun,
They live in peace, and all do them obey:
    In you fair Madam, are they richly placed,
    Where all their worth by eternity is graced.

You goddess-like unto the world appear,
Enriched with more than fortune can bestow,
Goodness and grace, which you do hold more dear
Than worldly wealth, which melts away like snow;

Your pleasure is the word of God to hear,
That his most holy precepts you may know:
    Your greatest honour, fair and virtuous deeds,
    Which from the love and fear of God proceeds.

Therefore to you (good Madam) I present
His lovely love, more worth than purest gold,
Who for your sake his precious blood hath spent,
His death and passion here you may behold,
And view this lamb, that to the world was sent,
Whom your fair soul may in her arms enfold:
    Loving his love, that did endure such pain,
    That you in heaven a worthy place might gain.

For well you know, this world is but a stage
Where all do play their parts, and must be gone;
Here's no respect of persons, youth, nor age,
Death seizeth all, he never spareth one,
None can prevent or stay that tyrant's rage,
But Jesus Christ the Just: by him alone
    He was o'ercome, He open set the door
    To eternal life, ne're seen, nor known before.

He is the stone the builders did refuse,
Which you, sweet lady, are to build upon;
He is the rock that holy church did choose,
Among which number, you must needs be one;
Fair shepherdess, 'tis you that he will use
To feed his flock, that trust in him alone:
    All worldly blessings he vouchsafes to you,
    That to the poor you may return his due.

And if deserts a lady's love may gain,
Then tell me, who hath more deserved than He?
Therefore in recompense of all his pain,
Bestow your pains to read, and pardon me,
If out of wants, or weakness of my brain,
I have not done this work sufficiently;
    Yet lodge him in the closet of your heart,
    Whose worth is more than can be showed by art.

'To the Virtuous Reader'

Often have I heard, that it is the property of some women, not only to emulate the virtues and perfections of the rest, but also by all their powers of ill speaking, to eclipse the brightness of their deserved fame: now contrary to this custom, which men I hope unjustly lay to their charge, I have written this small volume, or little book, for the general use of all virtuous ladies and gentlewomen of this kingdom; and in commendation of some particular persons of our own sex, such as for the most part, are so well known to myself, and others, that I dare undertake fame dares not to call any better. And this have I done, to make known to the world, that all women deserve not to be blamed though some, forgetting they are women themselves, and in danger to be condemned by the words of their own mouths, fall into so great an error, as to speak unadvisedly against the rest of their sex; which if it be true, I am persuaded they can show their own imperfection in nothing more: and therefore could wish (for their own ease, modesties, and credit) they would refer such points of folly, to be practised by evil disposed men, who forgetting they were born of women, nourished of women, and that if it were not by the means of women, they would be quite extinguished out of the world, and a final end of them all, do like vipers deface the wombs wherein they were bred, only to give way and utterance to their want of discretion and goodness. Such as these were they that dishonoured Christ, his apostles and prophets, putting them to shameful deaths. Therefore we are not to regard any imputations that they undeservedly lay upon us, no otherwise than to make use of them to our own benefits, as spurs to virtue, making us fly all occasions that may colour their unjust speeches to pass current. Especially considering that they have tempted even the patience of God himself, who gave power to wise and virtuous women, to bring down their pride and arrogancy. As was cruel Cesarus* by the discreet counsel of noble Deborah, judge and prophetess of Israel and resolution of Jael wife of Heber the Kenite; wicked Haman,* by the divine prayers and prudent proceedings of beautiful Hester; blasphemous Holofernes,* by the invincible courage, rare wisdom, and confident carriage of Judith; and the unjust judges, by the innocency of chaste Susanna,* with infinite others, which for brevity sake I will omit. As also in respect it pleased our Lord and Saviour Jesus Christ, without the assistance of man, being free from original and all other sins, from the time of his conception, till the hour of his death, to be begotten of a woman, born of a woman, nourished of a woman, obedient to a woman; and that he healed woman, pardoned women, comforted women; yea, even when he was in his greatest agony and bloody sweat, going to be crucified, and also in the last hour of his death, took care to dispose of a woman; after his resurrection, appeared first to a woman, sent a woman to declare his most glorious resurrection to the rest of his disciples. Many other examples I could allege of diverse faithful and virtuous women, who have in all ages, not only been confessors, but also endured most cruel martyrdom for their faith in Jesus Christ. All which is sufficient to enforce all good Christians and honourable minded men to speak reverently of our sex, and especially of all virtuous and good women. To the modest censures of both which, I refer these my imperfect endeavours, knowing that according to their own excellent dispositions, they will rather, cherish, nourish, and increase the least spark of virtue where they find it, by their favourable and best interpretations, than quench it by wrong constructions. To whom I wish all increase of virtue, and desire their best opinions.

'Salve Deus Rex Judaeorum'

Since Cynthia* is ascended to that rest
Of endless joy and true eternity,
That glorious place that cannot be expressed
By any wight* clad in mortality,
In her almighty love so highly blessed,
And crowned with everlasting sovereignty;
    Where saints and angels do attend her throne
    And she gives glory unto God alone.

To thee great countess now I will apply
My pen, to write thy never dying fame;
That when to Heaven thy blessed soul shall fly,
These lines on earth record thy reverend name:
And to this task I mean my muse to tie,
Though wanting skill I shall but purchase blame:
    Pardon (dear lady) want of woman's wit
    To pen thy praise, when few can equal it.

The lady Margaret countess dowager of Cumberland

And pardon (Madam) though I do not write
Those praiseful lines of that delightful place,
As you commanded me* in that fair night,
When shining Phoebe gave so great a grace,
Presenting paradise to your sweet sight,
Unfolding all the beauty of her face
With pleasant groves, hills, walks and stately trees,
Which pleasures with retired minds agrees.

Whose eagle's eyes behold the glorious sun
Of th'all-creating providence, reflecting
His blessed beams on all by him, begun;
Increasing, strengthening, guiding and directing
All worldly creatures their due course to run,
Unto His powerful pleasure all subjecting:
And thou (dear lady) by his special grace,
In these his creatures dost behold his face.

Whose all-reviving beauty, yields such joys
To thy sad soul, plunged in waves of woe,*
That worldly pleasures seems to thee as toys,
Only thou seek'st eternity to know,
Respecting not the infinite annoys
That Satan to thy well-staid mind can show;
Ne* can he quench in thee, the spirit of grace,
Nor draw thee from beholding Heaven's bright face.

Thy mind so perfect by thy maker framed
No vain delights can harbour in thy heart,
With his sweet love, thou art so much inflamed,
As of the world thou seem'st to have no part;
So, love him still, thou need'st not be ashamed,
'Tis He that made thee, what thou wert, and art:
'Tis He that dries all tears from orphans' eyes,
And hears from heaven the woeful widow's cries.

'Tis He that doth behold thy inward cares,
And will regard the sorrows of thy soul;
'Tis He that guides thy feet from Satan's snares,
And in his wisdom, doth thy ways control:
He through afflictions, still thy mind prepares,
And all thy glorious trials will enrol:

That when dark days of terror shall appear,
Thou as the sun shalt shine; or much more clear.

The Heavens shall perish as a garment old,
Or as a vesture* by the maker changed,
And shall depart, as when a scroll is rolled;
Yet thou from him shalt never be estranged,
When He shall come in glory that was sold
For all our sins; we happily are changed,
Who for our faults put on his righteousness,
Although full oft his laws we do transgress.

Long mayest thou joy in this almighty love,
Long may thy soul be pleasing in his sight,
Long mayest thou have true comforts from above,
Long mayest thou set on him thy whole delight,
And patiently endure when he doth prove,
Knowing that He will surely do thee right:
Thy patience, faith, long suffering, and thy love,
He will reward with comforts from above.

With majesty and honour is He clad,
And decked with light, as with a garment fair;
He joys the meek, and makes the mighty sad,
Pulls down the proud, and doth the humble rear:
Who sees this bridegroom, never can be sad;
None lives that can his wondrous works declare:
Yea, look how far the East is from the West,
So far he sets our sins that have transgressed.

He rides upon the wings of all the winds,
And spreads the heavens with his all powerful hand;
Oh! who can loose when the almighty binds,
Or in his angry presence dares to stand?
He searcheth out the secrets of all minds;
All those that fear him, shall possess the land:
He is exceeding glorious to behold,
Ancient of times; so fair, and yet so old.

He of the wat'ry clouds his chariot frames,
And makes his blessed angels powerful spirits,
His ministers are fearful fiery flames,
Rewarding all according to their merits;

The righteous for an heritage he claims,
And registers the wrongs of humble spirits:
    Hills melt like wax, in presence of the Lord,
    So do all sinners, in his sight abhorred.

He in the waters lays his chamber beams,
And clouds of darkness compass him about,
Consuming fire shall go before in streams,
And burn up all his en'mies round about:
Yet on these judgements worldlings never dreams,
Nor of these dangers never stand in doubt:
    While he shall rest within his holy hill,
    That lives and dies according to his will.

But woe to them that double-hearted be,
Who with their tongues the righteous souls do slay;
Bending their bows to shoot at all they see,
With upright hearts their maker to obey;
And secretly do let their arrows flee,
To wound true hearted people any way:
    The Lord will root them out that speak proud things,
    Deceitful tongues are but false slander's wings.

Froward are the ungodly from their birth,
No sooner born, but they do go astray;
The Lord will root them out from off the earth,
And give them to their en'mies for a prey,
As venomous as serpents is their breath,
With poisoned lies to hurt in what they may
    The innocent: who as a dove shall fly
    Unto the Lord, that he his cause may try.

The righteous Lord doth righteousness allow,
His countenance will behold the thing that's just;
Unto the mean he makes the mighty bow,
And raiseth up the poor out of the dust:
Yet makes no count to us, nor when, nor how,
But pours his grace on all, that puts their trust
    In him: that never will their hopes betray,
    Nor lets them perish that for mercy pray.

He shall within his tabernacle dwell,
Whose life is uncorrupt before the Lord,
Who no untruths of innocents doth tell,
Nor wrongs his neighbour, nor in deed, nor word,
Nor in his pride with malice seems to swell,
Nor whets his tongue more sharper than a sword,
    To wound the reputation of the just;
    Nor seeks to lay their glory in the dust.

That great Jehova, King of heaven and earth,
Will rain down fire and brimstone from above,
Upon the wicked monsters in their birth
That storm and rage at those whom he doth love:
Snares, storms, and tempests he will rain, and dearth,
Because he will himself almighty prove:
    And this shall be their portion they shall drink,
    That thinks the Lord is blind when he doth wink.

Pardon (good Madam) though I have digressed
From what I do intend to write of thee, *to the Countess*
To set his glory forth whom thou lov'st best, *of Cumberland*
Whose wondrous works no mortal eye can see;
His special care on those whom he hath blest
From wicked worldlings, how he sets them free:
    And how such people he doth overthrow
    In all their ways, that they his power may know.

The meditation of this monarch's love,
Draws thee from caring what this world can yield;
Of joys and griefs both equal thou dost prove,
They have no force, to force thee from the field:
Thy constant faith like to the turtle dove
Continues combat, and will never yield
    To base affliction; or proud pomp's desire,
    That sets the weakest minds so much on fire.

Thou from the court to the country art retired,
Leaving the world, before the world leaves thee:
That great enchantress of weak minds admired,
Whose all-bewitching charms so pleasing be
To worldly wantons; and too much desired
Of those that care not for eternity:

But yield themselves as preys to lust and sin,
Losing their hopes of Heav'n, Hell pains to win.

But thou, the wonder of our wanton age
Leav'st all delights to serve a heav'nly king:
Who is more wise? Or who can be more sage,
Than she that doth affection subject bring;
Not forcing for the world, or Satan's rage,
But shrouding under the almighty's wing;
Spending her years, months, days, minutes, hours,
In doing service to the heav'nly powers.

Thou fair example, live without compare,
With honour's triumphs seated in thy breast;
Pale envy never can thy name impair,
When in thy heart thou harbour'st such a guest:
Malice must live for ever in despair;
There's no revenge where virtue still doth rest:
All hearts must needs do homage unto thee,
In whom all eyes such rare perfection see.

An invective against outward beauty unaccompanied with virtue

That outward beauty which the world commends
Is not the subject I will write upon,
Whose date expired, that tyrant time soon ends;
Those gaudy colours soon are spent and gone:
But those faire virtues which on thee attends
Are always fresh, they never are but one:
They make thy beauty fairer to behold,
Than was that queen's* for whom proud Troy was sold.

As for those matchless colours red and white,
Or perfect features in a fading face,
Or due proportion pleasing to the sight;
All these do draw but dangers and disgrace:
A mind enriched with virtue, shines more bright,
Adds everlasting beauty, gives true grace,
Frames an immortal goddess on the earth,
Who though she dies, yet fame gives her new birth.

That pride of nature which adorns the fair,
Like blazing comets to allure all eyes,
Is but the thread, that weaves their web of care,
Who glories most, where most their danger lies;

For greatest perils do attend the fair,
When men do seek, attempt, plot and devise,
    How they may overthrow the chastest dame,
    Whose beauty is the white whereat they aim.

'Twas beauty bred in Troy the ten years' strife,
And carried Helen from her lawful lord;
'Twas beauty made chaste Lucrece* lose her life,
For which proud Tarquin's fact was so abhorred:
Beauty the cause Antonius* wronged his wife,
Which could not be decided but by sword:
    Great Cleopatra's beauty and defects
    Did work Octavia's wrongs, and his neglects.

What fruit did yield that fair forbidden tree,
But blood, dishonour, infamy, and shame?
Poor blinded queen, could'st thou no better see,
But entertain disgrace, instead of fame?
Do these designs with majesty agree?
To stain thy blood, and blot thy royal name.
    That heart that gave consent unto this ill,
    Did give consent that thou thyself should'st kill.

Faire Rosamund,* the wonder of her time,
Had been much fairer, had she not been fair;
Beauty betrayed her thoughts, aloft to climb,
To build strong castles in uncertain air,
Where th'infection of a wanton crime
Did work her fall; first poison, then despair,
    With double death did kill her perjured soul,
    When heavenly justice did her sin control.

Holy Matilda* in a hapless hour
Was born to sorrow and to discontent,
Beauty the cause that turned her sweet to sour,
While chastity sought folly to prevent.
Lustful King John refused, did use his power,
By fire and sword, to compass his content:
    But friends' disgrace, nor father's banishment,
    Nor death itself, could purchase her consent.

Here beauty in the height of all perfection,
Crowned this fair creature's everlasting fame,
Whose noble mind did scorn the base subjection
Of fears, or favours, to impair her name:
By heavenly grace, she had such true direction,
To die with honour, not to live in shame;
  And drink that poison with a cheerful heart,
  That could all heavenly grace to her impart.

. . . .

Let* barbarous cruelty far depart from thee,
And in true justice take affliction's part;
Open thine eyes, that thou the truth mayest see,
Do not the thing that goes against thy heart,
Condemn not him that must thy saviour be;
But view his holy life, his good desert.
  Let not us women glory in mens' fall,
  Who had power given to over-rule us all.

Eve's apology

Till now your indiscretion* sets us free,
And makes our former fault much less appear
Our Mother Eve, who tasted of the tree,
Giving to Adam what she held most dear,
Was simply good, and had no power to see,
The after-coming harm did not appear:
  The subtle serpent that our sex betrayed,
  Before our fall so sure a plot had laid.

That undiscerning ignorance perceived
No guile, or craft that was by him intended;
For had she known, of what we were bereaved,
To his request she had not condescended.
But she (poor soul) by cunning was deceived,
No hurt therein her harmless heart intended:
  For she alleged God's word, which he denies,
  That they should die, but even as gods, be wise.

But surely Adam cannot be excused,
Her fault though great, yet he was most to blame;
What weakness offered, strength might have refused,
Being lord of all, the greater was his shame:

Although the serpent's craft had her abused,
God's holy word ought all his actions frame,
For he was lord and king of all the earth,
Before poor Eve had either life or breath.

Who being framed by God's eternal hand,
The perfect'st man that ever breathed on earth;
And from God's mouth received that straight command,
The breach whereof he knew was present death:
Yea having power to rule both sea and land,
Yet with one apple won to lose that breath
Which God had breathed in his beauteous face,
Bringing us all in danger and disgrace.

And then to lay the fault on patience back,
That we (poor women) must endure it all;
We know right well he did discretion lack,
Being not persuaded thereunto at all;
If Eve did err, it was for knowledge sake,
The fruit being fair persuaded him to fall:
No subtle serpent's falsehood did betray him,
If he would eat it, who had power to stay him?

Not Eve, whose fault was only too much love,
Which made her give this present to her dear,
That what she tasted, he likewise might prove,
Whereby his knowledge might become more clear;
He never sought her weakness to reprove,
With those sharp words, which he of God did hear:
Yet men will boast of knowledge, which he took
From Eve's fair hand, as from a learned book.

If any evil did in her remain,
Being made of him, he was the ground of all;
If one of many worlds could lay a stain
Upon our sex, and work so great a fall
To wretched man, by Satan's subtle train;
What will so foul a fault amongst you all?
Her weakness did the serpent's words obey;
But you in malice God's dear son betray.

Whom, if unjustly you condemn to die,
Her sin was small, to what you do commit;

All mortal sins that do for vengeance cry,
Are not to be compared unto it:
If many worlds would altogether try,
By all their sins the wrath of God to get;
  This sin of yours, surmounts them all as far
  As doth the sun, another little star.

Then let us have our liberty again,
And challenge to yourselves no sovereignty;
You came not in the world without our pain,
Make that a bar against your cruelty;
Your fault being greater, why should you disdain
Our being your equals, free from tyranny?
  If one weak woman simply did offend,
  This sin of yours, hath no excuse, nor end.

To which (poor souls) we never gave consent,
Witness thy wife (O Pilate)* speaks for all;
Who did but dream, and yet a message sent,
That thou should'st have nothing to do at all
With that just man; which, if thy heart relent,
Why wilt thou be a reprobate with Saul?
  To seek the death of him that is so good,
  For thy soul's health to shed his dearest blood.*

'The Description of Cookham'*

Farewell sweet Cookham where I first obtained
Grace from that grace where perfect grace remained;
And where the Muses gave their full consent,
I should have power the virtuous to content:
Where princely palace willed me to indite
The sacred story of the soul's delight.
Farewell (sweet place) where virtue then did rest,
And all delights did harbour in her breast:
Never shall my sad eyes again behold
Those pleasures which my thoughts did then unfold.
Yet you (great lady) mistress of that place,
From whose desires did spring this work of grace,

Vouchsafe to think upon those pleasures past,
As fleeting worldly joys that could not last;
Or, as dim shadows of celestial pleasures,
Which are desired above all earthly treasures.
Oh how (me thought) against you thither came,
Each part did seem some new delight to frame!
The house received all ornaments to grace it,
And would endure no foulness to deface it.
The walks put on their summer liveries,
And all things else did hold like similes:
The trees with leaves, with fruits, with flowers clad,
Embraced each other, seeming to be glad,
Turning themselves to beauteous canopies,
To shade the bright sun from your brighter eyes:
The crystal streams with silver spangles graced,
While by the glorious sun they were embraced:
The little birds in chirping notes did sing,
To entertain both you and that sweet Spring.
And Philomela* with her sundry lays,
Both you and that delightful place did praise.
Oh how me thought each plant, each flower, each tree
Set forth their beauties then to welcome thee:
The very hills right humbly did descend,
When you to tread upon them did intend.
And as you set your feet, they still did rise,
Glad that they could receive so rich a prize.
The gentle winds did take delight to be
Among those woods that were so graced by thee.
And in sad murmur uttered pleasing sound,
That pleasure in that place might more abound:
The swelling banks delivered all their pride,
When such a Phoenix* once they had espied.
Each arbor, bank, each seat, each stately tree,
Thought themselves honoured in supporting thee.
The pretty birds would oft come to attend thee,
Yet fly away for fear they should offend thee:
The little creatures in the burrow by
Would come abroad to sport them in your eye;
Yet fearful of the bow in your fair hand,

Would run away when you did make a stand.
Now let me come unto that stately tree,
Wherein such goodly prospects you did see;
That oak that did in height his fellows pass,
As much as lofty trees, low growing grass:
Much like a comely cedar straight and tall,
Whose beauteous stature far exceeded all.
How often did you visit this fair tree,
Which seeming joyful in receiving thee,
Would like a palm tree spread his arms abroad,
Desirous that you there should make abode:
Whose fair green leaves much like a comely veil,
Defended Phoebus when he would assail:
Whose pleasing bowers did yield a cool fresh air,
Joying his happiness when you were there.
Where being seated, you might plainly see,
Hills, vales, and woods, as if on bended knee
They had appeared, your honour to salute,
Or to prefer some strange unlooked-for suit,
All interlaced with brooks and crystal springs,
A prospect fit to please the eyes of kings.
And thirteen shires appeared all in your sight,
Europe could not afford much more delight.
What was there then but gave you all content,
While you the time in meditation spent,
Of their creator's power, which there you saw,
In all his creatures held a perfect law;
And in their beauties did you plain descry,
His beauty, wisdom, grace, love, majesty.
In these sweet woods how often did you walk,
With Christ and his apostles there to talk;
Placing his holy writ in some fair tree,
To meditate what you therein did see:
With Moses you did mount his holy hill,
To know his pleasure, and perform his will.
With lovely David you did often sing,
His holy hymns to Heaven's eternal King.
And in sweet music did your soul delight,
To sound his praises, morning, noon, and night.

With blessed Joseph you did often feed
Your pined brethren, when they stood in need.
And that sweet lady sprung from Clifford's race,*
Of noble Bedford's blood, faire steam* of grace;
To honourable Dorset now espoused
In whose fair breast true virtue then was housed:
Oh what delight did my weak spirits find
In those pure parts of her well-framed mind:
And yet it grieves me that I cannot be
Near unto her, whose virtues did agree
With those fair ornaments of outward beauty,
Which did enforce from all both love and duty.
Unconstant fortune, thou art most to blame,
Who casts us down into so low a frame:
Where our great friends we cannot daily see,
So great a difference is there in degree.
Many are placed in those orbs of state,
Parters in honour,* so ordained by fate;
Nearer in show, yet farther off in love,
In which, the lowest always are above.
But whither am I carried in conceit?
My wit too weak to conster* of the great.
Why not? Although we are but born of earth,
We may behold the heavens, despising death;
And loving Heaven that is so far above,
May in the end vouchsafe us entire love.
Therefore sweet memory do thou retain
Those pleasures past, which will not turn again:
Remember beauteous Dorset's former sports,
So far from being touched by ill reports;
Wherein myself did always bear a part,
While reverend love presented my true heart:
Those recreations let me bear in mind,
Which her sweet youth and noble thoughts did find
Whereof deprived, I evermore must grieve,
Hating blind fortune, careless to relieve.
And you sweet Cookham, whom these ladies leave,
I now must tell the grief you did conceive
At their departure; when they went away,

How everything retained a sad dismay:
Nay long before when once an inkling came
Me thought each thing did unto sorrow frame:
The trees that were so glorious in our view,
Forsook both flowers and fruit, when once they knew
Of your depart, their very leaves did wither,
Changing their colours as they grew together.
But when they saw this had no power to stay you,
They often wept though, speechless, could not pray you;
Letting their tears in your fair bosoms fall,
As if they said, 'Why will ye leave us all?'
This being vain, they cast their leaves away,
Hoping that pity would have made you stay:
Their frozen tops like age's hoary hairs,
Shows their disasters languishing in fears:
A swarthy, rivelled rine all overspread,
Their dying bodies half alive, half dead.
But your occasions called you so away
That nothing there had power to make you stay:
Yet did I see a noble, grateful mind,
Requiting each according to their kind
Forgetting not to turn and take your leave
Of these sad creatures, powerless to receive
Your favour when with grief you did depart,
Placing their former pleasures in your heart;
Giving great charge to noble memory,
There to preserve their love continually:
But specially the love of that fair tree,
That first and last you did vouchsafe to see:
In which it pleased you oft to take the air
With noble Dorset, then a virgin fair;
Where many a learned book was read and scanned
To this fair tree, taking me by the hand,
You did repeat the pleasures which had passed
Seeming to grieve they could no longer last
And with a chaste, yet loving kiss took leave
Of which sweet kiss I did it soon bereave:
Scorning a senseless creature should possess
So rare a favour, so great happiness.

No other kiss it could receive from me
For fear to give back what it took of thee:
So I, ingrateful creature, did deceive it
Of that which you vouchsafed in love to leave it.
And though it oft had given me much content
Yet this great wrong I never could repent:
But of the happiest made it most forlorn
To show that nothing's free from fortune's scorn,
While all the rest with this most beauteous tree
Made their sad consort sorrow's harmony.
The flowers that on the banks and walks did grow
Crept in the ground, the grass did weep for woe.
The winds and waters seemed to chide together
Because you went away they know not whither.
And those sweet brooks that ran so fair and clear
With grief and trouble wrinkled did appear.
Those pretty birds that wonted were to sing
Now neither sing, not chirp, nor use their wing;
But with their tender feet on some bare spray
Warble forth sorrow, and their own dismay.
Faire Philomela leaves her mournful ditty
Drowned in dead sleep, yet can procure no pity:
Each arbour, bank, each seat, each stately tree,
Looks bare and desolate now for want of thee;
Turning green tresses into frosty grey,
While in cold grief they wither all away.
The sun grew weak, his beams no comfort gave,
While all green things did make the earth their grave.
Each briar, each bramble, when you went away,
Caught fast your clothes, thinking to make you stay.
Delightful Echo wonted to reply
To our last words, did now for sorrow die.
The house cast off each garment that might grace it,
Putting on dust and cobwebs to deface it.
All desolation then there did appear,
When you were going whom they held so dear.
This last farewell to Cookham here I give,
When I am dead thy name in this may live,
Wherein I have performed her noble hest,

Whose virtues lodge in my unworthy breast,
And ever shall, so long as life remains,
Tying my heart to her by those rich chains.

'To the Doubtful Reader'

Gentle Reader, if thou desire to be resolved, why I give this title, *Salve Deus Rex Judaeorum*, know for certain that it was delivered unto me in sleep many years before I had any intent to write in this manner, and was quite out of my memory until I had written the passion of Christ, when immediately it came into my remembrance, what I had dreamed long before, and thinking it a significant token that I was appointed to perform this work, I gave the very same words I received in sleep as the fittest title I could devise for this book.

ANNE CLIFFORD
(1590–1676)

From her Diary

[N.B. left-hand marginal annotations in Portland MS here follow in square brackets the entries they are originally alongside.]

JANUARY* 1616

Upon New Year's day I kept to my chamber all the day, my Lady Rich* and my sister Sackville* supping with me, but my Lord* and all the company at Dorset House went to see the masque at the court. [The first day, Sir George Villiers* was made Master of the Horse and my Lord of Worcester Lord Privy Seal.]

Upon the third died my Lady Thomas Howard's son.

Upon the fourth I went to see my Lady of Effingham* at my Lady Lumley's and went to sup at my Lady Shrewsbury's* where there was a great company and a play after supper. [Upon the fifth being twelfth eve* my Lord played at dice in the court and won nine hundred twenty shilling and gave me but twenty.]

Upon the 6th, being twelfth day, I supped with my Lady of Arundel* and sat with her in her Ladyship's box to see the masque, which was the second time it was presented before the King and Queen. [This twelfth day at night my Lady Arundel made a great supper to the Florentine ambassador, where I was and carried my sister Sackville along with me, so she sat with me in the box to see the masque. This night the queen wore a gown with a long train which my Lady Bedford bore up.]

Upon the eighth went to see Lady Raleigh* at the Tower.

Upon the 21st being Sunday, my Lord and I went to church to Sevenoak* to grace the Bishop of St David's prayers.

FEBRUARY 1616

All the time I stayed in the country I was sometimes merry and sometimes sad, as I heard news from London.

Upon Thursday the 8th of February I came to London, my Lord

Bishop of St David's riding with me in the Coach and Mary Neville.* This time I was sent up for by my Lord about the composition* with my uncle of Cumberland.

Upon Monday the 12th my Lord Roos* was married to Mrs Ann Lake the Secretary's Daughter. [Upon the fourteenth my lord supped at the Globe.]

Upon Thursday the fifteenth my Lord and I went to see my young Lady Arundel, and in the afternoon my Lady Willoughby came to see me. My Lady Gray brought my Lady Carr* to play at glecko* with me, when I lost fifteen pounds to them, they two and my Lady Grantham and Sir George Manners supping here with me.

Upon the sixteenth my Lady Grantham and Mrs Newton came to see me. My Lady Grantham told me, the Archbishop of Canterbury* would come to me the next day, and she persuaded me very earnestly to agree to this business which I took as a great argument of her love. Also my Coz. Russell* came to me the same day and chid me and told me of all my faults and errors in this business and he made me weep bitterly; then I spoke a prayer of ours* and went to see my Lady Wotten* at Whitehall, where we walked five or six turns, but spoke nothing of this business, though her heart and mine were both full of it.

From hence I went to the Abbey at Westminster where I saw the Queen of Scots her tomb and all the other tombs, and came home by water, where I took an extreme cold.

Upon the seventeenth being Saturday, my Lord Archbishop of Canterbury, my Lord William Howard,* my Lord Roos, my Coz. Russell, my brother Sackville* and a great company of men of note were all in the gallery at Dorset House,* where the Archbishop of Canterbury took me aside and talked with me privately one hour and a half, and persuaded me both by divine and human means to set my hand to these agreements.* But my answer to his Lordship was that I would do nothing till my Lady and I had conferred together. Much persuasion was used by him and all the company, sometimes terrifying me and sometimes flattering me, but at length it was concluded that I should have leave to go to my mother and send an answer by the 22nd of March next whether I will agree to this business or not, and to this prayer my Lord of Canterbury and the rest of the lords have set their hands. [After it was concluded I should go into the North to my mother, then my uncle Cumberland and my coz.

Clifford came down into the gallery, for they had all this while been in some other chamber with lawyers and others of their party.]

Next day was a marvellous day to me through the mercy of God, for it was generally thought that I must either have sealed to the agreement or else have parted with my Lord.

Upon the nineteenth I sent Tobias and Thomas Beddings to most of the ladies in the town of my acquaintance to let them know of my journey into the North.

Upon the twentieth came my Lord Russell and my coz. Gorge.* In all this time of my troubles my coz. Russell was exceeding careful and kind to me.

Upon the 21st my Lord and I began our journey Northward. The same day my Lord Willoughby* came and broke his fast with my Lord. We had two coaches in our company with four horses apiece and about six and twenty horsemen; I having no women to attend me, but Willoughby and Judith, Thomas Glenham going with my Lord. [At this meeting, my Lord's footman Acteon* won the race from the northern man and my Lord won both at XX* and stayed there a fortnight with my Lord of Essex and my Lord Willoughby. Before they came to London they heard that three of my Lord Abergavenny's sons were drowned between Gravesend and London and about this time the marriage between Sir Robert Sidney* and my Lady Dorothy Percy was openly known.]

Upon the 26th we went from Litchfield to Croxall, and about a mile from Croxall my Lord and I parted, he returning to Litchfield and I going on to Derby. I came to my lodgings with a heavy heart considering how things stood between my Lord and I. I had in my company ten persons and thirteen horses.

MARCH 1616

Upon the first we went from the parson's house over the dangerous moors, being eight miles, and afterwards the ways being so dangerous that the horses were fain to be taken out of the coach and the coach to be lifted down the hills. This day Rivers' horse fell from a bridge into the river. We came to Manchester about ten o'clock at night. Upon the twentieth in the morning my Lord William Howard with his son, my coz. William Howard and Mr John Dudley came hither to take the answer of my mother and myself which was a direct denial to stand to the judges' award.* The same day came Sir

Timothy Whittington hither who did all he could to mitigate the anger between my Lord William Howard and my mother, so as at the last we parted all good friends, and it was agreed upon that my men and horses should stay, and we should go up to London together after Easter. [This Lent I kept very strictly and did eat nothing that had butter in it.]

Upon the 22nd, my Lady and I went in a coach together to Whinfield and rid about the park and saw all the woods. [Upon the 24th my Lady Somerset was sent from Blackfriars by water as prisoner to the Tower.]

Upon the 27th my coz. William Howard sent me a dapple grey nag for my own saddle.

Upon the 31st being Easter day I received* with my Lady in the chapel at Broome.

APRIL 1616

Upon the first came my Coz. Charles Howard and Mr John Dudley with letters to show that it was my Lord's pleasure that the men and horses should come away without me, and so after much fallen out betwixt my Lady and them, all my folks went away, there being a paper drawn to show that their going was by my Lord's direction, contrary to my will. At night I sent two messengers to my folks to entreat them to stay. For some two nights my mother and I lay together and had much talk about this business. [As I came away I heard that John Digby who was late ambassador in Spain was made vice chamberlain to the King and swore one of the privy council.]

Upon the second I went after my folks in my Lady's coach, she bringing me a quarter of a mile in the way, where she and I had a heavy and grievous parting. Most part of the way I rid on horseback behind Mr Hodgson.

Upon the tenth we went from Ware to Tottenham where my Lord's coach with his men and horses met me and came to London to the lesser Dorset House. [Not long after this my coz. Sir Oliver St Johns* was made Lord Deputy of Ireland in the place of Sir Arthur Chichester.]

Upon the eleventh I came from London to Knole, where I had but a cold welcome from my Lord. My lady Margaret* met me at the outermost gate and my Lord came to me in the drawing chamber.

Upon the twelfth I told my Lord how I had left those writings which

the judges and my Lord would have me sign and seal behind with my mother.
Upon the thirteenth, my Lord and Thomas Glenham went up to London.
Upon the seventeenth came Tom Woodyatt from London, but brought no news of my going up, which I daily look for. [Upon the seventeenth my mother sickened as she came from prayers, being taken with a cold chillness in the manner of an ague, which afterwards turned to great heats and pains in her side, so as when she was opened it was plainly perceived to be an impostume.]*
Upon the eighteenth, Baskett came down hither and brought me a letter from my Lord to let me know this was the last time of asking me whether I would set my hand to this award of the Judges.
Upon the nineteenth being Friday, I returned my answer to my Lord that I would not stand to this award of the Judges what misery soever it brought me to. This morning the Bishop of St David's and my little child were brought to speak to me.
About this time I used to rise early in the morning and go to the standing* in the garden, and taking my prayer book with me, beseech God to be merciful towards me and to help me in this as He hath always done.

MAY 1616

Upon the first, Rivers came from London in the afternoon and brought me word that I should neither live at Knole or Bolebrooke.* [About this time I heard my sister Beauchamp* was with child.]
Upon the second came Mr Legg* and told diverse of the servants that my Lord would come down and see me once more, which would be the last time that I should see him again.
Upon the third came Basket down from London and brought me a letter from my Lord by which I might see it was his pleasure that the child should go the next day to London, which at the first was somewhat grievous to me, but when I considered that it would both make my Lord more angry with me and be worse for the child, I resolved to let her go, after I had sent for Mr Legg and talked with him about that and other matters and wept bitterly. [My Lady Margaret lay in the great house at Dorset House, for now my Lord and his whole company were removed from the little house where I lay when I was first married.]

Upon the fourth being Saturday, between ten and eleven o'clock the child went into the litter to go to London, Mrs Bathurst and her two maids with Mr Legge and a good company of the servants going with her. In the afternoon came a man called Hilton, born in Craven, from my Lady Willoughby to see me which I took as a great argument of her love, being in the midst of all my misery. [About this time died my Lord Shrewsbury at his house in Broad Street.]

Upon the eighth I dispatched a letter to my mother.

Upon the ninth I received a letter from Mr Bellasis how extreme ill my mother had been, and in the afternoon came Humphrey Godding's son with letters that my mother was exceeding ill, and as they thought, in some danger of death, so as I sent Rivers presently to London with letters to be sent to her and certain cordials and conserves.

At night was brought me a letter from my Lord to let me know that his determination was the child should live at Horsley,* not come hither any more, so as this was a very grievous and sorrowful day to me. [Upon the tenth early in the morning I writ a very earnest letter to my Lord to beseech him that I might not go to the little house which was appointed for me but that I might go to Horsley and sojourn there with my child and to the same effect I writ to my sister Beauchamps.]

Upon the tenth, Rivers came from London and brought me word from Lord William that she was not in such danger as I feared. The same day came the stewards from London whom I expected would have given warning to many of the servants to go away because the audit* was newly come up.

Upon the eleventh, being Sunday, before Mr Legg went away I talked with him an hour or two about all the business and matters between me and my Lord, so as I gave him better satisfaction and made him conceive a better opinion of me than ever he did.

A little before dinner came Matthew* down from London, my Lord sending me by him the wedding ring that my Lord Treasurer and my old Lady* were married withal, and a message that my Lord would be here the next week, and that the child would not as yet go down to Horsley, and I sent my Lord the wedding ring* that my Lord and I was married with. The same day came Mr Marsh from London and persuaded me much to consent to this agreement.

Twelfth at night, Grosvenor came hither and told me how my Lord had won two hundred pounds at the cocking,* and that my Lord of Essex and my Lord Willoughby who were on my Lord's side won a great deal and how there were some unkind words passed between my Lord and his side, and Sir William Herbert and his side. This day my Lady Grantham sent me a letter about these businesses between my uncle Cumberland and me, and I returned her an answer.

All this time my Lord was at London where he had infinite and great resort coming to him. He went much abroad to cocking, to bowling alleys, to plays and horse races, and commended by all the world. I stayed in the country, having many times a sorrowful and heavy heart and being condemned by most folks because I would not consent to the agreements, so as I may truly say, I am like an owl in the desert.*

Upon the thirteenth, being Monday, my Lady's footman Thomas Petty brought me letters out of Westmorland by which I perceived how very sick and full of grievous pain my dear mother was, so as she was not able to write herself to me, and most of her people about her feared she would hardly recover this sickness. At night I went out and prayed to God my only helper that she might not die in this pitiful case.

The 14th. Richard Jones came from London to see me and brought a letter with him from Matthew, the effect whereof was to persuade me to yield to my Lord's desire in this business at this time, or else I was undone for ever.

Upon the fifteenth my Lord and my coz. Cecily Neville came down from London my Lord lying in Lester['s] chamber and I in my own.

Upon the seventeenth my Lord and I after supper had some talk about these businesses, Matthew being in the room, where we all fell out and so we parted for that night. [My Lord was at London when my mother died, but he went to Lewes before he heard the news of her death.]

Upon the eighteenth, being Saturday, in the morning my Lord and I having much talk about these businesses, we agreed that Mr Marsh should go presently down to my mother and that by him I should write a letter to persuade her to give over her jointure presently to my Lord, and that he would give her yearly as much as it was worth. This day my Lord went from Knole to London. [Upon the twentieth went my child with Mary Neville and Mrs Bathurst to West Horsley from London. Mary Hitchin went with her, for still she lay in bed with Lady Margaret.]

Upon the twentieth, being Monday I dispatched Mr Marsh with letters to my mother about the business aforesaid. I sent them unsealed because my Lord might see them. [Upon the 24th, being Friday, between the hours of six and seven at night died my dear mother at Broome in the same chamber where my father was born, thirteen years and two months after the death of Queen Elizabeth and 10 years and four months after the death of my father, I being then twenty-six years old and four months and the child two years old wanting a month.]

My Brother Compton and his wife kept the House at West Horsley, and my brother Beauchamp and my sister his wife sojourned with them, so as the child was with both her aunts.

Upon the 22nd Mr Davys came down from London and brought me word that my mother was very well recovered of her dangerous sickness. By him I writ a letter to my Lord that Mr Amherst and Mr Davy might confer together about my jointure to free it from the payment of debts and all other encumbrances.

Upon the 24th my Lady Somerset was arraigned and condemned at Westminster Hall where she confessed her fault and asked the King's mercy, and was much pitied of all beholders.

Upon the 25th my Lord of Somerset was arraigned and condemned in the same place and stood much upon his innocency.

Upon the 27th being Monday, my Lord came down to Buckhurst. My Lord Vaux and his Uncle Sir Henry Neville and diverse others came with him, but the lords that promised to go with him stayed behind, agreeing to meet him the next day at Lewes. [At this great meeting at Lewes, my Lord Compton, my Lord Mordaunt, Tom Nevil, Jo. Herbert and all that crew with Wat. Raleigh,* Jack Lewis and a multitude of such company were there. There was bowling, bull-baiting, cards and dice with such sports to entertain the time. And on the 30th at night or the 31st my Lord was told the news of my mother's death he being then at Lewes with all this company.]

Upon the 28th my Lady Selby came hither to see me and told me that she had heard some folks say that I have done well in not consenting to the composition.

Upon the 29th Kendal came and brought me the heavy news of my mother's death, which I held as the greatest and most lamentable cross that could befall me.

Also he brought her will along with him, wherein she appointed her body should be buried in the parish church of Anwick, which was a double grief to me when I considered her body should be carried away and not interred at Skipton;* so I took that as a sign that I should be disinherited of the inheritance of my forefathers. The same night I sent Hammon away with the will to my Lord who was then at Lewes.

Upon the 30th the Bishop of St David's came to me in the morning to comfort me in these afflictions, and in the afternoon I sent for Sir William Selby to speak to him about the conveyance of my dear mother's body into Northumberland, and about the building of a little chapel wherein I intended she should be buried.

Upon the 31st came Mr Amherst from my Lord and brought me word that my Lord would be here on Saturday. The same day Mr James brought me a letter from Mr Woolrich wherein it seemed it was my mother's pleasure her body should be conveyed to what place I appointed and which was some contentment to my aggrieved soul.

JUNE 1616

Upon the first being Saturday, my Lord left all the company at Buckhurst and came hither about seven o' clock in the morning and so went to bed and slept till twelve, when I made Rivers write my letters to Sir Christopher Pickering, Mr Woolrich, Mr Dombvill and Ralph Conniston, wherein I told them that my Lord had determined to keep possession for my right and to desire that the body might be wrapped in lead till they heard from me. About four of the clock my Lord went to London.

Upon the 4th, Marsh and Rivers came from London and gave me to understand how my Lord, by the knowledge and consent of Lord William Howard and the advice of his learned counsel had sent a letter down into Westmorland to my Lady's Servants and tenants to keep possession for him and me, which was a thing I little expected, but gave me much contentment for I thought my Lord of Cumberland* had taken possession of her jointure quietly.

Upon the 8th being Saturday, Rivers and Mr Burridge were sent down into Westmorland with letters from the Council for restoring

the possession of Appleby Castle as it was at my Lady's decease. [About this time came my Lady Cavendish, Sir Robert Yately and Mr Watson so see me and comfort me after the loss of my mother and persuaded me much to consent to the agreement.]
At this time my Lord desired to have me pass my rights of the lands in Westmorland to him and my child, and to this end he brought my Lord William Howard to persuade me, and then my Lord told me I should go presently to Knole, and so I was sent away upon half an hour's warning, leaving my coz. Cecily Neville and Willoughby behind me at London, and so went down alone with Katherine Buxton about eight o'clock at night, so as it was twelve before we came to Knole.
Upon the 15th came the steward to Knole with whom I had much talk at this time. I wrought very hard and made an end of one of my cushions of Irish stitch work. [This Summer the King of Spain's eldest daughter, called Anna Maria, came into France and was married to the French King and the French King's eldest sister went into Spain and was married to the King of Spain's eldest son.]
Upon the 17th came down Dr Layfield, Ralph Conniston and Basket, Dr Layfield bringing with him the conveyance which Mr Walter had drawn, and persuaded me to go up and set my hand to it, which I refused because my Lord had sent me down so suddenly two days before.
Upon the nineteenth my Lord came down for me and Doctor Layfield with him, when my Lord persuaded me to consent to his business and assured me how good and kind a husband he would be to me.
Upon the twentieth my Lord and I, Doctor Layfield and Katherine Burton went up to London, and the same day I passed (by fine before my Lord Hubbard) the inheritance of Westmorland to my Lord if I had no heirs of my own body.
Upon the 21st, being Friday, my Lord wrote his letters to my Lord William and gave directions to Mr Marsh to go with them and that the possession of Brougham Castle should be very carefully looked to. The same day he went to Horsley to see the child at his sister's.
Upon Sunday the 23rd my Lord and I went in the morning to St Bride's church and heard a sermon.

Upon the 24th my Lord and my Lord XX,* my coz. Cecily Neville went by barge to Greenwich and waited on the King and Queen to Chapel and dined at my Lady Bedford's where I met Lady Hume, my old acquaintance. After dinner we went up to the gallery where the Queen used me exceeding well. [About this time I went to the tiltyard to see my Lady Knolles where I saw my Lady Somerset's little child,* being the first time I ever saw it.]
Upon the 28th came Kendall with letters from my Lord William, so as my Lord determined I should go presently into the North.
Upon the 30th, Sunday, presently after dinner my Lady Robert Rich, my coz. Cecily Neville and I went down by barge to Greenwich where in the gallery there passed some unkind words between my Lady Knolles and me. I took my leave of the Queen and all my friends here. About this time it was agreed between my Lord and me that Mrs Bathurst should go away from the child and that Willoughby should have charge of her till I should appoint it otherwise. He gave me his faithful promise that he would come after me into the North as soon as he could, and that the child should come out of hand, so that my Lord and I were never greater friends than at this time.

JULY 1616

Upon the first, my Lord Hobart came to Dorset House where I acknowledged a fine to him of a great part of my thirds in my Lord's land, but my Lord gave me his faithful word and promise that in Michaelmas Term next he would make me a jointure of the full thirds of his living. About one o'clock I set forward on my journey. My Lord brought me down to the coach side where we had a loving and kind parting.
Upon the 11th, Rafe brought me word that it* could not be buried at Appleby, so I sent Rivers away presently who got their consents. About five o'clock came my coz. William Howard and five or six of his. About eight we set forward, the body going in my Lady's own coach with my four horses and myself following it in my own coach with two horses and most of the men and women on horseback, so as there were about forty in the company, and we came to Appleby about half an hour after eleven o'clock, and about twelve the body was put into the grave. About three o'clock in the morning we came home, where I showed my cousin Howard my letter I writ to my

Lord. [About this time, Actaeon, my Lord's footman, lost his race to my Lord Salisbury's Irish footman and my Lord lost 200 twenty shilling pieces by betting on his side.]
Upon the 17th I rid into Whinfield park, and there I willed the tenants that were carrying of hay at Billian Bower that they should keep the money in their own hands till it were known who had a right to it.
Upon the 25th I signed a warrant for the killing of a stag in Stainsmore, being the first I ever had signed of that kind.
Upon the 29th I sent my folks into the park to make hay, when they being interrupted by my uncle Cumberland's people, two of my uncle's people were hurt by Mr Kidd, the one in the leg, the other in the foot, whereupon complaint was made to the judges at Carlisle, and a warrant sent forth for the apprehending of all my folks that were in the field at that time, to put in surety to appear at Kendal at the assizes.

AUGUST 1616

Upon the first day came Baron Bromley and Judge Nichols to see me as they came from Carlisle and ended the matter about the hurting of my uncle Cumberland's men and have released my folks that were bound to appear at the assizes.
Upon the fourth my coz. John Dudley supped here and told me that I had given very good satisfaction to the judges and all the company that was with them. [About this time my Lady Exeter was brought to bed of a daughter and my Lady Montgomery* of a son, being her first son.]
Upon the eleventh came Mr Marsh and brought a letter of the King's hand to it that I should not be molested in Brougham Castle and withal how all things went well and that my Lord would be here very shortly.
Upon the 22nd I met my Lord at Appleby town's end where he came with a great company of horse, Lord William Howard he and I riding in the coach together, and so we came that night to Brougham. There came with him Thomas Glenham, Coventry, Grosvenor, Grey Dick* etc etc. The same night Prudence, Bess, Penelope and some of the men came hither, but the stuff* was not yet come so as they were fain to lie three or four in a bed. [Upon Saturday and Sunday my Lord showed me his will, whereby he gave all his land to

the child, saving three thousand five hundred pound a year to my brother Sackville and fifteen hundred pounds a year which is appointed for the payment of his debts, and my jointure excepted, which was a matter I little expected.]
Upon the 24th in the afternoon I dressed the chamber where my Lady died and set up the green velvet bed, where the same night we went to lie there.
Upon the 26th came my coz. Clifford to Appleby, but with a far less train than my Lord.
Upon the 27th our folks being all at XXX* there passed some ill words betwixt Matthew, one of the keepers and William Punn, whereupon they fell to blows, & Grosvenor, Grey Dick, Thos., Todd Edwards' swords made a great uproar in the town, and three or four were hurt, and the man went to ring the bell fell from a ladder and was sore hurt.
Upon the 28th we made an end of dressing the house in the forenoon, and in the afternoon I wrought Irish stitch and my Lord sat and read by me.

SEPTEMBER 1616*

OCTOBER 1616

Upon the eleventh Mr Sandford went to London, by whom I sent a very earnest letter to my Lord that I might come up to London. [Upon the eighteenth being Friday died my Lady Margaret's old beagle.]
The seventeenth was the first day that I put on my black silk grogram gown.*
Upon the 22nd came Rivers down to Brougham and brought me word that I could not go to London all this winter.
Upon the 31st I rid into Whinfield in the afternoon. This month I spent in working and reading. Mr Dumbell read a great part of the History of the Netherlands.*

NOVEMBER 1616

Upon the first I rose betimes in the morning and went up to the Pagan tower to my prayers and saw the sun rise.
Upon the fourth I sat in the drawing chamber all the day at my work. [Upon the fourth Prince Charles was created Prince of Wales in the

great hall at Whitehall, where he had been created Duke of York about thirteen years before. There was barriers and running at the ring but it was not half so great pomp as was at the creation of Prince Henry.* Not long after this Lord Chancellor was created Viscount Brakely and my Lord Knolles Viscount Wallingford, my Lord Coke was displaced and Montague made Lord Chief Justice in his place]

Upon the ninth I sat at my work and heard Rivers and Marsh read Montaigne's Essays,* which book they have read almost this fortnight.

Upon the twelfth I made an end of the long cushion of Irish stitch* which my coz. Cecily Neville began when she went with me to the bath, it being my chief help to pass away the time to work.*

Upon the 19th William Pun came down from London with letters from my Lord, whereby I perceived there had passed a challenge between him and my coz. Clifford, which my Lord sent by my coz. Cheyney. The Lords of the Council sent for them both and the King made them friends, giving my Lord marvellous good words and willed him to send for me because he meant to make an agreement himself between us.

This going up to London of mine I little expected at this time. By him I also heard that my sister Sackville was dead.

Upon the twentieth I spent most of the day in playing at tables.* All this time since my Lord went away I wore my black taffety nightgown and a yellow taffety waistcoat, and used to rise betimes in the morning, and walk upon the leads* and afterwards to hear reading.

Upon the 22nd I did string the pearls and diamonds left me by my mother into a necklace.

Upon the 23rd I went to Mr Blink's house in Cumberland where I stayed an hour or two and heard music and saw all the house and gardens. [Upon the 23rd Baker, Hookfield, Harry the caterer, Will and Tom Fool went from hence toward London.]

Upon the 26th Thomas Hilton came hither and told me of some quarrels that would be between some gentlemen that took my Lord's part, and my coz. Clifford, which did much trouble me. [Upon the 24th Basket set out from London to Brougham Castle to fetch me up.]

Upon the 29th I bought of Mr Cliborne who came to see me a cloak and a saveguard* of cloth laced with black lace to keep me warm in my journey.

DECEMBER 1616

Upon the fourth came Basket with all the horses to carry me to London, but he left the coach behind him at Roos.

Upon the ninth I set out from Brougham Castle towards London. About 3 o'clock in the afternoon we came to Roos. All this day I rode on horseback on Rivers's mare, 29 miles that day.

Upon the eleventh I went to York. Three of Lord Sheffield's daughters and Mrs Matthews the Bishop's wife came to see me this night. Mrs Matthews lay with me. About this time died Mr Marshall, my Lord's auditor and surveyor, and left me a purse of ten angels as a remembrance of his love. [Upon the twelfth, William Dunn overtook us at Wentbridge, having found the diamond ring at Roos, which I was very glad of.]

[The fifteenth day was Mr John Tufton* just eight years old, being he what was after married to my first child in the church at St Bartholomew's.]

Upon the eighteenth I alighted at Islington where my Lord, who came in my Lady Withypole's coach which he borrowed, my Lady Effingham, the widow, my sister Beauchamp and a great many more came to meet me, so that we were in all ten or eleven coaches, and so I came to Dorset House where the child met me in the gallery. The house was well dressed up against I came. [The child was brought down to me in the gallery, which was the first time I had seen her after my mother died.]

Upon the 23rd my Lady Manners came in the morning to dress my head. I had a new black wrought taffety gown which my Lady St John's tailor made. She used often to come to me and I to her and was very kind one to another. About five o'clock in the evening my Lord and I and the child went in the great coach to Northampton House where my Lord Treasurer and all the company commended her, and she went down into my Lady Walden's chamber. My coz. Clifford saw her and kissed her, but I stayed with my Lady Suffolk. All this time of me being at London I was much sent to and visited by many, being unexpected that ever matters should have gone so well with me and my Lord, everybody persuading me to hear and to make an end, since the King had taken the matter in hand so as now I had a new part to play upon the stage of this world.

Upon the 26th I dressed myself in my green satin nightgown.

Upon the 27th I dined at my Lady Elizabeth Gray's lodgings at Somerset House where I met my Lady Compton and my Lady Fielding and spoke to them about my coming to the King. Presently after dinner came my Lord thither and we went together to my Lady Arundel's where I saw all the pictures in the gallery and the statues in the lower rooms.

Upon the 28th I dined above in my chamber and wore my night-gown because I was not very well, which day and yesterday I forgot it was fish day and ate flesh at both dinners. In the afternoon I played at glecko with my Lady Gray and lost £27 and odd money.

Upon the 31st this night I sent Thomas Woodyatt with a sweet bag* to the Queen for a New Year's gift, and a standish to Mrs Hanno, both cost me about 16 or 17 pounds.

JANUARY 1617

Upon New Year's day presently after dinner, I went to the Savoy to my Lord Carey's. From thence he and I went to Somerset House to the Queen where I met Lady Derby, my Lady Bedford, and my Lady Montgomery and a great deal of other company that came along with the King and the Prince. My Lord Arundel had much talk with me about the business and persuaded me to yield to the King in all things. From Somerset House we went to Essex House to see my Lady of Northumberland. [This was the last time I ever saw my Lady Northumberland.] From thence I went to see my Lady Rich and so came home. After supper I went to see my sister Beauchamp and stayed with her an hour or two, for my Lord was at the play at Whitehall that night. [As the King passed by he kissed me. Afterwards the Queen came out into the drawing chamber, where she kissed me and used me very kindly. This was the first time I either saw the King, Queen or Prince since my coming out of the North.]

Upon the second I went to the tower to see my Lady Somerset and my Lord. This was the first time I saw them since their arraignment.

Upon the fifth I went into the court. We went up into the King's presence chamber where my Lord Villiers was created Earl of Buckingham, my Lord, my Lord of Montgomery and diverse other earls bringing him up to the King. I supped with my Lord of Arundel and my Lady, and after supper I saw the play of the mad lover* in the hall.

Upon the sixth, being Twelfth Day, I went about four o'clock to the court with my Lord. I went up with my Lady Arundel and ate a scrambling supper with her and my Lady Pembroke at my Lord Duke's lodging. We stood to see the masque* in the box with my Lady Ruthven.

Upon the eighth we came down from London to Knole. This night my Lord and I had a falling out about the land.

Upon the ninth I went up to see the things in the closet* and began to have Mr Sandys's book* read to me about the government of the Turks, my Lord sitting the most part of the day reading in his closet.

Upon the tenth my Lord went up to London upon the sudden, we not knowing it till the afternoon.

Upon the sixteenth I received a letter from my Lord that I should come up to London the next day because I was to go before the King on Monday next.

Upon the seventeenth when I came up, my Lord told me I must resolve to go to the King the next day.

Upon the 18th being Saturday, I went presently after dinner to the Queen to the drawing chamber, where my Lady Derby told the Queen how my business stood, and that I was to go to the King, so she promised me she would do all the good in it she could. [The Queen gave me warning to take heed of putting my matters absolutely to the King, lest he should deceive me.] When I had stayed but a little while there I was sent for out, my Lord and I going through my Lord Buckingham's chamber, who brought us into the King, being in the drawing chamber. He put out all that were there, and my Lord and I kneeled by his chair side, when he persuaded us both to peace, and to put the whole matter wholly into his hands, which my Lord consented to, but I beseeched His Majesty to pardon me for that I would never part with Westmorland while I lived upon any condition whatsoever. Sometimes he used fair means and persuasions, and sometimes foul means, but I was resolved before so as nothing would move me.

From the King we went to the Queen's side and brought my Lady St John to her lodging, and so went home. At this time I was much bound to my Lord for he was far kinder to me in all these businesses than I expected, and was very unwilling that the King should do me any public disgrace.

Upon the nineteenth my Lord and I went to the court in the morning, thinking the Queen would have gone to the chapel, but she did not, so my Lady Ruthven and I and many others stood in the closet to hear the sermon. I dined with my Lady Ruthven. Presently after dinner she and I went up to the drawing chamber where my Lord Duke, my Lady Montgomery, my Lady Burleigh, persuaded me to refer these businesses to the King. About six o'clock my Lord came for me, so he and I and Lady St John went home in her coach. This night the masque* was danced at the court, but I would not stay to see it because I had seen it already.

Upon the twentieth, I and my Lord went presently after dinner to the court. He went up to the King's side about his business. I went up to my Aunt Bedford in her lodgings where I stayed in Lady Ruthven's chamber till towards three o'clock, about which time I was sent for up to the King into his drawing chamber, when the door was locked and nobody suffered to stay here but my Lord and I, my uncle Cumberland, my coz. Clifford, my Lord of Arundel, my Lord of Pembroke, my Lord of Montgomery and Sir John Digby. For lawyers there were my Lord Chief Justice Montague and Hobart, Yelverton, the King's Solicitor Sir Randal Crewe that was to speak for my Lord of Cumberland and Mr Ireland that was to speak for my Lord and me. The King asked us all whether we would submit to his judgement in this case, to which my uncle Cumberland, my coz. Clifford and my Lord answered they would, but I would never agree to it without Westmorland, at which the King grew in a great chaffe, my Lord of Pembroke and the King's Solicitor speaking much against me. At last when they saw there was no remedy, my Lord, fearing the King would do me some public disgrace, desired Sir John Digby to open the door, who went out with me and persuaded me much to yield to the King. My Lord Hay came to me to whom I told in brief how this business stood. Presently after my Lord came from the King where it was resolved that if I would not come to an agreement, there should be an agreement made without me. We went down, Sir Robert Douglas, and Sir George Chaworth bringing us to the coach. By the way my Lord and I went in at Worcester House to see my Lord and my Lady* and so came home. This day I may say I was led miraculously by God's providence, and next to that I must attribute all my good to the worth and nobleness of my Lord's disposition, for neither I nor anybody else thought I should have passed over this day so well as I thank God I have done.

Upon the 22nd the child had the sixth fit of her ague.* In the morning Mr Smith went up in the coach to London to my Lord to whom I wrote a letter to let him know in what case the child was, and to give him humble thanks for his noble usage towards me at London. The same day my Lord came down to Knole to see the child.

Upon the 23rd my Lord went up betimes to London again. The same day the child put on her red baize coats.

Upon the 25th I spent most of my time in working and in going up and down to see the child. About five or six o'clock her fits took her which lasted six or seven hours.

Upon the 28th at this time I wore a green plain tummel* gown that William Dunn made me, and my yellow taffety waistcoat. Rivers used to read to me in Montaigne Essays and Moll Nevill in the Fairy Queene.*

Upon the 30th Mr Amhurst the preacher came hither to see me, with whom I had much talk. He told me that now they began to think at London that I had done well in not referring this business to the King and that everybody said that God had a hand in it.

MARY WROTH

(*c.*1587–*c.*1653)

Love's Victory

CHARACTERS

Shepherds

Philisses: in love with Musella and beloved by her.
Lissius: in love with Simeana and beloved by her.
Forester: in love with Silvesta.
Lacon: in love with Musella.
Rustic: in love with Musella, marries Dalina.
Arcas: a villain.

Shepherdesses

Musella: in love with Philisses.
Simeana: sister to Philisses and in love with Lissius.
Silvesta: in love with Forester but has vowed chastity.
Climeana: in love with Lissius.
Dalina: a fickle lady marries Rustic
Phillis: in love with Philisses.
Mother to Musella.

Temple of Love

Venus
Cupid
Priests

ACT I

Venus and Cupid with her, in her temple, her priests attending her.

Venus. Cupid, methinks we have too long been still,
And that these people grow to scorn our will.
Mercy to those ungrateful breeds neglect;
Then let us grow our greatness to respect,
Make them acknowledge that our heavenly power
Cannot their strength, but even themselves, devour;

Let them not smile and laugh because thine eyes
Are covered,* as if blind, or love despise.
No, thou that scarce shalt from thine eyes take off,
Which gave them cause on thee to make this scoff.
Thou shalt discern their hearts, and make them know
That humble homage unto thee they owe;
Take thou the shaft which headed is with steel
And make them bow whose thoughts did lately reel;
Make them thine own, thou who didst me once harm,*
Cannot forget the fury of that charm;
Wound them, but kill them not, so may they live
To honour thee, and thankfulness to give;
Shun no great cross which may their crosses breed,
But yet, let blessed enjoying them succeed.
Grief is sufficient to declare thy might,
And in thy mercy glory will shine bright.

Cupid. Mother, I will no cross, no harm, forbear,
Of jealousy for loss, of grief or fear,
Which may my honour touched again repair;
But with their sorrows will my glory rear.
Friends shall mistrust their friends, lovers mistake,
And all shall for their folly woes partake;
Some shall love much, yet shall no love enjoy,
Others obtain, when lost is all their joy.
This will I do, your will and mind to serve,
And to your triumph will these rites preserve.

Venus. Then shall we have again our ancient glory;
And let this called be 'Love's Victory'.
Triumphs upon their travails* shall ascend,
And yet most happy ere they come to end.

Cupid. Joy and enjoying on some shall be set,
Sorrow on others caught by Cupid's net.

'Love's Victory'

*Philisses.** You pleasant flowery mead*
Which I did once well love,

Your paths no more I'll tread,
Your pleasures no more prove,
Your beauty more admire,
Your colours more adore,
Nor grass with daintiest store
Of sweets to breed desire.

Walks, once so sought for, now
I shun you for the dark;
Birds, to whose song did bow
Mine ears, your notes ne'er mark;
Brook, which so pleasing was,
Upon whose banks I lay,
And on my pipe did play,
Now unregarded pass.

Meadows, paths, grass, flowers,
Walks, birds, brook: truly find
All prove but as vain showers,
Wished welcome, else unkind.
You once I loved best,
But love makes me you leave,
By love I love deceive;
Joys lost for life's unrest.

Joys lost for life's unrest; indeed, I see.
Alas, poor shepherd, miserable me.
Yet, fair Musella, love and worthy be;
I blame thee not, but mine own misery.
Live you still happy and enjoy your love,
And let love's pain in me distressed move;
For since it is my friend thou dost affect,
Then wrong him once, myself I will neglect;
And thus in secret will my passion hide,
Till time or fortune doth my fear decide,
Making my love appear as the bright morn,
Without or mist, or cloud, but truly born.

Lissius. Joyful pleasant spring,
Which comforts to us bring,
Flourish in your pride
Never let decay

Your delights allay
Since joy is to you tied.

Philisses. No, joy is tied to you, you 'tis do prove
The pleasure of your friend's unhappy love
'Tis you enjoy the comfort of my pain,
'Tis I that love, and you that love obtain.

Lissius. Let no frost nor wind
Your dainty colours blind,
But rather cherish.
Your most pleasant sight,
Let never winter bite
Nor season perish.

Philisses. I cannot perish more than now I do,
Unless my death my miseries undo.
Lissius is happy, but Philisses cursed,
Love seeks to him, on me he doth his worst.
And do thy worst on me still, froward boy,*
More ill thou canst not, but poor life destroy,
Which do, and glory in thy conquest got;
All men must die, and love drew my ill lot.

Lissius. My dear Philisses. What, alone and sad?

Philisses. Neither, but musing why the best is bad.
But you were merry, I'll not mar your song,
My thoughts are tedious and for you too long. [*Exit*]

Lissius. Alas, what means this? Surely it is love
That doth in him this alteration move;
This is the humour makes our shepherds rave.
I'll none of this, I'll sooner seek my grave!
Love, by your favour, I will none of you,
I rather you should miss, than I should sue.
Yet Cupid, poor Philisses back restore
To his first wits, and I'll affect thee more

Silvesta. Fair shining day, and thou, Apollo* bright,
Which to these pleasant valleys gives thy light,
And with sweet showers mixed with golden beams
Enrich these meadows and these gliding streams,
Wherein thou seest thy face like mirror fair,

Dressing in them thy curling, shining hair;
This place with sweetest flowers still doth deck,
Whose colours show their pride, free from the check
Of fortune's frown, so long as Spring doth last;
But then, feel change, whereof all others taste.
As I, for one, who thus my habits change:
Once shepherdess, but now in woods must range
And after the chaste Goddess* bear her bow;
Though service once to Venus I did owe,
Whose servant then I was and of her band.
But farewell folly, I with Dian stand
Against love's changing and blind foolery
To hold with happy and blessed chastity.
For love is idle, happiness there's none
When freedom's lost and chastity is gone;
And where on earth most blessedness there is,
Love's fond desires never fail to miss.
And this, believe me, you will truly find,
Let not repentance therefore change your mind;
But change before your glory will be most,
When as the waggish boy can least him boast.
For he doth seek to kindle flames of fire,
But never thinks to quench a chaste desire;
He calls his foe, he hates none more than those
Who strive his law to shun, and this life chose.
All virtue hates his kingdom's wantonness
His crown, desires; his sceptre, idleness;
His wounds, hot fires are; his help's like frost,
Glad to hurt but never heals; thinks time lost
If any gain their long-sought joy with bliss;
And this the government of folly is.
But here Philisses comes, poor shepherd lad,
With love's hot fires, and his own, made mad.
I must away, my vow allows no sight
Of men, yet must I pity him, poor wight,
Though he, rejecting me, this change hath wrought,
He shall be no less worthy in my thought.
Yet, wish I do he were as free as I,
Then were he happy, now feels misery.

For thanks to heaven and to the gods above,
I have won chastity in place of love.
Now love's as far from me as never known;
Then basely tied, now freely am mine own;
Slavery and bondage with mourning care
Were then my living, sighs and tears my fare;
But all these gone now live I joyfully,
Free, and untouched of thought but chastity.

Philisses. Love being missed, in heaven at last was found
Lodged in Musella's fair, though cruel, breast;
Cruel, alas, yet whereon I must ground
All hopes of joy, though tired with unrest.
O hearest dear, let plaints which true felt are
Gain pity once, do not delight to prove
So merciless, still killing with despair;
Nor pleasure take so much to try my love;
Yet, if your trial will you milder make,
Try, but not long, lest pity come too late
But O, she may not, cannot, will not, take
Pity on me: she loves, and lends me hate

Lissius. Fie, my Philisses, will you ever fly
My sight that loves you and your good desires?

Philisses. Fly you, dear Lissius? No. But still a cry
I hear that says I burn in scorner's fires.
Farewell, good Lissius, I will soon return
But not to you a rival, like to burn.

Lissius. Ah, poor Philisses, would I knew thy pain,
That as I now lament might help obtain;
But yet in love they say none should be used
But self-deserts, lest trust might be abused.

[*Enter a forester*]

Forester. Did ever cruelty itself thus show?
Did ever heaven our mildness thus far move
All sweetness and all beauty to o'erthrow?
All joy deface and crop in Spring-time love?
Could any mortal breast invent such harm?
Could living creature think on such a loss?

No, no, alas, it was the Furies' charm
Who sought by this our best delights to cross,
And now in triumph glory in their gain.
Where was truc bcauty found, if not in thee,
O dear Silvesta? But accursed swain
That caused this change. O, miserable me,
Who live to see this day, and day's bright light.
To shine when pleasure's turned into despite.

Lissius. Another of Love's band ! O mighty Love
That can thy folly make in most to move.

Forester. Accursed shepherd, why wert thou e'er born
Unless it were to be true virtue's scorn?
Cursed be thy days, unlucky ever be,
Nor ever live, least happiness to see;
But where thou lov'st, let her as cruel prove
As thou wert to Silvesta, and my love.

Lissius. If one may ask, what is th'offence is done?

Forester. That cursed Philisses hath me quite undone.

Lissius. Undone, as how?

Forester. Sit down, and you shall know,
For glad I am that I my grief may tell,
Since 'tis some ease my sorrow's cause to show,
Disburdening my poor heart which grief doth swell.
Then know I loved, alas, and ever must,
Silvesta fair, sole mistress of my joy,
Whose dear affections were in surest trust
Laid up in flames, my hopes clean to destroy.
For as I truly loved and only she,
She for Philisses sighed, who did reject
Her love and pains, nor would she, cruel, see
My plaints, nor tears, but followed his neglect
With greater passion. I her followed still,
She ran from me, he flew from her as fast,
I after both did hie, though for my ill,
Who thus do live all wretchedness to taste.
Long time this lasted, still she constant loved,
And more she loved, more cruel still he grew;

Till at the length thus tyrant-like he proved,
Forcing that change which makes my poor heart rue.*
For she, perceiving hate so far to guide
His settled heart to nothing but disdain,
Having all manners and all fashions tried
That might give comfort to her endless pain,
But seeing nothing would his favour turn
From fondly flying of her truest love,
Led by those passions which did firmly burn
So hot as nothing could those flames remove,
But still increase, she for the last resolved
To kill this heat, this hopeless course to take,
Making a vow which cannot be dissolved,
As not obtaining love, will love forsake.
For she hath vowed unto Diana's life
Her pure virginity, as she who could
No more than once love, nor another's wife
Consent to be, nor his now, if he would.
This hath he done by his ungratefulness;
Would it might turn to his own wretchedness!

Lissius. O, curse him not, alas, it is his ill
To feel so much as doth his senses kill;
And yet, indeed, this cruelty and course
Is somewhat strange for shepherds here to use.
Yet, see I not how this can prove the worse
For you, whose love she ever did refuse,
But much the better, since your suffered pain
Can be no glory to another's gain

Forester. Would it could be to any's gain the most
Of glory, honour, fortune, and what more
Can added be, though I had ever lost
And he obtained the chief of beauty's store.
For then I might have her sometimes beheld
But now am barred; for my love placed was
In truest kind, wherein I all excelled;
Not seeking gain, but losing, did surpass
Those that obtain, for my thoughts did ascend
No higher than to look. That was my end.

Lissius. What strange effects doth fancy 'mong us prove,
Who still brings forth new images of love?
But this of all is strangest to affect
Only the sight and not the joys respect,
Nor end of whining love, since sight we gain
With small ado, the other with much pain;
Doubling the pleasure, having left despair,
And favour won, which kills all former care;
And sure, if ever I should chance to love,
The fruitful ends of love I first would move.

Forester. I wish you may obtain your heart's desire,
And I but sight, who waste in chastest fire. [*Exit*]

Lissius. These two to meet in one I ne'er did find,
Love and chastity linked in one man's mind,
But now I see Love hath as many ways
To win as to destroy when he delays.

[*Enter Philisses*, *Dalina*, *Rustic*, *Lacon*, *Lissius*.]

Dalina. Thc sun grows hot, 'twere best we did retire.

Lissius. There's a good shade.

Philisses. But here's a burning fire.

Lacon. Never did I see a man so changed as he.

Dalina. Truly nor I, what can the reason be?

Philisses. Love, love it is, which you in time may know,
But happy they can keep their love from show.

[*Enter Musella*]

Dalina. Musella welcome to our meeting is,
Of all our fellows you did only miss.

Musella. Small miss of me. For, oft'nest when I'm here
I am as if I were another where.
But where is Phillis? Seldom do I find
Her or Simena missing; yet, the blind
God Cupid late hath struck her yielding breast
And makes her lonely walk to seek for rest.

Philisses. Yet when the pain is greatest, 'tis some ease
To let a friend partake his friend's disease.

Musella. That were no friendly part, in this you miss,
Impart unto your friend no harm, but bliss.

Philisses. Some friend will ready be to ease one's smart.

Musella. So to befriend yourself they should bear part.

Dalina. Now we are met, what sport shall we invent
While the sun's fury somewhat more be spent?

Lacon. Let each one here their fortunes past relate,
Their loves, their froward chance, or their good fate.

Musella. And so discourse the secrets of their mind!
I like not this; thus sport may crosses find.

Philisses. Let one begin a tale.

Dalina. Nor that I like.

Lacon. What then will please? We see what doth dislike.

Philisses. Dislike is quickly known, pleasure is scant.

Musella. And where joys seem to flow, alas, there's want.

Climeana. O mine eyes, why do you lead
My poor heart thus forth to range
From the wonted course, to strange
Unknown ways and paths to tread?
Let it home return again,
Free, untouched of gadding thought,
And your forces back be brought
To the ridding of my pain.
But mine eyes, if you deny
This small favour to my heart
And will force my thoughts to fly,
Know yet you govern but your part.

Lissius. Climeana hath begun a pretty sport;
Let each one sing, and so the game is short.

Rustic. Indeed, well said, and I will first begin.

Dalina. And whosoever's out, you'll not be in!

Philisses. Sing they who have glad hearts or voice,
I can but patience to this pleasure bring.

Musella. Then you and I will sit, and judges be.

Philisses. Would fair Musella first would judge of me.

Musella. Will you then sing?

Philisses. No, I would only say.

Musella. Choose some time else. Who will begin this play?

Rustic. Why, that will I, and I will sing of thee.

Musella. Sorry I am I should be your subject be.

Rustic.
When* I do see
Thee, whitest thee,
Yea, whiter than lamb's wool;
How do I joy
That thee enjoy
I shall with my heart full.
Thy eyes do play
Like goats with hay,
And skip like kids flying
From the sly fox,
So eyelid's box
Shuts up thy sight's prying.
Thy cheeks are red
Like ochre spread
On a fatted sheep's back;
Thy paps are found
Like apples round,
No praises shall lack.

Musella. Well you have praises given enough; now let
Another come some other to commend.

Rustic. I had much more to say, but thus I'm met
And stayed; now will I harken and attend.

Lacon.
By a pleasant river's side,
Heart and hopes on pleasure's tide,
Might I see within a bower
Proudly dressed with every flower
Which the Spring doth to us lend,
Venus and her loving friend.
I upon her beauty gazed,
They, me seeing, were amazed;

Till at last up stepped a child,
In his face not actions mild.
'Fly away,' said he, 'for sight
Shall both breed and kill delight;
Fly away and follow me,
And I will let thee beauties see.'
I obeyed him, then he stayed
Hard beside a heavenly maid;
When he threw a flaming dart,
And unkindly struck my heart.

Musella. But what became then of the cruel boy?

Lacon. When he had done his worst he fled away.

Musella. And so let us. 'Tis time we do return
To tend our flocks, who all this while do burn.

Philisses. Burn, and must burn: this suddenly is said;
But heat not quenched, alas, but hopes decayed.

Dalina. What have you done, and must I lose my song?

Musella. Not lose it, though awhile we it prolong.

Dalina. I am content, and now let's all retire.

Philisses. And soon return, sent by Love's quickest fire.

[*Venus and Cupid, appearing in the clouds*]

Venus. Fie this is nothing! What? Is this your care?
That among ten, the half of them you spare!
I would have all to wail and all to weep;
Will you at such a time as this go sleep?
Awake your forces and make Lissius find
Cupid can cruel be as well as kind.
Shall he go scorning thee and all thy train,
And pleasure take he can thy force disdain?
Strike him, and tell him thou his lord wilt prove,
And he a vassal unto mighty Love;
And all the rest, that scorners be of thee,
Make with their grief, of thy might feelers be.

Cupid. 'Tis true that Lissius, and some others yet,
Are free and lively; but they shall be met
With care sufficient, for 'tis not their time

As yet into my pleasing pain to climb.
Let them alone, and let themselves beguile,
They shall have torment when they think to smile.
They are not yet in pride of all their scorn,
But ere they have their pleasures half-way worn,
They shall both cry, and sigh, and wail, and weep,
And for our mercy shall most humbly creep.
Love hath most glory whenas greatest sprites*
He downward throws unto his own delights.
Then take no care, Love's victory shall shine,
Whenas your honour shall be raised by mine.

Venus. Thanks, Cupid, if thou do perform thine oath
As needs thou must, for gods must want no troth,*
Let mortals never think it odd or vain
To hear that Love can in all spirits reign.
Princes are not exempted from our mights,
Much less should shepherds scorn us and our rights;
Though they as well can love and like affect,
They must not therefore our commands neglect.

Cupid. Nor shall. And mark but what my vengeance is:
I'll miss my force, or they shall want their bliss;
And arrows here I have of purpose framed
Which as their qualities so are they named:
Love, jealousy, malice, fear, and mistrust.
Yet all these shall at last encounter just;
Harm shall be none, yet all shall harm endure
For some small season, then of joy be sure.
Like you this, mother?

Venus. Son, I like this well
And fail not now in least part of thy spell.

ACT II SCENE I

Musella, Dalina, Simeana, Philisses, Lissius, Lacon, Silvesta, Forester.

Dalina. Methinks we now too silent are. Let's play
At something while we yet have pleasing day.

Lissius. Here's sport enough; view but her new attire
And see her slave who burns in chaste desire.

Dalina. Mark but their meeting.
Lissius. She, I'm sure, will fly
And he, poor fool, will follow still, and cry.
Musella. What pleasure you do take to mock at love;
Are you sure you cannot his power prove?
But look, he kneels, and weeps.
Lissius. And cries, 'Ay me!'
Sweet nymph have pity, or he dies for thee.
Forester. Alas, dear nymph, why fly you still my sight?
Can my true love and firm affection
So little gain me, as your fairest light
Must darkened be for my affliction?
O look on me and see if in my face
True grief and sorrow show not my disgrace;
If that despair do not by sighs appear;
If felt disdain do not with tears make show
My ever-wailing, ever-saddest cheer,
And mourning, which no breath can overblow?
Pity me not, else judge with your fair eyes
My loving soul which to you captive lies.
Silvesta. Alas, fond forester, urge me no more
To that which now lies not within my might;
Nor can I grant, or you to joy restore
By any means to yield you least delight,
For I have vowed, which vows I will obey,
Unto Diana. What more can I say?
Forester. O, this I know. Yet give me but this leave
To do as birds, and trees, and beasts may do;
Do not, O, do not me of sight bereave,
For without you I see not. Ah, undo
Not what is yours, o'erthrow not what's your own;
Let me, though conquered, not be quite o'erthrown.
I know you vowed have, and vows must stand;
Yet, though you chaste must be, I may desire
To have your sight, and this the strictest band*
Cannot refuse, and but this I require.
Then grant it me, which I on knees do seek,
Be not to nature, and yourself, unleek.*

Silvesta. No, no, I ne'er believe your fond-made oath.
I chastity have sworn, then no more move.
I know what 'tis to swear, and break it, both;
What to desire, and what it is to love.
Protest you may that there shall nothing be
By you imagined 'gainst my chastity,
But this I doubt; your love will make you curse,
If you so much do love, that cursed day
When I this vowed; attempt it may be worse.
Then follow not thus hopeless your decay,
But leave off loving, or some other choose
Whose state or fortune need not you refuse.

Forester. Indeed, sweet nymph, 'tis true that chastity
To one that loves may justly raging move.
Yet, loving you, those thoughts shall banished be:
Since 'tis in you, I chastity will love,
And now depart, since such is your pleasure.
Depart, O me, from joy, from life, from ease,
Go I must, and leave behind that treasure
Which all contentment gives. Now to displease
Myself with liberty I may free go,
And with most liberty, most grief, most woe. [*Exit*]

Musella. Lissius, I hope this sight doth something move
In you to pity so much constant love.

Lissius. Yes. Thus it moves: that man should be so fond
As to be tied t'a woman's faithless bond!
For we should women love but as our sheep,
Who, being kind and gentle, give us ease,
But cross, or straying, stubborn, or unmeek,
Shunned as the wolf, which most our flocks disease.

Musella. We little are beholding unto you,
In kindness, less. Yet, you these words may rue;
I hope to live to see you wail and weep,
And deem your grief far sweeter than your sleep.
Then, but remember this, and think on me,
Who truly told you could not still live free.

Lissius. I do not know, it may be very well,
But I believe I shall uncharm Love's spell.

And Cupid, if I needs must love,
Take your aim and shoot your worst.
Once more you rob your mother's dove,
All your last shafts sure were burst,
Those you stole, and those you gave,
Shoot not me till new you have.

Philisses. Rustic, faith, tell me, hast thou ever loved?

Rustic. What call you love? I've been to trouble moved,
As when my best cloak hath by chance been torn,
I have lived wishing till it mended were,
And but so lovers do; nor could forbear
To cry if I my bag or bottle lost,
As lovers do who by their loves are crossed,
And grieve as much for these, as they for scorn.

Philisses. Call you this love? Why, love is no such thing!
Love is a pain which yet doth pleasure bring,
A passion which alone in hearts do move,
And they that feel not this, they cannot love.
'Twill make one joyful, merry, pleasant, sad,
Cry, weep, sigh, fast, mourn, nay sometimes stark mad;
If they perceive scorn, hate, or else disdain
To wrap their woes in store, for others' gain,
For that (but jealousy) is sure the worst,
And then be jealous. Better be accursed!
But O, some are, and would it not disclose;
They silent love, and loving, fear. Ah, those
Deserve most pity, favour and regard;
Yet, are they answered but with scorn's reward,
This their misfortune. And the like may fall
To you, or me, who wait misfortune's call.
But if it do, take heed, be ruled by me:
Though you mistrust, mistrust not that she see.
For then she'll smiling say, 'Alas, poor fool,
This man hath learned all parts of Folly's school.'
Be wise, make love, and love, though not obtain,
For to love truly is sufficient gain.

Rustic. Sure you do love, you can so well declare
The joys and pleasures, hope and his despair.

Philisses. I love indeed.

Rustic. But who is she you love?

Philisses. She who best thoughts must to affection move;
If any love, none need ask who it is.
Within these plains, none loves that loves not this
Delight of shepherd's pride, of this fair place;
No beauty is that shines not in her face,
Whose whiteness whitest lilies doth excel,
Matched with a rosy morning to compel
All hearts to serve her. Yet, doth she affect
But only virtue, nor will quite neglect
Those who doth serve her in an honest fashion,
Which, sure, doth more increase, than decrease, passion.

Arcas. Here are they met, where beauty only reigns,
Whose presence gives the excellentest light,
And brightest, dimming Phoebus, who but feigns
To outshine these, it is not in his might.
Fair troop, here is a sport will well befit
This time and place, if you will license it.

Philisses. What is't, good Arcas?

Arcas. Why stay, and you shall see.
Here is a book wherein each one shall draw
A fortune, and, thereby, their luck shall be
Conjectured. Like you this? You ne'er it saw.

Rustic. It is no matter, 'tis a pretty one.
Musella, you shall draw.

Musella. Though choose alone.

Philisses. I never saw it, but I like it well.

Lissius. Then he, 'chieves* best of all, must bear the bell.*

Rustic. Pray thee, good Arcas, let me hold the book.

Arcas. With all my heart. Yet, you'll not some lots brook.*

Rustic. Fairest, sweetest, bonny lass,
You that love in mirth to pass,
Time delightful come to me
And you shall your fortune see.

Musella. You tell by book, then sure you cannot miss,
But shall I know what shall be, or what is?

Rustic. What shall be you need not fear,
Rustic doth thy fortune bear.
Draw, and when you chosen have,
Praise me who such fortune gave.

Musella. And so I will, if good; or if untrue,
I'll blame mine own ill choice, and not blame you.

Philisses. Pray, may I see the fortune you do choose.

Musella. Yes, and if right, I will it not refuse.

Philisses. None can be cross to you, except you will.

Musella. Read it.

Philisses. I will, although it were my ill.
Fortune cannot cross your will,
Though your patience much must be.
Fear not that your luck is ill,
You shall your best wishes see.
Refuse: believe me, no, you have no cause;
Thus hope brings longing, patience, passion draws.

Dalina. I'll try what mine shall be, good Rustic, hold.

Arcas. A man must follow.

Dalina. I am still too bold.

Philisses. Then I will try, though sure of cruelty.
And yet, this lot doth promise good at last,
That, though I now feel greatest misery,
My blessed days to come are not all past.

Dalina. Come, this fond lover knows not yet the play,
He studies while our fortunes run away!
What have you got? Let's see, do you this love?

Philisses. Read it, but heaven grant me the end to prove.

Dalina. You do live to be much crossed,
Yet esteem no labour lost,
Since you shall with bliss obtain
Pleasure for your suffered pain.
Truly, I cannot blame you. Like you this?
So I at last might gain, I well could miss.

Musella. After a rain the sweetest flowers do grow,
So shall your hap* be, as this book doth show.

Dalina. Now must I draw. Sweet Fortune be my guide.

Musella. She* cannot see. Yet, must your chance abide.

Dalina. Blind or no, I care not, this I take, and
If good, my luck, if not, a luckless hand.

Philisses. If Fortune guide, she will direct to love,
They cannot parted be. What now dost move ?

Dalina. Move? Did you ever see the like?

Philisses. Not I.

Dalina. Nay, read it out, it shows my constancy.

Philisses.
They that cannot steady be
To themselves, the like must see.
Fickle people, fickly choose,
Slightly like, and so refuse.
This your fortune, who can say,
Herein justice bears not sway!

In troth, Dalina, Fortune is proud-cursed
To you without desert.

Dalina. This is the worst
That she can do. 'Tis true I have fickle been,
And so is she; 'tis then the lesser sin.
Let her prove constant, I will her observe,
And then, as she doth mend, I'll good deserve.

Arcas. Who chooseth next?

Lissius. Not I, lest such I prove.

Silvesta. Nor I, it is sufficient I could love.

Arcas. I'll wish for one, but Fortune shall not try
On me her tricks, whose favours are so dry.

Dalina. None can wish, if they their wishes love not,
Nor can they love, if that their wishings move not.

Philisses. You fain would solve* this business.

Dalina. Who? Would I?
Nay, my care's past. I Love and his, deny.

Philisses. Love and Reason once at war,
Jove came down to end the jar.
'Cupid,' said Love, 'must have place';
Reason, that it was his grace.
Jove then brought it to this end:
Reason should on Love attend;
Love takes Reason for his guide,
Reason cannot from Love slide.
This agreed, they pleased did part,
Reason ruling Cupid's dart.
So as sure love cannot miss,
Since that reason ruler is.

Lissius. It seems he missed before he had this guide!

Philisses. I'm sure not me, I ne'er my heart could hide
But he it found; so, as I well may say,
Had he been blind I might have stolen away!
But so he saw, and ruled with Reason's might,
As he hath killed in me all my delight;
He wounded me, alas, with double harm,
And none but he can my distress uncharm;
Another wound must cure me, or I die.
But stay, this is enough, I hence will fly
And seek the boy that struck me. Fare you well,
Yet, make not still your pleasures prove my hell. [*Exit*]

Lissius. Philisses now hath left us, let's go back
And tend our flocks, who now our care do lack.
Yet would he had more pleasant parted hence,
Or that I could but judge the cause from whence
These passions grow; it would give me much ease
Since I perceive my sight doth him displease
I'll seek him yet, and of him truly know
What in him hath bred this unusual woe.
If he deny me, then I'll swear he hates
Me or affects that humour which debates
In his kind thought, which should the master be;
But, who the friend is, I will quickly see. [*Exit*]

Musella. Well let's away. And hither soon return
That sun to me, whose absence make me burn. [*Exit*]

SCENE 2

Philisses. Lissius.

Lissius. O, plainly deal with me! My love hath been
Still firm to you; then, let us not begin
To seem as strangers. If I have wronged you, speak,
And I'll forgiveness ask; else, do not break
That band of friendship of our long-held love,
Which did these plains to admiration move.

Philisses. I cannot change, but love thee ever will,
For no cross shall my first affection kill.
But give me leave that sight, once loved, to shun,
Since by the sight, I see myself undone.

Lissius. When this opinion first possessed thy heart
Would death had struck me with his cruel dart.
Live I to be mistrusted by my friend?
'Tis time for me my wretched days to end.
But what began this change in thee?

Philisses. Mistrust.

Lissius. Mistrust of me?

Philisses. I am not so unjust.

Lissius. What then? Pray tell, my heart doth long to know.

Philisses. Why then, the change and cause of all my woe
Proceeds from this: I fear Musella's love
Is placed in you; this doth my torments move,
Since if she do, my friendship bound to you
Must make me leave for love or joy to sue,
For though I love her more than mine own heart,
If you affect her, I will ne'er impart
My love to her; so, constant friendship binds
My love where truth such faithful biding finds.
Then truly speak, good Lissius, plainly say,
Nor shall a love make me your trust betray.

Lissius. O my Philisses! What, was this the cause?
Alas, see how misfortune on me draws.
I love; but vow 'tis not Musella's face
Could from my heart my freer thoughts displace.

Although, I must confess, she worthy is,
But she, alas, can bring to me no bliss.
It is your sister who must end my care;
Now do you see you need no more despair.

Philisses. Yet, she may love you, can you that deny?

Lissius. And swear I never yet least show could spy.
But well assured I am that she doth love,
And you, I venture dare, doth her heart move.
'Tis true she speaks to me, but for your sake,
Else for good looks from her I might leave take.
Her eyes cannot dissemble, though her tongue
To speak it hazards not a greater wrong;
Her cheeks cannot command the blood, but still
It must appear, although against her will.
Thus have I answered, and advice do give:
Tell her your love, if you will happy live;
She cannnot, neither will she, you deny.
And do as much for me, or else I die.

Philisses. What may I do that you shall not command?
Then here I 'gage* my word and give my hand;
If with my sister I but power have,
She shall requite you, and your sorrow save
With gift of her love. But, once more say this:
From fair Musella hope you for no bliss?

Lissius. None but her friendship, which I will require
From both, as equal to my best desire.

Philisses. Then, thus assured, that friendship shall remain,
Or let my soul endure eternal pain.

SCENE 3

Venus' priests to Love, or his praise, the Goddess and her son, appearing in glory.

Cupid, blessed be thy might,
Let thy triumph see no night;
Be thou justly God of Love,
Who thus can thy glory move.
Hearts, obey to Cupid's sway,

Princes, none of you say nay;
Eyes, let him direct your way,
For without him you may stray.
He your secret thoughts can spy,
Being hid else from each eye.
Let your songs be still of love;
Write no satires which may prove
Least offensive to his name.
If you do, you will but frame
Words against yourselves, and lines
Where his good, and your ill, shines.
Like him who doth set a snare
For a poor betrayed hare,
And that thing he best doth love
Lucklessly the snare doth prove.
Love, the king is of the mind,
Please him, and he will be kind;
Cross him, you see what doth come:
Harms which make your pleasure's tomb.
Then, take heed, and make your bliss
In his favour, and so miss
No content, nor joy, nor peace,
But in happiness, increase.
Love command your hearts and eyes,
And enjoy what pleasure tries;
Cupid govern, and his care,
Guide your hearts from all despair.

ACT III SCENE I

Silvesta. Silent woods with desert's shade,
Giving peace.
Where all pleasures first are made
To increase.
Give your favour to my moan.
Now my loving time is gone
Chastity my pleasure is,
Folly fled.
From hence, now I seek my bliss,

Cross love dead.
In your shadows I repose,
You, than Love, I rather chose.

Musella. Choice ill-made were better left,
Being cross.
Of such choice to be bereft,
Were no loss.
Chastity, you thus commend,
Doth proceed but from Love's end.
And if Love the fountain was
Of your fire,
Love must chastity surpass
In desire.
Love lost, bred your chastest thought,
Chastity by love is wrought.

Silvesta. O, poor Musella, now I pity thee;
I see thou'rt bound, who most have made unfree.
'Tis true, disdain of my love made me turn,
And happily I think. But you to burn
In love's false fires yourself, poor soul, take heed,
Be sure before you too much pine, to speed.
You know I loved have, but behold my gain:
This you dislike, I purchased with love's pain
And true-felt sorrow. Yet, my answer was
From my, then dear, Philisses: 'You must pass
Unloved by me, and for your own good leave
To urge that which, most urged, can but deceive
Your hopes. For know, Musella is my love.'
As then of duty I should no more move;
And this his will he got, but not his mind,
For yet it seems you are no less unkind.

Musella. Wrong me not, chaste Silvesta, 'tis my grief
That from poor me he will not take relief.

Silvesta. What, will he lose what he did most desire?

Musella. So is he led away with jealous fire.
And this, Silvesta, but to you I speak,
For sooner should my heart with silence break

Than any else should hear me thus much say
But you, who I know will not me betray.

Silvesta. Betray Musella? Sooner will I die.
No, I do love you, nor will help deny
That lies in me to bring your care to end,
Or service which to your content may tend.
For when I loved Philisses as my life,
Perceiving he loved you, I killed the strife
Which in me was. Yet, do I wish his good,
And for his sake, love you. Though I withstood
Good fortunes, this chaste life well pleaseth me,
And would joy more if you two happy be.
Few would say this, but fewer would it do,
But th'one I loved, and love the other too.

Musella. I know you loved him, nor could I the less
At that time love you. So did he possess
My heart, as my thought* all hearts sure must yield
To love him most and best; who in this field
Doth live and hath not had some kind of touch
To like him? But O, you and I too much!

Silvesta. Mine is now passed. Tell me now what yours is,
And I'll wish but the means to work your bliss.

Musella. Then know, Silvesta, I Philisses love.
But he, although, or that because, he loves,
Doth me mistrust. Ah, can such mischief move
As to mistrust her who such passion proves?
But so he doth, and thinks I have Lissius made
Master of my affections, which hath stayed
Him ever yet from letting me it know
By words, although he hides it not from show.
Sometimes I fain would speak, then straight forbear,
Knowing it most unfit; thus woe I bear.

Silvesta. Indeed a woman to make love is ill.
But hear, and you may all these sorrows kill;
He, poor distressed shepherd, every morn
Before the sun to our eyes new is born,
Walks in this place, and here alone doth cry

Against his life and your great cruelty.
Now, since you love so much, come here and find
Him in these woes, and show yourself but kind.
You soon shall see a heart so truly won
As you would not it miss to be undone.

Musella. Silvesta, for this love I can but say,
That piece of heart which is not given away
Shall be your own, the rest will you observe
As saver of two hearts, which, too, will serve
You ever with so true and constant love
Your chastity itself shall it approve.

Silvesta. I do believe it, for in so much worth
As lives in you, virtue must needs spring forth.
And for Philisses, I love him and will
In chastest service hinder still his ill.
Then keep your time, alas, let him not die
For whom so many suffered misery.

Musella. Let me no joy receive if I neglect
This kind advice, or him I so respect.

Silvesta. Farewell, Musella, love, and happy be. [*Exit*]

Musella. And be thou blessed that thus dost comfort me. [*Exit*]

SCENE 2

Philisses. O wretched man! And thou, all-conquering Love,
Which show'st thy power still on hapless me,
Yet give me leave in these sweet shades to move;
Rest but to show my killing misery;
And be once pleased to know my wretched fate,
And something pity my ill and my state.
Could ever Nature or the bright heavens frame
So rare a part so like themselves divine,
And yet that work be blotted with the blame
Of cruelty; and dark be, who should shine
To be the brightest star of dearest prize;
And yet to murder hearts which to her cries,
Cry; and even at the point of death for care,
Yet have I nothing left me but despair.

Despair! O, but despair! Alas, hath hope
No better portion? Nor a greater scope?
Well then, despair with my life coupled be,
And for my sudden end do soon agree.
Ah me, unfortunate; would I could die.
But so soon as this company I fly. [*Exit*]

[*Dalina, Climeana, Simeana, Phillis*]

Dalina. Now we're alone, let everyone confess
Truly to other what our lucks have been,
How often liked and loved, and so express
Our passions past; shall we this sport begin?
None can accuse us, none can us betray,
Unless ourselves, our own selves will bewray.*

Phillis. I like this, but will each one truly tell?

Climeana. Trust me, I will: who doth not, doth not well.

Simeana. I'll plainly speak, but who shall be the first?

Dalina. I can say least of all, yet I will speak.
A shepherd once there was, and not the worst
Of those were most esteemed, whose sleep did break
With love, forsooth, of me. I found it thought
I might have him at leisure, liked him not.
Then was there to our house a farmer brought,
Rich and lively, but those bought not his lot
For love. Two jolly youths at last there came,
Which both, methought, I very well could love.
When one was absent, t'other had the name;
In my stayed heart he present did most move,
Both at one time in sight, I scarce could say
Which of the two I then would wish away.
But they found how to choose, and as I was,
Like changing, like uncertain, let me pass.

Simeana. I would not this believe if other tongue
Should this report, but think it had been wrong;
But since you speak this, could not you agree
To choose someone, but thus unchosen be?

Dalina. Truly not I. I plainly tell the truth,
Yet do confess 'twas folly in my youth,

Which now I'll mend; the next that comes I'll have,
I will no more be foolish, nor delay,
Since I do see the lads will labour save.
One answer rids them, I'll no more say 'Nay'.
But if he say, 'Dalina, will you love?'
And, 'Thank you', I will say, 'If you will prove.'
The next go on, and tell what you have done.

Simeana. I am the next, and have but losses won.
Yet, still I constant was, though still rejected;
Loved and not loved I was, liked and neglected;
Yet, now some hope revives, when love, thought dead,
Proves like the Spring's young bud when leaves are fled.

Phillis. Your hap's the better, would mine were as good,
Though I as long as you despised stood.
For I have loved, and loved but only one;
Yet I, disdained, could but receive that moan
Which others do for thousands; so unjust
Is Love to those who in him most do trust.
Nor did I ever let my thoughts be shown
But to Musella, who all else hath known,
Which was, long time, I had Philisses loved,
And ever would, though he did me despise;
For then, though he had ever cruel proved,
From him, not me, the fault must needs arise.
And if, Simeana, thus your brother dear
Should be unkind, my love shall still be clear.

Simeana. 'Tis well resolved; but how liked she* your choice?
Did she, or blame, or else your mind commend?

Phillis. Neither she seemed to dislike or rejoice,
Nor did commend I did this love intend;
But smiling, said, 'twere best to be advised:
Comfort it were to win, but death despised.

Simeana. I do believe her. But Climeana yet
Hath nothing said, we must not her forget.

Climeana. Why, you have said enough for you and me!
Yet for your sakes, I will the order keep,
Who though a stranger here by birth I be

And in Arcadia* ever kept my sheep.
Yet, here it is my fortune with the rest
Of you to like, and loving be oppressed,
For since I came, I did a lover turn;
And turn I did indeed when I loved here,
Since for another I in love did burn,
To whom I thought I had been held as dear;
But was deceived. When I for him had left
My friends and country, was of him bereft,
And all, but that you kindly did embrace
And welcome me into this happy place.
Where, for your sakes, I meant to keep some sheep,
Not doubting ever to be more deceived;
But now, alas, I am anew bereaved
Of heart, now time it is myself to keep
And let flocks go, unless Simeana please
To give consent, and so give me some ease.

Simeana. Why, what have I to do with whom you love?

Climeana. Because 'tis he who doth your passion move.

Simeana. The lesser need I fear the winning of his love,
Since all my faith could never so much move.
Yet, can he not so cruel ever be
But he may live my misery to see.

Climeana. And when his eyes to love shall open be,
I trust he will turn pity unto me,
And let me have reward, which is my due.

Simeana. Which is your due? What pity's due to you?
Dream you of hope? O, you too high aspire!
Think you to gain by kindling an old fire?

Climeana. My love will be the surer when I know
Not love alone, but how love to bestow.

Simeana. You make him, yet for all this, but to be
The second in your choice. So was not he
In mine, but first, and last, of all the chief
That can to me bring sorrow or relief.

Climeana. This will not win him. You may talk and hope,
But in Love's passages there is large scope.

Simeana. 'Tis true, and you have scope to change and choose,
To take, and dislike, like, and soon refuse.

Climeana. My love as firm is to him as is thine.

Simeana. Yet mine did ever rise, never decline;
No other moved in me the flames of love,
Yet you dare hope as much as I to move.
Folly indeed is proud and only vain,
And you his servant feeds with hope of gain.

Climeana. I love him most.

Simeana. I love him best. Can you
Challenge reward, and cannot say you're true?

Climeana. In this you wrong me! False I have not been,
But changed on cause.*

Simeana. Well, now you hope to win
This second! Yet I, like those, lose no time;
But can you think that you can this way climb
To your desires? This shows you love have tried,
And that you can both choose and choice divide.
But take your course, and win him if you can,
And I'll proceed in truth as I began.

Dalina. Fie, what a life is here about fond love,
Never could it in my heart thus much move.
This is the reason men are grown so coy,
When they perceive we make their smiles our joy;
Let them alone, and they will seek and sue,
But yield to them and they'll with scorn pursue.
Hold awhile off, they'll kneel, nay, follow you,
And vow and swear. Yet all their oaths untrue!
Let them once see you coming, then they fly,
But strangely* look, and they'll for pity cry;
And let them cry, there is no evil done,
They gain but that which you might else have won.

Simeana. Is this your counsel? Why, but now you said
Your folly had your loves and good betrayed,
And that hereafter you would wiser be
Than to disdain such as have left you free.

Dalina. 'Tis true, that was the course I meant to take,
But this must you do, your own ends to make;
I have my fortunes lost, yours do begin,
And to cross those could be no greater sin.
I know the world, and hear me, this I advise:
Rather than too soon won, be too precise;
Nothing is lost by being carefull still,
Nor nothing so soon won as lover's ill.
Here Lissius comes. Alas, he is love-struck,
He's even now learning love without the book.

Lissius. Love, pardon me, I know I did amiss
When I thee scorned, or thought thy blame my bliss.
O pity me. Alas, I pity crave!
Do not set trophies on my luckless grave,
Though I, poor slave and ignorant, did scorn
Thy blessed name; let not my heart be torn
With thus much torture. O but look on me,
Take me a faithful servant unto thee!

Climeana. Dear Lissius, my dear Lissius, fly me not;
Let not both scorn and absence be my lot.

Lissius. Pray let me go, you know I cannot love;
Do not thus far my patience strive to move.

Climeana. Why, cruel Lissius, wilt thou never mend,
But still increase thy frowns for my sad end?

Lissius. Climeana, 'tis enough that I have said,
Begone and leave me. Is this for a maid
To follow and to haunt me thus? You blame
Me for disdain, but see not your own shame!
Fie, I do blush for you! A woman woo?
The most unfittest, shameful'st thing to do!

Climeana. Unfit and shameful I? Indeed, 'tis true,
Since suit is made too hard, relentless you.
Well, I will leave you and restore the wrong
I suffer for my loving you too long.
No more shall my words trouble you, nor I
Ere follow more, if not to see me die. [*Exit*]

Lissius. Farewell, you now do right; this is the way

To win my wish. For when I all neglect
That seek me, she must needs something respect
My love the more; and what though she should say
I once denied her, yet my true-felt pain
Must needs from her soft breast some favour gain.

Dalina. Lissius is taken, well said! Cupid, now
You partly have performed your taken vow.
Of all our shepherds, I ne'er thought that he
Would of thy foolish troop a follower be!
But this it is a Goddess to despise
And thwart a wayward boy who wants his eyes.
Come, let's not trouble him, he is distressed
Enough, he need not be with us oppressed.

Simeana. I'll stay, and ask him who 'tis he doth love.

Dalina. Do not a pensive heart to passion move.

Simeana. To passion? Would I could his passion find,
To answer my distressed and grieved mind.

Dalina. Stay then and try him, and your fortune try;
It may be he loves you. Come let's go by. [*Exit*]

Lissius. O, sweet Simeana, look but on my pain!
I grieve and curse myself for my disdain;
Now, but have pity, Love doth make me serve,
And for your wrong, and you, I will reserve
My life to pay, your love but to deserve,
And for your sake I do myself preserve.

Simeana. Preserve it not for me, I seek not now!
Nor can I credit this nor any vow
Which you shall make; I was too long despised
To be deceived. No, I will be advised
By my own reason; my love shall no more blind
Me, nor make me believe more than I find.

Lissius. Believe but that, and I shall have the end
Of all my pain, and wishes. I pretend
A virtuous love; then grant me my desire,
Who now do waste in true and faithful fire.

Simeana. How can I this believe?

Lissius. My faith shall tell
That in true love I will all else excel;
But then, will you love me, as I do you?

Simeana. I promise may, for you cannot be true!

Lissius. Then you will promise break.

Simeana. Not if I find
That as your words are, so you'll make your mind.

Lissius. Let me, nor speech, nor mind have, when that I
In this, or any else, do falsify
My faith and love to you.

Simeana. Then, be at rest;
And of my true affection be possessed.

Lissius. So, dear Simeana, be of me and mine.
Now do my hopes and joys together shine.

Simeana. Nor let the least cloud rise to dim this light,
Which Love makes to appear with true delight.

SCENE 3

Venus and Cupid.

Cupid. Is not this pretty? Who doth free remain
Of all this flock, that waits not in our train?
Will you have yet more sorrow? Yet more woe?
Shall I another bitter arrow throw?
Speak, if you will, my hand now knows the way
To make all hearts your sacred power obey.

Venus. 'Tis pretty, but 'tis not enough. Some are
Too slightly wounded, they had greater share
In scorning us. Lissius too soon is blessed,
And with too little pain hath got his rest;
Scarce had he learned to sigh before he gained,
Nor shed a tear ere he his hopes obtained.
This easy winning breeds us more neglect,
Without much pain, few do Love's joys respect;
Then are the sweetest purchased with felt grief,
To floods of woe sweet looks give full relief;
A world of sorrow is eased with one smile,

And heartwounds cured when kind words rule, the while.
That foregone wailings, in forgotten thought
Shall wasted lie disdained, once dearly bought;
One gentle speech more heals a bleeding wound
Than bawlings of pleasure, if from other ground.
Strike then to favour him, and let him gain
His love and bliss by Love's sweet pleasing pain.

Cupid. That shall be done. Nor had he this delight
Bestowed, but for his greater harm and spite;
You shall, before this act be ended, see
He doth sufficiently taste misery.
'Tis far more grief from joy to be down thrown,
Than joy to be advanced to Pleasure's throne.

Venus. Let me see that, and I contented am;
Such gracious favour would but get thy shame.

Cupid. He and others yet shall taste
Such distress as shall lay waste
All their hopes, their joys, and lives;
By such loss our glory thrives;
Fear not, then all hearts must yield
When our forces come to field.

ACT IV SCENE I

Musella. This is the place Silvesta 'pointed* me
To meet my joy, my sole felicity;
And here Philisses is. Ah me, this shows
The wounds by Love given are no childish blows.

Philisses. You blessed woods into whose secret guard
I venture dare my inward wounding smart,
And to you dare impart the crosses hard
Which harbour in my love-destroyed heart.
To you, and but to you, I durst disclose
These flames, these pains, these griefs, which I do find;
For your true hearts so constant are to those
Who trust in you, as you'll not change your mind.
No echo shrill shall your dear secrets utter,
Or wrong your silence with a blabbing tongue;

Nor will your springs against your private mutter,
Or think that counsel keeping is a wrong;
Then, since woods, springs, echoes, and all are true
My long-hid love, I'll tell, show, write in you.
Alas, Musella, cruel shepherdess,
Who takes no pity on me in distress.
For all my passions, plaints, and all my woes,
I am so far from gain as outward shows;
I never had could feed least hope to spring,
Or any while least comfort to me bring.
Yet pardon me, dear mistress of my soul,
I do recall my words, my tongue control,
For wronging thee; accuse my poor starved heart
Which withered is with Love's all-killing smart.
Since, truly, I must say I cannot blame
Thee, nor accuse thee with a scorner's name.
No, no, alas, my pains thou dost not know,
Nor dare I, wretch, my torments to thee show.
Why did I wrong thee then, who all must serve,
And happy he, by thee, thought to deserve?
Who heaven hath framed to make us here below
Deserve, they strive all worth in thee to show,
And doth these valleys and these meads* disgrace
When thou art present with excelling grace,
As now, who at this time doth show more bright
Than fair Aurora, when she lends best light.
O, that I might but now have heart to speak
And say I love, though after, heart did break.

Musella. I fain would comfort him, and yet I know
Not if from me 'twill comfort be or no,
Since causeless jealousy hath so possessed
His heart, as no belief of me can rest.
But why stay I? I came to give relief.
Should I then doubt? No, I may ease his grief,
And help will seek. None should one's good neglect,
Much more his bliss, who for me joys reject.
How now, Philisses, why do you thus grieve?
Speak, is there none that can your pains relieve?

Philisses. Yes, fair Musella, but such is my state,
Relief must come from her who can but hate.
What hope may I, wretch, have least good to move
Where scorn doth grow for me, for others, love?

Musella. But are you sure she doth your love disdain?
It may be for your love she feels like pain.

Philisses. Like pain for me! I would not crave so much.
I wish no more but that love might her touch,
And that she might discern by love to know
That kind respect is fit for her to show.

Musella. Sure this she knows.

Philisses. Prove it, and I may live.

Musella. Tell me who 'tis you love, and I will give
My word I'll win her if she may be won.

Philisses. Aye me, that doubt in me made me first run
Into this labyrinth of woe and care,
Which makes me thus to wed mine own despair.

Musella. But have you made it known to her you love,
That for her scorn you do these torments prove?

Philisses. Yes, now I have; and yet to ease some pain
I'll plainlier speak, though my own end I gain;
And so to end, it were to me a bliss.
Then know, for your dear sake my sorrow is.
It may be you will hate me, yet I have
By this some ease, though with it come my grave.
Yet, dear Musella, since for you I pine
And suffer welcome death, let favour shine
Thus far, that though my love you do neglect,
Yet sorry be I died. With this respect
I shall be satisfied, and so content
As I shall deem my life so lost well spent.

Musella. Sorry? Alas, Philisses, can it be
But I should grieve and mourn, nay, die for thee?
Yet, tell me why did you thus hide your love
And suffer wrong conceits thus much to move?
Now 'tis almost too late your wish to gain;
Yet you shall pity for your love obtain.

Philisses. Pity when helpless, 'tis endless given;
Am I to this unhappy bondage driven?
Yet truly pity, and 'twill be some ease
Unto my grief, though all things else displease;
But, do not yet, unless you can affect,
For forced pity's worse than is neglect;
And to be pitied but for pity's sake,
And not for love, do never pity take.

Musella. Well then, I love you, and so ever must,
Though time and fortune should be still unjust;
For we may love, and both may constant prove,
But not enjoy unless ordained above.

Philisses. Dost thou love me? O, dear Musella, say,
And say it still, to kill my late dismay.

Musella. More than myself, or love myself for thee
The better much. But wilt thou love like me?

Philisses. My only life, here do I vow to die
When I prove false or show unconstancy.

Musella. All true content may this to both procure.

Philisses. And when I break, may I all shame endure.

Musella. Nor doubt you me, nor my true heart mistrust,
For die I will before I prove unjust.
But here comes Rustic, whose encumbered brain
With love and jealousy must our loss gain,
For since he hopes, nay, says that I am his,
I cannot absent be but he'll me miss;
But when that is, let day no longer shine
Or I have life if live not truly thine.
But now, lest that our love should be found out,
Let's seek all means to keep him from this doubt,
And let none know it but your sister dear
Whose company I keep. So hold all clear,
Then let him watch and keep what he can get,
His plots must want their force our joys to let.
I'll step aside awhile, till you do meet
This welcome man, whose absence were more sweet;
For though that he, poor thing, can little find,

Yet I shall blush with knowing my own mind.
Fear and desire, still to keep it hid,
Will blushing show it when 'tis most forbid.

Philisses. None can have power against a powerful love;
Nor keep the blood, but in the cheeks 'twill move,
But not for fear or care it there doth show
But kind desire makes you blushing know
That joy takes place, and in your face doth climb
With leaping heart like lambkins in the prime.
But, sweet Musella, since you will away,
Take now my heart and let yours in me stay. [*Exit Musella*]
Could I express the joy I now conceive,
I were unworthy such bliss to receive;
But so much am I thine, as life and joy
Are in thy hands to nurse, or to destroy.
How now Rustic? Whither away so fast?

Rustic. To seek Musella.

Philisses. Now that labour's past;
See where she comes.

Musella. Rustic where were you?
I sought, but could not find you.

Rustic. Is that true?
Faith I was but, the truth to you to tell,
Marking some cattle and asleep I fell.

Musella. And I was seeking of a long-lost lamb,
Which now I found, ev'n as along you came

Rustic. I'm glad you found it.

Musella. Truly, so am I.

Rustic. Now let us go to find our company.

Philisses. See where some be.

Musella. It seems too soon, alas,
That love despised should come to such a pass.

Lissius and Simeana.
Love's beginning like the Spring,
Gives delight, in sweetness flowing;
Ever pleasant, flourishing,

Pride in her brave colours showing.
But Love ending is at last,
Like the storms of Winter's blast.

Musella. Lissius, methinks you are grown sad of late,
And privately with your own thoughts debate.
I hope you are not fallen in love; that boy
Cannot, I trust, your settled heart enjoy!

Lissius. 'Tis well, you may be merry at my fall!
Rejoice! Nay do, for I can lose but all.

Simeana. And so too much! [*Exit*]

Musella. Sure, some strange error is.

Philisses. Learn you it out.

Rustic. We'll leave you.

Musella. I'll know this.
Come Lissius, tell me, whence proceeds this grief?
Discover it and you may find relief.

Lissius. No, I'll go seek Philisses; he, I'm sure
Will comfort me, who doth the like endure.
Yet, fair Musella, do thus much for me:
Tell fierce Simeana she hath murdered me,
And gain but this, that she my end will bless
With some, though smallest, grief for my distress;
And that she will but grace my hapless tomb,
As to behold me dead by her hard doom.
This is a small request, and 'tis my last,
Whom to obey to my sad end will haste.

Musella. Nay Lissius, hear me. Tell me ere you go
What sudden matter moves in you this woe.

Lissius. Alas! 'Tis love of one I did disdain,
And now I seek, the like neglect I gain;
Yet at the first she answered me with love,
Which made my passions more increase and move.
But now she scorns me, and tells me I give
My love in equal sort to all; and drive
My sighs and plaints but from an outward part
Of feigned love, and never from my heart;

And when on knees I do her favour crave,
She bids me seek Climeana, where I gave
As many vows as then to her I did;
And thereupon her sight did me forbid,
Vowing that if I did more move or speak
Of love, she would not only speeches break,
But ever more her sight, and would be blind,
Rather than in my sight herself to find.
This is the cause, and this must be my end,
Which my sad days to saddest night must lend.

Musella. When grew this change?

Lissius. Alas too late, today,
And yet too early for my joy's decay.

Musella. Have no ill tongues reported false of you?

Lissius. I know not. But my heart was ever true
Since first I vowed, and that my death shall tell,
Which is my last hope that will please her well.

Musella. Soft, I will speak with her, and know her mind,
And why on such a sudden she's unkind;
Then truly bring you answer what she says.
Till then be quiet, for it can no praise
Bring to your death, when you shall wailing die,
Without so just a cause as to know why.

Lissius. But will Musella do thus much for me?
Shall I not of all friends forsaken be?

Musella. Never of me; and here awhile but stay,
And I shall comfort bring your care t'allay. [*Exit*]

Lissius. O no, I know she will not pity me,
Unfortunate and hapless must I be.
And now, thou powerful, conquering God of Love,
I do but thus much crave: thy forces prove
And cast all storms of thy just-caused rage
Upon me, vassal; and no heat assuage
Of greatest fury, since I do deserve
No favour or least grace, but here to starve.
Fed with sharp tortures, let me live to see
My former sin for so much slighting thee;

Death yet more welcome, were it not so meet
I oft should die, who knew not sour from sweet.
Simeana comes! Ah, most ungrateful maid,
Who answers love as one would welcome death:
The nearer that it comes, the more flies, stayed
Ne're but by limbs that tire, wanting breath.
So hastes she still from me whose love is fixed
In purest flames without all baseness mixed.

Musella. Simeana, this can be no ground to take
So great dislike, upon one man's report,
And what may well prove false, as thus to make
An honest loving heart die in this sort.
Say that he useth others well and smiles
On them, who't may be love of him beguiles;
Or that he used Climeana well, what then?
'Tis all, poor soul, she gets, who did condemn
And rail at her.

Simeana. 'Tis true, before my face
He did revile her with words of disgrace.
My back but turned, she was his only joy,
His best, his dearest life, and soon destroy
Himself he would if she not loved him still;
And just what he had vowed his heart did kill.
For my disdain, he shameless did protest
Within one hour to her caused his unrest!
Can I bear this? Who lived so long disdained,
Now to be mocked? I thought I love had gained
And not more scorn, but since thus much I find
I'm glad joy sank no deeper in my mind!

Musella. Fie, fie, Simeana, leave these doubts, too far
Already grown to breed so great a jar.*
'Twas but his duty kindly once to speak
To her, who for him would her poor heart break.
Would you not think it sin quite to undo
A silly maid with scorn! But let these go.
Think you if I did love, and that I saw
He used more well, would I my love withdraw
From him for that? O, no great cause may be

To move good looks; mistrust not, but be free
From this vile humour of base jealousy,
Which breedeth nothing but self-misery.
For this believe, while you yourself are just,
You cannot any way your love mistrust.
Let him discourse and smile, and what of this?
Is he the likelier in his faith to miss?
No, never fear him for his outward smiles,
'Tis private friendship that our trust beguiles.
And therefore let not Arcas' flattering skill
Have power in your breast his deserts to spill;
Lissius is worthy, and a worthy love
He bears to you; then these conceits remove.

Simeana. Arcas did see them sit too privately,
And kiss, and then embrace!

Musella. Well, if he did?

Simeana. And in her ear discourse familiarly,
When they did think it should from me be hid.

Musella. Lord, how one may conjecture if one fear;
All things they doubt to be the same they fear.
Though private, must it follow he's untrue,
Or that they whispered must be kept from you?
Fie, leave these follies, and begin to think
You have your love brought to death's river brink.
Repent, you have him wronged; and now cherish
The dying lad, who else soon will perish.
Go, ask him pardon.

Simeana. Pardon! Why? That he
The more may brag! He twice hath cozened me!

Musella. Nay, he is past all bragging. Mend your fault
And sorry be you have his torment wrought.
See where he lies, the truest sign of woe;
Go, haste and save him; Love's wings are not slow.

Simeana. O, dearest Lissius, look but up and speak
To me, most wretched, whose heart now must break
With self-accusing of a cursed wrong,
Which rashly bred, did win belief too strong.

Ah, cast but up thine eyes, see my true tears,
And view but her who now all torment bears.
Do but look up, and thou shalt see me die.
For having wronged thee with my jealousy.

Lissius. To see thee die? Alas, I die for thee!
What pleasure can thy death then bring to me?
Yet if love make you say this, then poor I
Shall much more happy and more blessed die.

Simeana. Nay, let me end before thy end I see!
Alas, I love you, and 'twas love in me
Bred this great ill, which jealousy confused;
I brought your harm, and my best love abused.

Lissius. O joy which now doth swell as much as grief,
And pleasing yet doth make me seek relief.
Am I myself? No, I am only joy,
Not Lissius, grief did lately him destroy;
I am Simeana's love, her slave revived,
Late hopeless dead, now have despair survived.

Musella. All care now past, let joy in triumph sit;
This for such lovers ever is most fit;
This doth become that happy loving pair,
Who seek to nurse the joys that kill all care;
Let those fall out, mistrust, wrangle and jar,
Who love for fashion not for love; but war
Not you, the couple Cupid best doth love,
Whose troubled hearts his godhead's self did move.

Lissius. Musella, you have turned this cloudy day
To sweet and pleasant light; nor can I say
So much as in my heart this kindness breeds,
For now delight all form and speech exceeds.
But let us, happy now, unhappy be
When in us least unthankfulness you see.

Simeana. Let me myself, nay, my dear Lissius leave,
When I in service or in faith deceive
Musella, sole restorer of this joy;
And jealousy anew strive to destroy
Our loves and hopes, if I forgetful be

Of this increase of lost felicity.
But now, my Lissius, have you me forgiven
My last offence, by love and fearing driven?

Lissius. Thou lov'st me, 'tis enough, and now enjoy
All rest, nor bring new doubts to cross our joy;
I all forget, and only hold thee dear,
And from thee all faults past my love doth clear.

Simeana. So let us, ever doubtless, live and love,
And no mistrust in least sort our hearts move.

Lissius. No doubt of thee shall ever stir in mine.

Simeana. Nor breed in me, so wholly I am thine.

Musella. Happy this time, and blessed be your loves,
And most accursed they that other moves.
Live both contented and live still as one,
Never divided till your lives be done.

[*Phillis, Dalina, Philisses, Arcas, Climeana, Rustic.*]

Musella. Here comes the flock.

Rustic. We're all here now.

Musella. 'Tis true,
We are all here, and one too much by you.

Dalina. Here be our fellows, now let us begin
Some pretty pastime, pleasure's sport to win.
Sweetest Musella, what think you is best?

Musella. That whereunto your fancy is addressed.

Dalina. Mine is to riddling.

Simeana. And, indeed that's good.

Climeana. But, methinks, not lest they be understood.

Simeana. Understood? Why so shall all be that I make.

Climeana. Tush, you'll say one thing, and another take.

Simeana. You'll still be wrangling.

Dalina. Aye, and for a man!
Would I might live till quarrel I began
On such a cause. But pray, now quiet be,
And, fair Musella, first begin with me.

Phillis. But must the riddles be expounded?

Dalina. No.

Musella. Then I'll begin, though scarce the play I know.

That I wish, which with most pain
I must gain;
That I shun, which with such ease
Cannot please;
That most easy still I fly,
Barred, I fainest would come by.

Dalina. I am the next, mark then what I will say.

Best is, my lovers cannot me betray!
What I seek can never be
Found in me,
Fain I would that try and find,
Which my mind,
Ever yet from my heart kept,
Till away my luck was stepped.

Philisses. Let them alone, the women still will speak;
Rustic come, you and I this course will break.

Late I saw a star to shine
Whose light methought was only mine,
Till a cloud came and did hide
That light from me, where light did bide.
Yet, tell me how can these agree:
That light, though dimmed, that light I see.

Now Rustic, Fortune's falling on your head,
Bring forth your riddle. Fie, in love, and dead
To such a sport! Think not upon the day,
There is no danger in it, I dare well say.

Rustic. Truly, I cannot riddle, I was not taught
These tricks of wit; my thoughts ne'er higher wrought
Than how to mark a beast, or drive a cow
To feed, or else with art to hold a plough,
Which if I knew, you surely soon would find
A matter more of worth than these odd things,
Which never profit, but some laughter brings;
These others be of body and of mind.

Philisses. Spoke like a husband, though you yet are none!
But come, what, is this sport already done?

Rustic. I cannot riddle.

Dalina. Whistle, 'tis as good,
For you sufficiently are understood!

Rustic. What mean you?

Dalina. Naught, but that you are
An honest man, and thrifty, full of care.

Rustic. I thought you had meant worse.

Dalina. Meant worse! What, I?
Fie, this doth show your doubt and jealousy;
Why should you take my meaning worse than 'tis?

Rustic. Nay, I but smile to see how all you miss,
But some shall find when I do seem to smile
And show best pleased, I oft'nest do beguile.

Dalina. Yourself you mean; for few else do respect
Your smiles or frowns; therefore, do not neglect
Your pleasant youth, ill will is too soon got,
And once that rooted, not so soon forgot.

Philisses. You grow too wise, dispute no more. Here be
Others who will let us their hearers be,
And give this sport some life again, which you
Almost made dead.

Dalina. I have done, let joy ensue.

Lissius. Guess you all what this can be:
A snake to suffer fire I see;
A fog and yet a clear bright day;
A light which better were away;
Two suns at once, both shining clear
And without envy hold each dear.

Phillis. A Spring I hoped for, but it died,
Then on the next my hopes relied;
But Summer past, the latter Spring,
Could me but former losses bring;
I died with them, yet still I live,
While Autumn can no comfort give.

Musella. Unmannerly, I must your presence leave,
Sent for in haste unto my mother. But

I hope in this sweet place soon to receive
Your most loved companies. And so to put
Good Rustic into better humours; say,
Will you be merry? [*Exit*]

Rustic. I'll not after stay. [*Exit*]

Philisses. No, follow. Shadows never absent be
When sun shines; in which blessing you may see
Your shadowed self, who nothing in truth are
But the reflection of her too great care.
What will you further do?

Dalina. Let us depart.

Arcas. Aye, let's away. But some ere long will smart.

Philisses. When shall we meet again?

Dalina. When day appears.

Lissius. No, not till sun, who all foul mists still clears.

Philisses. Why, then at sun, and who shall then miss here,
A punishment by us ordained shall bear.

Dalina. Let it be so.

Phillis. I'm very well agreed.

Lissius. So are we all, and sun appear with speed.

SCENE 2

Venus and Cupid.

Venus. Now have thy torments long enough endured,
And of thy force they are enough assured.
O, hold thy hand. Alas, I pity now
Those whose great pride did lately scorn to bow.
Thou hast performed thy promise, and thy state
Now is confessed. O, slacken then thy hate;
They humble do their hearts and thoughts to thee;
Behold them, and accept them, and mild be.
Thy conquest is sufficient, save the spoils
And let them only taken be in toils.
But set at liberty again, to tell
Thy might and clemency, which doth excel.

Cupid. I mean to save them; but some yet must try
More pain, ere they their blessings may come nigh;
But in the end most shall be well again,
And sweetest is that love obtained with pain.

[*The music or song of the priests*]

Priests.
Love, thy powerful hand withdraw;
And do yield unto thy law,
Rebels, now thy subjects be,
Bound they are who late were free.
Most confess thy power and might,
All hearts yield unto thy right.
Thoughts directed are by thee,
Souls do strive thy joys to see.
Pity then, and mercy, give
To those hearts where you do live;
They your images do prove,
In them may you see great Love;
They your mirrors, you their eyes,
By which they true Love do spy.
Ease awhile their cruel smarts
And behold their yielding hearts;
Greater glory 'tis to save,
When that you the conquest have,
Than with tyranny to press,
Which still makes the honour less.
Gods do princes' hearts direct,
Then, to those, have some respect.

ACT V

Musella and Simeana.

Musella. O eyes, that day can see and cannot mend
What my joys poison, must my wretched end
Proceed from love? And yet my true love crossed,
Neglected for base gain, and all worth lost
For riches?* Then 'tis time for good to die,
When wealth must wed us to all misery.

Simeana. If you will but stoutly tell your mother

You hate him and will match with any other,
She cannot, nor will, go about to cross
Your liking, so to bring your endless loss.

Musella. Alas, I've urged her, till that she with tears
Did vow and grieve she could not mend my state
Agreed on by my father's will, which bears
Sway in her breast and duty in me. Fate
Must have her courses, while that wretched I
Wish but so good a fate as now to die.

Simeana. Wish not such ill, which all we suffer must,
But take some hope the gods are not unjust;
My mind doth give me yet, you shall be blessed,
And seldom do I miss; then quiet rest.

Musella. Rest quiet! O heavens! Have you ever known
The pains of Love and been by him o'erthrown
To give this counsel and advise your friend
T'impossibilities? Why to what end
Speak you thus madly? Can it ere be thought
That quiet, or least rest, can now be brought
To me, while dear Philisses thus is crossed,
Whom missing all my happiness is lost?

Simeana. You have not missed, nor lost him yet.

Musella. I must,
And that's enough. Did I my blessings trust
In your kind breasts, you fatal sisters?* Now
By your decree to be bestowed, and bow
To base unworthy riches? O, my heart
That breaks not, but can suffer all this smart!

Simeana. Have patience.

Musella. I cannot, nor I will not
Patient be! Aye me, and bear this ill lot?
No! I will grieve in spite of grief, and mourn
To make those mad who now to pleasure turn.

Philisses. My dear Musella, what is it doth grieve
Your heart thus much? Tell me, and still believe
While you complain, I must tormented be;
Your sighs and tears, alas, do bleed in me.

Musella. I know it, 'tis your loss I thus lament.
I must be married. Would my days were spent!

Philisses. Married!

Musella. To Rustic. My mother so commands,
Who I must yield to, being in her hands.

Philisses. But will you marry? Or show love to me,
Or her obey, and make me wretched be.

Musella. Alas Philisses, will you this doubt make?
I would my life, to pleasure you, forsake;
Hath not my firmness hitherto made known
My faith and love? Which yet should more be shown
If I might govern but my mother's will.
Yet this last question even my heart doth kill.

Philisses. Grieve not my dearest, I speak but for love,
Then let not love your trouble so far move.
You weep not that it wounds not hapless me,
Nor sigh but in me all those sorrows be;
You never cry, but groans most truly show,
From deepest of my heart I feel your woe.
Then heap not now more sorrows on my heart,
By these dear tears which taste of endless smart;
No grief can be, which I have not sustained,
And must, for now despair hath conquest gained.
Yet, let your love in me still steady rest
And in that I sufficiently am blessed.
But must you marry? O, those words deny,
Or here behold your poor Philisses die!

Musella. I would I could deny the words I spake,
When I did Rustic's marriage offer take;
Hopeless of you, I gave my ill consent,
And we contracted were, which I repent.
The time now curse, my tongue wish out, which gave
Me to that clown with whom I wed my grave.

Philisses. I hear and see my end. O, Love unjust
And careless of my heart put in your trust,
Ungrateful and forgetful of the good
From me received, by whom thy fame hath stood,

Thy honour been maintained, thy name adored,
Which by all others with disgrace was stored.
Is this the great reward I shall receive
For all my service? Will you thus deceive
My hopes and joys?

Musella. Yet, let me one thing crave.

Philisses. Ask my poor life, all else long since I gave.

Musella. That will I ask, and yours requite with mine,
For mine cannot be, if not joined to thine.
Go with me to the temple and there we
Will bind our lives, or else our lives make free.

Philisses. To die for thee a new life I should gain,
But to die with thee were eternal pain;
So you will promise me that you will live,
I willingly will go, and my life give.
You may be happy.

Musella. Happy, without thee?
O, let me rather wretched, and thine, be!
Without thee no life can be, nor least joy,
Nor thought but how a sad end to enjoy.
But promise me, yourself you will not harm,
As you love me.

Philisses. Let me impose that charm
Likewise on you.

Musella. Content, I am agreed.

Philisses. Let's go alone, no company we need.

Musella. Simeana, she shall go, and so may tell
The good or heavy chance that us befell.

Philisses. I am content. Your will shall be obeyed
Till this life change and I in earth am laid.

At this point, the Huntington MS ends; the play continues in the Penshurst MS as follows: in the Temple of Love, Philisses and Musella drink poison provided by Silvesta. Rustic, on hearing the news, releases Musella from her vow. Musella's mother berates herself for causing the lovers' deaths. Forester asks Venus to forgive

Silvesta for her part in the suicides; but, as the priests announce: 'Venus hath caused this wonder for her glory, | And the triumph of Love's victory.' Venus then announces that this was all part of a trial of faith and Musella and Philisses are not dead at all. The play then moves towards its conclusion with this statement from Cupid:

Now my wars in love hath end,
Each one here enjoys their friend,
And so all shall henceforth say
Who my laws will still obey.
Mother, now judge Arcas' fault
All things else your will hath wrought.

Venus then consigns Arcas to exile in 'these fair plains' and the play ends with the following speeches:

Venus. Your doom is given, it may not be recalled,
But with your treachery you must be thralled.
And now all duties are performed to Love;
Look that no more our powers by scorn you move,
But be the treasures of Love's lasting glory,
And I, your princess, crowned with victory.

Arcas. Thus still is sin rewarded with all shame
And so let all be that deserve like blame.
I have offended in the basest kind
And more ill do deserve than ill can find.
I traitor was to Love, and to my love
Those who shall thus offend, like me, shame prove.

From 'Pamphilia to Amphilanthus'.

Sonnet 22

Like to the Indians scorched with the sun,
The sun which they do as their god adore,
So am I used by love for ever more
I worship him, less favours have I won.

Better are they who thus to blackness run,
And so can only whiteness' want deplore,

Than I who pale and white am with grief's store,
Nor can have hope but to see hopes undone;

Besides, their sacrifice received's* in sight
Of their chose saint, mine hid as worthless rite;
Grant me to see where I my offerings give,

Then let me wear the mark of Cupid's might
In heart, as they in skin of Phoebus' light,*
Not ceasing offerings to love while I live.

Sonnet 23

When everyone to pleasing pastime hies,*
Some hunt,* some hawk, some play,* while some delight
In sweet discourse, and music shows joy's might,
Yet I my thoughts do far above these prize.

The joy which I take is that, free from eyes,
I sit and wonder at this daylike night,
So to dispose themselves as void of right,*
And leave true pleasure for poor vanities.

When others hunt, my thoughts I have in chase;
If hawk, my mind at wished end doth fly,
Discourse, I with my spirit talk and cry,
While others, music choose as greatest grace.

'O God,' say I, 'can these fond* pleasures move?
Or music be but in sweet thoughts of love?'

Sonnet 34

Take heed mine eyes, how you your looks do cast,
Lest they betray my heart's most secret thought;
Be true unto yourselves, for nothing's bought
More dear than doubt which brings a lover's fast.*

Catch you all watching eyes ere they be past,
Or take yours fixed where your best love hath sought
The pride of your desires; let them be taught
Their faults for shame, they could no truer last;

Then look, and look with joy for conquest won
Of those that searched your hurt in double kind;

So you kept safe, let them themselves look blind
Watch, gaze and mark till they to madness run,

While you, mine eyes, enjoy full sight of love,
Contented that such happinesses move.

Sonnet 35

False hope which feeds but to destroy and spill
What it first breeds; unnatural to the birth
Of thine own womb; conceiving but to kill,
And plenty gives to make the greater dearth.

So tyrants do who falsely ruling earth
Outwardly grace them, and with profit's fill
Advance those who appointed are to death
To make their greater fall to please their will.

Thus shadow they their wicked vile intent
Colouring evil with a show of good,
While in fair shows their malice so is spent;
Hope kills the heart and tyrants shed the blood.

For hope deluding brings us to the pride
Of our desires* the farther down to slide.

Sonnet 48

How like a fire doth love increase in me,
The longer that it lasts, the stronger still,
The greater, purer, brighter, and doth fill
No eye with wonder more, then hopes still be

Bred in my breast, when fires of love are free
To use that part to their best-pleasing will,
And now impossible it is to kill,
The heat so great where Love his strength doth see.

Mine eyes can scarce sustain the flames, my heart
Doth trust in them my passions to impart,
And languishingly strive to show my love;

My breath not able is to breathe least part
Of that increasing fuel of my smart;
Yet love I will,* till I but ashes prove.*

'Song' from *Urania*

Love what art thou? A vain thought
In our minds by fancy wrought,
Idle smiles did thee beget
While fond wishes made the net
Which so many fools have caught.

Love what art thou? Light and fair
Fresh as morning, clear as th'air,
But too soon thy evening change
Makes thy worth with coldness range,
Still thy joy is mixed with care.

Love what art thou? A sweet flower
Once full blown, dead in an hour,
Dust in wind as stayed remains
As thy pleasure, or our gains
If thy humour change, to lour.

Love what art thou? Childish, vain,
Firm as bubbles made by rain,
Wantonness thy greatest pride,
These foul faults thy virtues hide
But babes can no stayedness gain.

Love what art thou? Causeless cursed,
Yet, alas, these not the worst,
Much more of thee may be said,
But thy law I once obeyed,
Therefore say no more at first.

ELEANOR DAVIES
(1590–1652)

*The Benediction. From The A:lmighty O:mnipotent.**

I have an Errand to thee O: Captain.
2 Kings 9.5.
Printed in the Year, 1651.
For the Army's General,* His Excellency.

My Lord,
Your interest in the nation's unparalleled troublesome times: the flaming sword for expelling the man in your hand, which crowns with no inferior honour that name of yours: hereof by her hand a touch presented. Derived from his own, namely A. & O. Letters of no mean latitude: armed beside with his sword: sun and moon* when as stood in admiration, witness ☉ ☾* their golden characters, styled eyes and horns of the lamb, &c. Their voice gone out into all lands, Psal. (Rev. 5.) Like theirs here, every one when the fifty days* at an end, heard in his proper language, &c. (Acts. 2). The prophet Joel as foresaw and others: By whom deciphered his thundering donative of the crown and bended bow (Rev. 6.). That seal or box of nard opened; as much to say, O: Cromwell, renowned, be victorious so long as sun moon continues or live ever.
Anagram, Howl Rome: And thus with one voice, come and see, O: C: Conquering and to Conquer went forth.
My Lord,
Your Humble Servant,
Eleanor.
O C tob. 28
A°* 1651.

Revelations
The Everlasting Gospel

Apocalypse 14.
And they sang a new Song before the Throne, and before the four

Beasts and the Elders; ver. 24. And no MAN could learn that Song, but the 144, &c.*

Printed in the Year of our Redemption, Decem. 1649.

The Holy Gospel. According to the Evangelist, By the Lady ELEANOR.

Even the same, that which was from the beginning, then believed in, magnified unto the end of the world, as until the consummation of the Age (saying) *Lo, I am with you, without end whose Kingdom.*

How it came to pass showing, in the first year of his reign, first of his name, *Charles* of *Great Britain*, in *Berks*. the first of shires, she* then at her house *Englefield* Manor, of *England's* realm, daughter of the first peer, *Anno* 25. the month of *July* in, so called after the first *Roman* emperor, he slain, *&c.*

Where the word of the Lord of Hosts, when came to her, the Heavenly voice descending, speaking as through a trumpet of a most clear sound these words:

Nineteen years and a half to the Judgement, and you as the meek Virgin.

Awakened by which alarm early in the morning, whereof thus, signed with *Division's* character,* the years being divided, this magnified morning star, story of *Jerusalem* of the *Gentiles*, *Great Britain's* blow foreshowing, *Anno* 44. accomplished:* The same though come to pass, who nevertheless in stead of their acknowledged error, like those *Priests* and *Elders*, first who *setting a Watch*, then underhand by such large doctrine endeavour to stop the people's mouths that do not do as they are taught, promised *to be saved harmless*, the old serpent's policy, &c. And with this revolution thus going on, in the first of his reign, the beginning in of the year, when a *Star* within the *Horns of the New Moon* enclosed, of some judgement at hand, the ominous forerunner: First, of the wise-men coming from the East, as follows; whose flight taken westward, through that heavy hand occasioned; the city's unparalleled plague,* bills to be cancelled never, or drowned in forgetfulness, increased to no less than weekly *Five thousand five hundred and odd*, the age of the world;* decreased as suddenly about the midst of Summer: all one as their being fed, that blessing thought upon, when the five thousand men with *those loaves five*, &c. no more than the fingers of their hand, any matter made of it, so thankful: Whereupon (the aforesaid visitation) the term* kept at *Reading*, County of *Berks*, other courts at *Maidenhead* town, the Parliament posting to *Oxford*, doing all homage to this *New born* BABE, *ruling with the iron sceptre*, them forewarning all in vain, *Be wise, O ye Kings, be learned, ye judges*; that in such security held themselves then, and so much first for that, and his powerful word displayed, the priority thereof, thou *Britain* not the least, *&c.* And of his wrath then kindled, showed great blessings and corrections inseparable companions: Wherewith proceeding, namely, *without it done nothing that was done*, its mouth the oracle, *Beginning* and *Ending* of *Monarchies*, inheritance whose from *East to West extends*; concerning the aforesaid golden number, *Nineteen years and a half*, being in a manuscript inserted, containing *Germany's* woeful occurrences,* and *Great Britain's* both, with what sign confirmed, showing further thus, who immediately after with her own hand within two days delivered it to the Archbishop *Abbot's*,* he then at *Oxford*, of university the first, in presence of no few; with this for a token given, *the plague presently to cease*; of whom took her leave, the Bishop's *Amen* whereto went round.

The Bills obeying the same before the month expired of *August*, witness when scarce deceased *one thousand* of all diseases, whereas afore so infectious, five children dying for one aged, next term supplied with others fled returned; so that of its late desolation appearance, no more then of change or amendment amongst them, none at all.

And so pursuing the prophetical history in the next place, that it might be fulfilled *out of the Low Countries, &c.* as the Virgin then undertook her voyage, she fleeing for the babe's* preservation thither; also constrained for printing the same, to go into *Holland*, those plain swathing-bands for wrapping it in, pretending in her husband's behalf the *Spaw* obtained a license, since none for printing to be had here, inquisition and hold such, among them imprisoned about it formerly, till afterward all free, *Cum Privilegio* out of date become.

Where thus passing on the meanwhile ere her return thence, *George* Archbishop deceased, *Anno* 33. unhappily whose hands imbrued in innocent blood,* Archbishop *Laud*, 19 of *Septemb.* translated, &c. reigning in his stead, successor of him, instead of the stag who shot the keeper, presaging what murders him coming after, when-as for another her soul pierced in no mean degree, what honour to be *a Prophet amongst their own nation and rank*;* for example as specified on record: no sooner arrived than apprehended,* of her child ravished, a greater than the parliament, *the Word of God*: And how recompensed for their service, referred, &c. where after a candle being sent for, about the third hour in the afternoon, that with his own hand had burnt it, saying, *She hath taken good long time, till 44. for dooms-day then; my Lords, I hope I have made you a smother of it*: in truth his own fatal hour, those years of *Nineteen and a half*, reaching to his execution month and year, *Anno* 44. *January*, when parted head and body, like that aforesaid divided year, showed afore sacrificed by his ungracious hand, author of this division or distraction, a cup filled to the brim afterward, as that Judgement day, *June Anno* forty four complete: The restrained four *Winds*, &c. (*Apoc*. 7.) signified by them, extending to forty eight,* that blow January also, all standing at the stroke of FOUR; the foursquare city *New Jerusalem* wherewith agrees: *Micah* the Prophet (cap. 5) his alarm to awaken the age, speaking no parable. So of her goods seized on, wherewith given the oath, such and such ARTICLES for answering to: In which case not much to seek, of *Scandalum Magnatum** in that kind, against *those little ones* (order of the prophets), the penalty of it, *touched by whomsoever, a millstone a fitter ornament*, &c. she not slow in appearing to receive their wild sentence; the dragon of *Lambeth,* Laud*, his venom discharging last of all, even *Anno Etatis* 33. measured out by our Lord's age, when as brought to his arraignment by wicked hands, how sacrificed this *Testimony* of his; a word also as ensues.

And of like measure *October* 23. she committed close prisoner,* excommunicated, fined to his Majesty's use three thousand pounds, and to make public recantation at *Paul's* Cross, as extant on record, twelve hands signed by; also *Edge* Hill fight, and the *Irish* massacre 23 of *October*,* and twelve of them at once voted to prison, for that order of theirs nothing to stand of force there done without them: His Majesty lastly fined his three Kingdoms to the use, &c. As for *Paul's*, a habitation for owls, those notes set up, to set forth the residue, where the time would fail how the first blow at *Edge Hill* in *Oxfordshire*, the second *Newbury*, fought within a stone's cast of her house at *Englefield*. And thou *Bedlam*-House, too little the thousandth part to contain of them distracted since thence her coming, *well knowing if the Master of the house called Devil, &c. what the Servant to expect;* where so much for this time, accompanied with the universal tax, no inferior rack set upon in these days *C. Stu** his reign, as sometimes in *Caes. August.* second of that monarchy, no small oppression, as the lineage of *David* a witness of it: closing it with these from her name, *Rachel's*,* signifying a sheep, rendering *Charles* his soil for the Golden fleece bearing the bell: so whom he hath joined of her lamentation, & this *Jacob's* saying, *Some evil Beast hath done it*, needs not ask *Whose Coat party-coloured?* also in pieces rent since our *British Union*, &c. not without cause *weeping, because they are not*; and so all doing they know not what, *even forgive*, &c. And again thus, since *Thus it was written, and thus it behoved to suffer, and to rise again.*

The New-Years-Gift to *all Nations and People*, Jubile.
Decemb. 1649.

PRISCILLA COTTON and MARY COLE
(fl. 1650s/1660s)

To the Priests and People of England, we discharge our consciences and give them warning. (1655)

Friends,
we have no envy nor malice to any creature, priest or people, but are to mind you of your condition, without any partiality or hypocrisy, and wish your eternal good. And what we contend against is your greatest enemy and will be your everlasting woe and torment if it be not destroyed in you. For know, there is the seed of the woman and the seed of the serpent in the world; there is the generation of Cain and righteous Abel. Now it lieth upon you all to know what generation you are of, for little did the false prophets and that generation that put to death the true prophets of the Lord think they were of Cain's race, nor did the Scribes and Pharisees, that with their priests put Christ to death, think they were of Cain's generation, for they garnished the sepulchres of the righteous and said if they had been in the days of their fathers they would not have slain them; yet Christ Jesus told them that all the blood spilt since righteous Abel should be required of that generation and that they were the children of them that murdered the prophets. Is it not strange that the learned Priests and Scribes that had the Hebrew and Greek besides Latin should not find out by all their high learning the original of the Scriptures of the prophets concerning Christ Jesus, that he was the true Messiah, but that they that read the gospel every Sabbath day, that spake of Christ, should murder and put him to death. Now Christ Jesus himself gives the reason and thanks his Father, that he had hid it from the wise, and prudent, and revealed it to babes,* because it was the Father's good pleasure, and the Scriptures declare them to be ignorant that had the Hebrew, Greek and Latin, for had they known it, they would not have crucified the Lord of life and glory.

Now people, this was the same generation of Cain in them after

Christ's death that persecuted the Apostles and put them to death; and it was the same spirit in them that put the martyrs to death, and of that generation were the bishops that persecuted, and so it continueth still to this day in the world; for Cain's generation is now still envying, hating and persecuting the righteous Abel. Now the persecuting Cainish generation would never acknowledge they were such, but in all ages persecuted the just under some false colour, as they of old said the true prophets were troublers of Israel; and Amaziel* the Priest of Bethel said of Amos, that the land was not able to bear his words; and Haman* said that the laws of the people of God were contrary to the laws and customs of all nations; and of Christ they said he was a deceiver and had a devil; and of Stephen, that he spake against the holy place and the law; and that Paul was a pestilent fellow, and a mover of sedition. So that all along it was on a false account the just were persecuted; so in the days of the bishops, the martyrs were burnt and butchered under the name of heretics; so now the seed of the serpent is subtle, and will not persecute the truth, as it is the truth, but under some false pretence or other, else all would see their deceit. But the truth is, it's from the first rise, because their own works are evil, and their brothers' good: they hated Christ Jesus, because he testified that their works were evil. So now Cain's generation hates the just and pure seed of God, because it declares that their works are evil.

Objection: But do not the priests declare against evil works?

Answer: Yes, they do so. The scribes and Pharisees spake good words, they spake of the Messiah, yet they killed the substance of what they spake; so the priests speak true words, good words, and yet kill, and persecute, pursue, and imprison the substance and life of what they speak, for he that departs from evil makes himself a prey to priest and people; and sometimes when the light in their consciences tells them, when they are persecuting the just seed, that they are innocent, yet they wilfully run on against the very light of their own consciences, as did Stephen's persecutors.*

And is it not so? I speak to that in your consciences, that though the priests speak true words, yet priests and people that live in Cain's race do pursue and persecute even to the very death, the life and power of what they do preach. And know you of a truth, that all the blood since Abel shall be required of this generation; for, as it groweth to the end, it heighteneth and ripeneth its malice and wickedness, and so shall its judgement be, for double plagues shall be poured out upon her.

Now to you all I speak: sin not against the light* in your own consciences, be not wilfully blind, but hearken to the light of Jesus Christ in your consciences, that you may come to see what generation you are of, whether of Cain or Abel, and if you did abide in the light, you should come to witness the life and power of what you profess, and so come to that life that gave forth the Scriptures, and not wrest them to your own opinions and lusts, one saying 'Lo, here in Presbytery';* another 'Lo, there in Independency'; and another in Prelacy; and another in baptism. But the Scriptures are not divided: they agree, and hold out one thing; but you divide them, because you live not in that life that gave them forth, yet you boast of your learning, that you have the Hebrew and Greek, and know the original. But you see Pilate and the Jews had the Hebrew, Greek and Latin, yet knew not the original, for had they known it, they would not have crucified the Lord of life and glory.

Therefore know you, that you may be, and are ignorant, though you think yourselves wise. Silly men and women may see more into the mystery of Christ Jesus than you, for the apostles, that the scribes called illiterate, and Mary and Susanna (silly women, as you would be ready to call them, if they were here now) these know more of the Messiah, than all the learned priests and rabbis; for it is the spirit that searcheth all things, yea, the deep things of God you may know and yet murder the just and think you do God good service.

This I warn you in love, for I cannot but think that there are some among you that ponder on this day, and if you would hearken to the light of Jesus Christ in your consciences, it would lead you from your own wisdom, learning, and self-conceitedness, into the simplicity of Jesus Christ, which is a mystery of faith hid in a pure conscience, for your own wisdom must be denied, if ever you will come to witness the life and power of true wisdom, which the fear of the Lord is the beginning of, for so did they of old.

Paul and Apollos* were very learned and eloquent, saith the Scriptures, yet Paul counted all his learning dung for the excellency of the knowledge of Christ, let his second chapter of his first Epistle to the Corinthians be a full witness of this; and Apollos was willing to be instructed of his hearers Aquila and Priscilla that were tentmakers, and the learned that studied curious arts burnt their books that were of great price when they came to the knowledge of Jesus Christ. So you now, would you hearken to Jesus Christ and obey his light in your consciences, you would come down to humility and the fear of the Lord, to the true wisdom and understanding, that you would not need so many authors, and books, you would not need to rent your heads with studying, but you would come to see your teacher in you which now is removed into a corner, you would come to live a preaching life, and witness that faith you talk of, to purify your hearts from envy, pride and malice, and to get the victory over the world's glory and honour that is so highly esteemed by you; and coming to see yourselves in the light of Jesus Christ, you will not lord it over God's heritage, nor lift yourselves up above your brethren in pride and arrogancy, but be a servant to all in love.

Therefore, come now to the light, sin no longer against that in your conscience; for Antichrist must be destroyed by the brightness of his coming, and God is gathering his people out from idol-shepherds into his own fold, to make them one flock and to give them one shepherd, that they may serve him with onc consent, for he hath fulfilled this Scripture in thousands this day whom he hath gathered out of Antichrist's opinions to worship one God in one way, in spirit and truth, speaking all the same things. If you speak with ten thousand of them, they all agree, having one king, one lawgiver. Now fret not at this, you that live at Babylon in confusion, in divisions, for the little stone cut out of the mountain* without hands, shall break Babylon's idols.

Now consider, friends and people, your conditions, for what good doth all your preaching and hearing do you? Break your sleep, rent your brains, and as it were, speak out your lungs, and alas who is bettered by it! Was there ever more pride, lightness, vanity, and wantonness manifested in your assemblies than now? You make it the place where you set forth your pride and vanity to the utmost. Was there ever the like injustice, violence, falsehood and deceit in any age, that scarce can a man tell what men mean by what they say any longer?

Men say in effect that God hath forsaken the earth by their wicked practices; the people cry out upon the priests, and say that their opinions have made them so wicked; and the priests cry out upon the people, and say that the fault is theirs; so that the Lord beheld, and instead of righteousness, equity and judgement, there is a cry.* So your whole religion is but a noise; the life, power and substance is not in it.

Oh apostate England, what shall the God of mercies do for thee? What shall he do unto thee? He hath tried thee with mercies, and with the sword, and then with peace again, and yet thou repentest not; he hath given thee his witness, his just one, to reprove thee, to convince thee of sin in thy conscience, but thou hast slain the witness, murdered and slain the just. He will not always strive with man, he will now roar from Sion, and the children of the west shall tremble, those that worship their idols; he will redeem Sion with judgement, and he will tear his flock out of the mouth of the greedy devouring shepherds, that have made a prey upon them, and the idol-shepherds shall have their arm dried up, and their right eye darkened.*

Come down thou, therefore, that hast built among the stars by thy arts and learning; for it's thy pride and thy wisdom that hath perverted thee; thou hast gone in the way of Cain, in envy and malice, and ran greedily after the reward of Balaam, in covetousness, and if thou repent not, shalt perish in the gainsaying of Kore.* For if a son or a daughter be moved from the Lord to go into the assembly of the people in a message from the Lord God, thou canst not endure to hear them speak sound doctrine, having a guilty conscience and fearing they would declare against thy wickedness. Thou incensest the people, telling them that they are dangerous people, Quakers, so making the people afraid of us, and incensest the magistrates, telling them that they must lay hold on us, as troublers of the people, and disturbers of the peace, and so makes them thy drudges to act thy malice, that thy filthiness may not be discovered, and thy shame appear; but God will make them in one day to forsake thee, and leave and fly from thee, though for the present thou lordest it over magistrates, people, meeting-house, and all, as though all were thine and thou sittest as a queen and lady over all, and wilt have the preeminence, and hast got into the seat of God, the consciences of the people, and what thou sayest must not be contradicted. If thou bid them fight and war, they obey it; if thou bid them persecute and imprison, they do it; so that they venture their bodies and souls to fulfil thy lusts of envy and pride, and in thy pride thou condemnest all others; thou tellest the people women must not speak in a church,* whereas it is not spoke only of a female, for we are all one, both male and female, in Christ Jesus, but it's weakness that is the woman by the Scriptures forbidden, for else thou puttest the Scriptures at a difference in themselves, as still it's thy practice out of thy ignorance; for the Scriptures do say that all the church may prophesy one by one,* and that women were in the church, as well as men, do thou judge; and the Scripture saith that a woman may not prophesy with her head uncovered, lest she dishonour her head.* Now thou wouldst know the meaning of that head, let the Scripture answer: the head of every man is Christ.* Man in his best estate is altogether vanity, weakness, a lie. If therefore any speak in the church, whether man or woman, and nothing appear in it but the wisdom of man, and Christ, who is the true head, be not uncovered, do not fully appear, Christ the head is then dishonoured. Now the woman, or weakness, that is man, which in his best estate or greatest wisdom is altogether vanity, that must be covered with the covering of the Spirit, a garment of righteousness, that its nakedness may not appear, and dishonour thereby come. Here mayest thou see from the Scriptures, that the woman or weakness, whether male or female, is forbidden to speak in the church; but it's very plain, Paul, nor Apollos, nor the true church of Christ, were not of that proud envious spirit that thou art of, for they owned Christ Jesus in man or woman; for Paul bid Timothy to help those women that laboured with him in the Gospel, and Apollos hearkened to a woman, and was instructed by her, and Christ Jesus appeared to the women first, and sent them to preach the resurrection to the apostles, and Philip had four virgins* that did prophesy. Now thou dost respect persons I know, and art partial in all things, and so judgest wickedly, but there is no respect of persons with God. Indeed, you yourselves are the women that are forbidden to speak in the church, that are become women; for two of your priests came to speak with us, and when they could not bear sound reproof and wholesome doctrine that did concern them, they railed on us with filthy speeches, as no other they can give to us, that deal plainly and singly with them, and so ran from us. So leaving you to the light in all your consciences to judge of what we have writ, we remain prisoners in Exeter gaol* for the word of God.

Priscilla Cotton,
Mary Cole.

HESTER BIDDLE

(*c.*1629–1696)

The Trumpet of the Lord Sounded Forth Unto These Three Nations, As a warning from the spirit of truth, especially unto thee, Oh England, who art looked upon as the seat of justice from whence righteous laws should proceed. Likewise unto thee, thou great and famous city of London, doth the Lord God of vengeance sound one warning more unto thine ear, that (if possible) haply thou mayest hearken unto him and amend thy life before it be too late.

With a word of wholesome counsel and advice unto thy kings, rulers, judges, bishops and priests, that they may prize the day of their visitation before it pass away. As also a word of prophesy of the sore destruction that is coming upon them if they repent not.

Together with a few words unto the royal seed,* which is chosen of God and separated from the world to do his will forever.

By one who is a sufferer for the testimony of Jesus in Newgate,* Esther Biddle. (1662)

One warning more from the Lord God of vengeance sounded forth unto thee, Oh city of London.

Oh London, London! The dreadful Lord God of everlasting strength, which faileth not, his notable, terrible and dreadful day is coming upon thee as at noon day, and from it thou canst not escape, neither canst thou quench God's fire, which burns as an oven, which is overtaking thee. Oh the burden of the Lord concerning this treacherous and backsliding city! Oh calamity upon calamity, misery upon misery, plagues upon plagues, sickness upon sickness, and one disease upon another will the Lord God of power bring upon thee, and the Lord will destroy thee from being inhabited unless thou dost repent from the bottom of thine heart and lead a new life and abhor thyself in dust and ashes. The everlasting counsellor and prince of peace is come, and coming to take peace from thee and to hide comfort from thine eyes.

Oh woe is me for thee, my heart is even broken within me and mine eyes as a fountain floweth forth before the Lord in thy behalf, that the bitter cup which thou and thy joining sister* hath to drink may be taken away, if it be his will. Oh that thou wouldst return to the Lord as Nineveh* did, who received the message of God. And the King came from his stately throne and humbled himself before the Lord and his soul was obedient unto the higher power, which is God, and all that had a being in that city, both man and beast, was covered with sackcloth and ashes. Three days and three nights they humbled themselves before the higher power, who is king of kings and lord of lords, who is governor amongst the gods, even he repented himself of the evil which he thought to bring upon them and accepted of their humiliation.

Oh London! It would be well for thee to consider thy ways and worship and religion and search with the light and let the light show thee whether thy ways and worship and Law is pure, which is given forth in thee; if it be not so, I pray thee as in Christ stead, let his light lead thee into his way and judgements and worship and religion, which are holy, that thy soul may be saved in the terrible day of the Lord, for there are hundreds in thee that do not know their right hand from their left, neither can they discern the power of the lamb from the power of the beast. Therefore hath the Lord stayed his fury from breaking forth upon thee yet a little while and the mighty hand and outstretched arm of the Lord, which is stretched forth from sea to sea, will come upon thee suddenly.

'Oh thou city!', saith the Lord, who formed thee in the womb and gave thee life and breath and hath been as a tender father and loving nurse even from thy cradle, 'have not I made the earth to bring forth her corn and oil and wine for thee?* Have not I clothed the earth with grass and the dew to descend upon it and the softly showers of rain? Have not I caused to distil upon thy flowers and vines that they might give a fragrant smell unto thee? How have thy streets and houses been dressed with the glory of them! And have not thine eyes beheld the glorious colours of the flowers and workmanship of my hands, the which many of you shall see no more because of my destroying angel?

'Oh London, have not I who am the God of the whole world placed a glorious burning fire in thee, which all the water in the sea cannot quench, which gives light in thee and unto thee and all nations, which is my witness in every man, which stands up for me against all manner of sin? Hath not the Lord broken up the seals of the great deep and opened the fountain of everlasting life in the midst of thee to wash thee from thy leprosy and to heal thy putrefying sores?* Oh thou art full of running sores from the crown of thine head to the sole of thy foot; there is not a free place. Have not I opened a well of pure water to bathe and make thee white? I the Lord of hosts hath caused my sons and daughters and handmaids to leave both father and mother, house and land, wife and children, and indeed all outward things, to come unto thee, rising up early in sore travels and labours to warn thee and call thee to repentance, that thou mightest be saved before my dreadful stroke be struck at thee which will not fail. Have not they showed thee many things which hath come to pass? I have shown and am showing signs in Heaven and earth in thee which shall make the keepers of the house to tremble; have not the dead been raised, the blind made to see, the lame to walk, the dumb to speak, the leopards* been cleansed in thee? Have not I made the elements to melt with fervent heat, the powers of Heaven have been shook by me, the sun have I turned into darkness and the moon hath lost her light. The old Heaven and the old earth hath the Lord made to pass away at the brightness of his coming, and as I have worked and suffered in you, so I will do until I have made up my jewels, which I am perfecting through sufferings in thee. And until I have gathered my seed from the four winds* in thee into my bosom from whence it came, until then will I work and bear the burden of iniquity, even until the seed suffering measure is come to an end, and then shall not my eye pity nor hands spare thee, but I will bathe my sword in thy blood and I will give thee blood to drink, even as thou hast done by my innocent lambs, even so will I do by thee, and as they have seen their blood lie in thy streets, so shalt thou see thine, and the day will be hot and terrible that is coming upon thee unless thou dost repent. I the everlasting God hath looked down out of my holy habitation and have beheld the sufferings of my people, notwithstanding the noble and worthy acts that have been done by my people in thee, how hast thou bruised, beaten and knocked down, killed and spilt the blood of my innocent lambs and haled them into thy nasty prisons* until they die. Oh, the blood of the innocent is found in thee, which crieth aloud for vengeance unto my throne. Drunkenness, whoredom and gluttony and all manner of ungodliness, tyranny and oppression is found in thee. Thy Priests preach for hire and thy people love to have it so; rioting and ungodly meetings, stage plays, ballad singing, cards and dice, and all manner of folly (not in corners only, but in the high places of thy streets) wicked works and actions are not punished by thee and hundreds may meet together to commit folly and take the name of the pure God in vain and cause his soul to mourn and abuse themselves with His creatures until they can neither go nor hardly speak. Taverns and alehouses are frequented day and night and are seldom disturbed by the magistrates or sent to prison or bruised or knocked down; but they that are innocent and cannot lift up a hand or bear arms for or against any man and have no evil or hard thought in their hearts against anyone, neither do they speak evil of things they know not, or condemn magistracy, but reprove sin in the gate and ungodliness in the streets, and so have made themselves a prey: these are they that are punished by thee and whose sufferings are deeper than any people upon the earth besides.

Oh London! The sins of the old world is found in thee; art thou guilty or not guilty? For thy time draweth near wherein thou must give an account unto me, who am a dreadful and terrible judge, unto that spirit which leadeth thee into persecution. Oh thou art grown numerous and very great, thy beam reacheth unto Heaven and thy glory unto the end of the earth and thou hast crowned thyself with dignity and hast built thy nest among the stars and sitteth as a queen; thou hast made thyself strong and hast said in thy heart 'Thou shalt not see sorrow'; thou seest no scarcity within thy gates, but fullness within thy palaces. But know this as from the Lord, thou bloody city, thou shalt know his terrible stroke, who is God almighty. He will plead with thee as in the valley of Jehosophat, even with the fire of his wrath and the glittering sword of his spirit.

Oh thou famous and beautiful harlot,* who art beautified with the glory of Egypt, thou hast played the whore with many lovers. Oh, thy bed is defiled and thou hast forgotten thy creator, which maketh my soul to mourn; thy strength shall become weakness and thy glory shall perish, thy beauty shall be turned into ashes and thy honour shall become contemptible because thou art covered with a dark cloud of sin and transgression and so cannot behold the Lord. Envy hath misled thy mind, which hath caused thee to imprison his messengers, not only them of thy own city but strangers who hath forsaken all to visit thee in bowels of everlasting love, and thus hast thou rewarded them, which is contrary to Christ's command, which is to love strangers.

In the days of old, they received strangers and washed their feet and gave them to eat and drink, but thou bruisest and knockest them down and keepest them in prison from their families and hast said 'The parish will look after them.' Oh thou merciless city! Dost thou think to obtain mercy from the Lord? How many families hast thou separated, the wife from the husband and the husband from the wife and the mother from her children and the servant from the master, not suffering them to see each other for a time. The Lord hath said, 'Cursed is he that separateth a man from his wife', and dost not thou bring that curse and many more upon thy head? We have been found in no plots nor risings, but have seeked the good of all souls and the prosperity of all nations; in Oliver's days* and ever since we have been gathered out of the worships and vanities of this city and could not bow unto Hammon;* we have been a suffering people and nothing could be found against us but concerning the worship of our God, which must disannul all unjust laws made by man. The Medes and Persians had nothing against Daniel but concerning his faith and I know Daniel's spirit liveth amongst us.

Therefore, consider what thou art doing, for in vain dost thou set up briars and thorns in battle against the terrible God, for by the brightness of his coming shall they be burnt up, for assuredly the Lord will arise mightily for his seed's sake, for as a lion roused up is he come, who is the munition of rocks, and as a she-bear bereaved of her young ones, will He roar and disquiet all thy inhabitants.

Oh London, God hath a remnant* in thee which he hath marked for His own, which shall escape the wrath that is to come. Glory, glory, songs of everlasting praises be rendered unto the living God, who hath not left himself without a witness in thee. Oh London, if thou wouldst return, saith the Lord God Almighty, I will heal thy backslidings and forgive thee all thy sins; I will withdraw my bitter cup which I have filled full of my indignation and I will cover thee with my garment of everlasting love and I will be married unto thee, even as a young man marrieth a virgin, never to be separated. I looked down from the throne of my glory and I saw thy distressed condition: thou art as a sheep without a shepherd; as upon the mountains of prey and art scattered hither and thither amongst the clouds of religions; thou knowest not which way to turn, thou art like the dove, thou canst find no rest nor footing for the sole of thy foot; thou art liable to be torn by the wolves and devoured by the lions; thy teachers are removed into corners and thou art dispossessed of thy wonted houses and service. Therefore, saith the Lord, do I pity thy condition, and if thou wilt hearken unto me, who am near thee in thy heart and in thy mouth; at thy down lying I am with thee and in the night season I visit thee, and at thy uprising I call thee to repentance. How many years have I born with thee, as I did with the old world? But my patience came to an end and my wrath waxed hot and so it will against thee if thou wilt not hear my beloved son, which I have sent a light into the world, and if thou wilt learn of the light which shines in thy heart, then thou wilt be on heaps no more, neither will thy teachers and worships and church be any more removed into corners, but thou wilt be built upon Christ, the pillar and ground of truth, who is the church of the first-born; then wilt thou have fellowship with the Lord and thy glory and crown and beauty shall never have an end, but thou shalt be the glory of the whole earth and the beauty of all nations and kings shall come to thy rising and princes to the brightness of thy glory. There is no city upon the earth can say, as thou canst in this latter day, for the power of the Lord hath been shed abroad in thee and thou hast been visited more than any, therefore prize the son of the Lord, lest thou art cast into utter darkness, for it is I, the Lord, that chaineth leviathan, which no man can tame, who am God, and there is none besides me; by my wisdom the world was made and the heavens framed; I created the sea and caused the rivers to run into it and have set the sands as swaddling bands that it cannot over pass, and this is my decree which I will have sealed unto my people. *I am the Quakers' God*, and will be with them unto the end of this world, and in the end they shall be with me in my glorious kingdom, where they shall be kept from their persecutors and lie down in joy, peace and tranquillity with the rest of my holy martyrs and prophets and apostles in years past, and I am utterly against all that do oppose them, who am a terrible God and will bring the wickedness of the wicked to an end, but the righteousness of the righteous doth live with me.

This is my decree and it shall live forever and remain world without end, and if thou canst cause the rain from raining or the stars from shining or the sun from going her course or giving light to the nations, then mayest thou alter my decree with my people, whose seed shall be for number as the sand upon the seashore, and for multitude as the stars of Heaven, and they shall shine in glory more brighter than the sun at noon day in the firmament of my power, when the generation of the wicked shall be cast into the lake which is prepared of God for the king of darkness and his subjects.

The Trumpet of the Lord sounded forth unto England, Scotland and Ireland, with a word of wholesome advice and counsel to the King, rulers and judges thereof.

Oh King,* this is my counsel unto thee and thy rulers and judges. Oh hearken unto the light of Christ in your consciences that it may bear rule in your hearts, that you may judge for the Lord and oppression may be expelled in your dominions. Oh that you would do justice and love mercy and walk humbly with the God of Heaven, then would the Lord give you length of days and a long life, peace and plenty shall be in your dominions, everyone shall sit under his own vine and fig tree and none shall make them afraid; joy and tranquillity shall be in your palaces. This shall you see and know to be accomplished if you will leave off oppressing the righteous and set the captive free.

Oh ye rulers, judges and justices and all people high and low! Be it known unto you from the mighty judge of powerful majesty that he is risen who will scatter rulers in his anger and will pluck down kings in his wrath. Oh, the anger of the Lord waxeth hot against all workers of iniquity and he will set his oppressed seed free, which crieth unto him for deliverance; and know this, what cruelty soever be in your hearts against us, the Lord will confound it and bring it to nothing, for the Lord is on our sides and we fear not imprisonment, banishment, fire or tortures, or whatever the wrath of man can inflict upon us, for our hearts are firmly fixed upon the Lord and we are freely given up in body, soul and spirit to suffer for God's cause. Oh you rulers, if the Lord suffereth you to banish us, I know that the Lord will go along with us, as he did with Abraham in a strange land. But know this, we shall leave a seed behind us which shall be your tormentor and shall witness for us when we are gone.

Oh Lord, I commit our case unto thee, who art faithful and keepeth covenant forever, and I know thou wilt fight our battle and plead our cause with the mighty on earth, who would destroy us from being a people if thy power did not preserve us. Glory and honour be given unto thee, who hath compassed us about with songs of everlasting praises, and we may bless the hour and time that thou raised up a people in the North,* even a dreadful and terrible army, who marched swiftly in thy power through the nations and by them we were convinced and turned towards the Lord, and they shall be the dread of all nations and God hath crowned them with an everlasting crown which neither men nor devils shall be able to take from them.

Oh you rulers and judges of these nations! Do you think to overcome us or make us yield by keeping them in prison which you think are our teachers and ringleaders? Nay, Christ is our teacher and he cannot be removed into a corner, who is the ancient of days and will cause us to increase daily and to grow as calves in the stall.* We are not like the world, who must have a priest to interpret the Scriptures to them, and when he is removed they are scattered and know not what to do, but my friends, we witness the Scriptures fulfilled, who hath said in latter days He would pour out his spirit upon sons and daughters and they should prophesy and they shall all be taught of me and great shall be their peace and in righteousness shall they be established.* So the Lord doth not speak unto us in an unknown tongue, but in our own language do we hear Him perfectly, whose voice is better than life; and for this cause doth the unlearned hate us and the uncircumcised revile us, because we cannot own the teaching that is of this world, but that which cometh immediately from God and that is pure and refresheth the soul and holdeth up the head in the day of battle, and it causeth us to meet together, to worship the Lord as we ought to do. And oh you rulers and people, it is in vain for you to strive against us, for the God of heaven is with us!

Oh England, Scotland and Ireland, but more especially thou, O England, that art the most fruitful and famous land, in which the Lord hath been pleased to make manifest His life and power, beauty and glory, more than in any nation under the heavens, in so much that he hath raised his sons and daughters from death to life and hath made them bold and valiant soldiers for his testimony, which he hath given them to bear forth unto all nations, and by the glorious and powerful word of life, which hath proceeded out of their mouths, hath thy judges and rulers been convinced of the evil of their way and have been made to confess to the truth, both priests and people, both high and low, rich and poor, hath the Lord visited in this day of great salvation and everlasting love, so that none could plead ignorance, but many like Demas* hath denied the truth and embraced this present evil world. And now, oh England, will the Lord try and prove all thy inhabitants, from the king that sitteth upon his throne unto the beggar that sitteth upon the dunghill, even all sorts of professors* and profane. Oh, the fire is kindled and the furnace is even hot, in the which your works and worships, faith and religion, must be tried, and that which will not remain in the furnace must be consumed by the fire of the Lord, for the most high and glorious king is a-trying and purifying his children in the furnace, as Jerusalem, that they may come forth as polished silver* and well-refined gold, and he hath brought many through the furnace and hath set them as pillars in his house to bear forth a valiant and noble testimony of what they have seen, tasted and handled of the word of life unto thy inhabitants and unto the whole world, that they may fear that dreadful God who made Heaven and earth, in whose sight the whole world is but as the drop of a bucket* and at whose presence the heavens shall wax old as a garment that moths* have eat and the element shall pass away with a great noise, the earth shall be dissolved and all things therein shall mourn and the souls shall fail before him which he hath made.

Oh, let your king and queen, dukes and earls, lords and ladies, judges and rulers, and all bishops, deacons, priests and people in these three nations and all the world consider their ways, worships and religions and fear and tremble before the mighty God, who hath the hearts of kings and rulers in his hand; times and seasons are with him, the dominions of the world are at his disposing, who is the high and lofty one and doth inhabit eternity. What is the Pope or the kings of the earth; will he not bring them to judgement and turn them to dust again from whence they came?

Oh you high and lofty ones, who spendeth God's creation upon your lusts and doth not feed the hungry, nor clothe the naked, but they are ready to perish in the streets; both old and young, lame and blind, lieth in your streets and at your mass-house doors, crying for bread, which even melteth my heart and maketh the soul of the righteous to mourn. Did not the Lord make all men and women upon the earth of one mould? Why then should there be so much honour and respect unto some men and women and not unto others, but they are almost naked for want of clothing and almost starved for want of bread? And are you not all brethren and all under the government of one king? Oh repent, lest the Lord consume you, and be ashamed and clothe the naked and feed the hungry and set the oppressed free!

Oh King, thou art as head under God over these three nations and the Lord hath set thee as overseer to see justice and true judgement executed in thy dominions. Oh let all unjust laws and unrighteous decrees made in thy days and before thy days be all disannulled and made of none effect and henceforth let there be good and wholesome laws established that all the honest-hearted in thy dominions may worship the God of their life without any molestation; and if thou decreest anything, let it not grieve the Lord, for the Lord God of Israel looketh for better fruit at thy hands than he did of all that are gone before thee, for in the time of ignorance God winked, but now is the glorious light of the morning risen and God calleth all men everywhere to repentance.

Oh you rulers, priests and people of these three lands! I most humbly entreat you to learn wisdom before it be too late, and prudence before it be hid from your eyes. Oh leave off your old ways and worships and observing days, times and seasons, and learn the new and living way, which is the way in the wilderness, though a wayfaring man or a fool shall not err therein; this calls for holiness and purity, without which you cannot see the Lord. Therefore, consider you are but men and made of the dust of the earth and you know not how soon you may return to your long homes* and shall be seen no more; have you the length of your life or the number of your days in your own hands? Have you the command of death or can you stay its stroke? Nay, you are but as potsherds broken by the hand of the potter, you are here today and gone tomorrow; your beauty is as the grass and your glory as the flower thereof, cut down by the hand of the mower; your crown is mortal and will fade away. Ah, poor dust and ashes, why do you persecute us even to death for no other cause but worshipping the God of Heaven? Oh, do you think that the Lord is such a one as yourselves? Or are you so vain to believe that he winks or joins with you in persecuting, knocking down and spilling our blood in your streets and murdering of us in your prisons? Nay, nay, although He hath suffered such things to be done for the trial of our faith and the filling up of the measure of your iniquity, which is near full, now will I arise, saith the dreadful and terrible God, who am clothed with vengeance as with a robe and with zeal as with a garment, and I will tear and devour and for Sion's sake I will not be quiet, and for my beloved Jerusalem I will not be silent, but I will roar and thunder forth my voice out of my holy mountain and the beasts shall tremble, the earth shall be as a smoke, the tall cedars shall fall and the sturdy oaks shall be plucked up by the roots and all things of this world shall be afraid; the bats shall go into their holes and the lions into their dens when the Lord appeareth in his beauty to make inquisition for blood; then shall your hearts fail you for fear of those things that are coming upon you; in that terrible day, all your lovers will do you no good and your familiars will stand afar off. Then must you be left to the judge of judges, where you shall see the book of conscience opened, where your indictments will be read at large, and he will judge you according as your deeds shall be. Oh then, if you have not done justice nor loved mercy, or did the thing that was just in the sight of the Lord, then shall you be banished from the presence of the King of Heaven for ever more into utter darkness where is weeping, wailing and gnashing of teeth and you shall be a stink to ages to come.

Oh blessed and happy will it be for those judges and rulers and people who hath clean hands and pure hearts and have not joined with the wicked in persecuting the innocent. Surely their reward will be great in Heaven.

My friends, I was once of this religion which is now in power. I was signed with the sign of the cross and baptised into the faith; my godfathers and godmothers promised and vowed that I should forsake the devil and all his works, the pomps and vanities of this wicked world and all the sinful lusts of the flesh and that I should keep God's holy will and commandment all the days of my life; and when I was young, my father had me bishoped,* thinking thereby to gain a blessing for me. I spent many years in Oxford, where the carriages of the scholars did trouble me in that day, they were so wild. After the best sort of religion and custom of the nation was I brought up; then the Lord drew me to this city, where I applied my heart both evening and morning and at noon day unto reading and hearing the Common Prayer. When there was but one place of worship left in this city, I went to it, and when their books were burned I stood for them, for my heart was wholly joined unto them; and when the King's head was taken off,* my heart and soul was burdened that

I was even weary of my life and the enemy waited to devour me. Then did the Lord take away my hearing that I was deaf as to all teachings of men for a year. Then that faith which I was baptised in did no good, for all that the man and woman had promised and vowed I should do, I could not forsake the pomps and vanities and sinful lusts of the flesh I run into, and they stood always before my eyes. My cry was continually unto the Lord that I might put off that body of death which hindered me from his presence. Then did the Lord carry me to a meeting of the people called Quakers, where I was filled with the dread and power of the Lord and it raised my soul to bear testimony to the truth, and after a little season, the Lord set my sins in order before me and every idle word which I had spoken was brought to my remembrance, where I received a just reward from the Lord and so came to have peace of conscience with my Saviour, which I never could obtain whilst I walked with those people.

Oh my friends, I can truly say, ever since I was a child the witness of God pursued me, and whatever I did, I had no peace in this worship or service which is now in being; it tired and vexed my tender soul to see what a sad estate I was in. But now, glory be to the Lord, I am set at liberty from this vain religion, which never profited me at all; and would you have me to conform to this religion which keepeth the soul in the grave? Nay, I shall never conform unto this worship whilst I have any breath, but shall bear my testimony against it, for I know the powerful God is risen to throw it down and woe be to all that uphold it.

Oh you rulers! Be it known unto you, if you will not do justice and ease the oppressed and set the captives free, the Lord will overturn you and destroy you from being a people, as he hath done in years past; for his sword is in his hand and it will cut you down; unless you do repent ye shall likewise perish.

One warning more to the bishops, priests, deacons, friars and Jesuits.

Oh, woe be unto you, bishops, priests, deacons, friars and Jesuits, and all other officers under you, for the Lord is risen in power, yea, he is risen in dreadful and terrible wrath. Oh I have seen, I have seen this night the dreadful flames which the Lord God will cast you into. Oh, your communion tables which you sacrifice upon unto devils and not unto the living God, your altars which you bow down unto and make an image of, will the dreadful Lord of vengeance overthrow in his fiery indignation; your surplices and tippets and all your loathsome robes which you dress yourselves withal which are like unto a menstrous cloth* before the eye of the pure Jehovah, he will rent them all off, who is the bishop of our souls. Oh you bishops, priests, deacons, friars and Jesuits! Once more will the judge of heaven and earth plead with you because you are a bloodthirsty generation, you are a-building of Zion with blood and Jerusalem with iniquity, as your forefathers did in the days of old. Therefore will the Lord of the harvest cast you in heaps upon heaps as stones in the street and as mire in the highway; the Lord of heaven and earth loathes your worships; your singing and the noise of your organs doth the Lord abhor; and instead of your instruments of music will the Lord make you howl and lament bitterly, in so much that the earth shall be astonished and your downfall shall be so great that nations shall fear and tremble before our God; your communion and union is with devils and unclean spirits and not with the powerful God, which creates a new heaven and a new earth, and this shall you see fulfilled in its time and season, for the Lord hath determined your utter destruction, both Pope and bishops, both root and branch, from off the face of the earth. Oh, it hastens, it hastens, and wrath will not stay.

> In this glorious day, in which Zion is rayed in beauty bright,
> To stand in her strength against this dark night;
> Whose clouds are so many, and sky so dim,
> That Zion's beauty can hardly be seen;
> But the Lord is risen in this his glorious day,
> To sweep bishops, prelates and clouds away.

Babylon's destruction is very near; let all the world fear for ever more.

A few words unto the royal seed, which is chosen of God and separated from the world to do his will for ever.

Oh Friends! Blessed are you of the immortal God, who are centred in the city of refuge, which is made without hands, which indeed is the lot and inheritance of the unspotted lambs, whose hearts are after nothing but the glory of God, which is the crown and cause of rejoicing of his sons and daughters who do inhabit in and about this city, who are come to the church of the first born and to the innumerable company of angels, and to the spirits of just men made perfect. Oh my beloved ones, your life is above this city and denies the vanity of it and it loathes the worship that abounds in it! Oh, it is well with you, for the Lord hath made you up as his jewels and pillars in his house forever! Oh my friends, who do inhabit in and about this city, who are convinced of the abominations and uncleanness that is committed in her, I am moved of the dreadful and terrible God to warn you that you do not join with her spirit, neither in word nor thought, for assuredly the day of her pain and sorrow is at hand, in the which she shall weep bitterly and shall make all astonished who are from the power and life of God. Oh my friends, keep to the power and to the judgements of the just judge, that that eye and thought that would look out at her glory and that would think to sit at ease in her borders, let that be judged and accursed for ever that would have any life below the son of God. Oh my friends, call to mind the years past: how precious and fresh was the love of the Lord in your hearts, when he first visited you in this city? Oh, did you think anything too dear for him? Could you not have laid down your lives for His truth? Were you not glad when you were robbed of your glory and bereaved of your choicest jewels even for the Lord's sake? Oh my friends, I can bear you record in the sight of God, who was a fellow feeler of your integrity and faithfulness unto the lamb.

Oh you tender ones, with whom my soul hath union, keep to that pure and undefiled love, even to the measure of God's grace, that it may teach you continually to deny all things that is of this world and unclean in this city, that you may stand every one in your measures as lights in this dark city, for the Lord of the heavens and the earth hath placed you in and about this city as he hath done the sun, moon and stars, and there you in the firmament are to stand fixed in him, who is the glorious morning star. You must not wander lest you cease to give light in the place where you are set, for remember they that wandered were reserved in chains of darkness until the judgement of the great day which is near at hand, to give unto everyone a just reward.

Oh you beloved friends of God, this I have to say unto you from the mighty God, although you are set as marks for the mighty men to shoot at, and as a byword in the mouth of the beggars, and are reckoned the worst of all people, not worthy to live upon the earth, yet know this: that the covenant of the Lord is made with you and his power and life shall not depart from you nor from your seed for ever more; glory, praises and power eternally be rendered unto the Lord, who reigneth in the heavens, who never altereth, but liveth a God forever. Oh my friends, this is the earnest desire of my soul: that we may keep close unto our maker, even to bear a pure, holy and faithful testimony in our generation against all that do oppose the lamb in this city, as the prophets and apostles and holy martyrs have done in their day against all false gods, worships and worshippers; we have the same spirit to fight against in this city as they had in the world before. Therefore, my companions and fellow sufferers, have we not need to stand up for God's cause, for the which we have, and are called to bear forth our testimony in so deep sufferings as we have come through? And if we are to drink of a deeper cup, yet let us be thankful unto the Lord of the harvest, for it is for the gathering of the exiles unto Abraham's bosom and the poor thirsty souls unto the place of broad rivers. Oh rejoice and give praises unto God on high, who hath begun his work and will finish it in his time. Oh my friends, let us keep clear of this city, let us not taste nor handle any of her works, for her works are vanity and falsehood, the poison of asps* is under her tongue and deceit is in her hands; therefore it is good that we bear a faithful testimony for the most high against this generation and if our lot be to die, and we appointed to be slain for the same, it will be well with us, our souls shall be received into the bosom of the father, where we shall glorify God day and night and shall be free from oppression. Oh dear hearts, be not afraid of the threatenings or proud looks of vain man, which is but like a bubble, he can but kill the body, but cannot kill the soul! Oh, be continually prepared to die that none may be afraid of death when it comes, for it may come suddenly, when ye are asleep, or in the twinkling of an eye! Oh that then the rest which God hath prepared for his people may be entered into, or else misery and pain will be found, which is the reward of the slothful and disobedient! The way of the righteous is life eternal and the path of the just is a burning and a shining light, which our eyes have seen and our hands have handled of the word of life, by which we have been preserved unto this day; and I am certain if thousands of thousands should rise up against us, they shall not prevail, for the Lord the mighty Jehovah is with us and will fight our battle and plead our cause with the mighty ones of the earth; we need do nothing but stand still in God's salvation, which is the saving health of all nations, and will plead with all tongues and kindreds of the earth who do oppose him: and his lambs and babes who walketh in his holy path, which is life to the upright in heart.

Oh, the wisdom, power and glory of the unlimited God, what tongue is able to declare it or what heart can conceal the infiniteness of the riches of the judge of heaven and earth? It even fills the heart with love and life, and overshadows the soul and mind with the glory and beauty of the unspotted lamb, which taketh away the sins of the world. Oh the weight of his glory, I am even swallowed up with the incomprehensibleness of it! Oh the height and depth of it is past finding out by the wisdom of this world! Oh my friends, is not that God amongst us who created Adam in innocency and Eve of the dust of the earth? Did not he cause Abraham to leave the land of his nativity and go into a strange land? And did he not compass him about with strength and power and gave him favour in the sight of the people? And is He not the same God still? Yes, although the earth may wax old and heavens vanish away as smoke and the elements with fervent heat, yet he remains unchangeable who is our head. Oh, what is all the world before him, who is judge of judges and king of kings? It's but as the drop of a bucket in his sight and a thousand years is but as one day with our God. Therefore it is expedient for all friends to watch and wait and pray, lest they enter into temptation. And this have I seen, my beloved friends, this night as from the Lord, that there must be a watching and waiting for the invisible power of the lamb to arise, to move, to pray, to speak and then it will be a pure and a holy sacrifice which the Lord will accept. Oh my friends, let us whilst we have breath sacrifice our sighs, tears and groans, prayers and fastings, upon God's holy altar, that a sweet savour may ascend into the nostrils of the most high God, that so we may receive a blessing from heaven for evermore. And this the Lord hath put into my heart, and I cannot forebear but write, that if any prayeth or speaketh unless in the holy power of the dreadful God amongst us, it is as water spilt upon the ground and it will bring a curse rather than a blessing. The Lord looketh for a holy and clean sacrifice from us, above all the people in the world, because he hath raised up his own life in us and chosen us to be his people, and the lot of his inheritance and the place where his honour dwelleth is with us; and I know sacrifices have been offered by us and is* to this day, which the Lord's soul loves and He doth delight to make us his choice. He is our God and we have none in heaven nor in earth to plead our cause but He, that suffered and laid down His life on earth, but now sits in majesty and glory in the highest heavens, who is our chief leader and guide and doth lead us into his power to meet together and to stand in awe and sin not. And if, friends, we should not meet together, we should sin against God and should miss of His presence, who hath said 'where two or three are met together in my name, there will I be',* saith the Lord. And this is my testimony as a witness to this thing: I never went to any meeting since I knew the truth, even from the first meeting to this day, but I was filled with the living power of the Lord. Oh, the sweet showers that doth descend from the presence of the Lord, and the pleasant rains that falleth from his throne like silver drops; it doth distil upon our hearts whilst we are in our meetings in the name and power of Jesus, who is amongst us and hath raised us and is raising us from the dead and hath and is quickening our mortal bodies, that they may be like unto His glorious body. He hath and doth turn us from darkness to light, from Satan's power to his own. Oh, can we forget or refuse such glorious benefits which we have received from the God of our life in our meetings together? I know my friends you are not unsensible of this great gain: by losing the love of the world, to meet together with the king of heaven and earth, whose presence is better than life. Oh, how hath he opened the sluice of everlasting mercies and love, that it hath poured down from the crown of our head to the sole of our foot, so that we have been washed throughout by the endless goodness of the Lord in our meetings. And this is my mind, and I hope you are and will be of the same with me, and I do believe the Lord will carry me on to the end; I had rather die the cruellest death that ever was or can be devised by man, than to neglect or abstain from meeting together in his name, for I know whoever doth it neglects their own salvation and the day of their visitation. Oh my beloved friends, if we suffer imprisonment or loss of life upon the account of meeting together, let us rejoice, for it is for Christ['s] sake that we are persecuted, for great is our reward in Heaven. Oh, Christ is our meat and drink, he is become our table in the midst of our persecutors, our cup doth overflow; when we are in close prisons, Christ is with us, who cannot be exposed from us by the wrath of wicked men; when we are brought out of prison and had before the rulers, then

Christ goeth along with us and teacheth us what to say. He is a mouth and wisdom and utterance, we take no care what to do; when we are sent back again to prison from the rulers, if it be into a nasty hole or dungeon, our saviour goeth with us and he teacheth us patience and meekness and poureth upon our head and hearts his holy oil, which maketh us sing for joy of heart that he hath counted us worthy to suffer for his name. So my friends, if they fight against us, they fight against God, for God is with us and it is His cause we stand for and suffer in goods, body and spirit. And therefore, seeing it is so weighty a thing that we lie at stake for, we value not what men or devils, spirits or angels can do unto us, for our hearts and spirits are firmly fixed upon the Lord and his cause, and for meeting together as long as we are moved of the Lord, the which will be, I hope, as long as we have breath. Oh all you my friends who are young and tender, and all you who are looking abroad to see what will become of us and cannot join with us because of persecution, have a care; I warn you in the presence of the dreadful God, stand not in that slippery place, lest the day of mercy pass over you whilst you stand gazing and repentance be hid from your eyes; then would you give the whole world, if you had it, for one hour to repent it, but then it will be too late. Therefore I beseech you not to look at us, but to mind your own salvation and what the Lord saith unto you by his witness in you, for everyone in the day of God's account shall answer for himself and receive a reward according to their works; the Lord is no respecter of persons: the king as well as the beggar shall know the stroke of God's hand, when the book of conscience is opened wherein their sins are written as with the point of a diamond, and I know that there is nothing can blot them out but the blood of the lamb; and therefore do we utterly deny and abhor any pardons from the bishops, for I know they cannot pardon themselves, not keep their own soul alive; our confidence is in God, who hath tried our reins and searched our hearts by His living power. Glory everlasting shall be given unto the higher power, to whom our souls are subject and in whom we live and shall do, world without end.

O Zion's king, thy beauty bright
Hath filled our hearts with great delight;
Thy city pure our eye doth see,
In which alone dwells purity.

Oh rejoice ye saints of Zion all
For God hath saved you from the fall;
It's no matter if our bodies die,
Our souls shall live eternally
With God, who ruleth in the heavens high.

A city pure God hath prepared for us,
When our enemies hath laid us in the dust.
Thy day and beauty doth declare
An open war with sin and sinner
Who doth thy name defame.

O Lord, unto the glorious name all knees shall bow
Of things in heaven and things below,
Thy seed royal, that glorious plant,
Which thou into the world hath sent
A light, is content with punishment
From sinners' hands, who like iron bands
Against thy own seed stands,
Their hearts is* bent, with full consent, thy seed to rent.
O Lord, thy seed to heaven doth cry for delivery
In this day of perplexity;
Thou righteous judge, thy suffering lambs in prisons lie
Until they die for thy testimony,
Which shall remain when all is slain,
Which doth increase our joy and peace.
Oh blessed be the day our sins were washed away
And we set free to follow thee
From the gulf of misery, who art a God of purity.
O Lord we will serve thee whilst we have breath
For thou art judge of heaven and earth,
Honour and glory is thine alone
And be it rendered to thee for ever more.

MARGARET CAVENDISH
(1623–1673)

'A World Made by Atoms'*

Small atoms of themselves a world may make,
For being subtle, every shape they take;
And as they dance about, they places find,
Of forms that best agree, make every kind.
For when we build an house of brick, or stone
We lay them even, every one by one:
And when we find a gap that's big, or small,
We seek out stones to fit that place withal.
For when as they too big, or little be,
They fall away, and cannot stay, we see;
So atoms, as they dance, find places fit,
And there remaining close and fast will knit.
Those which not fit the rest that rove about,
Do never leave, until they thrust them out.
Thus by their forms and motions they will be
Like workmen, which amongst themselves agree
And so, by chance, may a new world create:
Or else predestinate, may work by fate.

'Of the Ant'

Mark but the little ant, how she doth run,
In what a busy motion she goes on:
As if she ordered all the world's affairs,
When 'tis but only one small straw she bears.
And when a fly doth on the ground lie dead
Lord, how they stir; how full is every head!
Some it along with feet and mouths do trail
And some thrust on with shoulder and with tail.
And if a stranger ant comes on that way,
She helps them straight, ne'er asketh if she may,

Nor stays to have rewards, but is well pleased:
T'have labour for her pains, so they be eased.
They live as the Lacedemonians* did,
All is common, nothing is forbid.
No private feast, but all together meet,
And wholesome food, though plain, in public eat.
They have no envy, all ambition's down,
There is neither superior nor clown.
No palaces for pride erect they will,
Their house is common, called the ants' hill.
All help to build, and keep it in repair
No special workmen, but all labourers are;
No markets kept, no meat have they to sell
But what each eats, all welcome are, and well.
No jealousy, each takes his neighbour's wife,
Without offence, which never breedeth strife.
They fight no duels, nor do give the lie,*
Their greatest honour is to live, not die.
For they, to keep up life, through dangers venture
To get provisions in against the Winter,
But many lose their life, as chance doth fall
None is perpetual, death devoureth all.

'The Hunting of the Hare'

Betwixt two ridges of plowed land sat Wat
Whose body pressed to th'earth, lay close and squat
His nose upon his two fore-feet did lie,
With his grey eyes he glared obliquely;
His head he always set against the wind;
His tail when turned, his hair blew up behind,
And made him to get cold; but he being wise
Doth keep his coat still down, so warm he lies.
Thus rests he all the day, till th'sun doth set,
Then up he riseth his relief to get,
And walks about until the sun doth rise,
Then coming back in's former posture lies.
At last, poor Wat was found as he there lay,
By huntsmen, which came with their dogs that way.

Whom seeing, he got up, and fast did run,
Hoping some ways the cruel dogs to shun
But they by nature had so quick a scent,
That by their nose they traced what way he went
And with their deep, wide mouths set forth a cry
Which answered was by echo in the sky.
Then Wat was struck with terror, and with fear,
Seeing each shadow thought the dogs were there,
And running out some distance from their cry
To hide himself, his thoughts he did employ;
Under a clod of earth in sand-pit wide,
Poor Wat sat close, hoping himself to hide.
There long he had not been but straight in's ears
The winding horns, and crying dogs he hears:
Then starting up with fear, he leaped, and such
Swift speed he made, the ground he scarce did touch;
Into a great thick wood straightways he got
And underneath a broken bough he sat.
Where every leaf that with the wind did shake,
Brought him such terror that his heart did ache.
That place he left, to champain* plains he went
Winding about, for to deceive their scent.
And while they snuffling were, to find his track,
Poor Wat, being weary, his swift pace did slack.
On his two hinder legs for ease he sat
His fore-feet rubbed his face from dust, and sweat,
Licking his feet, he wiped his ears so clean,
That none could tell that Wat had hunted been.
But casting round about his fair, grey eyes,
The hounds in full career he near him 'spies;
To Wat it was so terrible a sight;
Fear gave him wings and made his body light.
Though he was tired before, by running long,
Yet now his breath he never felt more strong.
Like those that dying are, think health returns,
When 'tis but a faint blast, which life out burns.
For spirits seek to guard the heart about,
Striving with death, but death doth quench them out.
The hounds so fast came on, and with such cry,

That he no hopes had left, nor help could spy;
With that the winds did pity poor Wat's case,
And with their breath the scent blew from that place,
Then every nose was busily employed
And every nostril was set open, wide,
And every head did seek a several way,
To find the grass, or track where the scent lay
For witty industry is never slack,
'Tis like to witchcraft, and brings lost things back.
But though the wind had tied the scent up close,
A busy dog thrust in his snuffling nose:
And drew it out, with that did foremost run,
Then horns blew loud, th'rest to follow on.
The great, slow hounds, their throats did set a base,
The fleet, swift hounds, as tenors next in place;
The little beagles did a treble sing,
And through the air, their voices round did ring,
Which made a consort, as they ran along;
That, had they spoken words, 't had been a song;
The horns kept time, the men did shout for joy,
And seemed most valiant, poor Wat to destroy;
Spurring their horses to a full career
Swum rivers deep, leaped ditches without fear;
Endangered life, and limbs, so fast they'd ride,
Only to see how patiently Wat died;
At last the dogs so near his heels did get,
That their sharp teeth they in his breech did set.
Then tumbling down, he fell with weeping eyes,
Gave up his ghost, and thus poor Wat he dies.
Men whooping loud, such acclamations made,
As if the Devil they imprisoned had,
When they but did a shiftless creature kill;
To hunt there needs no valiant soldier's skill.
But men do think that exercise, and toil,
To keep their health, is best, which makes most spoil.
Thinking that food, and nourishment so good,
Which doth proceed from others' flesh, and blood.
When they do lions, wolves, bears, tigers see,
Kill silly sheep, they say they cruel be.

But for themselves all creatures think too few,
For luxury, wish God would make more new.
As if God did make creatures for man's meat,
And gave them life, and sense, for man to eat;
Or else for sport, or recreation's sake,
For to destroy those lives that God did make,
Making their stomachs graves, which full they fill,
With murdered bodies, that in sport they kill.
Yet man doth think himself so gentle and mild,
When of all creatures he's most cruel, wild,
Nay, so proud, that he only thinks to live,
That God a God-like nature him did give.
And that all creatures for his sake alone
Were made for him to tyrannise upon.

Bell in Campo (1662)

THE ACTORS NAMES

The Lord General.
Seigneur Valeroso.
Monsieur la Hardy.
Monsieur Companion.
Monsieur Comrade.
Monsieur la Gravity.
Captain Ruffle.
Captain Whiffle, and several other Gentlemen.
Doctor Educature.
Doctor Comfort.
Stewards, Messengers and Servants.

Lady Victoria.
Madam Jantil.
Madam Passionate.
Madam Ruffle.
Madam Whiffle.
Doll Pacify, Madam Passionate's Maid.
Nell Careless, Madam Jantil's Maid, other
Servants and Heroicesses.

The First Part of Bell in Campo.

ACT I SCENE I

Enter two Gentlemen.

1 Gent. You hear how this kingdom of Reformation* is preparing for war against the kingdom of Faction.

2 Gent. Yea, for I hear the kingdom of Faction resolves to war with this kingdom of Reformation.

1 Gent. 'Tis true, for there are great preparations of either side, men are raised of all sorts and ages fit to bear arms, and of all degrees to command and obey, and there is one of the gallantest and noblest persons in this kingdom, which is made general to command in chief, for he is a man that is both valiant and well experienced in wars, temperate and just in peace, wise and politic in public affairs, careful and prudent in his own family, and a most generous person.

2 Gent. Indeed I have heard that he is a most excellent soldier.

1 Gent. He is so, for he is not one that sets forth to the wars with great resolutions and hopes, and returns with maskered* fears, and despairs; neither is he like those that take more care, and are more industrious to get gay clothes, and fine feathers, to flaunt in the field, and vapour in their march, than to get useful and necessary provision; but before he will march, he will have all things ready, and proper for use, as to fit himself with well-tempered arms, which are light to be worn, yet musket proof; for he means not to run away, nor to yield his life upon easy terms unto his enemy, for he desires to conquer, and not vain-gloriously to show his courage by a careless neglect or a vain carelessness; also he chooses such horses as are useful in war, such as have been made subject to the hand and heel, that have been taught to trot on the haunches, to change, to gallop, to stop, and such horses* as have spirit and strength, yet quiet and sober natures; he regards more the goodness of the horses than the colours or marks, and more the fitness of his saddles than the embroidery; also he takes more care that his wagons should be easy to follow, and light in their carriage, than to have them painted and gilded; and he takes greater care that his tents should be made, so as to be suddenly put up, and as quickly pulled down, than for the setting and embroidering his arms thereupon; also he takes more care to have useful servants than numerous servants; and as he is industrious and careful for his particular affairs, so he is for the general affairs.

2 Gent. A good soldier makes good preparations, and a good general doth both for himself and army; and as the general hath showed himself a good soldier by the preparations he had made to march, so he hath shown himself a wise man by the settlement he hath made, in what he hath to leave behind him; for I hear he hath settled and ordered his house and family.

1 Gent. He hath so, and he hath a fair young and virtuous lady that he must leave behind him, which cannot choose but trouble him.

2 Gent. The wisest man that is, cannot order or have all things to his own contentment.

Exeunt.

SCENE 2

Enter the Lord General, and the Lady Victoria his wife.

General. My dear heart, you know I am commanded to the wars, and had I not such [a] wife as you are, I should have thought fortune had done me a favour to employ my life in heroical actions for the service of my country, or to give me an honourable death, but to leave you is such a cross as my nature sinks under; but wheresoever you are, there will be my life, I shall only carry a body which may fight, but my soul and all the powers thereof will remain with thee.

Lady Victoria. Husband, I shall take this expression of love but for feigning words, if you leave me; for 'tis against nature to part with that we love best, unless it be for the beloved's preservation, which cannot be mine, for my life lives in yours, and the comfort of that life in your company.

Lord General. I know you love me so well, as you had rather part with my life than I should part from my honour.

Lady Victoria. 'Tis true, my love persuades me so to do, knowing fame is a double life, as infamy is a double death; nay I should persuade you to those actions, were they never so dangerous, were you unwilling thereunto, or could they create a world of honour, fully inhabited with praises; but I would not willingly part with your life for an imaginary or supposed honour, which dies in the womb before it is born; thus I love you the best, preferring the best of what is yours, but I am but in the second place in your affections, for you prefer your honour before me; 'tis true, it is the better choice, but it shows I am not the best beloved, which makes you follow and glue to that and leave me.

Lord General. Certainly wife, my honour is your honour, and your honour will be buried in my disgrace, which Heaven avert; for I prefer yours before my own, insomuch as I would have your honour to be the crown of my glory.

Lady Victoria. Then I must partake of your actions, and go along with you.

Lord General. What, to the wars?

Lady Victoria. To any place where you are.

Lord General. But wife, you consider not, as that long marches, ill lodgings, much watching, cold nights, scorching days, hunger and danger are ill companions for ladies: their acquaintance displeases; their conversation is rough and rude, being too boisterous for ladies; their tender and strengthless constitutions cannot encounter nor grapple therewith.

Lady Victoria. 'Tis said, that love overcomes all things: in your company, long marches will be but as a breathing walk, the hard ground feel as a feather-bed, and the starry sky a spangled canopy, hot days a stove to cure cold agues, hunger as fasting days or an eve to devotion, and danger is honour's triumphant chariot.

Lord General. But nature hath made women like china, or porcelain: they must be used gently, and kept warily, or they will break and fall on death's head; besides, the inconveniencies in an army are so many, as put patience herself out of humour; besides, there is such inconveniences as modesty cannot allow of.

Lady Victoria. There is no immodesty in natural effects, but in unnatural abuses; but contrive it as well as you can, for go I must, or either I shall die, or dishonour you; for if I stay behind you, the very imaginations of your danger will torture me, sad dreams will affright me, every little noise will sound as your passing bell, and my fearful mind will transform every object like as your pale ghost, until I am smothered in my sighs, shrouded in my tears, and buried in my griefs; for whatsoever is joined with true love, will die absented, or else their love will die, for love and life are joined together; as for the honour of constancy, or constant fidelity, or the dishonour of inconstancy, the lovingest and best wife in all story that is recorded to be, the most perfectest and constantest wife in her husband's absence was Penelope, Ulysses' wife, yet she did not barricado* her ears from love's soft alarms, but parleyed and received amorous treaties, and made a truce until she and her lovers could agree and conclude upon conditions, and questionless there were amorous glances shot from loving eyes of either party; and though the siege of her chastity held out, yet her husband's wealth and estate was impoverished, and great riots committed both in his family and kingdom, and her suitors had absolute power thereof; thus though she kept the fort of her chastity, she lost the kingdom, which was her husband's estate and government, which was a dishonour both to her and her husband; so if you let me stay behind you, it will be a thousand to one but either you will lose me in death, or your honour in life, where if you let me go you will save both; for if you will consider and reckon all the married women you have heard or read of, that were absented from their husbands, although upon just and necessary occasions, but had some ink of aspersions flung upon them, although their wives were old, ill favoured, decrepit and diseased women, or were they as pure as light, or as innocent as Heaven; and wheresoever this ink of aspersion is thrown, it sticks so fast, that the spots are never rubbed out; should it fall on saints, they must wear the marks as a badge of misfortunes, and what man had not better be thought or called an uxorious husband, than to be despised and laughed at, as being but thought a cuckold?* The first only expresses a tender and noble nature, the second sounds as a base, cowardly, poor dejected, forsaken creature; and as for the immodesty you mentioned, there is none, for there can be no breach of modesty, but in unlawful actions, or at least unnecessary ones; but what law can warrant, and necessity doth enforce, is allowable amongst men, pure before angels, religious before gods, when unchoosing persons, improper places, unfit times, condemn those actions that are good in themselves, make them appear base to men, hateful to angels, and wicked to gods, and what is more lawful, fitting, and proper, than for a man and wife to be inseparable together?

Lord General. Well, you have used so much rhetoric to persuade, as you have left me none to deny you, wherefore I am resolved you shall try what your tender sex can endure; but I believe when you hear the bullets fly about you, you will wish yourself at home, and repent your rash adventure.

Lady Victoria. I must prove false first, for love doth give me courage.

Lord General. Then come along, I shall your courage try.

Lady Victoria. I'll follow you, though in death's arms I lie.

Exeunt.

SCENE 3

Enter the two former Gentlemen.

1 Gent. Well met, for I was going to thy lodging to call thee to make up the company of good fellows, which hath appointed a meeting.

2 Gent. Faith you must go with the odd number, or get another in my room, for I am going about some affairs which the Lord General hath employed me in.

1 Gent. I perceive by thee that public employments spoil private meetings.

2 Gent. You say right, for if everyone had good employment, vice would be out of fashion.

1 Gent. What do you call vice?

2 Gent. Drinking, wenching, and gaming.

1 Gent. As for two of them, as drinking and wenching, especially wenching, no employment can abolish them, no, not the most severest, devotest, nor dangerest: for the statesman divines, and soldiers, which are the most and greatest employed, will leave all other affairs to kiss a mistress.

2 Gent. But you would have me go to a tavern and not to a mistress.

1 Gent. Why, you may have a mistress in a tavern if you please.

2 Gent. Well, if my other affairs will give me any leisure, I will come to you.

Exeunt.

SCENE 4

Enter four or five other Gentlemen.

1 Gent. The Lord General was accounted a discreet and wise man, but he shows but little wisdom in this action of carrying his wife along with him to the wars, to be a clog at his heels, a chain to his hands, an encumbrance in his march, obstruction in his way; for she will be always puling and sick, and whining, and crying, and tired, and froward, and if her dog should be left in any place, as being forgotten, all the whole army must make a halt whilst the dog is fetched, and trooper after trooper must be sent to bring intelligence of the dog's coming, but if there were such a misfortune that the dog could not be found, the whole army must be dispersed for the search of it, and if it should be lost, then there must seem to be more lamentation for it than if the enemy had given us an entire defeat, or else we shall have frowns instead of preferments.

2 Gent. The truth is, I wonder the General will trouble himself with his wife, when it is the only time a married man hath to enjoy a mistress without jealousy, a sprightly sound wench, that may go along without trouble, with bag and baggage, to wash his linen, and make his field bed, and attend to his call, when a wife requires more attendance than sentries to watch the enemy.

3 Gent. For my part I wonder as much that any man should be so fond of his wife as to carry her with him; for I am only glad of the wars because I have a good pretence to leave my wife behind me; besides, an army is a quiet, solitary place, and yields a man a peaceable life compared to that at home: for what with the faction and mutiny amongst his servants, and the noise the women make, for their tongues like as an alarm beat up quarters in every corner of the house, that a man can take no rest; besides every day he hath a set battle with his wife, and from the army of her angry thoughts, she sends forth such volleys of words with her gunpowder anger, and the fire of her fury, as breaks all the ranks and files of content, and puts happiness to an utter rout, so as for my part I am forced to run away in discontent, although some husbands will stay, and fight for the victory.

4 Gent. Gentlemen, gentlemen, pray condemn not a man for taking his lawful delight, or for ordering his private affairs to his own humour: every man is free to himself, and to what is his, as long as he disturbs not his neighbours, nor breaks the peace of the kingdom, nor disorders the commonwealth, but submits to the laws and obeys the magistrates without dispute; besides gentlemen, 'tis no crime nor wonder, for a man to let his wife go along with him when he goeth to the wars, for there hath been examples; for Pompey had a wife with him, and so had Germanicus, and so had many great and worthy heroics, and as for Alexander the Great he had a wife or two with him; besides, in many nations men are not only desired, but commanded by the chiefs to let their wives go with them, and it hath been a practice by long custom, for women to be spectators in their battles, to encourage their fights, and so give fire to their spirits; also to attend them in their sicknesses, to cleanse their wounds, to dress their meat; and who is fitter than a wife? What other woman will be so lovingly careful, and industriously helpful as a wife? And if the Greeks had not left their wives behind them, but had carried them along to the Trojan wars, they would not have found such disorders as they did at their return, nor had such bad welcome home, as witness Agamemnon's;* besides, there have been many women that have not only been spectators, but actors, leading armies, and directing battles with good success, and there have been so many of these heroics, as it would be tedious at this time to recount; besides the examples of women's courage in death, as also their wise conduct, and valiant actions in wars are many, and pray give me leave to speak without your being offended thereat, it is not noble, nor the part of a gentleman, to censure, condemn, or dispraise another man's private actions, which nothing concerns him, especially when there is so gallant a subject to discourse of as the discipline and actions of these wars we are entering into.

1 Gent. In troth Sir, you have instructed us so well, and have chid us so handsomely, as we are sorry for our error, and ask pardon for our fault, and our repentance shall be known by that we will never censure so again.

Exeunt.

ACT II SCENE 5

Enter Captain Whiffle and Madam Whiffle his Wife.

Captain Whiffle. I have heard our General's lady goeth with the General her husband to the wars, wherefore I think it fit for the rest of the commanders, if it were only for policy, to let our General see that we approve of his actions so well, as to imitate him in ours, carrying our wives along with us; besides the General's lady cannot choose but take it kindly to have our wives wait upon her. Wherefore wife, it is fit you should go.

Madam Whiffle. Alas husband, I am so tender, that I am apt to catch cold if the least puff of wind do but blow upon me; wherefore to lie in the open fields will kill me the first night; if not, the very journey will shatter my small bones to pieces.

Captain Whiffle. Why, our General's lady is a very fine young lady, and she ventures to go.

Madam Whiffle. There let her venture, for you must excuse me, for I will stay at home, go you where you please.

Captain Whiffle. Well wife, consider it.

Exeunt.

SCENE 6

Enter Captain Ruffle, and his wife Madam Ruffle.

Captain Ruffle. Wife, prepare your self to follow the army, for 'tis now the fashion for wives to march, wherefore pack up and away.

Madam Ruffle. What, with a knapsack behind me as your trull?* Not I, for I will not disquiet my rest with inconveniences, nor divert my pleasures with troubles, nor be affrighted with the roaring cannons, nor endanger my life with every potgun, nor be frozen up with cold, nor stewed to a jelly with heat, nor be powdered up with dust, until I come to be as dry as a neats-tongue;* besides, I will not venture my complexion to the wrath of the sun, which will tan me like a sheep's skin.

Captain Ruffle. Faith wife, if you will not go, I will have a laundry-maid to ride in my wagon, and lie in my tent.

Madam Ruffle. Prithee husband, take thy kitchen maid along too, for she may have as much grease about her as will serve to make soap to wash your linen with, and while you ride with your laundry-maid in your wagon, I will ride with my gentleman-usher in my coach.

Captain Ruffle. Why wife, it is out of love that I would have thee go.

Madam Ruffle. And 'tis out of love that I will stay at home; besides, do you think I mean to follow your General's lady as a common trooper doth a commander, to feed upon her reversions, to wait for her favour, to watch for a smile; no, no, I will be a generalissimo myself at home, and distribute my colours to be carried in the hats of those that will fight in my quarrel, to keep or gain the victory of my favour and love.

Captain Ruffle. So I may chance to be a cuckold before I return home.

Madam Ruffle. You must trust to fortune for that, and so I wish you a good journey.

SCENE 7

*Enter Seigneur Valeroso and his friend Monsieur la Hardy, to take their leaves of their Wives, Madam Jantil, and Madam Passionate, Madam Jantil young and beautiful, Madam Passionate in years.**

Madam Jantil. I cannot choose but take it unkindly that you will go without me; do you mistrust my affection, as that I have not as much love for you as the General's lady hath for her husband, or do you desire to leave me because you would take a mistress along with you, one that perchance hath more beauty than you think me to have, with whom you may securely and freely sit in your tent, and gaze upon, or one that hath more wit than I, whose sweet, smooth, and flattering words may charm your thoughts and draw your soul out of your ears to sit upon her lips, or dancing with delight upon her tongue?

Seigneur Valeroso. Prithee wife, be not jealous, I vow to Heaven no other beauty can attract my eyes but thine, nor any sound can please my brain, but what thy charming tongue sends in; besides, I prize not what thy body is, but how thy soul's adorned. Thy virtue would make me think thee fair, although thou wert deformed, and wittier far than Mercury, hadst thou Midas's ears, but thou hast all that man can wish of women kind and that is the reason I will leave thee safe at home; for I am loath to venture all my wealth and happiness in Fortune's unconstant barque,* suffering thy tender youth and sex to float on the rough waves of chance, where dangers like Northern winds blow high, and who can know but that fatal gusts may come, and overwhelm thee, and drown all my joys? Wherefore, for my sake, keep thyself safe at home.

Madam Jantil. I shall obey you, but yet I think it were not well I should be a long time from you, and at a great distance.

Seigneur Valeroso. I will promise you, if I perceive the war is like to be prolonged, and that there be garrison-towns so safe as you may securely live in, I will send for you, placing you so where sometimes I may visit you,

Madam Jantil. Pray do not forget me so much as to cancel your promise.

Seigneur Valeroso. Forget thee, sweet? I should sooner forget life, and if I do whilst I have memory, Heaven forget me.

Madam Jantil. I must ask you a question, which is to know why you will take an under-command, being so nobly born, and bearing a high title of honour yourself, and being master of a great estate?

Seigneur Valeroso. To let the world see my courage is above my birth, wealth, or pride, and that I prefer inward worth before outward title, and I had rather give my life to the enemy on honourable terms, than basely to stay at home in time of general wars, out of an ambitious discontent: for valour had rather have dangers to fight with, than offices to command in.

Seigneur Valeroso and his lady whispers, while the other two, Monsieur la Hardy and his Lady speaks.

Madam Passionate. Why should you go to the wars now you are in years, and not so fit for action as those that are young, and have their strengths about them? Besides, we have lived a married pair above these thirty years, and never parted, and shall we now be separated when we are old?

She weeps.

Monsieur la Hardy. Alas wife, what would you have me do? When I am commanded out I must obey; besides, I would not have my country fight a battle whilst I live, and I not make one, for all the world, for when I cannot fight, my body shall serve to stop a breach; wherefore leave your crying wife, and fall to praying for our safe return, and here my noble friend is desirous you should stay with his lady to comfort one another, and to divert melancholy and the longing hours of our return.

Madam Passionate. Farewell, I fear I shall never see you again, for your absence will soon kill me.

She cries.

Exeunt.

SCENE 8

Enter two Gentlemen.

1 Gent. O you are welcome from the army, what news?

2 Gent. Why our army marched until they came unto the frontiers of the kingdom, where they found the army of the enemy ready to encounter them. The Lord General, seeing they must of necessity fight a battle, thought best to call a council of war, that there might be nothing of ill conduct laid to his charge, but that all might be ordered by a wise and experienced council, whereupon he made an election of counsellors, joining together three sorts, as grave, wise, and prudent men, subtle and politic men, and valiant, skilful martial men, that the cold temper of the prudent, might allay the hot temper of the valiant, and that the politic might be as ingenious to serve them together by subtle devises, and to make traps of stratagems to catch in the enemy; and at this council many debates there were, but at last they did conclude a battle must be fought; but first they did decree that all the women should be sent into one of their garrison towns, some two days' journey from the army. The reasons were, that if they should be overcome by their enemies, the women might be taken by their enemies, and made slaves, using or abusing them as they pleased;

but when the women were sent away, they did not shed tears of sorrow, but sent such volleys of angry words as wounded many men's hearts; but when they were almost at the town that was to be their abode, the General's lady was so extremely incensed against the counsellors, by reason they decreed her departure with the others, as she strove to raise up the spirits of the rest of her sex to the height of her own; but what the issue will be I know not.

1 Gent. Have you been with the King?

2 Gent. Yes, I was sent to give him an account of the army.

Exeunt

SCENE 9

Enter the Lady Victoria and a number of women of all sorts with her; she takes her stand upon a heap of green turfs, as being in the fields before the garrison town, and then speaks to those women.

Lady Victoria. Most heroical spirits of most chaste and loving wives, mistresses, sisters, children or friends, I know you came not from your several houses and homes into this army merely to enjoy your husbands, lovers, parents and friends in their safe and secure garrisons, or only to share of their troublesome and tedious marches, but to venture also in their dangerous and cruel battles, to run their fortunes, and to force destiny to join you to their periods;* but the masculine sex hath separated us, and cast us out of their companies, either out of their loving care and desire of preserving our lives and liberties, lest we might be destroyed in their confusions, or taken prisoners in their loss, or else it must be out of jealousy we should eclipse the fame of their valours with the splendour of our constancy; and if it be love, let us never give the pre-eminence, for then we should lose that prerogative that belongs to the crown of our sex; and if it be through jealous mistrust of their fame, it were poor for us to submit and quit that unto men, that men will not unto us, for fame makes us like the gods, to live for ever; besides, those women that have stayed at home will laugh at us in our return, and their effeminate lovers and carpet knights,* that cowardly and luxuriously coin excuses to keep and stay them from the wars, will make lampoons* of us for them to sing of our disgrace, saying, our husbands, lovers and friends were so weary of us, as they were forced to take that pretence of affectionate love to be rid of our companies; wherefore if you will take my advice, let us return, and force those that sent us away to consent that we shall be partakers with them, and either win them by persuasions, or lose ourselves by breaking their decrees; for it were better we should die by their angry frowns, than by the tongue of infamy.

All the women call to her.

All the women. Let us return, let us return!

Lady Victoria waves her hand to them to keep silence.

Lady Victoria. Noble Heroicesses, I am glad to hear you speak all as with one voice and tongue, which shows your minds are joined together, as in one piece, without seam or rent; but let us not return unfit to do them service, so we may cause their ruin by obstruction, which will wound us more than can their anger; wherefore let us strive by our industry to render ourselves useful to their service.

All the women. Propound the way, and set the rules, and we will walk in the one, and keep strictly to the other.

Lady Victoria. Then thus: we have a body of about five or six thousand women, which came along with some thirty thousand men, but since we came, we are not only thought unuseful, but troublesome, which is the reason we were sent away, for the masculine sex is of an opinion we are only fit to breed and bring forth children, but otherwise a trouble in a commonwealth, for though we increase the commonwealth by our breed, we encumber it by our weakness, as they think, as by our incapacities, as having no ingenuity for inventions, nor subtle wit for politicians; nor prudence for direction, nor industry for execution; nor patience for opportunity, nor judgment for counsellors, nor secrecy for trust; nor method to keep peace, nor courage to make war, nor strength to defend our selves or country, or to assault an enemy; also that we have not the wisdom to govern a commonwealth, and that we are too partial to sit in the seat of justice, and too pitiful to execute rigorous authority when it is needful, and the reason of those erroneous opinions of the masculine sex to the effeminate, is, that our bodies seem weak, being delicate and beautiful, and our minds seem fearful, being compassionate and gentle-natured, but if we were both weak and fearful, as they imagine us to be, yet custom, which is a second nature, will encourage the one and strengthen the other, and had our educations been answerable to theirs, we might have proved as good soldiers and privy counsellors, rulers and commanders, navigators and architectors, and as learned scholars both in arts and sciences, as men are; for time and custom is the father and mother of strength and knowledge, they make all things easy and facil, clear and propitious; they bring acquaintance, and make friendship of every thing; they make courage and fear, strength and weakness, difficulty and facility, dangers and securities, labours and recreations, life and death, all to take and shake as it were hands together; wherefore if we would but accustom ourselves we may do such actions as may gain us such a reputation, as men might change their opinions, insomuch as to believe we are fit to be copartners in their governments, and to help to rule the world, where now we are kept as slaves forced to obey; wherefore let us make ourselves free, either by force, merit, or love, and in order, let us practise and endeavour, and take that which fortune shall proffer unto us, let us practise I say, and make these fields as schools of martial arts and sciences, so shall we become learned in their disciplines of war, and if you please to make me your tutoress, and so your Generalless, I shall take the power and command from your election and authority, otherwise I shall most willingly, humbly, and obediently submit to those whom you shall choose.

All the women. You shall be our Generalless, or instructress, ruler and commanderess, and we will every one in particular, swear to obey all your commands, to submit and yield to your punishments, to strive and endeavour to merit your rewards.

Lady Victoria. Then worthy heroicesses, give me leave to set the laws and rules I would have you keep and observe, in a brass tablet.

All. We agree and consent to whatsoever you please. [*Exeunt*]

SCENE 10

Enter the Lady Jantil alone.

Madam Jantil. How painful is true love absented from what is loved, 'tis strange that that which pleaseth most should be the greatest torment.

Enter Madam Passionate.

Madam Passionate. What, all times walking by yourself alone? When your lord returns I will complain, and tell him what dull company you are.

Madam Jantil. I hope I shall not be from him so long, for he promised to send for me.

Madam Passionate. Nay faith, when you go, as old as I am, I will travel with you to see my husband too.

Madam Jantil. You will be so much the more welcome, by how much you were unexpected.

Madam Passionate. You look pale on the sudden, are not you well?

Madam Jantil. Yes, only on a sudden I had a chill of cold that seized my spirits.

Madam Passionate. Beshrew me, their coldness hath nipped the blood out of your cheeks and lips.

Madam Jantil. If they had been painted, they would have kept their colour.

Exeunt.

ACT III SCENE II

Enter the Lady Victoria with a great company of women, after a table of brass carried before her. She stands upon the heap of turfs, and another woman that carried the table, wherein the laws and rules are inscribed; she bids her read them.

Reader. Noble Heroics, these are the laws our Generalless hath caused to be inscribed and read for every one to observe and keep.

First, be it known, observed and practised, that no woman that is able to bear arms, shall go unarmed, having arms to wear, but shall wear them at all times, but when they put them off to change their linen; they shall sleep, eat and rest, and march with them on their bodies.

Lady Victoria. Give me leave, noble heroics, to declare the reason of this law or command, as to wear an iron or steel habit, and to be constantly worn, is, that your arms should not feel heavy, or be troublesome or painful for want of use, as they will be when you shall have an occasion to put them on; and certainly, for want of practice, more masculine soldiers are overcome by their arms, than by their enemies, for the unaccustomedness makes them so unwieldy, as they can neither defend themselves, nor assault their foes, whereas custom will make them feel as light as their skins on their flesh, or their flesh on their bones; nay custom hath that force, as they will feel as if their bodies were naked whenas their arms are off, and as custom makes the cold and piercing air to have no power over the naked bodies of men, for in cold countries as well as hot men have been accustomed to go naked, and have felt no more harm, nor so much, by the cold, than those that are warmly clothed, so custom will make your arms seem as light as if you had none on, when for want of use their weight will seem heavy, their several pieces troublesome and incombersome, as their gorgets will seem to press down their shoulders, their back and breast-plates and the rest of the several pieces to cut their waist, to pinch their body, to bind their thighs, to tie their arms, and their headpiece to hinder their breath, to darken their sight, and to stop their hearing, and all for want of use and custom. But enough of this, read on.

Reader. Secondly, be it known, observed and practised, that every company must watch by turns, whether they have enemies near or no, and at all times, and whosoever drinks anything but water, or eats anything but bread, all the time they are on the watch, shall be punished with fasting.

Lady Victoria. Give me leave to declare the reason of this law: the reason is, that strong drinks and nourishing meats send many vapours to the brain, which vapours are like several keys, which lock up the senses so fast, as neither loud noises, bright lights, nor strong scents can enter either at the ears, eyes, or nostrils, insomuch as many times their enemies send death to break them asunder.

Reader. Thirdly, be it known, observed and practised, that none of the troopers march over corn fields if it can be avoided, unless the Enemy should be behind, and then the more spoil the better.

Lady Victoria. The reason of this is, that it were a great imprudence to destroy through a careless march of horse and foot, that which would serve to feed and nourish us in the Winter time, and in our Winter quarters, when it is laid in the barns and granaries, by the labour and the industry of the farmers.

Reader. Fourthly, be it known, observed and practised, that none shall plunder those things which are weighty of carriage, unless it be for safety or necessity.

Lady Victoria. The reason is of this, that all that is heavy in the carriage is a hindrance in our march.

Reader. Fifthly, be it known, observed and practised, that no soldiers shall play at any game for money or drink, but only for meat to eat.

Lady Victoria. The reason of is this, that those that play for drink, the winners will be drunk, and those that are drunk are unfit for service; besides, many disorders are caused by drunkenness; and to play for money, the losers grow choleric, and quarrels proceed therefrom, which quarrels many times cause great mutinies through their side-taking,* and factious parties; besides, having lost their money and not their appetites, they become weak and faint for want of that nourishing food their money should get them, having nothing left to buy them victuals withal; besides, it forces them to forage further about, where by straggling far from the body of the army, they are subject to be catched by the enemy, but when they play for meat their winnings nourish their bodies, making them strong and vigorous, and when their appetites are satisfied, and their stomachs are filled, their humours are pleasant, and their minds courageous; besides, it is the nature of most creatures, either to distribute or at least to leave the remaining pieces to the next takers, so that the losers may have a share with the winners, and part of what was their own again.

Reader. Sixthly, be it known, observed and practised, that no captains or colonels, shall advance beyond their company, troop, regiment or brigade, but keep in the middle of the first rank, and the lieutenant, or lieutenant colonel to come behind in the last rank.

Lady Victoria. The reason of this is, that colonels and captains going a space before their troops, companies or regiments, for to encourage and lead on their soldiers, do ill to set themselves as marks for the enemy to shoot at, and if the chief commanders should be killed, the common soldiers would have but faint hearts to fight, but for the most part they will run away, as being afraid and ashamed to see the enemy when their chief commander is killed, and if they have no officer or commander behind them, the common soldiers will be apt to run away, having no worthy witnesses or judges, to view and condemn their base cowardly actions, which otherwise they are ashamed of, choosing rather to fight their enemies than to make known their fears.

Reader. Seventhly, be it known, observed and practised, that none of the army lie in garrison towns, but be always entrenched abroad.

Lady Victoria. The reason of this is, that towns breed or beget a tenderness of bodies, and laziness of limbs, luxurious appetites, and soften the natural dispositions, which tenderness, luxury, effeminacy, and laziness, corrupts and spoils martial discipline, whereas the open fields and casting up trenches makes soldiers more hardy, laborious and careful, as being more watchful.

[*Reader*]. Eighthly, be it known, observed and practised, that none unless visibly sick to be idle, but employed in some masculine action, as when not employed against an enemy, and that they are not employed about the works, forts or trenches, but have spare time to employ themselves, in throwing the bar, tripping, wrestling, running, vaulting, riding, and the like exercise.

Ninthly, be it known, observed and practised, that every commander when free from the enemy's surprisals, shall train their men thrice a week at least, nay every day if they can spare so much time, as putting their soldiers into several ranks, files and figures, in several bodies apart, changing into several places, and the like.

Lady Victoria. The reason of this is, that the soldiers may be expert and ready, and not be ignorant when they encounter their enemies, for many a battle is lost more through the ignorance of the soldiers not being well and carefully trained by their commanders, or having such commanders that know not how to train or draw them up. There are more battles, I say, lost thus, than for want of men or courage.

Reader. Tenthly, be it known, observed and practised, that every morning when encamped, that every commander shall make and offer in the midst of his soldiers a prayer to Mars, another to Pallas, a third to fortune, and a fourth to fame; these prayers to be presented to these gods and goddesses with great ceremony, both from the commander and common soldiers.

Lady Victoria. The reason of is this, that ceremony strikes a reverence and respect into every breast, raising up a devotion in every heart, and devotion makes obedience, and obedience keeps order, and order is the strength and life to an army, state, or commonwealth; and as for the prayers presented to these particular gods and goddesses is, that Mars would give us courage and strength, Pallas give us prudent conduct, fortune give us victory, and fame give us glory and renown.

Reader. Eleventhly, be it known, observed and practised, that the most experienced, practiced, and ingenioust* commanders shall preach twice a week of martial discipline, also those errors that have been committed in former wars, and what advantages have been taken, to be cited in their sermons, as also what was gained or lost by mere fortune.

Twelfthly, be it known, observed and practised, that when the army marches, that the soldiers shall sing in their march the heroical actions done in former times by heroical women.

Lady Victoria. The reason of this is, that the remembrance of the actions of gallant persons inflames the spirit to the like, and begets a courage to a like action, and the reason of singing of heroical actions only of women, is that we are women ourselves.

Reader. Thirteenthly, be it known, observed and submitted to, that no council shall be called, but that all affairs be ordered and judged by the Generalless herself.

Lady Victoria. The reason of this is, that all great councils, as of many persons, confounds judgments, for most being of several opinions, and holding strongly and stiffly, nay obstinately thereunto, as everyone thinking themselves wisest, cause a division, and wheresoever a division is, there can be no final conclusion.

Reader. Fourteenthly, be it know, observed and practised, that none of this effeminate army admits of the company of men, whilst they are in arms or warlike actions, not so much as to exchange words, without the Generalless her leave or privilege thereto.

Lady Victoria. The reason of this is, that men are apt to corrupt the noble minds of women, and to alter their gallant, worthy, and wise resolutions, with their flattering words, and pleasing and subtle insinuations, and if they have any authority over them, as husbands, fathers, brothers, or the like, they are apt to fright them with threats into a slavish obedience; yet there shall be chosen some of the most inferior of this female army, to go into the masculine army, to learn their designs, and give us intelligence of their removals, that we may order our encampings and removings according as we shall think best; but these women shall neither be of the body of our army, nor keep amongst the army, nor come within the trenches, but lie without the works in huts, which shall be set up for that purpose.

Reader. Lastly, whosoever shall break any of these laws or orders, shall be put to death, and those that do not keep them strictly, shall be severely punished.

Lady Victoria. But I am to advise you, noble heroics, that though I would not have a general council called to trouble our designs in war with tedious disputes, and unnecessary objections, and over-cautious doubts, yet in case of life and death, there shall be a jury chosen to sit and judge their causes, and the whole army shall give their votes, and the most voices shall either condemn, or reprieve, or save them, lest I should hereafter be only called in question, and not the rest, as being not accessary thereunto; and now you have heard these laws or orders, you may assent or dissent therefrom as you please; if you assent, declare it by setting your hands thereto, if you dissent, declare it by word of mouth, and the tables shall be broken.

All the women. We assent, and will set our hands thereto.

Exeunt.

SCENE 12

Enter Doctor Educature the Lady Jantil's Chaplain, and Nell Careless her maid.

Doctor Educature. Nell, how doth your good lady?

Nell Careless. Faith she seems neither sick nor well, for though her body seems in health, her mind seems to be full of trouble, for she will rise in the midst of the night, and walk about her chamber only with her mantle about her.

Doctor. Why doth she so?

Nell Careless. I asked her why she broke her sleep so as to walk about, and she answered me, that it was frightful dreams that broke her sleep, and would not let her rest in quiet.

Doctor. Alas she is melancholic in the absence of my Lord.

Exeunt.

SCENE 13

Enter the Lady Victoria and a number of other women.

Lady Victoria. Now we are resolved to put ourselves into a warlike body, our greatest difficulty will be to get arms, but if you will take my advice we may be furnished with those necessaries, as thus: the garrison we are to enter is full of arms and ammunition, and few men to guard them, for not only most of the soldiers are drawn out to strengthen the General's army, and to fight in the battle, but as many of the townsmen as are fit to bear arms, wherefore it must of necessity be very slenderly guarded, and when we are in the town, we will all agree in one night, when they shall think themselves most secure, to rise and surprise those few men that are left, and not only disarm them and possess ourselves of the town and all the arms and ammunition, but we will put those men out of the town or in safe places, until such time as we can carry away whatsoever is useful or needful for us, and then to go forth and entrench, until such time as we have made ourselves ready to march, and being once master, or mistress, of the field we shall easily master the peasants, who are for the most part naked and defenceless, having not arms to guard them, by which means we may plunder all their horses, and victual ourselves out of their granaries; besides, I make no question but our army will increase numerously by those women that will adhere to our party, either out of private and home discontents, or for honour and fame, or for the love of change, and as it were a new course of life; wherefore let us march to the town and also to our design, but first I must have you all swear secrecy.

All the women. We are all ready to swear to what you will have us.

Exeunt.

SCENE 14

Enter Madam Jantil alone as rising out of her bed, her mantle wrapped about her, and in her night linen.

Madam Jantil. I saw his face pale as a lily white
His wounds fresh bleeding blood like rubies bright;
His eyes were looking steadfastly on me,
Smiling as joying in my company;
He moved his lips as willing was to speak,
But had no voice, and all his spirits weak;
He shaked his hand as if he bid farewell,
That brought the message which his tongue would tell;
He's dead, he's dead, asunder break my heart,
Let's meet in death, though wars our lives did part.

After she had walked silently a turn or two about her chamber, her eyes being fixed on the ground, she returned as to her bed.

Exit.

SCENE 15

Enter a gentleman, and another meets him as in great haste.

1 Gent. What news, what news?

2 Gent. Sad news, for there hath been a battle fought betwixt the two armies, and our army is beaten, and many of our gallant men slain.

1 Gent. I am sorry for that.

The second gentleman goeth out.

Enter a third gentleman.

1 Gent. Sir I suppose you are come newly from the army; pray report the battle.

3 Gent. Truly I came not now from the army, but from the town the General's heroical lady and the rest of the heroics did surprise, seize and plunder.

1 Gent. What, the garrison town they were sent to for safety?

3 Gent. Yes.

1 Gent. And doth their number increase?

3 Gent. O very much, for after the surprisal of the town, the women in that town did so approve of their gallant actions, as everyone desired to be enlisted in the roll and number of the Amazonian army, but in the meantime of the forming of their army, intelligence was brought of the battle which was fought, and that there was such loss of both sides as each army retired back, being both so weak as neither was able to keep the field, but that the loss was greater on the reformed army, by reason there was so many of their gallant men slain; but this news made many a sad heart and weeping eyes in the female army; for some have lost their husbands, some their fathers, others their brothers, lovers and friends.

1 Gent. Certainly this will fright them out of the field of war, and cause them to lay by their heroic designs.

3 Gent. I know not what they will do, for they are very secret to their designs, which is strange, being all women.

ACT IV SCENE 16

*Enter two women like Amazons.**

1 Woman. Our Generalless seems to be troubled, perceiving how heavily this female army takes their losses.

2 Woman. She hath reason, for it may hinder or at least obstruct her high designs.

Exeunt.

SCENE 17

Enter the Lady Victoria and her Amazons;
she takes her stand and speaks to them.

Lady Victoria. Noble Heroics, I perceive a mourning veil over the face of this female army, and it becomes it well, for 'tis both natural and human to grieve for the death of our friends; but consider, constant Heroics, tears nor lamentations cannot call them out of the grave, no petitions can persuade death to restore them, nor threats to let them go, and since you cannot have them alive, being dead, study and be industrious to revenge their quarrels upon their enemies' lives, let your justice give them death for death, offer upon the tombs of your friends the lives of their foes, and instead of weeping eyes, let us make them weep through their veins; wherefore take courage, cast off your black veil of sorrow, and take up the firematch of rage, that you may shoot revenge into the hearts of their enemies, to which I hope fortune will favour us; for I hear that as soon as the masculine army have recovered strength, there will be another battle fought, which may be a means to prove our loves to our friends, our hate to our enemies, and an aspiring to our honour and renown; wherefore let us employ our care to fit ourselves for our march.

All the women. We shall follow and obey you, where, and when, and how you please.

SCENE 18

Enter Doctor Educature, and Nell Careless; the Doctor weeps.

Doctor. Doth my Lady hear of my Lord's death?

Nell Careless. The messenger or intelligencer of my Lord's death is now with her.

Exeunt.

SCENE 19

Enter Madam Jantil, and a gentleman intelligencer;
the lady seems not disturbed, but appears as usually.

Madam Jantil. How died my Lord?

Gentleman. Madam, he fought with so much courage, as his actions will never die, and his valour will keep alive the memory of this war: for though he died, his death was crowned with victory; he digged his grave out of his enemy's sides, and built his pyramid with heaps of their bodies; the groans of those he slew did ring his dying knell.

Madam Jantil. What became of his body?

Gentleman. He gave order before the armies joined to fight, that if he were killed, his body should be sought out, and delivered to you: for he said it was yours whilst he lived, and he desired it might be disposed of by you when he was dead; his desires and commands were obeyed, and his body is coming in a litter lapped in cerecloth.*

Madam Jantil. Worthy Sir, I give you many thanks for your noble relation, assuring myself it is true because you report it, and it is my husband that is the subject and ground of that honourable relation, whom I always did believe would out-act all words.

Gentleman. He hath so, Madam.

Madam Jantil. Sir, if I can at any time honourably serve you, I shall be ready whensoever you will command me.

Gentleman. Your servant, Madam.

(*He was going forth and returns*)

If your Ladyship hath not heard of Monsieur la Hardy's death, give me leave to tell you he is slain.

Madam Jantil. I am sorry, and for his Lady, for she loved him most passionably.

The gentleman goes out.

Enter as running and calling out Doll Pacify, Madam Passionate's maid.

Doll Pacify. Help, help, my Lady is dead, my Lady is fallen into a swoon at the report of my Master's being killed.

The lady goeth out and the maid, then they enter straight again with two or three servants more, bringing in the Lady Passionate as in a swoon.

Madam Jantil. Alas poor lady, her spirits are drowned in sorrow, and grief hath stopped her breath; loosen her garments, for she is swelled with troubled thoughts, her passions lie on heaps, and so oppress life; it cannot stir, but makes her senseless.

Upon the loosing of her garments she revives, and cries out.

Madam Passionate. O my husband, my husband!

She swoons again.

Madam Jantil. Bow her forward, bow her forward.

Madam Passionate revives again.

Madam Passionate. O let me die, let me die, and bury, bury me with him.

Swoons again.

Madam Jantil. Alas poor lady, put her to bed, for her life will find most ease there.

The servants go out with Madam Passionate.

Madam Jantil alone.

Madam Jantil. O life what art thou? And death, where doest thou lead us, or what dissolv'st thou us into?

Exeunt.

SCENE 20

Enter two gentlemen.

1 Gent. I wonder there is no news or messenger come from the army yet, when there usually comes one every day.

Enter a Messenger.

2 Gent. O Sir, what news?

Messenger. Faith there hath been nothing acted since the last battle, but it is said there will be another battle very suddenly, for the enemy provokes our men to fight, by reason our Lord General lies sick of his wounds, having had a fever, caused by the anguish of his hurts, and by his sickness the enemies hope to gain an advantage of his absence, but he hath put a deputy in his place to command in chief until he recovers.

1 Gent. What is become of the female army?

Messenger. I hear they are marched towards the masculine army, but upon what design I cannot understand.

Exeunt.

SCENE 21

Enter Madam Jantil, and her maid, Nell Careless.

Madam Jantil. Call my steward.

The maid goes out.

The Lady walks in a musing posture, her eyes fixed on the ground.

Enter the steward, weeping.

Steward. O Madam, that I should live to hear this cursed news of my dear Lord and Master's death.

Madam Jantil. Life is a curse, and there's none happy but those that die in the womb before their birth, because they have the least share of misery; and since you cannot weep out life, bear it with patience. But thy tears have almost washed out the memory of what I was to say, but this it is: that I would have you sell all my jewels, plate, and household furniture to the best advantage, and to turn off all my servants, but just those to attend my person, but to reward all of them with something more than their wages, and those servants that are old, and have spent their youth with my Lord's predecessors and in his service, but especially those he favoured most, give them so much during their lives as may keep them from the miseries of necessity, and vexations of poverty. Thirdly, I would have you hire the best and curioust* carvers or cutters of stones to make a tomb after my direction; as first, I will have a marble piece raised from the ground about half a man's height or something more, and something longer than my husband's dead body, and then my husband's image carved out of marble to be laid thereupon, his image to be carved with his armour on, and half a head-piece on the head, that the face might be seen, which face I would have to the life as much as art can make it; also let there be two statues, one for Mercury, and another for Pallas, these two statues to stand at his head, and the hands of these statues to join and to be laid under as carrying the head of my husband's figure, or as the head lay thereupon, and their hands as his pillow; on the right side of his figure, let there be a statue for Mars, and the hand of Mars's statue holding the right hand of my husband's figure, and on the left hand a statue for Hymen,* the hand on the place of the heart of my husband's figure, and at the feet of the figure let there be placed a statue for Fortune also, about a yard distance from the tomb; at the four corners thereof, let there be four marble pillars raised of an indifferent height, and an arched marble cover thereupon, and let all the ground be paved underneath with marble, and in the midst on the outside of the marble roof let the statue of fame be placed in a flying posture, and as blowing a trumpet; then some two yards distance square from those pillars let the ground be paved also with marble, and at the four corners four other marble pillars raised as high as the former, with capitals at top, and the body of those pillars round, and the statues of the four cardinal virtues placed on those capitals, sitting as in a weeping posture, and at the feet of those pillars the statues of the graces embracing each pillar; as the statue of charity, the pillar whereon the statue of justice sits, and the statue of patience, the pillar of temperance, and the statue of hope, the pillar of prudence, and the statue of faith, the pillar of fortitude; then set a grove of trees all about the outside of them, as laurel, myrtle, cyprus, and olive, for in death is peace, in which trees the birds may sit and sing his elegy; this tomb placed in the midst of a piece of ground of some ten or twenty acres, which I would have encompassed about with a wall of brick of a reasonable height. On the inside of the wall at one end, I would have built a little house divided into three rooms, as a gallery, a bed-chamber, and a closet, on the outside of the wall a house for some necessary servants to live in, to dress my meat,* and to be ready at my call, which will be but seldom, and that by the ring of a bell, but the three rooms I would have furnished after this manner: my chamber and the bed therein to be hung with white, to signify the purity of chastity, wherein is no colours made by false lights; the gallery with several colours intermixed, to signify the varieties, changes and encumbrances of life; my closet to be hung with black, to signify the darkness of death, wherein all things are forgotten and buried in oblivion. Thus will I live a signification, not as a real substance but as a shadow made betwixt life and death; from this house which shall be my living tomb, to the tomb of my dead husband, I would have a cloister built, through which I may walk freely to my husband's tomb, from the injuries of the weather, and this cloister I would have all the sides thereof hung with my husband's pictures drawn to the life by the best painters, and all the several accidents, studies and exercise of his life; thus will I have the story of his life drawn to the life. See this my desire speedily, carefully and punctually done, and I shall reward your service as a careful and diligent steward and servant.

Steward. It shall be done, but why will not your Ladyship have my Lord's figure cast in brass?

Madam Jantil. Because the wars ruin tombs before time doth, and metals being useful therein are often taken away by necessity, and we seldom find any ancient monuments but what are made of stone, for covetousness is apt to rob monuments of metal, committing sacrileges on the dead, for metals are soonest melted into profit, but stone is dull and heavy, creeping slowly, bringing but a cold advantage, wherein lies more pains than gains.

Steward. But your Ladyship may do all this without selling your jewels, plate, and household furniture.

Madam Jantil. It is true, but I would not let so much wealth lie dead in vanity when, exchanging them for money, I can employ it to some good use.

Steward. Your Ladyship hath forgotten to give order for blacks.*

Madam Jantil. No I have not, but I will give no mourning until my husband's body be carried to the tomb; wherefore I have nothing more to employ you in at this time, but only to send hither my chaplain, Doctor Educature.

The Steward goes out.

Enter Doctor Educature.

Madam Jantil. Doctor, although it is not the profession of a divine to be an historian, yet you knowing my husband's life and natural disposition best, being in his childhood under your tutorage, and one of his family ever since, I know none so proper for that work as you; and though you are naturally an eloquent orator, yet the bare truth of his worthy virtues and heroical actions will be sufficient to make the story both profitable, delightful, and famous; also I must entreat you to choose out a poet, one that doth not merely write for gain, or to express his own wit, so much as to endeavour to pencil with the pen virtue to the life, which in my Lord was so beautiful as it was beyond all draughts, but the theme will inspire his muse, and when both these works are writ, printed and set out, as divulged to the world as a pattern for examples, which few will be able to imitate, then I would have these books lie by me as registers of memory, for next unto the gods my life shall be spent in contemplation of him. I know I shall not need to persuade you to do this, for your affection to his memory is ready of itself; but love and duty binds me to express my desires for his fame, leaving nothing which is for my part thereunto.

Doctor Educature. Madam, all the service I can do towards the memory of my dear pupil, and noble Lord and patron, shall be most devoutly observed and followed; for Heaven knows, if I had as many lives to dispose of as I have lived years, I would have sacrificed them all for to have redeemed his life from death.

Doctor Educature goes out.

Madam Jantil alone.

Madam Jantil. When I have interred my husband's body, and all my desires thereunto be finished, I shall be at some rest, and like an executrix to myself executing my own will, distributing the rites and ceremonies, as legacies to the dead, thus the living gives the dead; but O my spirits are tired with the heavy burden of melancholy, and grow faint for want of rest, yet my senses invite me thereunto, yet I cannot rest in my bed, for frightful dreams disturb me; wherefore I will lie down on this floor, and try if I can get a quiet sleep on the ground, for from earth I came, and to earth I would willingly return.

She lays herself down upon the ground on one side of her arm bowing, leaning upon her elbow, her forehead upon the palm of her hand bowing forwards, her face towards the ground; but her grief elevating her passion, thus speaks.

Madam Jantil. Weep cold earth, through your pores weep,
Or in your bowels my salt tears fast keep;
Inurn* my sighs which from my grief is sent,
With my hard groans build up a monument;
My tongue like as a pen shall write his name,
My words as letters to divulge his fame;
My life like to an arch over his ashes bend,
And my desires to his grave descend;
I warn thee life keep me not company,
I am a friend to death thy enemy;
For thou art cruel, and everything torments,
Wounding with pain all that the world presents;
But death is generous and sets us free,
Breaks off our chains, and gives us liberty;
Heals up our wounds of trouble with sweet rest,
Draws our corrupted passions from our breast;
Lays us to sleep on pillows of soft ease,
Rocks us with silence nothing hears nor sees.

She fetches a great sigh.

O that I may here sleep my last.

After a short slumber she wakes.

If it were not for dreams, sleep would be a happiness next unto death, but I find I cannot sleep a long sleep in death; I shall not die so soon as I would.

Love is so strong and pure it cannot die,
Lives not in sense, but in the soul doth lie;
Why do I mourn? His love with mine doth dwell,
His love is pleased mine entertains it well;
But mine would be like his one embodied,
Only an essence or like a Godhead.

Exeunt.

SCENE 22

Enter Doctor Comfort and Doll Pacify.

Doctor Comfort. How doth our Lady, Doll?

Doll Pacify. Today she began to sit up, but yet she is very weak and faint.

Doctor Comfort. Heaven help her.

Doll Pacify. You that are Heaven's almoner* should distribute Heaven's gifts out of the purse of your mouth and give her single godly words instead of single silver pence, to buy her some heavenly food to feed her famished mind.

Doctor Comfort. Thou art a full-fed wench.

Doll Pacify. If I were no better fed than you feed me, which is but once a week, as on Sundays, I should be starved.

Doctor Comfort. You must fast and pray; fast and pray.

ACT V SCENE 23

Enter two Gentlemen.

1 Gent. All the young gallants in the town are preparing themselves with fine cloths and feathers to go a-wooing to the two rich widows, the Lady Jantil, and the Lady Passionate.

2 Gent. Riches are the lodestone* of affection, or at least professions.

1 Gent. The truth is, riches draw more suitors, than youth, beauty, or virtue.

Exeunt.

SCENE 24

Enter two or three gentlemen: Monsieur Comrade, Monsieur Companion, and Monsieur la Gravity.

Mr Comrade. For Heaven's sake, let us go and address ourselves to the two rich widows.

Mr Companion. For my part, I will address myself to none but the young widow, the Lady Jantil, and to her let us go without delay.

Mr la Gravity. It will be uncivil to go so soon after their husbands' death, for their husbands are not yet laid in their graves.

Mr Companion. If they were we should come too late, for I knew a man which was a great friend of mine, who was resolved to settle himself in a married course of life, and so he went a-wooing to a widow, for a widow he was resolved to marry, and he went a-wooing to one whose husband was but just cold in his grave, but she told him she was promised before, so he wooed another whilst she followed her husband's corpse, but she told him he came too late, whereat he thought with the third not to be a second in his suit, and so expressed his desires in her husband's sickness; she told him she was very sorry that she had passed her word before to another, for if she had not, she would have made him her choice, whereat he cursed his imprudence, and wooed the fourth on her wedding day, who gave him a promise after her husband was dead to marry him, and withal she told him, that if she had been married before, it had been ten to one but he had spoke too late, 'For,' said she, 'when we are maids, we are kept from the free conversation of men by our parents or guardians, but on our wedding day we are made free and set at liberty, and like as young heirs on the day of one and twenty, we make promises like bonds for two or three lives.' Wherefore I fear we shall miss of our hopes, for these two widows will be promised before we address our suit.

Mr Gravity. No, no, for I am confident all do not so, for some love to have the freedom of their wills, for every promise is a bondage to those that make a conscience to keep their promise; besides, it is not only variety that pleaseth women, but new changes, for stale acquaintance is as unpleasant as want of change, and the only hopes I have to the end of my suit is that I am a stranger and unknown, for women fancy men beyond what they are when unknown, and prize them less than their merits deserve when they are acquainted.

Mr Comrade. Well, we will not stay, but we will do our endeavour to get admittance.

Exeunt.

SCENE 25

Enter Madam Passionate as very ill, sitting in a chair groaning. Enter Madam Jantil as to see her.

Madam Jantil. Madam, how do you find your health?

Madam Passionate. Very bad, for I am very ill, but I wonder at your fortitude, that you can bear such a cross as the loss of your husband so patiently.

Madam Jantil. O Madam, I am like those that are in a dropsy,* their face seems full and fat, but their liver is consumed, and though my sorrow appears not outwardly, yet my heart is dead within me.

Madam Passionate. But your young years is a cordial to restore it, and a new love will make it as healthful as ever it was.

*Enter Doll Pacify, the Lady Passionate's maid, with a porringer of caudle.**

Doll Pacify. Pray Madam eat something, or otherwise you will kill yourself with fasting, for you have not eaten any thing since the beginning of your sorrow.

Madam Passionate. O carry that caudle away, carry it away, for the very sight doth overcome my stomach.

Doll Pacify. Pray Madam, eat but a little.

Madam Passionate. I care not for it, I cannot eat it: wherefore carry it away, or I will go away.

Both the ladies go out.

Enter Nell Careless, Madam Jantil's maid.

Nell Careless. Prithee, if thy lady will not eat this caudle, give it me, for I have an appetite to it; but I wonder you will offer your lady anything to eat, but rather you should give her something to drink, for I have heard sorrow is dry, but never heard it was hungry.

Doll Pacify. You are mistaken, for sorrow is sharp, and bites upon the stomach, which causes an eager appetite.

Nell Careless. I am sure weeping eyes make a dry throat.

(*She eats and talks between each spoonful.*)

Doll Pacify. But melancholy thoughts make a hungry stomach. But faith, if thou wert a widow, by thy eating thou wouldst have another husband quickly.

Nell Careless. Do you think I would marry again?

Doll Pacify. Heaven forbid that a young woman should live a widow.

Nell Careless. Why, is it a sin for a young woman to live a widow?

Doll Pacify. I know not what it would be to you, but it would be a case of conscience to me if I were a widow.

Nell Careless. By thy nice conscience thou seemest to be a Puritan.

Doll Pacify. Well, I can bring many proofs; but were it not a sin, it is a disgrace.

Nell Careless. Where lies the disgrace?

Doll Pacify. In the opinion of the world, for old maids and musty widows are like the plague, shunned of by all men, which affrights young women so much, as by running from it they catch hold on whatsoever man they meet, without consideration of what or whom they are, by which many times they fall into poverty and great misery.

Nell Careless. You teach a doctrine that to escape one mischief they fall on another, which is worse than the first; wherefore it were better to live a musty widow, as you call them, than a miserable wife; besides, a man cannot intimately love a widow, because he will be a cuckold, as being made one by her dead husband, and so live in adultery, and so she live in sin herself by cuckolding both her husbands, having had two.

Doll Pacify. I believe if you were a widow you would be tempted to that sin.

Nell Careless. Faith I should not, for should I commit that sin, I should deserve the Hell of discontent.

Doll Pacify. Faith you would marry if you were young, and fair, and rich.

Nell Careless. Those you mention would keep me from marrying: for if any would marry me for the love of youth and beauty, they would never love me long, because time ruins both soon; and if anyone should marry me merely for my riches, they would love my riches so well and so much as there would be no love left for me that brought it, and if my husband be taken prisoner by my wealth, I shall be made a slave.

Doll Pacify. No, not if you be virtuous.

Nell Careless. Faith there is not one in an age that takes a wife merely for virtue, nor values a wife anything the more for being so; for poor virtue sits mourning unregarded and despised, not anyone will so much as cast an eye towards her, but all shun her as you say they do old maids or musty widows.

Doll Pacify. Although you plead excellently well for not marrying, yet I make no question but you would willingly marry if there should come a young gallant.

Nell Careless. What's that, a fool that spends all his wit and money on his clothes? Or is it a gallant young man, which is a man enriched with worth and merit?

Doll Pacify. I mean a gallant both for bravery and merit.

Nell Careless. Nay, they seldom go both together.

Doll Pacify. Well, I wish to Heaven that Hymen would give thee a husband, and then that Pluto would take him away to see whether you would marry again. O I long for that time!

Nell Careless. Do not long too earnestly, lest you should miscarry of your desires.

Enter Madam Passionate, whereat Nell Careless, hearing her come, she runs away.

Madam Passionate. Who was it that run away?

Doll Pacify. Nell Careless, Madam Jantil's maid.

Madam Passionate. O that I could contract a bargain for such an indifferent mind as her young lady hath, or that the pleasures of the world could bury my grief.

Doll Pacify. There is no way for that, Madam, but to please yourself still with the present times, gathering those fruits of life that are ripe, and next to your reach, not to endanger a fall by climbing too high, nor to stay for that which is green, nor to let it hang whilst it is rotten with time, nor to murmur for that which is blown down by chance, nor to curse the weather of accidents for blasting the blossoms, nor the birds and worms of death, which is sickness and pain, for picking and eating the berries, for nature allows them a part as well as you, for there is nothing in the world we can absolutely possess to ourselves, for time, chance, fortune and death, hath a share in all things, life hath the least.

Madam Passionate. I think so, for I am weary of mine.

The lady goes out.

Enter a man.

Man. Mistress Dorothy, there are two or three gentlemen that desire to speak with one of the widow's maids, and you belong to one.

Doll Pacify. Well, what is their business?

Man. I know not, but I suppose they will only declare that to yourself.

She goeth out, and enters again as meeting the gentlemen.

Doll Pacify. Gentlemen, would you speak with me?

Monsieur la Gravity. Yes, for we desire you will help us to the honour of kissing your lady's hands, thereon to offer our service.

Doll Pacify. Sir, you must excuse me, for the sign of widowhood is not as yet hung out, mourning is not on, nor the scutcheons* are not hung over the gate, but if you please to come two or three days hence I may do you some service, but now it will be to no purpose to tell my lady, for I am sure she will receive no visits.

Exeunt.

The Second Part of Bell in Campo

ACT I SCENE I

Enter Doctor Comfort, and Doll Pacify.

Doll Pacify. Good Master Priest, go comfort my old Lady.

Dr Comfort. If you will comfort me, I will strive to comfort her.

Doll Pacify. So we shall prove the crumbs of comfort.

Dr Comfort. But is my Lady so sad still?

Doll Pacify. Faith, today she hath been better than I have seen her, for she was so patient as to give order for blacks; but I commend the young lady Madam Jantil, who bears out the siege of sorrow most courageously, and on my conscience I believe will beat grief from the fort of her heart, and become victorious over her misfortunes.

Dr Comfort. Youth is a good soldier in the warfare of life, and like a valiant cornet or ensign, keeps the colours up, and the flag flying, in despite of the enemies, and were our lady as young as Madam Jantil, she would grieve less, but to lose an old friend after the loss of a young beauty is a double, nay a treble affliction, because there is little or no hopes to get another good husband, for though an old woman may get a husband, yet ten thousand to one but he will prove an enemy, or a devil.

Doll Pacify. It were better for my Lady if she would marry again, that her husband should prove a Devil than a mortal enemy, for you can free her from the one though not from the other, for at your words, the great Devil will avoid or vanish, and you can bind the lesser devils in chains, and whip them with holy rods until they roar again .

Dr Comfort. Nay, we are strong enough for the Devil at all times, and in all places, neither can he deceive us in any shape, unless it be in the shape of a young beauty, and then I confess he overcomes us, and torments our hearts in the fire of love, beyond all expression.

Doll Pacify. If I were a Devil I would be sure to take a most beautiful shape to torment you, but my Lady will torment me if I stay any longer here.

Exeunt.

SCENE 2

Enter two gentlemen.

1 Gent. Sir, you being newly come from the army, pray what news?

2 Gent. I suppose you have heard how our army was forced to fight by the enemy's provocations, hearing the Lord General lay sick, whereupon the General's lady the Lady Victoria, caused her Amazonians to march towards the masculine army, and to entrench some half a mile distance therefrom, which when the masculine army heard thereof, they were very much troubled thereat, and sent a command for them to retreat back, fearing they might be a disturbance, so a destruction unto them, doing some untimely or unnecessary action; but the female army returned the masculine army an answer, that they would not retreat unless they were beaten back, which they did believe the masculine sex would not, having more honour than to fight with the female sex; but if the men were so base, they were resolved to stand upon their own defence; but if they would let them alone, they would promise them upon the honour of their words not to advance any nearer unto the masculine army, as long as the masculine army could assault their enemies, or defend themselves, and in this posture I left them.

Exeunt.

SCENE 3

Enter the Lady Victoria and her heroicesses.

Lady Victoria. Noble Heroicesses, I have intelligence that the army of Reformations begins to flag, wherefore now or never is the time to prove the courage of our sex, to get liberty and freedom from the female slavery, and to make ourselves equal with men: for shall men only sit in honour's chair, and women stand as waiters by? Shall only men in triumphant chariots ride, and women run as captives by? Shall only men be conquerors, and women slaves? Shall only men live by fame, and women die in oblivion? No, no, gallant heroics raise your spirits to a noble pitch, to a deatical* height, to get an everlasting renown, and infinite praises, by honourable, but unusual actions, for honourable fame is not got only by contemplating thoughts which lie lazily in the womb of the mind, and prove abortive, if not brought forth in living deeds;

but worthy Heroicesses, at this time fortune desires to be the midwife, and if the gods and goddesses did not intend to favour our proceedings with a safe deliverance, they would not have offered us so fair and fit an opportunity to be the mothers of glorious actions, and everlasting fame, which if you be so unnatural to strangle in the birth by fearful cowardice, may you be blasted with infamy, which is worse than to die and be forgotten; may you be whipped with the torturing tongues of our own sex we left behind us, and may you be scorned and neglected by the masculine sex, whilst other women are preferred and beloved, and may you walk unregarded until you become a plague to yourselves; but if you arm with courage and fight valiantly, may men bow down and worship you, birds taught to sing your praises, kings offer up their crowns unto you, and honour enthrone you in a mighty power.

May time and destiny attend your will,
Fame be your scribe to write your actions still;
And may the gods each act with praises fill.

All the women. Fear us not, fear us not, we dare and will follow you wheresoever and to what you dare or will lead us, be it through the jaws of death.

THE PRAYER

Lady Victoria. Great Mars thou god of war, grant that our squadrons may like unbroken clouds move with entire bodies, let courage be the wind to drive us on, and let our thick swelled army darken their sun of hope with black despair, let us pour down showers of their blood, to quench the fiery flames of our revenge.

And where those flowers fall, their deaths as seeds
Sown in time's memory sprout up our deeds;
And may our acts triumphant garlands make,
Which fame may wear for our heroics' sake.

Exeunt.

SCENE 4

Enter Doctor Comfort and Doll Pacify.

Doctor Comfort. Doll, how doth our Lady since the burying of my patron?

Doll Pacify. Faith she begins now to have regard to her health, for she takes jackalato* every morning in her bed fasting, and then she hath a mess of jelly broth for her breakfast, and drinks a cup of sack* before dinner, and eats a white wine caudle every afternoon, and for her supper she hath new-laid eggs, and when she goes to bed, she drinks a hearty draught of muskadine* to make her sleep well; besides, if she chances to wake in the night, she takes comfortable spirits, as angelica, aniseeds, besor,* aquamirabilis, and the like hot waters, to comfort her heart, and to drive away all melancholy thoughts.

Dr Comfort. Those things will do it if it be to be done, but I am sorry that my Lady hath sold all my patron's horses, saddles, arms, cloths, and such like things at the drum's head,* and by out-cries, to get a little the more money for them. I fear the world will condemn her, as believing her to be covetous.

Doll Pacify. O that's nothing, for what she loses by being thought covetous, she will regain by being thought rich, for the world esteems and respects nothing so much as riches.

Exeunt.

ACT II SCENE 5

Enter two gentlemen.

1 Gent. Pray Sir, what news from the army? You are newly come from thence.

2 Gent. I suppose you have heard how the effeminate army was some half a mile from the masculine armies; but the masculine army being very earnest to fight, not only to get victory and power, but to revenge each other's losses, as their friends slain in the former battle, which thoughts of revenge did so fire their minds and inflame their spirits, that if their eyes had been as much illuminated as their flaming spirits were, there might have been seen two blazing armies thus joining their forces against each other. At last began a cruel fight, where both the armies fought with such equal courages and active limbs, as for a long time neither side could get the better, but at last the army of Faction broke the ranks and files of the army of Reformation, whereupon every squadron began to fall into a confusion, no order was kept, no charge was heard, no command obeyed, terror and fear ran maskered about, which helped to rout our army, whereupon the enemy killed many of our men, and wounded many more, and took numbers of prisoners; but upon this defeat came in the female army, in the time that some of the enemy was busy in gathering up the conquered spoils, others in pursuit of thc remainders of our men, others were binding up the prisoners, others driving them to their quarters like a company of sheep to a market there to be sold; but when as some of the commanders perceived a fresh army coming towards them, their General commanded the trumpets to sound a retreat to gather them together, and also made haste to order and settle his men in battle array, and desirous their General was to have all the prisoners slain; but the female army came up so fast and so close to prevent that mischief, as they had not time to execute that design; but their General encouraged his soldiers, and bid them not to be disheartened, persuading them not to lose what they had got from an army of men to an army of boys, 'For,' said he, 'they seem to be no other by appearance of their shapes and statures.' But when the female army came to encounter them, they found their charge so hot and furious as made them give place, which advantage they took with that prudence and dexterity, as they did not only rout this army of Faction, killing and wounding many, and set their own countrymen at liberty, and recovered their losses, and gained many spoils, and took numbers of prisoners of their enemies with bag and baggage, but they pursued those that fled into their trenches, and beat them out of their works, and took possession thereof, where they found much riches; these trenches being taken, the Lady Victoria took possession, and made them her quarters, calling all her female soldiers to enter therein by the sound of flutes, which they always used instead of trumpets, and their drums were kettle-drums; but upon this victory the masculine sex of the army of Reformation was much out of countenance, being doubly or trebly overcome, twice by their enemy, and then by the gallant actions of the females which out-did them, yet they thought it best to take their advantage whilst the victory was fresh and flourishing, and their enemies weak and fearful, to lay siege to the next towns in the enemy's country; whereupon the Lady Victoria and her female soldiers hearing of the army of Reformation's designs, for they had sent the men to their own quarters as soon as the battle was won and victory got, also the masculine prisoners they sent to the men's quarters, not intermixing themselves with the men, but as I said they, hearing the design they had to besiege the towns, were much enraged for not making them of their councils, whereupon they sent a messenger like as an ambassador to tell the masculine army they did wonder at their ingratitude, that they should forget so much their relievers as to go upon any warlike design without making them acquainted therewith, striving as it were to steal the victory out of their hands, 'But,' said they, 'since we are become victorious over our enemies and masters, and mistresses of the field, by our own valiant actions and prudent conducts, we will maintain our power by our own strengths, for our army is become now numerous, full and flourishing, formed and conformable by our discipline, skilful by our practice, valiant by our resolutions, powerful by our victory, terrible to our enemies, honourable to our friends, and a subject of envy to the masculine sex; but your army is weak and decrepit, fitter for an hospital than for a field of war, your power is lost, your courage is cold, your discipline disorderous, and your command slighted, despised by your enemies, pitied by your friends, forsaken of good fortune, and made subject unto our effeminate sex, which we will use by our power like slaves.' But when our Lord General, who was recovered out of sickness, and all his commanders about him, heard this message, which was delivered in a full assembly, according as the Lady Victoria had commanded the message should be, the men could not choose but smile at the women's high and mighty words, knowing they had all sweet and gentle dispositions and complying natures, yet they were at a stand which to be pleased at most, as in hearing them disparage their masculine sex, or in advancing their own female sex by their self-commendations, but howsoever, so well pleased the men were with the women's gallant actions, that every man was proud that had but a female acquaintance in the female army; but our Lord General was mightily taken with their bravadoes, and much mirth amongst the commanders was about it; but when they were to advise what to do in the affairs of war, and the warring women, the General told them he made no question but that most men knew by experience that women were won by gentle persuasions and fair promises, and not by rigid actions or angry frowns, 'Besides,' said he, 'all noble natures strive to assist the weakest in all lawful actions,' and that he was no gallant man that submits not to a woman in all things that are honourable, and when he doth dissent it must be in a courtly manner, and a complimental behaviour and expression, for that women were creatures made by nature for men to love and admire, to protect and defend, to cherish and maintain, to seek and to sue to, and especially such women which have out-done all their sex which nature ever made before them; 'Wherefore,' said he, ' 'tis fit to these women above all others we should yield ourselves prisoners, not only in love but in arms; wherefore let us treat fairly with them, and give them their own conditions.' But in the meantime the Lady Victoria thought it best not to lose any opportunity with talking out the time, wherefore she besieged a considerable fort, a place which was as it were the key that unlocked the passage into the heart of the enemy's kingdom, and at this siege they were when I came away. But the General and his council had sent a messenger unto them, but what his message was I cannot give you an account.

Exeunt.

SCENE 6

Enter two men in mourning.

1 Man. Now my Lord is entombed, our Lady will enanchor herself by his ashes.

2 Man. 'Tis strange so young and beautiful a lady should bury herself from the world, and quit all the pleasures thereof, to live with dead ashes.

1 Man. A grieved mind, melancholy thoughts, and an oppressed heart, considers not the body, nor the world.

2 Man. But yet I think 'tis an example that few of her sex will imitate.

1 Man. Because few of the female sex can truly grieve or be melancholy.

2 Man. No, it is that few of the female sex can truly and constantly love.

Exeunt.

SCENE 7

A tomb being thrust on the stage, enter Madam Jantil and a company of mourners, but the Lady Jantil was attired in a garment of rich cloth of gold girt loosely about her, and a mantle of crimson velvet lined with powdered ermines* over that, her woman bearing up the train thereof, being long; her hair all unbound hung loose upon her shoulders and back, upon her head a rich crown of jewels, as also pendant jewels in her ears, and on her wrists costly bracelets. When she came in she goeth towards the tomb, and bows with great respect and devotion thereto, then speaks, directing her speech to every several figure.*

*The following verses or speeches were written by my Lord Marquess of Newcastle.**

Madam Jantil. Pallas and Mercury at thy death mourned,
So as to marble statues here th'are turned;
Mars sheaths his sword, and begs of thee a room,
To bury all his courage in thy tomb;
Hymen amazed stands, and is in doubt,
Thy death his holy fire hath put out;
What various shapes of fortune thou didst meet,
Thou scorn'st her frowns and kicks her with thy feet,
Now sound aloud the trumpet of good fame,
And blow abroad his everlasting name.

After this she directs her speech to the outward figures about the tomb.

The cardinal virtues, pillars of thy fame,
Weep to see now each but an empty name
Only for painters and for carvers be,
When thy life sustained them more than they thee;
Each capital a sadder virtue bears,
But for the graces would be drowned in tears;
Faith strengthens fortitude lest she should faint,
Hope comforts prudence as her only saint;
And charity to justice doth advance
To counsel her, as patience temperance;
But woeful counsellors they are each one,
Since grief for thy death turned them all to stone.

Then putting off her rich garments and ornaments before mentioned, as she was undressing she spake thus.

Now I depose myself, and here lay down,
Titles, not honour, with my richer crown;
This crimson velvet mantle I throw by,
There ease and plenty in rich ermines lie;
Off with this glittering gown which once did bear
Ambition and fond pride, lie you all there
Bracelets and pendants which I now do wear,
Here I divest my arms and so each ear;
Cut off these dangling tresses once a crime,
Urging my glass* to look away my time;
Thus all these worldly vanities I wave,
And bury them all in my husband's grave.

After this she calls for her other garments, which was a pure white light silk loose garment, girt about her with a white silk cord, and then puts on a thin black veil over it, and then takes a book in her hand, but speaks as they were a-putting on those latter garments.

More of my Lord Marquess's, are these.

Lady Jantil. Put on that pure and spotless garment white,
To show my chaster thoughts, my soul's delight;
Cord of humility about my waist,
A veil of obscure mourning about me cast;
Here by this sadder tomb shall be my station,
And in this book my holy contemplation.

She turns herself to her servants.

Farewell my servants, farewell every one,
As you all love me, pray leave me alone.

They all go forth weeping.

When they were all gone and she alone, she turns herself to the tomb.

No dust shall on thy marble ever stay,
But with my sadder sighs I'll blow 't away;
And the least spot that any pillar bears,
I'll wash it clean with grief of dropping tears;
Sun fly this hemisphere, and feast my eyes,
With melancholy night, and never rise,
Nor by reflection, for all light I hate,

Therefore no planet do illuminate;
The twinkling stars that in cold nights are seen,
Clouds muster up and hide them as a screen,
The centric* fire raise vapours from the earth,
Get and be midwife for those fogs their birth;
Then chilling colds freeze up thy pores without,
That trembling earthquakes nowhere may get out;
And that our mother earth may nothing wear,
But snow and icicles to curl her hair;
And so Dame Nature barren, nothing bring,
Wishing a chaos, since despair's a spring;
Since all my joys are gone, what shall I do,
But wish the whole world ruined with me too?

Here ends my Lord Marquess's verses.
Exeunt.

ACT III SCENE 8

Enter the Lady Victoria, and many of her Amazons, then enters a messenger from the masculine army.

Messenger. May it please your Excellence, our Lord General and the rest of the commanders have sent you and your heroics a letter, desiring it may be read in a full assembly.

Lady Victoria. One of you take the letter and read it.

One of the women takes the letter and reads it to all the company.

THE LETTER

To the most excellent of her sex, and her most worthy heroicesses. You goddesses on earth, who have the power and dominion over men, 'tis you we worship and adore, we pray and implore your better opinions of us, than to believe we are so unjust as to take the victory out of your fair hands, or so vain-glorious as to attribute it to ourselves, or so ungrateful as not to acknowledge our lives and liberties from your valours, wisdoms, and good fortune, or so imprudent as to neglect your power, or so ill-bred as to pass by you without making our addresses, or so foolish as to go about any action without your knowledge, or so unmannerly as to do anything without your leave; wherefore we entreat and pray you to believe that we have so much honour in us, as to admire your beauties, to be attentive to your discourses, to dote on your persons, to honour your virtues, to divulge your sweet graces, to praise your behaviours, to wait your commands, to obey your directions, to be proud of your favours, and we wear our lives only for your service, and believe we are not only taken captives by your beauties, but that we acknowledge we are bound as your slaves by your valours; wherefore we all pray that you may not misinterpret our affections and care to your persons, in believing we sent you away because we were weary of you, which if so, it had been a sin unpardonable, but we sent you away for your safety, for Heaven knows your departure was our Hell, and your absence our torments; but we confess our errors and do humbly beg your pardons, for if you had accompanied us in our battles, you had kept us safe, for had we fought in your presence, our enemies had never overcome us, since we take courage from your eyes, life from your smiles, and victory from your good wishes, and had become conquerors by your encouragements, and so we might have triumphed in your favours, but hereafter your rules shall be our methods, by which we will govern all our actions, attending only wholly your directions. Yet give us leave humbly to offer our advice as subjects to their princess: if you think fit, we think it best to follow close the victory, lest that our enemies recruit their forces with a sufficient strength to beat us out of what we have gained, or at least to hinder and oppose our entrance and hopes of conquering them, where if you will give us leave, we will besiege and enter their towns, and raze their walls down to the ground, which harbour their disorders, offending their neighbours' kingdoms; yet we are not so ambitious as to desire to be commanders, but to join our forces to yours, and to be your assistants, and as your common soldiers; but leaving all these affairs of war to your discretion, offering our selves to your service,

we kiss your hands, and take our leaves for this time.

All the women fall into a great laughter: ha, ha, ha, ha.

Lady Victoria. Noble heroicesses, by your valours, and constant, and resolute proceedings, you have brought your tyrants to be your slaves; those that commanded your absence, now humbly sue your presence, those that thought you a hindrance have felt your assistance, the time is well altered since we were sent to retreat back from the masculine army; and now nothing to be done in that army without our advice, with an humble desire they may join their forces with ours. But gallant heroicesses, by this you may perceive we were as ignorant of ourselves as men were of us, thinking ourselves shiftless, weak, and unprofitable creatures, but by our actions of war we have proved ourselves to be every way equal with men; for what we want of strength, we have supplied by industry, and had we not done what we have done, we should have lived in ignorance and slavery.

All the female commanders. All the knowledge of ourselves, the honour of renown, the freedom from slavery and the submission of men, we acknowledge from you, for you advised us, counselled us, instructed us, and encouraged us to those actions of war, wherefore to you we owe our thanks, and to you we give our thanks.

Lady Victoria. What answer will you return to the masculine army?

All the commanders. What answer you will think best.

Lady Victoria. We shall not need to write back an answer, for this messenger may deliver it by word of mouth; wherefore Sir, pray remember us to your General and his commanders, and tell them that we are willing upon their submissions to be friends, and that we have not neglected our good fortune, for we have laid siege to so considerable a fort, which if taken, may give an easy passage into the kingdom, which fort we will deliver to their forces when they come, that they may have the honour of taking it; for tell them, we have got honour enough in the battle we fought, and victory we did win.

Exeunt.

SCENE 9

Enter Monsieur la Gravity, Monsieur Companion, and Monsieur Comrade.

Monsieur Companion. We are bound to curse you, Monsieur Gravity, for retarding our visits to the widows, for I told you we should come too late if we did not go before their husbands were buried.

Mr la Gravity. But I do not hear they have made a promise to marry any as yet.

Mr Companion. That's all one unto us, but the noblest, youngest, richest, and fairest widow is gone; for though she is not promised or married, yet she is encloistered, and that is worse than marriage, for if she had been married there might have been some hopes her husband would have died, or been killed, or some ways or other death would have found to have taken him away.

Mr Comrade. Let us comfort ourselves with hopes that it is but a lady's humour, which she will be soon weary of, for when her melancholy fit is over, she will come forth of her cloister, and be fonder to marry than if she had never gone in.

Mr la Gravity. Well, since she is gone, let us assault the other.

Mr Companion. What, the old woman that hath never a tooth in her head?

Mr Comrade. Why, she is rich, and she will kiss the softer for having no bones in her mouth.

Mr Companion. The Devil shall kiss her before I will; besides, an old woman is thought a witch.

Mr la Gravity. Pish, that is because they are grown ill-favoured with age, and all young people think whatsoever is ill-favoured belongs to the Devil.

Mr Companion. An ancient man is a comely sight, being grave and wise by experience, and what he hath lost in his person, he hath gained in his understanding; besides, beauty in men looks as unhandsome as age in women, as being effeminate; but an old woman looks like the picture of envy, with hollow eyes, fallen cheeks, lank sides, black pale complexion,* and more wrinkles than time hath minutes.

Mr Comrade. Nay by your favour, some old women look like the full moon, with a red, swelled, great, broad face, and their bodies like as a spongy cloud, thick and gross, like our fat hostess.

Mr la Gravity. Gentlemen, why do you rail against ancient women so much, since those that are wise will never marry such boys as you?

Mr Companion. It is to be observed that always old girls match themselves with young boys.

Mr la Gravity. None but fools will do so.

Mr Companion. Why, did you or any man else ever know a wise old woman, or a chaste young woman, in their lives? For the old one dotes with age, the other is corrupted with flattery, which is a bawd to self-conceit.

Mr la Gravity. Grant it be so, yet it is better to marry an old doting fool, than a wanton young fille.*

Mr Companion. For my part, I think now it is the best way to marry none, since Madam Jantil is gone, but to live like the Lacedemonians, all in common.

Mr la Gravity. I am of another opinion, wherefore if you will go along with me to the old widow, Madam Passionate, and help to countenance my suit, I shall take it as an act of friendship.

Mr Comrade. Come, we will be thy pillars to support thee.

Exeunt.

SCENE 10

Enter Nell Careless, and Doll Pacify.

Doll Pacify. What, doth thy lady resolve to live an anchoret?*

Nell Careless. I think so.

Doll Pacify. How doth she pass away her time in her solitary cell?

Nell Careless. Why, as soon as she rises she goeth to my Lord's tomb, and says her prayers, then she returns and eats some little breakfast, as a crust of bread and a draught of water, then she goeth to her gallery and walks and contemplates all the forenoon, then about twelve a clock at noon she goeth to the tomb again and says more prayers, then returns and eats a small dinner of some spoon-meats,* and most of the afternoon she sits by the tomb and reads, or walks in the cloister, and views the pictures of my Lord that are placed upon the walls, then in the evening she says her evening prayers at the tomb, and eats some light supper, and then prays at the tomb before she goeth to bed, and at midnight she rises and takes a white waxen torch lighted in her hand, and goeth to the tomb to pray, and then returns to bed.

Doll Pacify. Faith she prays often enough in the day, she shall not need to pray at midnight; but why doth she rise just at midnight?

Nell Careless. I know not, unless she is of that opinion which some have been of, which is that the souls or spirits of the dead rise at that hour out of their graves and tombs to visit the face of the earth, and perhaps my Lady watches or hopes to converse by that means with my Lord's ghost: for since she cannot converse with him living, she desires to converse with him dead, or otherwise she would not spend most of her time at this tomb as she doth; but how doth thy lady spend her time now?

Doll Pacify. Faith as a lady should do: with nourishing her body with good hearty meats and drink. And though my Lady doth not pray at midnight, yet she converses with spirits at that time of night.

Nell Careless. What spirits?

Doll Pacify. Marry, spirits distilled from wine and other cordials, which she drinks when she wakes, which is at midnight; but do you watch, fast and pray as thy Lady doth?

Nell Careless. No truly, for I feed with the rest of my Lady's servants, which live within the house without the cloister, and they eat and drink more liberally.

Exeunt.

SCENE 11

Enter Monsieur la Gravity, Monsieur Companion and Monsieur Comrade as to Madam Passionate's house.
Enter Madam Passionate's gentleman usher.

Mr la Gravity. Sir, we come to kiss the hands of the Lady Passionate, if you please to inform your lady of us.

Usher. I shall, if't please you to enter into another room.

SCENE 12

Enter Doll Pacify, as to her Madam Passionate in her chamber where her cabinets were.

Doll Pacify. Madam, there are three gentlemen come to visit you, desiring you would give them leave to kiss your hands.

Madam Passionate. Shut down the lid of the cellar of strong waters and rid away the loose things that lie about, that my chamber may appear in some order.

The maid sets things in order, whilst the old lady is trimming herself in the looking-glass.

Madam Passionate. Bring in those gentlemen!

The maid goes out, then enters with the gentlemen; the two younger men speak to each other the time that Monsieur la Gravity is saluting.

Monsieur Companion. Aye, marry Sir, here is a comfortable smell indeed.

Monsieur Comrade. Faith, the smell of these spirits overcomes my spirits, for I am ready to swoon.

They go and salute the lady.

Madam Passionate. Pray gentleman, sit down.

They sit.

Truly I have had so great a wind in my stomach as it hath troubled me very much.

Companion speaks softly to Comrade.

Mr Companion. Which to express the better, she rasps* at every word to make a full stop.

Mr la Gravity. Perchance Madam you have eaten some meat that digests not well.

Mr Companion. [*speaks aside*] A toad.

Lady Passionate. No, truly I cannot guess what should cause it, unless it be an old pippin,* and that is accounted a great restorative. [*She fetches a great sigh*] But I believe it is the drugs of my sorrow which stick in my stomach, for I have grieved mightily for my dead husband, rest his soul; he was a good man and as kind a husband as ever woman had.

Mr la Gravity. But the destinies, Madam, are not to be controlled. Death seizes on all, be it early or late, wherefore everyone is to make their life as happy as they can, since life is so short, and in order to that, you should choose a new companion to live withal, wherefore you must marry again.

Lady Passionate. 'Tis true, the destinies are not to be controlled, as you say, wherefore if my destiny be to marry, I shall marry, or else I shall die a widow.

Mr Companion [*aside softly, as in the ear of Monsieur Comrade*]. She will lay the fault of her second marriage on destiny, as many the like foolish actions are laid to destiny's charge, which she was never guilty of.

Mr la Gravity. If I should guess at your destiny, I should judge you will marry again, by the quickness of your eyes, which are fair and lovely.

She simpers.

Lady Passionate. O Sir, you flatter me!

Mr Companion [*aside*]. I'll be sworn that he doth.

Lady Passionate. But my eyes were good, as I have been told both by my glass and friends, when I was young, but now my face is in the autumnal.

Mr Companion [*softly to Comrade aside*]. Nay faith, it is in the midst of winter!

Lady Passionate. But now you talk of eyes, that young gentleman's eyes [*points to Companion*] do so resemble my husband's as I can scarce look off from them. They have a good aspect.

Mr Companion. I am glad they have an influence upon your Ladyship.

Lady Passionate [*She speaks as softly to herself*]. By my faith, wittily answered; I dare say he is a notable youth.

Sir, for resemblance of him which is dead, I shall desire your continued acquaintance.

Companion [*softly to Comrade*]. She woos me with her husband's dead skull.

I shall render my service to your Ladyship.

She bows him thanks with simpering and smiling countenance and a bridled head.

Mr la Gravity [*softly so himself*]. Those young youths, I perceive, will be my ruin if not prevented.

Madam, will your Ladyship honour me so much as to give me the private hearing of a few words?

Lady Passionate. Yes Sir.

She removes with him a little space.

Mr la Gravity. Madam, although I am not such a one as I could wish myself for your sake, yet I am a gentleman, and what I want in person or estate, my affection, respect and tender regard to your person, worth and merit shall make good. Besides, Madam, my years suiting to your Ladyship's will make the better agreement in marriage.

Lady Passionate. Sir, you must excuse me, for though you merit a better wife than I, yet I cannot answer your affections, wherefore I desire you will desist in your suit, for I am resolved, if I do marry, to please my fancy.

Mr la Gravity. If your Ladyship cannot love me, Heaven forbid I should marry you, wherefore I wish your Ladyship such a husband as you can fancy best and love most.

They return to the other two gentlemen; they all take their leaves.

Madam, your most humble servant.

They go through the stage and come upon it again, as it were at the street door.

Mr la Gravity. Where is our coach?

Enter a footman.

Call the coach to the door.

Enter Doll Pacify as from her Lady to Monsieur Companion.

Doll Pacify. Sir, pray give me leave to speak a word or two with you.

Mr Companion. As many as you please.

Doll Pacify. Sir, my Lady desires your company tomorrow to dinner, but she desires you will come alone.

Mr Companion. Pray give your lady thanks for her favours and tell her if I can possibly I will wait on her Ladyship.

Doll Pacify goes out.

Mr Comrade. Now, what encouragement have you from the old lady?

Mr Companion. Faith, so much as I am ashamed of it, for she invited me to come alone.

Mr Comrade. On my life, if thou wilt not woo her, she will woo thee.

Mr Companion. Like enough, for there is nothing so impudent as an old woman, they will put a young man, be he never so debauched, out of countenance.

Mr Comrade. But faith consider of it, for she is rich.

Mr Companion. So is the Devil: as poets say, Pluto, the God of riches.

Mr Comrade. I grant it, and is not he best served? For everyone bows with respect, nay worships and adores riches and they have reason so to do, since all are miserable that have it not, for poverty is a torment beyond all sufferance, which causes many to hang themselves, either in the chain of infamy or in a hempen rope, or to do acts against the strict laws of a commonwealth, which is to commit self-murder. Besides, poverty is the slave and drudge, the scorn and reproach of the world, and it makes all younger brothers shirks and mere cheats, whereas this old lady's riches will not only give you an honest mind and create noble thoughts, but will give you an honourable reputation in the world, for everyone will think you wise, although you were a fool, valiant although you were a coward, and you shall have the first offers of all offices and all officers will be at your devotion: they will attend you as slaves, the lawyers will plead on your side, and judges will give sentence according as you desire. Courtiers will flatter you and divines will pray for you in their pulpits, and if your old lady die and leave you her wealth, you shall have all the young, beautiful virgins in the kingdom gather to that city, town or village where you live, omitting no art that may prefer them to your affection.

Mr Companion. You say well, and I could approve of your counsel if she would die soon after I had married her.

Mr Comrade. Why, put the case she should live a great while, as the truth is, old women are tough and endure long, yet you will have her estate to please yourself withal, which estate will buy you fine horses, great coaches, maintain servants and great retinues to follow you.

Mr Companion. But she is so devilish old!

Mr Comrade. Why, let her keep her age to herself, whilst you keep a young mistress to yourself, and it is better to have an old wife that will look after your family and be careful and watchful therein, and a young mistress, than a young wife, which will be a tyrannical mistress, which will look after nothing but vanities and love servants, while you, poor wretch, look like a contented cuckold, and so out of countenance as you dare not show your face whilst she spends your estate running about with every vain, idle fellow to plays, masques, balls, exchanges, taverns, or meets at a private friend's private lodging, also making great feasts and entertainments, where after dinner and supper there must be gaming at cards and dice, where for her honour, or at least seeming so, to lose five hundred or a thousand pounds away and when they rise with or from their losses, singing with a feigned voice as if it were a trifle not to be considered or considerable. Thus if you marry an old and rich lady you may live and spend her estate, but if you marry for youth and beauty, your wife will live and spend your estate. Besides, the husband of an old lady lives like the great Turk, having a seraglio, but marrying a young wife, you live like a prisoner: never durst show your head.

Mr la Gravity. He gives you good counsel and let me advise you to go to this lady as she hath invited you, for I perceive she hath a young tooth in her old head by refusing me and there is none so fit to pull it out as you are, wherefore go!

Mr Companion. Well gentlemen, I will try if my reason and your counsel can prevail in my choice.

Exeunt.

ACT IV SCENE 13

Enter Madam Jantil in her habit with a white taper lighted in her hand, the tomb being thrust upon the stage. She goeth to the tomb, then kneels down and seems as praying. After that she rises, holding out the torch with the other hand: speaks as follow[s].

These verses being writ by my Lord, the Marquess of Newcastle.

Madam Jantil. Welcome sad thoughts that's heaped up without measure,
They're joys to me and wealthy sons* of treasure;
Were all my breath turned into sighs 'twould ease me,
And showers of tears to bathe my griefs would please me;
Then every groan so kind to take my part

To vent some sorrows still thus from my heart,
But there's no vacuum, O my heart is full,
As it vents sorrows new griefs in doth pull.
Is there no comfort left upon the earth?
Let me consider vegetable birth;
The new-born virgin lily of the day
In a few hours dies, withers away,
And all the odoriferous flowers that's sweet
Breathe but a while and then with death do meet,
The stouter oak at last doth yield, and must
Cast his rough skin and crumble all to dust;
But what do sensitives?* Alas, they be
Beasts, birds and flesh to die as we;
And harder minerals, though longer stay
Here for a time, yet at the last decay,
And die as all things else that's in this world
For into death's arms everything is hurled.
Alas poor man, thou'rt in the worst estate,
Thou diest as these, yet an unhappier fate;
Thy life's but trouble still of numerous passions,
Torments thyself in many various fashions;
Condemned thou art to vexing thoughts within,
When beasts both live and die without a sin.
O happy beasts than grazing look no higher,
Or are tormented with thought's flaming fire;
Thus by thyself and others still annoyed
And made a purpose but to be destroyed.
Poor man!

Here ends my Lord Marquess's verses.

Muses some short time, then kneels to the tomb again and prays as to herself, then rises and bows to the tomb, so exit.

SCENE 14

Enter two gentlemen.

1 Gent. What news, Sir, of our armies abroad?

2 Gent. Why Sir, this: in the time of our masculine army's recruiting, the female army had taken the fort they besieged, where, upon the taking of that fort, many considerable towns and strongholds surrendered and submitted to the female army, whereupon the Lady Victoria sent to her husband to bring his army. When the General and all the masculine army came to the female army, much mirth and jesting there was between the heroics and heroicesses and so well they did agree as the female army feasted the masculine army and then gave the possession of the surrendered towns to the Lord General, and the Lady Victoria and all her army kept themselves in and about the fort, laying all their victorious spoils therein, and whilst the masculine army is gone to conquer the kingdom of Faction, they stay there upon the frontiers, passing their time in heroic sports, as hunting the stags, wild boars and the like, and those that have the good fortune to kill the chase is brought to the fort and trenches in triumph and is queen until another chase is killed. But we hear the masculine army goeth on with victorious success.

1 Gent. I am very glad to hear it.

Exeunt.

SCENE 15

Enter Doll Pacify and Nell Careless.

Nell Careless. O Doll, I hear thy lady is married, and not only married, but she hath married a very young man, one that might be her grandson, or son at least.

Doll Pacify. Yes, yes, my lady doth not intend to live with the dead, as your lady doth, but to have the company and pleasure of that which hath most life, which is a young man.

Nell Careless. Her marriage was very sudden.

Doll Pacify. So are all inconsiderated marriages, but happy is the wooing that is not long a-doing.

Nell Careless. If I had been your lady, I would have prolonged the time of my wooing, for the wooing time is the happiest time.

Doll Pacify. Yes, if she had been as young as you or your lady, but time bids my lady make haste.

Exeunt.

SCENE 16

Enter two gentlemen.

1 Gent. Do you hear the news?

2 Gent. What news?

1 Gent. Why, the news is that all the kingdom of Faction hath submitted to the kingdom of Reformation and that the armies are returning home.

2 Gent. I am glad of it.

Exeunt.

SCENE 17

Enter Madam Passionate alone.

Madam Passionate. O unfortunate woman that I am! I was rich and lived in plenty, none to control me. I was mistress of myself, estate and family. All my servants obeyed me, none durst contradict me, but all flattered me, filling my ears with praises, my eyes with their humble bows and respectful behaviours, devising delightful sports to entertain my time, making delicious meats to please my palate, sought out the most comfortable drinks to strengthen and increase my spirits. Thus did I live luxuriously, but now I am made a slave and in my old age, which requires rest and peace, which now Heaven knows I have little of, for the minstrels keep me waking, which play whilst my husband and his whores dance, and he is not only contented to live riotously with my estate, but sits amongst his wenches and rails on me, or else comes and scoffs at me to my face. Besides, all my servants slight and neglect me, following those that command the purse, for this idle young fellow which I have married first seized on all my goods, then let leases for many lives out of my lands, for which he had great fines, and now he cuts down all my woods and sells all my lands of inheritance which I foolishly and fondly delivered by deed of gift the first day I married, divesting myself of all power, which power, had I kept in my own hands, I might have been used better. Whereas now when he comes home drunk he swears and storms and kicks me out of my warm bed and makes me sit shivering and shaking in the cold whilst my maid takes my place. But I find I cannot live long, for age and disorders bring weakness and sickness and weakness and sickness bring death, wherefore my marriage bed is like to prove my grave, whilst my husband's curses are my passing bell. Hey ho!

Exit.

SCENE 18

Enter two gentlemen.

1 Gent. I hear the army is returning home.

2 Gent. Yes, for they are returned as far back as to the effeminate army and all the masculine commanders have presented all the female commanders with their spoils got in the kingdom of Faction as a tribute to their heroical acts and due for their assistance and safety of their lives and country.

1 Gent. And do not you hear what privileges and honours the King and his council hath resolved and agreed upon to be given to the female army, and the honours particularly to be given to the Lady Victoria?

2 Gent. No.

1 Gent. Why then, I will tell you some. The Lady Victoria shall be brought through the city in triumph, which is a great honour, for never anyone makes triumphs in a monarchy but the king himself. Then, that there shall be a blank for the female army to write their desires and demands; also there is an armour of gold and a sword a-making, the hilt being set with diamonds and a chariot all gilt and embroidered to be presented to the Lady Victoria, and the city is making great preparation against her arrival.

2 Gent. Certainly she is a lady that deserves as much as can be given, either from kings, states, or poets.

Exeunt.

SCENE 19

Enter the Lady Jantil as being sick, brought by two men in a chair and set by the tomb of her dead lord, and many servants and friends about her weeping.

Madam Jantil. Where is my secretary?

Secretary. Here, Madam.

Madam Jantil. Read the will I caused you to write down.

The will read.

I Jantil, the widow of Seigneur Valeroso, do here make a free gift of all these following.

Item: all my husband's horses and saddles and whatsoever belongs to those horses, with all his arms, pikes, guns, drums, trumpets, colours, wagons, coaches, tents and all he had belonging to the war, to be distributed amongst his officers of war, according to each degree, I freely give.

Item: all his library of books I give to that college he was a pupil in when he was at the university.

Item: to all his servants I give the sum of their yearly wages to be yearly paid to them during their lives.

Item: I give two hundred pounds a year pension to his chaplain, Doctor Educature during his life.

Item: I give a hundred pound a year pension to his steward during his life.

Item: I give fifty pound a year pension to his secretary during his life.

Item: I give a hundred pound per annum for the use and repair of this tomb of my dead husband's.

Item: I give a thousand pounds a year to maintain ten religious persons to live in this place or house by this tomb.

Item: I give three thousand pounds to enlarge the house and three thousand pounds more to build a chapel by my husband's tomb.

Item: two hundred pounds a year I give for the use and repair of the house and chapel.

Item: I give my maid, Nell Careless, a thousand pound to live a single life.

Item: I give the rest of my estate which was left to me by my husband, Seigneur Valoroso, to the next of his name.

The following speeches and songs of hers
my Lord the Marquess of Newcastle writ.

Jantil. So 'tis well.
O death hath shaked me kindly by the hand,

To bid me welcome to the silent grave;
'Tis dead and numb, sweet death how thou dost court me,
O let me clap thy fallen cheeks with joy
And kiss the emblem of what once was lips,
Thy hollow eyes I am in love withal,
And thy balled* head beyond youth's best-curled hair,
Prithee embrace me in thy colder arms
And hug me there to fit me for thy mansion;
Then bid our neighbour worms to feast with us,
Thus to rejoice upon my holy day.
But thou art slow. I prithee, hasten death,
And linger not my hopes thus with thy stay,
'Tis not thy fault thou sayest, but fearful nature
That hinders death's progress in his way.
Oh foolish nature thinks thou canst withstand
Death's conquering and inevitable hand.
Let me have music for divertissement,
This is my masque, death's ball, my soul to dance
Out of her frail and fleshly prison here.
Oh could I now dissolve and melt; I long
To free my soul in slumbers with a song;
In soft and quiet sleep here as I lie,
Steal gently out, O soul, and let me die.

Lies as asleep.

SONG

O you gods, pure angels send her,
Here about her to attend her,
Let them wait and here condole
Till receive her spotless soul,
So serene it is and fair
It will sweeten all the air,
You this holy wonder bears
With the music of the spheres
Her soul's journey in a trice
You'll bring safe to paradise
And rejoice the saints that say
She makes heaven's holy day.

The song ended, she opens her eyes, then speaks.

Death hath not finished yet his work, he's slow
But he is sure, for he will do't at last;
Turn me to my dear lord, that I may breathe
My last words unto him. My dear,
Our marriage joined our flesh and bone
Contracted by those holy words made one,
But by our loves we joined each other's heart
And vowed that death should never us depart;
Now death doth marry us, since now we must
Ashes to ashes be mingling our dust,
And our joyed souls in Heaven married then
When out frail bodies rise, we'll wed again,
And now I am joyed to lie by thy loved side,
My soul within thy soul shall in Heaven reside.
For that is all my . . .

In this last word, she dies, which when her servants saw, they cried out 'she is dead, she is dead.'

Here ends my Lord Marquess's writing.

Doctor Educature. She is dead, she is dead, the body hence convey,
And to our mistress our last rites we'll pay.

So they lay her by her husband upon the tomb and, drawing off the tomb, go out.

ACT V SCENE 20

Enter citizens' wives and their apprentices.

1 Wife. Where shall we stand to see this triumphing?

2 Wife. I think, neighbour, this is the best place.

3 Wife. We shall be mightily crowded there!

2 Wife. For my part, I will stand here and my apprentice Nathaniel shall stand by me and keep off the crowd from crowding me.

Nathaniel. Truly mistress, that is more than I am able to do.

3 Wife. Well neighbour, if you be resolved to stand here, we will keep you company. Timothy, stand by me.

Timothy. If you stand here mistress, the squibs* will run under your clothes.

3 Wife. No matter Timothy, let them run where they will.

They take their stand.

1 Wife. I hope, neighbour, none will stand before us, for I would not but see this Lady Victoria for anything, for they say she hath brought articles for all women to have as many husbands as they will, and all tradesmen's wives shall have as many apprentices as they will.

2 Wife. The gods bless her for it.

Enter a crowd of people.

She is coming; she is coming!

Officers come.

Stand up close; make way!

Enter many prisoners which march by two and two, then enter many that carry the conquered spoils, then enters the Lady Victoria in a gilt chariot drawn with eight white horses, four on abreast, the horses covered with cloth of gold and great plumes of feathers on their heads.

The Lady Victoria was adorned after this manner: she had a coat on, all embroidered with silver and gold, which coat reached no further than the calves of her legs, and on her legs and feet she had buskins and sandals embroidered suitable to her coat. On her head she had a wreath or garland of laurel, and her hair curled and loosely flowing; in her hand a crystal bolt headed with gold at each end, and after the chariot marched all her female officers with laurel branches in their hands, and after them the inferior she-soldiers, then going through the stage as through the city and so entering again, where on the midst of the stage as if it were the midst of the city, the magistrates meet her, so her chariot makes a stand and one as the recorder speaks a speech to her.*

Victorious lady, you have brought peace, safety and conquest to this kingdom by your prudent conduct and valiant actions, which never any of your sex in this kingdom did before you. Wherefore our gracious King is pleased to give you that which was never granted nor given to any before, which is to make you triumphant, for no triumph is ever made in monarchies but by the king thereof. Besides, our gracious King hath caused an act to be made and granted to all your sex, which act I have order to declare, as:

First: that all women shall hereafter in this kingdom be mistress in their own houses and families.

Secondly: they shall sit at the upper end of the table, above their husbands.
Thirdly: that they shall keep the purse.
Fourthly: they shall order their servants, turning from or taking into their service what numbers they will, placing them how they will and ordering them how they will and giving them what wages they will or think fit.
Fifthly: they shall buy in what provisions they will.
Sixthly: all the jewels, plate and household furniture they shall claim as their own and order them as they think good.
Seventhly: they shall wear what fashioned clothes they will.
Eighthly: they shall go abroad when they will, without control or giving of any account thereof.
Ninthly: they shall eat when they will and of what they will, and as much as they will and as often as they will.
Tenthly: they shall go to plays, masques, balls, churchings, christenings, preachings, whensoever they will and as fine and bravely attired as they will.
Lastly: that they shall be of their husband's counsel.

When those were read, all the women cried out: 'God save the King; God save the King, and Heaven reward the Lady Victoria.'

Then an act was read concerning the Lady Victoria.

As for you, most gallant lady, the King hath caused to be enacted that:
First: all poets shall strive to set forth your praise.
Secondly: that all your gallant acts shall be recorded in story and put in the chief library of the kingdom.
Thirdly: that your arms you fought in shall be set in the King's armoury.
Fourthly: that you shall always wear a laurel garland.
Fifthly: you shall have place next to the King's children.
Sixthly: that all those women that have committed such faults as is a dishonour to the female sex shall be more severely punished than heretofore, in not following your exemplary virtues and all those that have followed your example shall have respective honour done to them by the state.
Seventhly and lastly: your figure shall be cast in brass and then set in the midst of the city armed as it was in the day of battle.

The Lady Victoria rises up in her chariot and then bows herself to the magistrates.

Lady Victoria. Worthy Sir, the honour and privileges my gracious king and sovereign hath bestowed upon me is beyond my merit.

Then was read the Acts concerning the rest of the female army.

Our gracious King hath caused to be enacted as:

First: all the chief female commanders shall have place, as every lord's wife shall take place of an earl's wife that hath not been a soldier in the army; every knight's wife before a baron's wife that hath not been a soldier in the army; an esquire's wife before a knight's wife; a doctor's wife before an esquire's wife that hath not been a soldier in the army; a citizen's wife before a doctor's wife; a yeoman's wife before a citizen's wife that hath not been a soldier in the army; and all tradesmen's wives that have been soldiers in the army shall be free in all the corporations in this kingdom. These acts during their lives and all the chief commanders shall be presented according to their quality and merit.

All the female soldiers cried out 'God save the King; God save the King!'

After this, the Lady Victoria is drawn on her chariot and the rest walk after all.

Exeunt.

SCENE 21

Enter Doll Pacify and Nell Careless.

Doll Pacify. O Nell, I hear thy lady is dead and hath left thee a thousand pound.

Nell weeps.

[*Doll Pacify*]. What, dost thou weep for joy of thy thousand pound, or for grief of thy lady's death?

Nell Careless. I wish my lady had lived, although I had begged all my life.

Doll Pacify. I am not of your mind. I had rather live well myself as to live in plenty than to live poor for the life of anybody, and if upon that condition my lady would leave me a thousand pound, I care not if she died tomorrow—but my young master hath robbed me of all. But Nell, for all thou art left a thousand pound, it is upon such a condition as, for my part, had it been to me, I should not thank the giver, for they say it is given thee upon condition to live a single life.

Nell Careless. Truly I have seen so much sorrow in my lady, and so much folly in your lady, concerning husbands, that had not my lady enjoined me to live a single life, I would never have married, wherefore my lady's generosity did not only provide for my bodily life and for my plentiful living, but provided for the tranquillity of my mind, for which I am trebly obliged to reverence her memory.

Exeunt.

SCENE 22

Enter two gentlemen.

1 Gent. The Lady Victoria hath been at court and hath had public audience.

2 Gent. Yes, and the Lady Victoria and her officers and commanders hath distributed all the spoils got in these wars amongst the common she-soldiers.

1 Gent. All the ladies that were not with the army look most pitifully out of countenance.

2 Gent. Yes, and they are much troubled that the heroics shall take place.

1 Gent. The Lord General seems to be very proud of his lady; methinks he looks upon her with a most pleased eye.

2 Gent. He hath reason, for never man had so gallant and noble a lady, nor more virtuous and loving a wife, than the Lord General hath.

Exeunt.

FINIS.

The Preface to the Ensuing Treatise [*Observations Upon Experimental Philosophy* (1666)]

It is probable, some will say, that my much writing is a disease, but what disease they will judge it to be I cannot tell. I do verily believe they will take it to be a disease of the brain, but surely they cannot call it an apoplectical or lethargical disease. Perhaps they will say it is an extravagant, or at least a fantastical disease; but I hope they will rather call it a disease of wit. But let them give it what name they please, yet of this I am sure: that if much writing be a disease, then the best philosophers, both moral and natural, as also the best divines, lawyers, physicians, poets, historians, orators, mathematicians, chemists and many more have been grievously sick, and Seneca, Plinius, Aristotle, Cicero, Tacitus, Plutarch, Euclid, Homer, Virgil, Ovid, St Augustine, St Ambrose, Scotus, Hippocrates, Galen, Paracelsus and hundreds more have been at death's door with the disease of writing. Now to be infected with the same disease which the devoutest, wisest, wittiest, subtlest, most learned and eloquent men have been troubled withal is no disgrace, but the greatest honour, even to the most ambitious person in the world, and next to the honour of being thus infected it is also a great delight and pleasure to me, as being the only pastime which employs my idle hours, in so much that, were I sure nobody did read my works, yet I would not quit my pastime for all this, for although they should not delight others, yet they delight me; and if all women that have no employment in worldly affairs should but spend their time as harmlessly as I do, they would not commit such faults as many are accused of.

I confess there are many useless and superfluous books and perchance mine will add to the number of them; especially it is to be observed that there have been in this latter age as many writers of natural philosophy as in former ages there have been of moral philosophy, which multitude, I fear, will produce such a confusion of truth and falsehood as the number of moral writers formerly did with their over-nice divisions of virtues and vices, whereby they did puzzle their readers so that they knew not how to distinguish between them. The like, I doubt, will prove amongst our natural philosophers, who by their extracted, or rather distracted, arguments, confound both divinity and natural philosophy, sense and reason, nature and art, so much as in time we shall have rather a chaos than a well-ordered universe by their doctrine. Besides, many of their writings are but parcels taken from the ancient. But such writers are like those unconscionable men in Civil Wars which endeavour to pull down the hereditary mansions of noblemen and gentlemen to build a cottage of their own, for so do they pull down the learning of ancient authors to render themselves famous in composing books of their own. But though this age does ruin palaces to make cottages, churches to make conventicles and universities to make private colleges, and endeavour not only to wound but to kill and bury the fame of such meritorious persons as the ancient were, yet I hope God of his mercy will preserve state, church and schools from ruin and destruction. Nor do I think their weak works will be able to overcome the strong wits of the ancient, for setting aside some few of our moderns, all the rest are but like dead and withered leaves in comparison to lovely and lively plants. And as for arts, I am confident that where there is one good art found in these latter ages, there are two better old arts lost, both of the Egyptians, Grecians, Romans and many other ancient nations. (When I say lost, I mean in relation to our knowledge, not in nature, for nothing can be lost in nature.)

Truly the art of augury was far more beneficial than the lately invented art of micrography,* for I cannot perceive any great advantage this art doth bring us. The eclipse of the sun and moon was not found out by telescopes, nor the motions of the lodestone, or the art of navigation, or the art of guns and gunpowder, or the art of printing and the like, by microscopes. Nay, if it be true that telescopes make appear the spots in the sun and moon, or discover some new stars, what benefit is that to us? Or if microscopes do truly represent the exterior parts and superficies of some minute creatures, what advantageth it our knowledge? For unless they could discover their interior, corporeal, figurative motions and the obscure actions of nature, or the causes which make such or such creatures, I see no great benefit or advantage they yield to man. Or if they discover how reflected light makes loose and superficial colours, such as no sooner perceived but are again dissolved, what benefit is that to man? For neither painters nor dyers can enclose and mix that atomical dust and those reflections of light to serve them for any use. Wherefore, in my opinion it is both time and labour lost, for the inspection of the exterior parts of vegetables doth not give us any knowledge how to sow, set, plant and graft, so that a gardener or husbandman will gain no advantage at all by this art. The inspection of a bee through a microscope will bring him no more honey, nor the inspection of a grain more corn; neither will the inspection of dusty atoms and reflections of light teach painters how to make and mix colours, although it may perhaps be an advantage to a decayed lady's face by placing herself in such or such a reflection of light where the dusty atoms may hide her wrinkles. The truth is, most of these arts are fallacies, rather than discoveries of truth, for sense deludes more than it gives a true information, and an exterior inspection through an optic glass is so deceiving that it cannot be relied upon. Wherefore regular reason is the best guide to all arts, as I shall make it appear in this following treatise.

It may be the world will judge it a fault in me that I oppose so many eminent and ingenious writers, but I do it not out of a contradicting or wrangling nature, but out of an endeavour to find out truth, or at least the probability of truth, according to that proportion of sense and reason nature has bestowed upon me; for as I have heard my noble lord say that in the art of riding and fencing there is but one truth, but many falsehoods and fallacies, so it may be said of natural philosophy and divinity, for there is but one fundamental truth in each and I am as ambitious of finding out the truth of nature as an honourable dueller is of gaining fame and repute, for as he will fight with none but an honourable and valiant opposite, so am I resolved to argue with none but those which have the renown of being famous and subtle philosophers, and therefore as I have had the courage to argue heretofore with some famous and eminent writers in speculative philosophy, so have I taken upon me in this present work to make some reflections also upon some of our modern experimental and dioptrical* writers. They will perhaps think me an inconsiderable opposite because I am not of their sex, and therefore strive to hit my opinions with a side-stroke, rather covertly than openly and directly. But if this should chance, the impartial world, I hope, will grant me so much justice as to consider my honesty and their fallacy and to pass such a judgement as will declare them to be patrons not only to truth but also to justice and equity, for which Heaven will grant them their reward and time will record their noble and worthy actions in the register of fame to be kept in everlasting memory.

'The Matrimonial Agreement' from *Nature's Pictures* (2nd edn. 1671)

A handsome young man fell in love with a fair young lady, insomuch that if he had her not, he was resolved to die, for live without her he could not. So wooing her long, at last, although she had no great nor good opinion of a married life, being afraid to enter into so strict bonds, observing the discords therein that trouble a married life, being raised by a disagreement of humours and jealousy of rivals, but considering withal that marriage gave a respect to women, although beauty were gone, and seeing the man personable and knowing him to have a good fortune, which would help to counterpoise the inconveniences and troubles that go along with marriage, she was resolved to consent to his request.

The gentleman coming as he used to do and persuading her to choose him for her husband, she told him she would, but that she found herself of that humour that she could not endure a rival in wedlock, and the fear of having one would cause jealousy, which would make her very unhappy, and the more because she must be bound to live with her enemy (for so she should account of her husband when he had broken his faith and promise to her).

He, smiling, told her she need not fear and that death was not more certain to man than he would be constant to her, sealing it with many oaths and solemn protestations. 'Nay,' said he, 'when I am false, I wish you may be so, which is the worst of ills.'

She told him words would not serve her turn, but that he should be bound in a bond, that not only whensoever she could give a proof, but when she had cause of suspicion, she might depart from him with such an allowance out of his estate as she thought fit to maintain her.

He told her he was so confident and knew himself so well that he would unmaster himself of all his estate and make her only mistress.

She answered, a part would serve her turn. So the agreement was made and sealed; they married and lived together as if they had but one soul, for whatsoever one did or said, the other disliked not, nor had they reason, for their study was only to please each other.

After two years, the wife had a great fit of sickness which made her pale and wan and not so full of lively spirits as she was wont to be, but yet as kind and loving to her husband as she was afore, and her husband, at her first sickness, wept, watched and tormented himself beyond all measure. But the continuance made him so dull and heavy that he could take no delight in himself, nor in anything else.

His occasions calling him abroad, he found himself so refreshed that his spirits revived again. But returning home, and finding not that mirth in the sick, as was in the healthy, wife, it grew wearisome to him, insomuch that he always would have occasions to be abroad and thought home his only prison. His wife, mourning for his absence, complained to him at his return and said she was not only unhappy for her sickness, but miserable in that his occasions were more urgent to call him from her when she had most need of his company to comfort her in the loss of her health than in all the time they had been married. 'And therefore, pray husband,' said she, 'what is this unfortunate business that employs you so much and makes me see you so seldom?' He told her, the worldly affairs of men, women did not understand, and therefore it were a folly to recite them. 'Besides,' said he, 'I am so weary in following them that I hate to repeat them.' She, like a good wife, submitted to her husband's affairs and was content to sit without him.

The husband returning home one day from jolly company, whose discourse had been merry and wanton, he met with his wife's maid at the door and asked her how her mistress did. She said, 'Not very well.' 'Thou lookest well,' said he, and chucks her under the chin. She, proud of her master's kindness, smirks and smiles upon him, insomuch that, the next time he met her, he kissed her. Now she begins to despise her mistress and only admires herself, and is always the first person or servant that opens the door to her master. And through the diligence of the maid, the master's great affairs abroad were ended, and his only employment and busy care is now so much at home that whensoever he was abroad, he was in such haste that he could scarce salute anybody by the way and when his friends spoke to him his head was so full of thoughts that he would answer quite from the question, insomuch that he was thought one of the best and carefullest husbands in the world.

In the meantime, his wife grew well and his maid grew pert and bold towards her mistress, and the mistress, wondering at it, began to observe more strictly what made her so, for she perceived the wench came oftener than accustomed where her husband and she were, and found also that her husband had always some excuse to turn his head and eyes to that place where she was, and that whensoever the wench came where they were, he would alter his discourse, talking extravagantly.

Whereupon, not liking it, she examined her husband whether his affections were as strong to her as ever they were. He answered he was the perfectest good husband in the world, and so he should be until he died.

It chanced he was employed by the state into another country, where, at parting, his wife and he lamented most sadly, and many tears were shed. But when he was abroad, being in much company who took their liberty and had many mistresses, he then considered with himself he was a most miserable man that must be bound only to one; but withal did consider what promises he made his wife and what advantages she had on him in his estate, which kept him in good order for a time.

But at last he was persuaded by his companions to fling off all care and take his pleasure whilst he might. 'For,' said they, 'what do our wives know what we do? Besides,' said they, 'wives are only to keep our house, to bring us children, not to give us laws.' Thus preaching to him, he at last followed their doctrine and improved it so well that he became the greatest libertine of them all, like a horse that, having broken his reins, when he finds himself loose, skips over hedges, ditches, pales or whatsoever is in his way and runs wildly about until he hath wearied himself.

But his wife having some intelligence (as most commonly they want none), or maybe out of pure love, comes to see him. He receives her with the greatest joy and makes the most of her in the world, carrying her to see all the country and towns thereabouts and all the varieties, curiosities and sights that were to be seen. But when she had been there a month or such a time, he tells her how dangerous it is to leave his house to servants who are negligent, and his estate to be entrusted he knows not to whom, so that there is no way but to return, both for his and her good, especially if they had children. 'Although,' said he, 'I had rather part with my life than be absent from you, but necessity hath no law.' So she, good woman, goeth home to care and spare whilst he spends, for in the meantime he follows his humours and custom making confidence, and confidence carelessness, begins to be less shy and more free, insomuch as, when he returned home, his maid, whom he did but eye and friendly kiss, now he courts in every room, and were it not for his having his estate made over, even before his wife's face, but that made him fawn and flatter, and somewhat for quietness' sake.

But his wife one day being in his closet, by chance opened a cabinet wherein she found a letter from a mistress of his, whereat she was much amazed, and being startled at it, at last calling herself to herself again, showed it to her husband. He fain would have excused it but that the plainness of truth would not give him leave, whereupon he craved pardon, promising amendment and swearing he would never do so again.

'No,' said she, 'I never will trust a broken wheel. Do you know what is in my power?' said she.

'Yes,' said he, 'a great part of my estate.'

'O how I adore Dame Nature,' said she, 'that gave me those two eyes, prudence to foresee, and providence to provide. But I have not only your estate, but your honour and fame in my power, so that, if I please, all that see you shall hiss at you and condemn whatsoever you do. For if you had the beauty of Paris, they would say you were but a fair cuckold. If you had the courage of Hector, they would say you were but a desperate cuckold. Had you the wisdom of Ulysses or Solomon, they would laugh and say "There goes he that is not yet so wise as to keep his wife honest." If you had the tongue of Tully* and made as eloquent orations, they would say "There is the prating cuckold." If you were as fine a poet as Virgil or as sweet as Ovid, yet they would laugh and scorn and say "He makes verses whilst his wife makes him a cuckold."'

Now jealousy and rage are her two bawds to corrupt her chastity, the one persuading her to be revenged, to show her husband she could take delight and have lovers as well as he. This makes her curl, paint, prune, dress, make feasts, plays, balls, masques, and have merry-meetings abroad, whereupon she began to find as much pleasure as her husband in variety and now begins to flatter him and to dissemble with him that she may play the whore more privately, finding a delight in obscurity, thinking that most sweet which is stolen. So they play, like children, at bo-peep in adultery and face it out with fair looks and smooth it over with sweet words and live with false hearts and die with large consciences. But these, repenting when they died, made a fair end.

'Of a Civil War', from *The World's Olio*

The greatest storm that shipwrecks honest education, good laws and decent customs is civil-wars, which splits the vessel of a common-wealth and buries it in the waves of ruin. But civil-wars may be compared to a pair of cards which, when they are made up in order, every several suit is by itself, as from one, two and three and so to the tenth card, which is like the commons in several degrees, in order, and the coat cards by themselves, which are the nobles; but factions, which are like gamesters when they play, setting life at the stake, shuffle them together, intermixing the nobles and commons, where loyalty is shuffled from the crown, duty from parents, tenderness from children, fidelity from masters, continencies from husbands and wives, truth from friends, from justice innocency, charity from misery. Chance plays and fortune draws the stakes.

DOROTHY OSBORNE
(1627–1695)

Letters

[SATURDAY 8 OF SUNDAY 9 JANUARY 1653]

There is nothing moves my charity like gratitude, and when a beggar's thankful for a small relief, I always repent it was not more. But seriously, this place* will not afford much towards the enlarging of a letter, and I am grown so dull with living in't (for I am not willing to confess that I was always so) as to need all helps. Yet you shall see I will endeavour to satisfy you, upon condition you will tell me why you quarrelled so, at your last letter; I cannot guess at it, unless it were that you repented you told me so much of your story, which I am not apt to believe neither because it would not become our friendship, a great part of it consisting (as I have been taught) in a mutual confidence, and to let you see that I believe it so, I will give you an account of myself, and begin my story, as you did yours, from our parting at Goring House.*

I came down hither not half so well pleased as I went up, with an engagement upon me that I had little hope of ever shaking off, for I had made use of all the liberty my friends would allow me to preserve my own and 'twould not do, he was so weary of his,* that he would part with 't upon any terms. As my last refuge, I got my brother to go down with him to see his house, who when he came back made the relation I wished. He said the seat was as ill, as so good a country would permit, and the house so ruined for want of living in it, as it would ask a good proportion of time, and money, to make it fit for a woman to confine herself to. This (though it were not much) I was willing to take hold of, and made it considerable enough to break the agreement. I had no quarrel to his person or his fortune, but was in love with neither, and much out of love with a thing called marriage, and have since thanked God I was so, for 'tis not long since one of my brothers writ me word of him, that he was killed in a duel, though since I hear 'twas the other that was killed and he is fled upon't, which does not mend the matter much. Both made me glad I had 'scaped him, and sorry for his misfortune, which in earnest was the least return his many civilities to me could deserve.

Presently after this was at an end, my mother died and I was left at liberty to mourn her loss a while. At length, my aunt (with whom I was when you last saw me) commanded me to wait on her at London, and when I came she told me how much I was in her care, how well she loved me for my mother's sake, and something for my own, and drew out a long, set speech, which ended in a good motion (as she called it) and truly I saw no harm in it, for by what I had heard of the gentleman* I guessed he expected a better fortune than mine, and it proved so, yet he protested he liked me so well, that he was very angry my father would not be persuaded to give up £1000 more with me, and I him so ill, that I vowed if I had had £1000 less I should have thought it too much for him, and so we parted. Since, he has made a story with a new mistress that is worth you knowing, but too long for a letter. I'll keep it for you.

After this, some friends that had observed a gravity in my face, which might become an elderly man's wife (as they termed it) and a mother-in-law,* proposed a widower* to me that had four daughters, all old enough to be my sisters. But he had a great estate, was as fine a gentleman as ever England bred, and the very pattern of wisdom. I that knew how much I wanted it, thought this the safest place for me to engage in, and was mightily pleased to think I had met with one at last that had wit enough for himself and me too. But shall I tell you what I thought when I knew him? (You will say nothing on't.) 'Twas the vainest, impertinent, self-conceited, learned, coxcomb that ever yet I saw—to say more were to spoil his marriage, which I hear he is towards with a daughter of my Lord of Coleraine's, but for his sake I shall take heed of a fine gentleman as long as I live. Before I had quite ended with him, coming to town about that, and some other occasions of my own, I fell in Sir Thomas's* way, and what humour took him I cannot imagine, but he made very formal addresses to me, and engaged his mother and my brother to appear in't. This bred a story pleasanter than any I have told you yet, but so long a one that I must reserve it till we meet, or make it a letter of itself, only by this you may see 'twas not for nothing he commended me;* though to speak seriously, it was, because it was to you, otherwise I might have missed off his praises, for we have hardly been cousins since the breaking up of that business.*

The next thing I desired to be rid on was a scurvy spleen* that I have ever been subject to, and to that purpose was advised to drink the waters.* There I spent the latter end of the Summer, and at my coming here, found that a gentleman* (who had some estate in this country) had been treating with my brother, and it yet goes on fair and softly. I do not know him so well as to give you much of his character: 'tis a modest, melancholy, reserved man, whose head is so taken up with little philosophical studies that I admire how I found a room there. 'Twas sure by chance, and unless he is pleased with that part of my humour which other people think the worst, 'tis very possible the next new experiment may crowd me out again.

Thus you have all my late adventures, and almost as much as this paper will hold.* The rest shall be employed in telling you how sorry I am that you have got such a cold. I am the more sensible of your trouble by my own, for I have newly got one myself; but I will send you that which uses to cure me. 'Tis like the rest of my medicines: if it do no good, 'twill be sure to do no harm, and 'twill be no great trouble to you to eat a little on't now and then, for the taste as it is not excellent, so 'tis not very ill. One thing more I must tell you, which is that you are not to take it ill that I mistook your age* by my computation of your journey through this country, for I was persuaded t'other day that I could not be less than 30 year old by one that believed it himself, because he was sure 'twas a great while since he had heard of such a one in the world

as, your humble Servant

[SATURDAY] 22 JANUARY [1653]

Not to confirm you in your belief of dreams, but to avoid your reproaches, I will tell you a pleasant one of mine. The night before I received your first letter, I dreamt one brought me a packet and told me 'twas from you. I, that remembered you were by your own appointment to be in Italy at that time, asked the messenger where he had it, who told me my Lady your mother sent him with it to me. There my memory failed me a little, for I forgot you had told me she was dead, and meant to give her many humble thanks if ever I were so happy as to see her. When I had opened the letter, I found in it two rings; one was as I remember an emerald doublet, but broken in the carriage I suppose, as it might well be coming so far, t'other was plain gold, with the longest and the strangest posy* that ever was. Half on't was Italian, which for my life I could not guess at, though I spent much time about it. The rest was, there was a marriage in Cana of Galilee,* which though it was Scripture, I had not that reverence for it in my sleep, that I should have had I think if I had been awake, for in earnest the oddness on't put me into that violent laughing, that I waked myself with it and as a just punishment upon me, from that hour to this, I could never learn whom those rings were for, nor what was in the letter besides.

This is but as extravagant as yours, for 'tis as likely your mother should send me letters as that I should make a journey to see poor people hanged, or that your teeth should drop out at this age. And now I am out of your dreaming debt, let me be bold to tell you I believe you have been with Lilly* yourself; nothing but he could tell you my knight's strange name.* I'll swear I could never remember it when I was first concerned in't, and when people asked it me and were not satisfied with truth, (for they took my ignorance for a desire to conceal him) I was fain to make names for him and so instead of one odd servant I had gotten twenty. But in earnest now, where have you fished him out, for I think he is as little known in the world as I could have wished he should have been if I had married him?

I am sorry you are not satisfied with my exceptions to your friend:* I spake in general terms of him, and was willing to spare him as much as I could, but everybody is allowed to defend themselves. You may remember a quality that you discovered in him when he told you the story of his being at St Malo, and in earnest he gave me so many testimonies that it was natural to him, as I could not hope he would ever leave it, and consequently could not believe anything he ever had or should say. If this be not enough I can tell you more, hereafter. And to remove the opinion you have of my niceness* or being hard to please, let me assure you, I am so far from desiring my husband should be fond of me at threescore, that I would not have him so at all; 'tis true I should be glad to have him always kind, and know no reason why he should be wearier of being my master than he was of being my servant. But it is very possible I may talk ignorantly of marriage. When I come to make sad experiments on't in my own person, I shall know more, and say less, for fear of disheartening others (since 'tis no advantage to foreknow a misfortune that cannot be avoided) and for fear of being pitied, which of all things I hate. Lest you should be of the same humour, I will not pity you, as lame as you are, and to speak truth, if you did like it you shall not have it, for you do not deserve it: would anybody in this world but you make such haste for a new cold before the old one has left him, in a year too when mere colds kill as many as a plague uses to do.

Well, seriously, either resolve to have more care of yourself, or I renounce my friendship, and as a certain king (that my learned knight is well acquainted with) who, seeing one of his confederates in so happy a condition as it was not likely to last, sent his ambassador presently to break off the league betwixt them, lest he should be obliged to mourn the change of his fortune if he continued his friend. So I: with a great deal more reason do I declare that I will no longer be a friend to one that's none to himself, nor apprehend the loss of what you hazard every day at tennis. They had served you well enough if they had crammed a dozen ounces of that precious medicine down your throat to have you remember a quinsy.* But I have done and am now at leisure to tell you that it is that daughter of my Lord of Holland's* (who makes, as you say, so many sore eyes with looking on her) that is here, and if I know her at all, or have any judgement, her beauty is the least of her excellencies. And now I speak of her, she has given me the occasion to make a request to you. It will come very seasonably after my chiding and I have great reason to expect you should be in the humour of doing anything for me. She says that seals are much in fashion and by showing me some that she has, has set me a-longing for some too. Such as are oldest, and oddest, are most prized, and if you know anybody that is lately come out of Italy, 'tis ten to one but they have store, for they are very common there. I do remember you once sealed a letter to me with as fine a one as I have seen. It was a Neptune I think, riding upon a dolphin, but I'm afraid it was not yours, for I saw it no more. Any old Roman head is a present for a prince; if such things come your way, pray remember me.

I am sorry the new carrier* makes you rise so early, 'tis not good for your cold. How might we do that you might lie a-bed, and yet I have your letter? You must use to write before he comes, I think, that it may be sure to be ready against he goes. In earnest consider on't, and take some course that your health and my letters may be both secured, for the loss of either would be very sensible to your humble*

[SATURDAY 5 OR SUNDAY 6 MARCH 1653]

Your last letter came like a pardon to one upon the block.* I had given over the hopes on't, having received my letters by the other carrier, who uses always to be last. The loss put me hugely out of order, and you would both have pitied and laughed at me, if you could have seen how woodenly I entertained the widow* who came hither the day before, and surprised me very much. Not being able to say anything, I got her to cards, and there with a great deal of patience lost my money to her, or rather I gave it as my ransom. In the midst of our play in comes my blessed boy* with your letter, and in earnest I was not able to disguise the joy it gave me, though one was by that is not much your friend* and took notice of a blush that for my life I could not keep back. I put up the letter in my pocket, and made what haste I could to lose the money I had left, that I might take occasion to go fetch some more. But I did not make such haste back again, I can assure you: I took time enough to have coined myself some money if I had had the art on't and left my brother enough to make all his addresses to her, if he were so disposed. I know not whether he was pleased or not, but I am sure I was.

You make so reasonable demands, that 'tis not fit you should be denied. You ask my thoughts but at one hour; you will think me bountiful, I hope, when I shall tell you that I know no hour when you have them not. No, in earnest my very dreams are yours, and I have got such a habit of thinking of you, that any other thought intrudes and grows uneasy to me. I drink your health every morning in a drench that would poison a horse I believe, and 'tis the only way I have to persuade myself to take it. 'Tis the infusion of steel* and makes me so horridly sick that every day at ten a clock I am making my will, and taking leave of all my friends—you will believe you are not forgot then. They tell me I must take this ugly drink a fortnight, and then begin another as bad, but unless you say so too I do not think I shall, 'tis worse than dying by the half.

I am glad your father is so kind to you; I shall not dispute it with him because 'tis much more in his power than in mine, but I shall never yield that 'tis more in his desires. Sure, he was much pleased with that which was a truth when you told it him, but would have been none if he had asked the question sooner. He thought there was no danger of you, since you were more ignorant and less concerned in my being in town than he; if I were Mrs Cl.* he would be more my friend, but howsoever, I am much his servant as he is your father.

I have sent you your book, and since you are at leisure to consider the moon, you may be enough to read *Cleopatra*,* therefore I have sent you three tomes. When you have done with those you shall have the rest, and I believe they will please. There is a story of Artemise* that I will recommend to you; her disposition I like extremely, it has a great deal of gratitude in't, and if you meet with one Britomart pray send me word how you like him.

I am not displeased that my Lord makes no more haste, for though I am very willing you should go the journey* for many reasons, yet two or three months hence sure will be soon enough to visit so cold a country and I would not have you endure two winters in one year. Besides, I look for my eldest brother and my cousin Moll here shortly and I should be glad to have nobody to entertain but you whilst you are here. Lord that you had the invisible ring or Fortunatus* his wishing hat! Now, at this instant, you should be here. My brother is gone to wait upon the widow homewards, she that was born to persecute you and I, I think. She has so tired me with being here (but two days) that I do not think I shall accept of the offer she has made me of living with her in case my father dies before I have disposed of myself. Yet we are very great, and for my comfort she says she will come again about the latter end of June, and stay longer with me.

My aunt is still in town, kept by her business which I am afraid will not go well, they do so delay it, and my precious uncle does so visit her, and is so kind, that without doubt some mischief will follow. Do you know his son, my cousin Harry?* 'Tis a handsome youth, and well natured, but such a goose, and he has bred him so strangely, that he needs all his ten thousand pound a year. I would fain have him marry my Lady Diana, she was his mistress when he was a boy. He had more wit then than he has now I think, and I have less wit than he, sure, for spending my paper upon him when I have so little. Here is hardly room for Your affectionate friend and servant.

[TUESDAY 29 MARCH 1653]

There shall be two posts this week, for my brother sends his groom up and I am resolved to make some advantage of it. Pray what the paper denied me in your last let me receive by him. Your fellow servant* is a sweet jewel to tell tales of me. The truth is, I cannot deny but that I have been very careless of myself, but alas, who would have been other. I never thought my life a thing worth my care whilst nobody was concerned in't but myself, now I shall look upon't as something that you would not lose, and therefore shall endeavour to keep it for you. But then you must return my kindness with the same care of a life that's much dearer to me. I shall not be so unreasonable as to desire that for my satisfaction you should deny yourself a recreation* that is pleasing to you, and very innocent sure, when 'tis not used in excess, but I cannot consent you should disorder yourself with it, and Jane was certainly in the right when she told you I would have chid if I had seen you so endanger a health that I am so much concerned in. But for what she tells you of my melancholy, you must not believe. She thinks nobody in good humour unless they laugh perpetually as Nan* and she does, which I was never given to much, and now I have been so long accustomed to my own natural dull humour, nothing can alter it. 'Tis not that I am sad, for as long as you and the rest of my friends are well, I thank God I have no occasion to be so, but I never appear to be very merry, and if I had all that I could wish for in the world, I do not think it would make any visible change in my humour. And yet with all my gravity I could not but laugh at your encounter in the park, though I was not pleased that you should leave a fair lady, and go lie upon the cold ground. That is full as bad as over-heating yourself at tennis and therefore remember 'tis one of the things you are forbidden.

You have reason to think your father kind and I have reason to think him very civil; all his scruples are very just ones, but such as time and a little good fortune (if we were either of us lucky to it) might satisfy. He may be confident I can never think of disposing myself without my father's consent, and though he has left it more in my power than almost anybody leaves a daughter, yet certainly I were the worst natured person in the world if his kindness were not a greater tie upon me than any advantage he could have reserved. Besides that, 'tis my duty, from which nothing can ever tempt me.

Nor could you like it in me if I should do otherwise; 'twould make me unworthy of your esteem. But if ever that may be obtained or I left free, and you in the same condition, all the advantages of fortune or person imaginable met together in one man should not be preferred before you. I think I cannot leave you better than with this assurance. 'Tis very late and having been abroad all this day I knew not till e'en now of this messenger. Good night to you. There needed no excuse for the conclusion of this letter: nothing can please me better. Once more good night, I am half in a dream already. Your

For Mr Temple—

[THURSDAY 14 APRIL 1653]

Sir

I received your letter today when I thought it almost impossible that I should be sensible of anything but my father's sickness and my own affliction in it. Indeed he was then so dangerously ill that we could not reasonably hope he should outlive this day, yet he is now I think, thank God, much better, and I am come so much to myself with it as to undertake a long letter to you whilst I watch by him. Towards the latter end it will be excellent stuff I believe, but alas you may allow me to dream sometimes: I have had so little sleep since my father was sick that I am never thoroughly awake. Lord how have I wished for you! Here do I sit all night by a poor moped* fellow that serves my father, and have much ado to keep him awake and myself too. If you heard the wise discourse that is between us, you would swear we wanted sleep, but I shall leave him tonight to entertain himself and try if I can write as wisely as I talk.

I am glad all is well again. In earnest it would have lain upon my conscience if I had been the occasion of making your poor boy* lose a service that, if he has the wit to know how to value it, he would never have forgiven it me while he had lived. But while I remember it, let me ask you if you did not send my letter and *Cleopatra* where I directed you for my Lady.* I received one from her today full of the kindest reproaches that she has not heard from me this three weeks. I have writ constantly to her, but I do not so much wonder that the rest are lost as that she seems not to have received that which I sent to you, nor the books. I do not understand it, but I know there is no fault of yours in't. But hark you, if you think to 'scape with sending me such bits of letters you are mistaken. You say you are often interrupted and I believe it, but you must use then to begin to write before you receive mine, and whensoever you have any spare time, allow me some of it. Can you doubt that anything can make your letters cheap. In earnest 'twas unkindly said, and if I could be angry with you, it should be for that. No certainly they are, and ever will be, dear to me, as that which I receive a huge contentment by. How shall I long when you are gone your journey to hear from you, how shall I apprehend a thousand accidents that are not likely, nor will never happen, I hope. O if you do not send me long letters then, you are the cruellest person that can be. If you love me, you will, and if you do not, I shall never love myself. You need not fear such a command as you mention, alas I am too much concerned that you should love me ever to forbid it you; 'tis all that I propose of happiness to myself in the world.

The turning* of my paper has waked me: all this while I was in a dream, but 'tis no matter, I am content you should know they are of you, and that when my thoughts are left most at liberty, they are the kindest. I'll swear my eyes are so heavy that I hardly see what or how I write, nor do I think you will be able to read it when I have done. The best on't is 'twill be no great loss to you if you do not, for sure the greatest part on't is not sense and yet on my conscience I shall go on with it. 'Tis like people that talk in their sleep: nothing interrupts them but talking to them again and that you are not like to do at this distance—besides that, at this instant you are, I believe, more asleep than I, and do not so much as dream that I am writing to you. My fellow watchers have been asleep too till just now. They begin to stretch and yawn; they are going to try if eating and drinking can keep them awake and I am kindly invited to be of their company. My father's man has got one of the maids to talk nonsense too* tonight and they have got between them a bottle of ale. I shall lose my share if I do not take them at their first offer; your patience till I have drunk and then I am for you again.

And now in the strength of this ale I believe I shall be able to fill up this paper that's left with something or other. And first let me ask you if you have seen a book of poems newly come out, made by my Lady Newcastle.* For God sake if you meet with it send it me, they say 'tis ten times more extravagant than her dress. Sure the poor woman is a little distracted, she could never be so ridiculous else as to venture at writing books, and in verse too! If I should not sleep this fortnight I should not come to that. My eyes grow a little dim, though, for all the ale, and I believe if I could see it this is most strangely scribbled. Sure I shall not find fault with you writing in haste for anything but the shortness of your letter, and 'twould be very unjust in me to tie you to a ceremony that I do not observe myself. No, for God sake, let there be no such thing between us, a real kindness is so far beyond all compliment that it will never appear's more than when there is least of t'other mingled with it. If then you would have me believe yours to be perfect, confirm it to me by a kind freedom; tell me if there be anything that I can serve you in; employ me as you would do that sister that you say you love so well; chide me when I do anything that is not well, but then make haste to tell me that you have forgiven me, and that you are what I shall ever be,

a faithful friend.

[SATURDAY 18 or SUNDAY 19 JUNE 1653]

Sir, you are more in my debt than you imagine: I never deserved a long letter so much as now, when you sent me a short one. I could tell you such a story ('tis too long to be written) as would make you see (what I never discovered in myself before) that I am a valiant lady in earnest: we have had such a skirmish and upon so foolish an occasion as I cannot tell which is strangest; the emperor* and his proposals began it. I talked merrily on't till I saw my B.* put on his sober face and could hardly then believe he was in earnest. It seems he was, for when I had spoke freely my meaning, it wrought so much with him as to fetch up all that lay upon his stomach; all the people that I have ever in my life refused were brought again upon the stage, like Richard the Third's ghosts, to reproach me withal, and all the kindness his discoveries could make I had for you was layed to my charge. My best qualities (if I had any that are good) served but for aggravations of my fault, and I was allowed to have wit and understanding and discretion in other things, that it might appear I had none in this. Well 'twas a pretty lecture, and I grew warm with it after a while, and in short we came so near an absolute falling out, that 'twas time to give over and we said so much then that we have hardly spoken a word together since; but 'tis wonderful to see what courtesies and legs* pass between us, and as before we were thought the kindest brother and sister, we are certainly now the most complimental couple in England. 'Tis a strange change and I am very sorry for it, but I'll swear I know not how to help it—I look upon't as one of my great misfortunes, and I must bear it, as that which is not my first, nor likely to be my last. 'Tis but reasonable (as you say) that you should see me, and yet I know not, now, how it can well be; I am not for disguises: it looks like guilt, and I would not do a thing I durst not own. I cannot tell whether (if there were a necessity of your coming) I should not choose to have it when he is at home, and rather expose him to the trouble of entertaining a person whose company here would not be pleasing to him and perhaps an opinion that I did it purposely to cross him, than that your coming in his absence should be thought a concealment. 'Twas one reason more than I told you, why I resolved not to go to Epsom this Summer, because I knew he would imagine it an agreement between us, and that something besides my spleen carried me thither. But whether you see me or not you may be satisfied I am safe enough and you are in no danger to lose your prisoner, since so great a violence as this has not broke her chains. You will have nothing to thank me for after this, my whole life will not yield such another occasion to let you see at what rate I value your friendship and I have been much better than my word in doing but what I promised you, since I have found it a much harder thing not to yield to the power of a near relation and a great kindness than I could then imagine it. To let you see I did not repent me of the last commission, I'll give you another. Here is a seal that Walker set for me, and 'tis dropped out; pray give it him to mend.

If anything could be wondered at in this age, I should very much, how you come by your information: 'tis more than I know if Mr Freeman* be my servant. I saw him not long since and he told me no such thing. Do you know him? In earnest he's a pretty gentleman and has a great deal of good nature, I think, which may oblige him perhaps to speak well of his acquaintances without design. Mr Fish* is the Squire of Dames and has so many mistresses that anybody may pretend a share in him and be believed; but though I have the honour to be his near neighbour, to speak freely I cannot brag much that he makes any court to me, and I know no young woman in the country that he does not visit oftener.

I have sent you another tome of *Cyrus*; * pray send the first to Mr Hollingsworth for my Lady.* My cousin Moll went from hence to Cambridge on Thursday and there's an end of Mr B.* I have no company now but my niece Peyton.* My brother will be shortly for the Term,* but will make no long stay in town. I think my youngest brother* comes down with him; remember that you owe me a long letter and something for forgiving your last. I have no room for more than Your

[SATURDAY 8 or SUNDAY 9 OCTOBER 1653]

Sir,

You would have me say something of my coming.* Alas, how fain I would have something to say, but I know no more than you saw in that letter that I sent you. How willingly would I tell you anything that I thought would please you, but I confess I do not love to give uncertain hopes because I do not care to receive them, and I thought there was no need of saying I would be sure to take the first occasion and that I waited with impatience for it, because I hoped you had believed all that already. And so you do, I am sure. Say what you will, you cannot but know my heart enough to be assured that I wish myself with you for my own sake as well as yours. 'Tis rather that you love to hear me say it often than that you doubt it, for I am no dissembler. I could not cry for a husband that were indifferent to me (like your cousin).* No, nor for a husband that I loved neither. I think 'twould break my heart sooner than make me shed a tear; 'tis ordinary griefs that only make me weep. In earnest, you cannot imagine how often I have been told that I had too much franchise in my humour and that 'twas a point of good breeding to disguise handsomely, but I answered still for myself that 'twas not to be expected I should be exactly bred, that had never seen a court since I was capable of anything. Yet I know so much that my Lady Carlisle* would take it very ill if you should not let her get the point of honour. 'Tis all she aims at: to go beyond everybody in compliment. But are you not afraid of giving me a strange vanity with telling me that I write better than the most extraordinary person in the kingdom? If I had not the sense to understand that the reason why you like my letters better is only because they are kinder than hers, such a word might have undone me.

But my Lady Isabella* that speaks and looks and sings and plays, and all so prettily: why cannot I say that she is as free from faults as her sister believes her? No, I am afraid she is not and sorry that those she has are so generally known. My B. did not bring them for an example, but I did, and made him confess she had better have married a beggar than that beast with all his estate; she cannot be excused, but certainly they run a strange hazard that have such husbands as makes them think they cannot be more undone, whatever course they take. Oh, 'tis ten thousand pities. I remember she was the first woman that ever I took notice of for extremely handsome, and in earnest she was then the loveliest thing that could be looked on, I think. But what should she do with beauty now? Were I as she, I would hide myself from all the world; I should think all people that looked on me read it in my face and despised me in their hearts, and at the same time they made me a leg or spoke civilly to me, I should believe they did not think I deserved their respect. I'll tell you who he urged for an example though: my Lord Pembroke* and my Lady, who they say are upon parting after all his passion for her, and his marrying her against the consent of all his friends. But to that I answered that, though he pretended great kindness he had for her, I never heard of much she had for him, and knew she married him merely for advantage. Nor is she a woman of that discretion as to do all that might become her, when she must do it rather as things fit to be done than as things she is inclined to; besides, that what with a splenatic side and a chimical* head, he is but an odd body himself. But is it possible what they say: that my Lord Liec.* and my Lady are in great disorder, and that after forty years patience he has now taken up the cudgels and resolves to venture for the mastery? Methinks he wakes out of his long sleep like a froward child that wrangles and fights with all that comes near it. They say he has turned away almost every servant in the house and left her at Penshurst* to digest it as she can. What an age do we live in where 'tis a miracle if, in ten couple that are married, two of them live so as not to publish it to the world that they cannot agree.

I begin to be of the opinion of him that (when the Roman Church first propounded whether it were not convenient for priests not to marry) said that it might be convenient enough, but sure it was not our Saviour's intention, for he commanded that all should take up their cross and follow him, and for his part he was confident there was no such cross as a wife. This is an ill doctrine for me to preach, but to my friends I cannot but confess that I am afraid much of the fault lies in us, for I have observed that generally in great families the men seldom disagree, but that the women are always scolding, and 'tis most certain that, let the husband be what he will, if the wife have but patience (which sure becomes her best) the disorder cannot be great enough to make a noise. His anger alone when it meets with nothing that resists it cannot be loud enough to disturb the neighbours and such a wife may be said to do as a kinswoman of ours that had a husband who was not always himself, and when he was otherwise, his humour was to rise in the night and, with two bedstaves,* tabor* upon the table an hour together. She took care every night to lay a great cushion upon the table for him to strike on that nobody might hear him and so discover his madness. But 'tis a sad thing when all one's happiness is only that the world does not know you are miserable. For my part, I think it were very convenient that all such as intend to marry should live together in the same house some years of probation and if in all that time they never disagreed, they should then be permitted to marry if they pleased—but how few would do it then! I do not remember that I ever saw or heard of any couple that were bred up so together (as many you know are, they that are designed for one another from children), but they always disliked one another extremely and parted if it were left in their choice. If people proceeded with this caution, the world would end sooner than is expected, I believe, and because with all my wariness 'tis not impossible but I may be caught, nor likely that I should be wiser than everybody else, 'twere best, I think, that I said no more in this point.

What would I give to know that sister* of yours that is so good at discovery. Sure she is excellent company. She has reason to laugh at you when you would have persuaded her the moss was sweet. I remember Jane brought some of it to me to ask me if I thought it had no ill smell and whether she might venture to put it in the box* or not. I told her as I thought she could not put a more innocent thing there, for I did not find that it had any smell at all; besides, that I was willing it should do me some service in requital of the pains I had taken for it. My niece and I wandered through some six hundred acres of wood in search of it to make rocks and strange things that her head is full of, and she admires it more than you did. If she had known I had consented it should have been used to fill up a box, she would have condemned me extremely. I told Jane that you liked her present, and she, I find, is resolved to spoil your compliment and make you confess at last that they are not worth the eating. She threatens to send you more, but you would forgive her if you saw how she baits me every day to go to London. All that I can say will not satisfy her. When I urge (as 'tis true) that there is a necessity of my stay here, she grows furious, cries you will die with melancholy, and confounds me so with stories of your ill humour that I'll swear I think I should go merely to be at quiet, if it were possible, though there were no other reason for it. But I hope 'tis not so ill as she would have me believe it, though I know your humour is strangely altered from what it was, and I am sorry to see it. Melancholy must needs do you more hurt than to another to whom it may be natural, as I think it is to me, therefore if you loved me you would take heed on't. Can you believe that you are dearer to me than the whole world besides and yet neglect yourself? If you do not, you wrong a perfect friendship, and if you do, you must consider my interest in you and preserve yourself to make me happy. Promise me this, or I shall haunt you worse than she does me.

Scribble how you please, so you make your letters long enough. You see I give you good example. Besides I can assure you we do perfectly agree if you receive no satisfaction but from my letters; I have none but what yours give me.

[SATURDAY 22 OR SUNDAY 23 OCTOBER 1653]

You say I abuse you and Jane says you abuse me when you say you are not melancholy. Which is to be believed? Neither I think, for I could not have said so positively as (it seems) she did, that I should not be in town till my B. came back. He was not gone when she writ, nor is not yet, and if my B. Peyton* had come before his going, I had spoiled her prediction. But now it cannot be, for he goes on Monday or Tuesday at farthest. I hope you deal truly with me too in saying that you are not melancholy (though she does not believe it). I am thought so many times when I am not at all guilty on't. How often do I sit in company a whole day and when they are gone am not able to give an account of six words that was said, and many times could be so much better pleased with the entertainment my own thoughts give me that 'tis all I can do to be so civil as not to let them see they trouble me. This may be your disease. However, remember you have promised me to be careful of yourself and that if I secure what you have entrusted me with, you will answer for the rest. Be this our bargain then, and look that you give me as good an account of one as I shall give you of t'other.

In earnest, I was strangely vexed to see myself forced to disappoint you* so and felt your trouble and my own too. How often have I wished myself with you, though but for a day for an hour. I would have given all the time I am to spend here for it with all my heart. You could not but have laughed if you had seen me last night. My Br. And Mr Gibson* were talking by the fire and I sat by, but as no part of the company. Amongst other things (which I did not at all mind) they fell into a discourse of flying and both agreed that it was very possible to find out a way that people might fly like birds and dispatch their journeys. So I, that had not said a word all night, started up at that and desired they would say a little more in it, for I had not marked the beginning. But instead of that they both fell into so violent a laughing that I should appear so much concerned in such an art. But they little knew of what use it might have been to me. Yet I saw you last night; but 'twas in a dream, and before I could say a word to you, or you to me, the disorder my joy to see you had put me into waked me.

Just now I was interrupted too and called away to entertain two dumb gentlemen. You may imagine whether I was pleased to leave my writing to you for their company. They have made such a tedious visit too, and I am so tired with making signs and tokens for everything I had to say—good God, how do those that live always with them? They are brothers and the eldest is a baronet, has a good estate, a wife and three or four children. He was my servant heretofore and comes to see me still for old love's sake, but if he could have made me mistress of the world I could not have had him, and yet I'll swear he has nothing to be disliked in him but his want of tongue, which in a woman might have been a virtue.

I sent you a part of *Cyrus* * last week, where you will meet with one Doralize in the story of Abradate and Panthée; the whole story is very good, but her humour makes the best part of it. I am of her opinion in most things that she says in her character of l'honnest homme* that she is in search of, and her resolution of receiving no heart that had been offered to anybody else. Pray tell me how you like her, and what fault you find in my Lady Car's letter;*

methinks* the hand and the style both show her a great person, and 'tis writ in the way that's now affected by all that pretend to wit and to good breeding, only I am a little scandalised, I confess, that she uses that word faithful, she that never knew how to be so in her life.

I have sent you my picture* because you wished for it, but pray let it not presume to disturb my Lady Sunderland's.* Put it in some corner where no eyes may find it out but yours, to whom it is only intended. 'Tis no very good one, but the best I shall ever have drawn of me, for as my Lady says, my time for pictures is past, and therefore I have always refused to part with this because I was sure the next would be a worse. There is a beauty in youth that everybody has once in their lives, and I remember my mother used to say there was never anybody (that was not deformed) but were handsome to some reasonable degree once between fourteen and twenty. It must hang with the light on the left hand of it, and you may keep it if you please till I bring you the original, but then I must borrow it, (for 'tis no more mine if you like it) because my Br. is often bringing people into my closet where it hangs to show them other pictures that are there and if he should miss this long from thence 'twould trouble his jealous head.

You are not the first that has told me I knew better what quality I would not have in a husband, than what I would, but it was more pardonable in them; I thought you had understood better what kind of person I liked than anybody else could possibly have done, and therefore did not think it necessary to make you that description too. Those that I reckoned up were only such as I could not be persuaded to have, upon no terms, though I had never seen such a person in my life as Mr T.,* not but that all those may make very good husbands to some women, but they are so different from my humour that 'tis not possible we should ever agree, for though it might be reasonable enough expected that I should conform mine to theirs, (to my shame be it spoken) I could never do it, and I have lived so long in the world and so much at my own liberty that whosoever has me must be content to take me as they find me, without hope of ever making me other than I am: I cannot so much as disguise my humour. When it was designed that I should have had Sir Jus.* my Br. used to tell me he was confident that with all his wisdom, any woman that had wit and discretion might make an ass of him and govern him as she pleased. I could not deny but possibly it might be so, but 'twas that I was sure I could never do, and though 'twas likely I should have forced myself to so much compliance as was necessary for a reasonable wife, yet farther than that no design could ever have carried me, and I could not have flattered him into a belief that I admired him to gain more than he and all his generation are worth. 'Tis such an ease (as you say) not to be solicitous to please others; in earnest, I am no more concerned whether people think me handsome or ill-favoured, whether they think I have wit or that I have none, than I am whether they think my name Eliz. or Dor. I would do nobody no injury, but I should never desire to please above one and that one I must love too, or else I should think it a trouble and consequently not do it. I have made a general confession to you, will you give me absolution? Methinks you should, for you are not much better by your own relation, therefore 'tis easiest for us to forgive one another. When you hear anything from your father, remember that I am his humble servant and much concerned in his health. I am Yours

[SATURDAY 17 OR SUNDAY 18 DECEMBER 1653]

I am extremely sorry that your letter miscarried, but I am confident my B. has it not. As cunning as he is, he could not hide it so from me, but that I should discover it some way or other. No, he was here, and both his men, when this letter should have come and not one of them stirred out that day; indeed the next day they went all to London. The note you writ to Jane came in one of Nan's by Collins, but nothing else. It must be lost by the porter that was sent with it, and 'twas very unhappy that there should be anything in it of more consequence than ordinary. It may be numbered amongst the rest of our misfortunes, all which an inconsiderate passion has occasioned. You must pardon me, I cannot be reconciled to it, 't has been the ruin of us both. 'Tis true that nobody must imagine to themselves ever to be absolute masters on't, but there is great difference betwixt that and yielding to it, between striving with it, and soothing it up till it grows too strong for one. Can I remember how ignorantly and innocently I suffered it to steal upon me by degrees, how under a mask of friendship I cozened myself into that which, had it appeared to me at first in its true shape, I had feared and shunned? Can I discern that it has made the trouble of your life, and cast a cloud upon mine that will help to cover me in my grave? Can I know that it wrought so upon us both as to make neither of us friends to one another, but agree in running wildly to our own destructions and perhaps of some more innocent persons who might live to curse our folly that gave them so miserable a being? Ah, if you love yourself or me, you must confess that I have reason to condemn this senseless passion that wheresoe'er it comes destroys all that entertain it; nothing of judgement or discretion can live with it, and puts everything else out of order, before it can find a place for itself.* What has it not brought my poor Lady Anne Blunt* to, she is the talk of all the footmen and boys in the street, and will be company for them shortly, who yet is so blinded by her passion as not at all to perceive the misery she has brought herself to, and this fond love of hers has so rooted all sense of nature out of her heart, that they say she is no more moved than a statue with the affliction of a father and mother that doted on her, and had placed the comfort of their lives in her preferment. With all this, is it not manifest to the whole world that Mr Blunt could not consider anything in this action but his own interest, and that he makes her a very ill return for all her kindness. If he had loved her truly, he would have died rather than have been the occasion of this misfortune to her.

My Cousin Fr.* (as you observe very well) may say fine things now she is warm in Moor Park, but she is very much altered in her opinions since her marriage, if these be her own. She left a gentleman that I could name whom she had much more of kindness for than ever she had for Mr Fr. because his estate was less, and upon the discovery of some letters that her mother intercepted, suffered herself to be persuaded that 23 hundred pound a year was better than twelve, though with a person she loved, and has recovered it so well that you see she confesses there is nothing in her condition she desires to alter at the charge of a wish. She's happier by much than I shall ever be, but I do not envy her. May she long enjoy it, and I, an early, and a quiet grave, free from the trouble of this busy world, where all with passion pursue their own interests at their neighbours' charges, where nobody is pleased but somebody complains on't, and where 'tis impossible to be without giving and receiving injuries.

You would know what I would be at, and how I intend to dispose of myself. Alas, were I in my own disposal you should come to my grave to be resolved, but grief alone will not kill. All that I can say then is, that I resolve on nothing but to arm myself with patience, to resist nothing that is laid upon me, not struggle for what I have no hope to get. I have no ends nor no designs, nor will my heart ever be capable of any, but like a country wasted by a Civil War, where two opposing parties have disputed their right so long till they have made it worth neither of their conquests, 'tis ruined and desolated by the long strife within it to that degree as 'twill be useful to none, nobody that knows the condition 'tis in will think it worth the gaining, and I shall not cozen anybody with it. No really, if I may be permitted to desire anything it shall be only that I may injure nobody but myself. I can bear anything that reflects only upon me, or if I cannot, I can die, but I would fain die innocent, that I might hope to be happy in the next world, though never in this.

I take it a little ill that you should conjure me by anything with a belief that 'tis more powerful with me than your kindness. No, assure yourself, what that alone cannot gain, will be denied to all the world. You would see me, you say. You may do so if you please, though I know not to what end. You deceive yourself if you think it would prevail upon me to alter my intentions. Besides, I can make no contrivances, all must be here and I must endure the noise it will make and undergo the censures of a people that choose ever to give the worst interpretation that anything will bear. Yet if it can be any ease to you to make me more miserable than I am, never spare me, consider yourself only and not me at all; 'tis no more than I deserve for not accepting what you offered me whilst 'twas in your power to make it good, as you say it then was. You were prepared, it seems, but I was surprised, I confess it. 'Twas a kind fault though, and you may pardon it with more reason than I have to forgive it myself. And let me tell you this too: as lost and as wretched as I am, I have still some sense of my reputation left in me. I find that to my last I shall attempt to preserve it as clear as I can, and to do that I must, if you see me thus, make it the last of our interviews. What can excuse me if I should entertain any person that is known to pretend to me, when I can have no hope of ever marrying him, and what hope can I have of that when the fortune that can only make it possible to me depends upon a thousand accidents and contingencies: the uncertainty of the place 'tis in,* and the government it may fall under, your father's life, or his success, his disposal of himself and then of his fortune, besides the time that must necessarily be required to produce all this, and the changes that may probably bring with it which 'tis impossible for us to foresee. All this considered, what have I to say for myself when people shall ask what 'tis I expect? Can there be anything vainer than such a hope upon such grounds? You must needs see the folly on't yourself, and therefore examine your own heart what 'tis fit for me to do, and what you can do for a person you love, and that deserves your compassion if nothing else: a person that will always have an inviolable friendship for you, a friendship that shall take up all the room my passion held in my heart and govern there as master till death come to take possession and turn it out.

Why should you make an impossibility where there is none? A thousand accidents might have taken me from you and you must have born it. Why should not your own resolution work as much upon you, as necessity and time does infallibly upon all people? Your father would take it very ill, I believe, if you should pretend to love me better than he did my Lady, yet she is dead and he lives, and perhaps may do to love again. There is a gentlewoman in this country that loved so passionately for six or seven years, that her friends, who kept her from marrying, fearing her death, consented to it, and within half a year her husband died, which afflicted her so strangely nobody thought she would have lived. She saw no light but candles in three year, nor came abroad in five, and now that 'tis some nine years past, she is passionately taken again with another and how long she has been so nobody knows but herself. This is to let you see 'tis not impossible what I ask, nor unreasonable. Think on't and attempt it at least, but do it sincerely and do not help your passion to master you. As you have ever loved me, do this. The carrier shall bring you[r] letters to Suffolk House to Jones. I shall long to hear from you, but if you should deny me the only hope that's left me, I must beg you will defer it till Christmas day be past, for to deal freely with you, I have some devotions to perform then which must not be disturbed with anything, and nothing is like to do it so much as so sensible an affliction. Adieu.

[SUNDAY] APRIL the 2d 1654

There was never anybody more surprised than I was with your last. I read it so coldly and was so troubled to find that you were no forwarder on your journey; but when I came to the last, and saw Dublin at the date, I could scarce believe my eyes. In earnest it transported me so that I could not forebear expressing my joy in such a manner as, had anybody been by to have observed me, they would have suspected me no very sober person. You are safe arrived you say, and pleased with the place already only because you meet with a letter of mine there. In your next I expect some other commendations on't, or else I shall hardly make such a haste to it as people here believe I will. All the servants have been to take their leaves on me and say how sorry they are to hear I am going out of the land; some beggars at the door has* made so ill a report of Ireland to them, that they pity me extremely. But you are pleased, I hope, to hear I am coming to you; the next fair wind, expect me. 'Tis not to be imagined the ridiculous stories they have made, nor how J.B.* cries out on me for refusing him and choosing his chamber fellow. Yet he pities me too and swears I am condemned to be the miserablest person upon earth. With all his quarrel to me, he does not wish me so ill as to be married to the proudest, imperious, insulting, ill-natured man that ever was, one that before he has had me a week shall use me with contempt, and believe that the favour was of his side. Is not this very comfortable? But pray make it no quarrel; I make it none, I can assure you, and though he knew you before I did, I do not think he knows you so well; besides that, his testimony is not of much value. I am to spend this next week in taking leave of this country and all the company in't, perhaps never to see it more. From hence I must go into Northamptonshire to my Lady R.* and so to London, where I shall find my aunt and my B. P.,* betwixt whom I think to divide this Summer.

Nothing has happened since you went worth your knowledge. My Lord Marquess Hartford has lost his eldest son, my Lord Beaucham, who has left a fine young widow. In earnest 'tis great pity; at the rate of our young nobility he was an extraordinary person, and remarkable for an excellent husband. My Lord Campden has fought too, with Mr Stafford, but there's no harm done. You may discern the haste I am in by my writing. There will come a time for long letters again, but there will never come any wherein I shall not be Yours

For Mr William Temple
at Sir John Temple's house
in Damask Street
Dublin.

KATHERINE PHILIPS
(1632–1664)

'Epitaph: On Hector Philips.* At St Sith's Church'*

What on earth deserves our trust?
Youth and beauty both are dust.
Long we gathering are with pain,
What one moment calls again.
Seven years childless marriage past,
A son, a son is born at last;
So exactly limbed and fair,
Full of good spirits, mien, and air,
As a long life promised;
Yet, in less than six weeks, dead.
Too promising, too great a mind
In so small room to be confined:
Therefore, fit in Heaven to dwell,
Quickly broke the prison shell.
So the subtle alchemist,
Can't with Hermes' seal* resist
The powerful spirit's subtler flight,
But 'twill bid him long good night.
So the sun, if it arise
Half so glorious as his eyes,
Like this infant, takes a shroud,
Buried in a morning cloud.

'On the Death of my First and Dearest Child, Hector Philips, born the 23rd of April, and died the 2nd of May 1655. Set by Mr Lawes'*

Twice forty months in wedlock I did stay,
Then had my vows crowned with a lovely boy.
And yet in forty days he dropped away;
O swift vicissitude of human joy!

I did but see him, and he disappeared,
  I did but touch the rosebud, and it fell;
A sorrow unforeseen and scarcely feared,
  So ill can mortals their afflictions spell.

And now (sweet babe) what can my trembling heart
  Suggest to right my doleful fate or thee?
Tears are my muse, and sorrow all my art,
  So piercing groans must be thy elegy.

Thus whilst no eye is witness of my moan,
  I grieve thy loss (ah, boy too dear to live!)
And let the unconcerned world alone,
  Who neither will, nor can refreshment give.

An offering too for thy sad tomb I have,
  Too just a tribute to thy early hearse;
Receive these gasping numbers to thy grave,
  The last of thy unhappy mother's verse.

'To Mrs Mary Awbrey* at Parting'

1

I have examined, and do find,
    Of all that favour me,
There's none I grieve to leave behind
    But only, only thee.
To part with thee I needs must die,
Could parting separate thee and I.

2

But neither chance nor compliment
    Did element our love;
'Twas sacred sympathy was lent
    Us from the choir above.
That friendship fortune did create,
Which fears a wound from time or fate.

3

Our changed and mingled souls are grown
 To such acquaintance now,
That if each would assume their own,
 Alas! we know not how.
We have each other so engrossed,
That each is in the union lost.

4

And thus we can no absence know,
 Nor shall we be confined;
Our active souls will daily go
 To learn each other's mind.
Nay, should we never meet to sense,
Our souls would hold intelligence.

5

Inspired with a flame divine,
 I scorn to court a stay;
For from that noble soul of thine
 I can ne're be away.
But I shall weep when thou dost grieve;
Nor can I die whilst thou dost live.

6

By my own temper I shall guess
 At thy felicity,
And only like my happiness
 Because it pleaseth thee.
Our hearts at any time will tell
If thou, or I, be sick, or well.

7

All honour sure I must pretend,
 All that is good or great;
She that would be Rosania's friend,
 Must be at least complete.
If I have any bravery,
'Tis cause I am so much of thee.

8

Thy lieger* soul in me shall lie,
And all thy thoughts reveal;
Then back again with mine shall fly,
And thence to me shall steal.
Thus still to one another tend;
Such is the sacred name of friend.

9

Thus our twin souls in one shall grow,
And teach the world new love;
Redeem the age and sex, and show
A flame fate dares not move:
And courting death to be our friend,
Our lives together too shall end.

10

A dew shall dwell upon our tomb
Of such a quality,
That fighting armies, thither come,
Shall reconciled be.
We'll ask no epitaph, but say
Orinda* and Rosania.

'A Retired Friendship: To Ardelia.* 23d August 1651'*

1

Come, my Ardelia, to this bower,
Where kindly mingling souls awhile,
Let's innocently spend an hour,
And at all serious follies smile.

2

Here is no quarrelling for crowns,
Nor fear of changes in our fate;
No trembling at the great ones' frowns,
Nor any slavery of state.

3

Here's no disguise, nor treachery,
  Nor any deep concealed design;
From blood and plots this place is free,
  And calm as are those looks of thine.

4

Here let us sit and bless our stars
  Who did such happy quiet give,
As that removed from noise of wars
  In one another's hearts we live.

5

Why should we entertain a fear?
  Love cares not how the world is turned
If crowds of dangers should appear,
  Yet friendship can be unconcerned.

6

We wear about us such a charm
  No horror can be our offence,
For mischief's self can do no harm
  To friendship and to innocence.

7

Let's mark how soon Apollo's beams
  Command the flock to quit their meat,
And not entreat the neighbour streams
  To quench their thirst, but cool their heat.

8

In such a scorching age as this
  Whoever would not seek a shade
Deserve their happiness to miss,
  As having their own peace betrayed.

9

But we (of one another's mind
  Assured)* the boisterous world disdain;
With quiet souls, and unconfined,
  Enjoy what princes wish in vain.

'To My Excellent Lucasia* On Our Friendship, 17 July 1651'

I did not live until this time
    Crowned my felicity,
When I could say without a crime
    I am not thine, but thee.
This carcass breathed and walked and slept,
    So that the world believed
There was a soul the motions kept,
    But they were all deceived.
For as a watch by art is wound
    To motion, such was mine:
But never had Orinda found
    A soul till she found thine;
Which now inspires, cures and supplies
    And guides my darkened breast,
For thou art all that I can prize,
    My joy, my life, my rest.
Nor bridegroom's nor crowned conqueror's mirth
    To mine compared can be:
They have but pieces of this earth,
    I've all the world in thee.
Then let our flame still light and shine,
    (And no bold fear control)
As innocent as our design,
    Immortal as our soul.

'Friendship's Mysteries: To My Dearest Lucasia' (Set by Mr H. Lawes)*

I

Come, my Lucasia, since we see
    That miracles men's faith do move
By wonder and by prodigy,
    To the dull, angry world let's prove
    There's a religion in our love.

2

For though we were designed t'agree,
 That fate no liberty destroys,
But our election is as free
 As angels, who with greedy choice
 Are yet determined to their joys.

3

Our hearts are doubled by their loss,
 Here mixture is addition grown;
We both diffuse, and both engross,
 And we, whose minds are so much one,
 Never, yet ever, are alone.

4

We court our own captivity,
 Than thrones more great and innocent
'Twere banishment to be set free,
 Since we wear fetters whose intent
 Not bondage is, but ornament.

5

Divided joys are tedious found,
 And griefs united easier grow:
We are ourselves but by rebound,
 And all our titles shuffled so,
 Both princes, and both subjects too.

6

Our hearts are mutual victims layed,
 While they (such power in friendship lies)
Are altars, priests, and offerings made,
 And each heart which thus kindly dies,
 Grows deathless by the sacrifice.

'Content: To My Dearest Lucasia'

1

Content, the false world's best disguise,
The search and faction of the wise,
Is so abstruse and hid in night,
That like that fairy Red-Cross knight,*
Who treacherous falsehood for clear truth had got,
Men think they have it, when they have it not.

2

For courts content would gladly own,
But she ne're dwelt about a throne;
And to be flattered, rich or great,
Are things that do man's senses cheat;
But grave experience long since this did see,
Ambition and content could ne're agree.

3

Some vainer would content expect
From what their bright outsides reflect;
But sure content is more divine
Than to be digged from rock or mine;
And they that know her beauties will confess,
She needs no lustre from a glittering dress.

4

In mirth some place her, but she scorns
Th'assistance of such crackling thorns,
Nor owes herself to such thin sport,
That is so sharp, and yet so short;
And painters tell us they the same strokes place
To make a laughing and a weeping face.

5

Others there are that place content
In liberty from government;
But who his passions do deprave,
Though free from shackles, is a slave.
Content and bondage differ only then,
When we are chained by vices, not by men.

6

Some think the camp content does know,
And that she sits o' th' victor's brow;
But in his laurel there is seen
Often a cypress bough between.
Nor will content herself in that place give,
Where noise and tumult and destruction live.

7

But the most discreet believe
The schools* this jewel do receive,
And thus far's true, without dispute,
Knowledge is still the sweetest fruit.
But while men seek for truth they lose their peace;
And who heaps knowledge, sorrow doth increase.

8

But now some sullen hermit smiles,
And thinks he all the world beguiles,
And that his cell and dish contain
What all mankind do wish in vain.
But yet his pleasure's followed with a groan,
For man was never made to be alone.

9

Content herself best comprehends
Betwixt two souls, and they two friends,
Whose either joys in both are fixed,
And multiplied by being mixed;
Whose minds and interests are so the same,
Their very griefs, imparted, lose that name.

10

These, far removed from all bold noise,
And (what is worse) all hollow joys,
Who never had a mean design,
Whose flame is serious and divine,
And calm, and even, must contented be,
For they've both union and society.

11

Then, my Lucasia, we who have
What ever love can give or crave,
With scorn or pity can survey
The trifles which the most betray;
With innocence and perfect friendship fired,
By virtue joined, and by our choice retired.

12

Whose mirrors are the crystal brooks,
Or else each other's hearts and looks;
Who cannot wish for other things
Than privacy and friendship brings;
Whose thoughts and persons changed and mixed are one,
Enjoy content, or else the world has none.

'Orinda to Lucasia, Parting, October 1661, at London'

Adieu, dear object of my love's excess,*
And with thee all my hopes of happiness,
With the same fervent and unchanged heart
Which did its whole self once to thee impart,
(And which, though fortune has so sorely bruised,
Would suffer more, to be from this excused)
I to resign thy dear converse submit,
Since I can neither keep, nor merit it.
Thou hast too long to me confined been,
Who ruin am without, passion within.

My mind is sunk below thy tenderness,
And my condition does deserve it less;
I'm so entangled and so lost a thing
By all the shocks my daily sorrows bring,
That wouldst thou for thy old Orinda call,
Thou hardly couldst unravel her at all.
And should I thy clear fortunes interline
With the incessant miseries of mine?
No, no, I never loved at such a rate,
To tie thee to the rigours of my fate.
As from my obligations thou art free,
Sure thou shalt be so from my injury;
Though every other worthiness I miss,
Yet I'll at least be generous in this.
I'd rather perish without sigh or groan,
Than thou shouldst be condemned to give me one;
Nay, in my soul I rather could allow
Friendship should be a sufferer, than thou;
Go then, since my sad heart has set thee free,
Let all the loads and chains remain on me.
Though I be left the prey of sea and wind,
Thou, being happy, wilt in that be kind;
Nor shall I my undoing much deplore,
Since thou art safe, whom I must value more.
Oh! mayst thou ever be so, and as free
From all ills else, as from my company;
And may the torments thou hast had from it,
Be all that heaven will to thy life permit;
And that they may thy virtue service do,
Mayest thou be able to forgive them too:
But though I must this sharp submission learn,
I cannot yet unwish thy dear concern.
Not one new comfort I expect to see,
I quit my joy, hope, life, and all but thee;
Nor seek I thence aught that may discompose
That mind where so serene a goodness grows.
I ask no inconvenient kindness now,
To move thy passion, or to cloud thy brow;
And thou wilt satisfy my boldest plea

By some few soft remembrances of me,
Which may present thee with this candid thought,
I meant not all the troubles that I brought.
Own not what passion rules, and fate does crush,
But wish thou couldst have done't without a blush;
And that I had been, ere it was too late,
Either more worthy, or more fortunate.
Ah, who can love the thing they cannot prize?
But thou mayst pity though thou dost despise.
Yet I should think that pity bought too dear,
If it should cost those precious eyes a tear.
  Oh, may no minute's trouble thee possess,
But to endear the next hour's happiness;
And mayst thou when thou art from me removed,
Be better pleased, but never worse beloved:
Oh, pardon me for pouring out my woes
In rhyme, now that I dare not do't in prose:
For I must lose whatever is called dear,
And thy assistance all that loss to bear,
And have more cause than ere I had before,
To fear that I shall never see thee more.

'Orinda to Lucasia'

I

Observe the weary birds ere night be done,
How they would fain call up the tardy sun,
    With feathers hung with dew,
    And trembling voices too,
They court their glorious planet to appear,
That they may find recruits of spirits there.
    The drooping flowers hang their heads,
    And languish down into their beds:
While brooks more bold and fierce than they,
    Wanting those beams, from whence
    All things drink influence,
Openly murmur, and demand the day.

2

Thou, my Lucasia, art far more to me,
Than he to all the under-world can be;
From thee I've heat and light,
Thy absence makes my night.
But ah! my friend, it now grows very long,
The sadness weighty, and the darkness strong:
My tears (its dew) dwell on my cheeks,
And still my heart thy dawning seeks,
And to thee mournfully it cries,
That if too long I wait,
Even thou mayest come too late,
And not restore my life, but close my eyes.

APHRA BEHN
(*c.*1640–1689)

The City-Heiress: Or, Sir Timothy Treat-All

To the Right Honourable Henry, Earl of Arundel, and Lord Mowbray.*

MY LORD,

’Tis long that I have with great impatience waited some opportunity to declare my infinite respect to your Lordship; coming, I may say, into the world with a veneration for your illustrious family, and being brought up with continual praises of the renowned actions of your glorious ancestors, both in war and peace, so famous over the Christian world for their virtue, piety, and learning, their elevated birth, and greatness of courage, and of whom all our English history are full of the wonders of their lives: a family of so ancient nobility, and from whom so many heroes have proceeded to bless and serve their King and country, that all ages and all nations mention ’em even with adoration. Myself have been in this our age an eye and ear-witness, with what transports of joy, with what unusual respect and ceremony, above what we pay to mankind, the very name of the great Howards of Norfolk and Arundel, have been celebrated on foreign shores. And when anyone of your illustrious family have passed the streets, the people thronged to praise and bless him, as soon as his name has been made known to the glad crowd. This I have seen with a joy that became a true English heart, (who truly venerate its brave countrymen) and joined my dutiful respects and praises with the most devout; but never had the happiness yet of any opportunity to express particularly that admiration I have and ever had for your Lordship and your great family. Still, I say, I did admire you, still I wished and prayed for you; ’twas all I could or durst. But as my esteem for your Lordship daily increased with my judgment, so nothing could bring it to a more absolute height and perfection than to observe in these troublesome times, this age of lying, peaching, and swearing,* with what noble prudence, what steadiness of mind, what loyalty and conduct you have evaded the snare* that 'twas to be feared was laid for all the good, the brave, and loyal, for all that truly loved our best of kings and this distracted country. A thousand times I have wept for fear that impudence and malice would extend so far as to stain your noble and ever-loyal family with its unavoidable imputations; and as often for joy, to see how undauntedly both the illustrious Duke your father, and yourself, stemmed the raging torrent that threatened, with yours, the ruin of the King and kingdom; all which had not power to shake your constancy or loyalty, for which may Heaven and earth reward and bless you, the noble examples to thousands of failing hearts, who from so great a precedent of loyalty, became confirmed. May Heaven and earth bless you for your pious and resolute bravery of mind, and heroic honesty, when you cried, 'Not guilty!',* that you durst, like your great self, speak conscientious truths in a junta* so vicious, when truth and innocence was criminal, and I doubt not but the soul of that great sufferer bows down from Heaven in gratitude for that noble service done it. All these and a thousand marks you give of daily growing greatness; every day produces to those like me, curious to learn the story of your life and actions, something that even adds a lustre to your great name, which one would think could be made no more splendid; some new goodness, some new act of loyalty or courage, comes out to cheer the world and those that admire you. Nor would I be the last of those that daily congratulate and celebrate your rising glory; nor durst I any other way approach you with it, but this humble one, which carries some excuse along with it.

Proud of the opportunity then, I most humbly beg your Lordship's patronage of a comedy which has nothing to defend it but the honour it begs; and nothing to deserve that honour but its being in every part true Tory! Loyal all over, except one knave, which I hope nobody will take to himself; or if he do, I must e'en say, with Hamlet, 'Then let the stricken deer go weep'.*

It has the luck to be well received* in the town, which not from my vanity pleases me, but that thereby I find honesty begins to come in fashion again, when loyalty is approved, and Whigism becomes a jest where're 'tis met with. And no doubt on't, so long as the royal cause has such patrons as your Lordship, such vigorous and noble supporters, his Majesty will be great, secure and quiet, the nation flourishing and happy, and seditious fools and knaves that have so long disturbed the peace and tranquillity of the world will become the business and sport of comedy, and at last the scorn of that rabble that fondly and blindly worshiped 'em; and whom nothing can so well convince as plain demonstration, which is ever more powerful and prevalent than precept, or even preaching itself. If this have edified effectually, 'tis all I wish; and that your Lordship will be pleased to accept the humble offering is all I beg, and the greatest glory I care should be done,

MY LORD,

Your Lordship's most humble and most obedient servant,

A. BEHN

THE ACTORS' NAMES*

Sir Timothy Treat-All: An old seditious knight that keeps open house for Commonwealthsmen* and true blue Protestants.—He is Uncle to *Tom Wilding*.

Tom Wilding: A Tory, his discarded nephew.

Sir Anthony Meriwill: An old Tory Knight of Devonshire.

Sir Charles Meriwill: His nephew, a Tory also, in love with *Lady Galliard*, and friend to *Wilding*.

Dresswell: A young gentleman, friend to *Wilding*.

Fopington: A hanger-on on *Wilding*.

Jervice: Man to *Sir Timothy*.

Laboir: Man to *Wilding*.

[*Valet*: to *Wilding*.

William: Page/footman to *Lady Galliard*.

Page/Boy: to *Diana*.

Footmen, Guests, Servants, Music, etc.]

Lady Galliard: A rich city-widow, in love with *Wilding*.

Charlotte: The city-heiress, in love with *Wilding*.

Diana: Mistress to *Wilding*, and kept by him.

Mrs Clacket: A city-bawd and Puritan.

Mrs Closet: Woman to *Lady Galliard*.

[*Mrs Censure*: Housekeeper to *Sir Timothy*.

Betty: Maid to *Diana*.]

SCENE: within the walls of London.

PROLOGUE (Written by Mr Otway)*
Spoken by *Mrs Barry*

How vain have proved the labours of the stage,
In striving to reclaim a vicious age!
Poets may write the mischief to impeach,
You care as little what the poets teach
As you regard at church what parsons preach.
But where such follies and such vices reign,
What honest pen has patience to refrain?
At church, in pews, ye most devoutly snore,
And here, got dully drunk, ye come to roar;
Ye go to church to gloat, and ogle there,
And come to meet more lewd convenient* here:
With equal zeal ye honour either place,
And run so very evenly your race,
Y'improve in wit just as you do in grace.
It must be so, some demon has possessed
Our land, and we have never since been blest.
Y' have seen it all, or heard of its renown,
In reverend shape* it stalked about the town,
Six Yeomen tall attending on its frown.
Sometimes with humble note and zealous lore,
'Twould play the apostolic function o'er:
But, Heaven have mercy on us when it swore.*
Whene'er it swore, to prove the oaths were true,
Out of its mouth at random halters flew
Round some unwary neck, by magic thrown,
Though still the cunning devil saved its own:
For when the enchantment could no longer last,
The subtle pug, most dexterously uncast,
Left aweful form for one more seeming pious,
And in a moment varied to defy us:
From silken doctor,* home-spun Ananias*
Left the lewd court, and did in city fix,
Where still by its old arts it plays new tricks,
And fills the heads of fools with politics.
This demon lately drew in many a guest,

To part with zealous guinea for—no feast.*
Who, but the most incorrigible fops,
For ever doomed in dismal cells, called shops,
To cheat and damn themselves to get their livings,
Would lay sweet money out in sham-thanksgivings?
Sham-plots you may have paid for o'er and o'er;
But who ere paid for a sham-treat before?
Had you not better sent your offerings all,
Hither to us, than sequestrators' hall?*
I being your steward, justice had been done ye;
I could have entertained you worth your money.

ACT I SCENE I

The Street

Enter Sir Timothy Treat-All followed by Tom Wilding bare, Sir Charles Meriwill, Fopington, and Footman with a cloak*

Sir Timothy. Trouble me no more: for I am resolved, deaf and obdurate, d'ye see, and so forth.

Wilding. I beseech ye, Uncle, hear me.

Sir Timothy. No.

Wilding. Dear Uncle—

Sir Timothy. No.

Wilding. You will be mortified—

Sir Timothy. No.

Wilding. At least hear me out, Sir.

Sir Timothy. No, I have heard you out too often, Sir, till you have talked me out of many a fair thousand; have had ye out of all the bailiffs, sergeants, and constables' clutches about town, Sir; have brought ye out of all the surgeons, apothecaries, and pocky doctors'* hands that ever pretended to cure incurable diseases, and have crossed ye out of the books of all the mercers, silk-men, exchange-men,* tailors, shoemakers, and sempstresses,* with all the rest of the unconscionable city-tribe of the long bill,* that had but faith enough to trust, and thought me fool enough to pay.

Sir Charles. But, Sir, consider, he's your own flesh and blood.

Sir Timothy. That's more than I'll swear.

Sir Charles. Your only heir.

Sir Timothy. That's more than you or any of his wise associates can tell, Sir.

Sir Charles. Why his wise associates? Have you any exception to the company he keeps? This reflects on me and young Dresswell, Sir, men both of birth and fortune.

Sir Timothy. Why, good Sir Charles Meriwill, let me tell you, since you'll have it out, that you and young Dresswell are able to debauch, destroy, and confound all the young imitating fops in town.

Sir Charles. How, Sir!

Sir Timothy. Nay, never huff, Sir, for I have six thousand pound a year, and value no man. Neither do I speak so much for your particular, as for the company you keep, such termagant Tories as these, (*to Fopington*) who are the very vermin of a young heir, and for one tickling give him a thousand bites.

Fopington. Death! Meaning me, Sir?

Sir Timothy. Yes, you, Sir. Nay, never stare, Sir, I fear you not: no man's hectoring signifies this—in the city, but the constable's; nobody dares be saucy here, except it be in the King's name.

Sir Charles. Sir, I confess he was to blame .

Sir Timothy. Sir Charles, thanks to Heaven, you may be lewd, you have a plentiful estate, may whore, drink, game, and play the devil; your uncle Sir Anthony Meriwill intends to give you all his estate too. But for such sparks as this, and my fop in fashion here, why with what face, conscience, or religion, can they be lewd and vicious, keep their wenches, coaches, rich liveries, and so forth, who live upon charity, and the sins of the nation?

Sir Charles. If he have youthful vices, he has virtues too.

Sir Timothy. Yes, he had; but I know not, you have bewitched him amongst ye (*weeping.*) Before he fell to Toryism, he was a sober civil youth, and had some religion in him, would read the prayers night and morning with a laudable voice, and cry 'Amen' to 'em; 'twould have done one's heart good to have heard him; wore decent clothes, was drunk but upon fasting-nights, and swore but on Sundays and holy-days: and then I had hopes of him. *Still weeping*

Wilding. Aye, Heaven forgive me.

Sir Charles. But, Sir, he's now become a new man, is casting off all his women, is drunk not above five or six times a week, swears not above once in a quarter of an hour, nor has not gamed this two days.—

Sir Timothy. 'Twas because the devil was in's pocket then.

Sir Charles. —Begins to take up at coffee-houses,* talks gravely in the city, speaks scandalously of the government, and rails most abominably against the Pope and the French King.*

Sir Timothy. Aye, aye, this shall not wheedle me out of one English guinea; and so I told him yesterday.

Wilding. You did so, Sir.

Sir Timothy. Yes; by a good token you were witty upon me, and swore I loved and honoured the King nowhere but on his coin.

Sir Charles. Is it possible, Sir?

Wilding. God forgive me, Sir, I confess I was a little overtaken.

Sir Timothy. Aye, so it should seem: for he mistook his own chamber and went to bed to my maid's.

Sir Charles. How! to bed to your maid's! Sure, Sir, 'tis scandal on him.

Sir Timothy. No, no, he makes his brags on't, Sir. Oh that crying sin of boasting! Well fare, I say, the days of old Oliver;* he by a wholesome act,* made it death to boast; so that then a man might whore his heart out, and nobody the wiser.

Sir Charles. Right, Sir, and then the men passed for sober religious persons, and the women for as demure saints—

Sir Timothy. Aye, then there was no scandal, but now they do not only boast what they do, but what they do not.

Wilding. I'll take care that fault shall be mended, Sir.

Sir Timothy. Aye, so will I, if poverty have any feats of mortification; and so farewell to you, Sir.

Going.

Wilding. Stay, Sir, are you resolved to be so cruel then, and ruin all my fortunes now depending?

Sir Timothy. Most religiously—

Wilding. You are?

Sir Timothy. I am.

Wilding. Death, I'll rob.

Sir Timothy. Do and be hanged.

Wilding. Nay, I'll turn Papist.

Sir Timothy. Do and be damned.

Sir Charles. Bless me, Sir, what a scandal would that be to the family of the Treat-alls!

Sir Timothy. Hum! I had rather indeed he turned Turk or Jew, for his own sake, but as for scandalising me, I defy it: my integrity has been known ever since Forty One;* I bought three thousand a year in bishops' lands,* as 'tis well known, and lost it at the King's return; for which I'm honoured by the city. But for his farther satisfaction, consolation, and destruction, know, that I Sir Timothy Treat-all, Knight and Alderman, do think myself young enough to marry, d'ye see, and will wipe your nose with a son and heir of my own begetting, and so forth. *Going away.*

Wilding [*Aside*]. Death! Marry!

Sir Charles [*Aside*]. Patience, dear Tom, or thou't spoil all.

Wilding [*Aside*]. Damn him, I've lost all patience, and can dissemble no longer, though I lose all.—Very good, Sir; hark ye, I hope she's young and handsome, or if she be not, amongst the numerous lusty-stomached Whigs that daily nose your public dinners, some may be found that either for money, charity, or gratitude, may requite your treats. You keep open house to all the party, not for mirth, generosity, or good nature, but for roguery. You cram the brethren, the pious city-gluttons, with good cheer, good wine, and rebellion in abundance, gormandising all comers and goers, of all sexes, sorts, opinions, and religions, young half-witted fops, hot-headed fools, and malcontents. You guttle* and fawn on all, and all in hopes of debauching the King's liege-people into commonwealths-men; and rather than lose a convert, you'll pimp for him. These are your nightly debauches.—Nay, rather than you shall want it, I'll cuckold you myself in pure revenge.

Sir Timothy. How! Cuckold his own natural uncle!

Sir Charles. Oh, he cannot be so profane.

Wilding. Profane! Why, he denied but now the having any share in me, and therefore 'tis lawful. I am to live by my wits, you say, and your old rich good-natured cuckold is as sure a revenue to a handsome young cadet, as a thousand pound a year. Your tolerable face and shape is an estate in the city, and a better bank than your six per cent at any time.

Sir Timothy. Well, Sir, since nature has furnished you so well, you need but up and ride, show and be rich; and so your Servant, witty Mr. Wilding. *Goes out*, [*Wilding*] *looks after him.*

Sir Charles. Whilst I am labouring another's good, I quite neglect my own. This cursed, proud, disdainful Lady Galliard is ever in my head; she's now at church, I'm sure, not for devotion, but to show her charms and throw her darts amongst the gazing crowd, and grows more vain by conquest. I'm near the church, and must step in, though it cost me a new wound. *Wilding stands pausing.*

Wilding. I am resolved.—Well, dear Charles, let's sup together tonight, and contrive some way to be revenged of this wicked uncle of mine. I must leave thee now, for I have an assignation here at church.

Sir Charles. Hah! At church!

Wilding. Aye, Charles, with the dearest she-saint and, I hope, sinner.

Sir Charles [*Aside*]. What, at church? Pox, I shall be discovered now in my amours. That's an odd place for love-intrigues.

Wilding. Oh, I am to pass for a sober discreet person to the relations, but for my mistress, she's made of no such sanctified materials; she is a widow, Charles, young, rich, and beautiful.

Sir Charles [*Aside*]. Hah! If this should prove my widow now!

Wilding. And though at her own dispose, yet is much governed by honour, and a rigid mother, who is ever preaching to her against the vices of youth, and t'other end of the town sparks; dreads nothing so much as her daughter's marrying a villainous Tory.

So the young one is forced to dissemble religion, the best mask to hide a kind mistress in.

Sir Charles [*Aside*]. This must be my Lady Galliard.

Wilding. There is at present some ill understanding between us; some damned honourable fop lays siege to her, which has made me ill received, and I having a new intrigue elsewhere, return her cold disdain, but now and then she crosses my heart too violently to resist her. In one of these hot fits I now am, and must find some occasion to speak to her.

Sir Charles [*Aside*]. By Heaven, it must be she!—I am studying now, amongst all our she-acquaintance, who this should be.

Wilding. Oh, this is of quality to be concealed: but the dearest loveliest hypocrite, white as lilies, smooth as rushes and plump as grapes after showers, haughty her mien, her eyes full of disdain, and yet bewitching sweet; but when she loves: soft, witty, wanton, all that charms a soul, and but for now and then a fit of honour (oh, damn the nonsense!), would be all my own.

Sir Charles [*Aside*]. 'Tis she, by Heaven! Methinks this widow should prove a good fortune to you, as things now stand between you and your uncle.

Wilding. Ah, Charles, but I am otherways disposed of. There is the most charming young thing in nature fallen in love with this person of mine, a rich city-heiress, Charles; I have her in possession.

Sir Charles. How can you love two at once? I've been as wild, and as extravagant, as youth and wealth could render me, but ne're arrived to that degree of lewdness, to deal my heart about: my hours I might, but love should be entire.

Wilding. Ah, Charles, two such bewitching faces would give thy heart the lie:—but love divides us, and I must into church. Adieu till night. [*Exit*]

Sir Charles. And I must follow to resolve my heart in what it dreads to learn. Here, my cloak (*Takes his cloak from his man, and puts it on.*) Hah, church is done! See, they are coming forth!

Enter people cross the stage, as from church; amongst 'em Sir Anthony Meriwill followed by Sir Timothy Treat-All

Hah, my Uncle! He must not see me here.

Throws his cloak over his face.

Sir Timothy. What, my old friend and acquaintance, Sir Anthony Meriwill!

Sir Anthony. Sir Timothy Treat-all!

Sir Timothy. Whe!* How long have you been in town, Sir?

Sir Anthony. About three days, Sir.

Sir Timothy. Three days, and never came to dine with me! 'Tis unpardonable! What, you keep close to the church, I see. You are for the surplice still, old orthodox you. The times cannot mend you, I see.

Sir Anthony. No, nor shall they mar me, Sir.

Sir Charles [*Aside*]. They are discoursing; I'll pass by.

Exit Sir Charles

Sir Anthony. As I take it, you came from church too.

Sir Timothy. Aye, needs must when the Devil drives. I go to save my bacon, as they say, once a month,* and that too, after the porridge* is served up.

Sir Anthony. Those that made it, Sir, are wiser than we. For my part, I love good wholesome doctrine that teaches obedience to my King and superiors, without railing at the government, and quoting scripture for sedition, mutiny, and rebellion. Why here was a jolly fellow this morning made a notable sermon. By George, our country-vicars are mere scholars to your gentlemen town-parsons! Hah, how he handled the text, and run divisions upon't! 'Twould make a man sin with moderation, to hear how he clawed away the vices of the town, whoring, drinking and conventicling,* with the rest of the deadly number.

Sir Timothy. Good lack! An he were so good at whoring and drinking, you'd best carry your nephew, Sir Charles Meriwill, to church; he wants a little documentizing that way.

Sir Anthony. Hum! You keep your old wont still; a man can begin no discourse to you, be it of Prester John,* but you still conclude with my nephew.

Sir Timothy. Good Lord! Sir Anthony, you need not be so purty;*

what I say is the discourse of the whole city, how lavishly you let him live, and give ill examples to all young heirs.

Sir Anthony. The city!* The city's a grumbling, lying, dissatisfied city, and no wise or honest man regards what it says. Do you, or any of the city, stand bound to his scrivener* or tailor? He spends what I allow him, Sir, his own; and you're a fool or knave, choose ye whether, to concern yourself.

Sir Timothy. Good lack! I speak but what wiser men discourse.

Sir Anthony. Wiser men! Wiser coxcombs. What, they would have me train my nephew up a hopeful youth, to keep a merchant's book, or send him to chop logic in a university, and have him return an errant learned ass, to simper, and look demure, and start at oaths and wenches, whilst I fell his woods, and grant leases; and lastly, to make good what I have cozened him of, force him to marry Mrs. Crump, the ill-favoured daughter of some right worshipful.—A pox of all such guardians!

Sir Timothy. Do, countenance sin and expenses, do.

Sir Anthony. What sin, what expenses? He wears good clothes: why, tradesmen get the more by him; he keeps his coach: 'tis for his ease; a mistress: 'tis for his pleasure; he games: 'tis for his diversion. And where's the harm of this? Is there aught else you can accuse him with?

Sir Timothy [*Aside*]. Yes,—a pox upon him, he's my rival too. Why then I'll tell you, Sir, he loves a lady.

Sir Anthony. If that be a sin, Heaven help the wicked!

Sir Timothy. But I mean honourably.—

Sir Anthony. Honourably! [*Angrily*] Why, do you know any infirmity in him, why he should not marry?

Sir Timothy. Not I, Sir.

Sir Anthony. Not you, Sir? Why then you're an ass, Sir. But is the lady young and handsome?

Sir Timothy. Aye, and rich too, Sir.

Sir Anthony. No matter for money, so she love the boy.

Sir Timothy. Love him! No, Sir, she neither does, nor shall love him.

Sir Anthony. How, Sir, nor shall love him! By George, but she shall, and lie with him too, if I please, Sir.

Sir Timothy. How, Sir! Lie with a rich city-widow, and a lady, and to be married to a fine reverend old gentleman within a day or two?

Sir Anthony. His name, Sir, his name; I'll dispatch him presently.

Offers to draw.

Sir Timothy. How, Sir, dispatch him!—Your Servant, Sir.

Offers to go.

Sir Anthony. Hold, Sir! by this abrupt departure, I fancy you the boy's rival. Come, draw!* *Draws.*

Sir Timothy. How, draw, Sir?

Sir Anthony. Aye draw, Sir. Not my nephew have the widow!

Sir Timothy. With all my soul, Sir, I love and honour your nephew. I his rival! Alas, Sir, I'm not so fond of cuckoldom. Pray, Sir, let me see you and Sir Charles at my house; I may serve him in this business. And so I take my leave, Sir.—[*Aside*] Draw quoth a! A pox upon him for an old Tory-rory!* *Exit.*

Enter as from Church, Lady Galliard, Closet, and footman: Wilding passes carelessly by her, Sir Charles Meriwill following wrapped in his cloak

Sir Anthony. Who's here? Charles, muffled in a cloak, peering after a woman? My own boy to a hair! She's handsome too. I'll step aside, for I must see the meaning on't. *Goes aside.*

Lady Galliard. Bless me! How unconcerned he passed!

Closet. He bowed low, Madam.

Lady Galliard. But 'twas in such a fashion, as expressed indifferency, much worse than hate from Wilding.

Closet. Your Ladyship has used him ill of late; yet if your Ladyship please, I'll call him back.

Lady Galliard. I'll die first.—Hah, he's going!—Yet now I think on't, I have a toy of his, which to express my scorn, I'll give him back now:—this ring.

Closet. Shall I carry it, Madam?

Lady Galliard. You'll not express disdain enough in the delivery; and you may call him back.

Closet goes to Wilding

Sir Charles [*Aside*]. By Heaven, she's fond of him.

Wilding. Oh, Mrs Closet, is it you?—Madam, your servant: By this disdain, I fear your woman, Madam, has mistaken her man. Would your Ladyship speak with me?

Lady Galliard. Yes.—[*Aside*] But what? The god of love instruct me.

Wilding. Command me quickly, Madam, for I have business.

Lady Galliard. [*Aside*] Nay, then I cannot be discreet in love.
—Your business once was love, nor had no idle hours
To throw away on any other thought.
You loved as if you'd had no other faculties,
As if you'd meant to gain eternal bliss
By that devotion only, and see how now you're changed.

Wilding. Not I, by Heaven; 'tis you are only changed.
I thought you'd love me too, curse on the dull mistake;
But when I begged to reap the mighty joy
That mutual love affords,
You turned me off for honour,
That nothing framed by some old sullen maid,
That wanted charms to kindle flames when young.

Sir Anthony [*Aside*]. By George, he's i'th'right.

Sir Charles. Death! Can she hear this language?

Lady Galliard. How dare you name this to me any more?
Have you forgot my fortune, and my youth?
My quality, and fame?

Wilding. No, by Heaven, all these increase my flame.

Lady Galliard. Perhaps they might, but yet I wonder where
You got the boldness to approach me with it.

Wilding. Faith, Madam, from your own encouragement.

Lady Galliard. From mine! Heavens, what contempt is this!

Wilding. When first I paid my vows, (good Heaven forgive me)
They were for honour all;
But wiser you, thanks to your mother's care too,
Knowing my fortune an uncertain hope,
My life of scandal, and my lewd opinion,

Forbid my wish that way. 'Twas kindly urged;
You could not then forbid my passion too,
Nor did I ever from your lips or eyes,
Receive the cruel sentence of my death.

Sir Anthony [*Aside*]. Gad, a fine fellow this!

Lady Galliard. To save my life, I would not marry thee.

Wilding. That's kindly said:
But to save mine, thou't do a kinder thing;
—I know thou wo't.

Lady Galliard. What, yield my honour up!
And after find it sacrificed anew,
And made the scorn of a triumphing wife!

Sir Anthony [*Aside*]. Gad, she's i'th' right too; a noble girl I'll warrant her.

Lady Galliard. But you disdain to satisfy those fears;
And like a proud and haughty conqueror,
Demand the town, without the least conditions.

Sir Charles [*Aside*]. By Heaven, she yields apace,

Sir Anthony [*Aside*]. Pox on't, would I'd ne're seen her; now have I a legion of small Cupids at hot-cockles in my heart.

Wilding. Now am I pausing on that word 'conditions'.
Thou sayest thou wouldst not have me marry thee;
That is, as if I loved thee for thy eyes,
And put 'em out to hate thee:
Or like our stage-smitten youth, who fall in love with a woman for acting finely, and by taking her off the stage, deprive her of the only charm she had, then leave her to ill luck.

Sir Anthony [*Aside*]. Gad, he's i'th' right again too! A rare fellow!

Wilding. For, widow, know, hadst thou more beauties, yet not all of 'em were half so great a charm as thy not being mine.

Sir Anthony [*Aside*]. Hum! How will he make that out now?

Wilding. The stealths of love, the midnight kind admittance,
The gloomy bed, the soft-breathed murmuring passion;
Ah, who can guess at joys thus snatched by parcels!
The difficulty makes us always wishing,

Whilst on thy part, fear still makes some resistance;
And every blessing seems a kind of rape.

Sir Anthony [*Aside*]. H'as done't!—A divine fellow this; just of my religion. I am studying now whether I was never acquainted with his mother.

Lady Galliard walks away, Wilding follows

Lady Galliard. Tempt me no more! What dull unwary flame
Possessed me all this while! [*In rage*] Confusion on thee,
And all the charms that dwell upon thy tongue.
Diseases ruin that bewitching form,
That with thy soft feigned vows debauched my heart.

Sir Charles [*Aside*]. Heavens! Can I yet endure!

Lady Galliard. By all that's good, I'll marry instantly;
Marry, and save my last stake, honour, yet,
Or thou wilt rook me out of all at last.

Wilding. Marry! Thou canst not do a better thing:
There are a thousand matrimonial fops,
Fine fools of fortune,
Good-natured blockheads too, and that's a wonder.

Lady Galliard. That will be managed by a man of wit.

Wilding. Right.

Lady Galliard. I have an eye upon a friend of yours.

Wilding. A friend of mine! Then he must be my cuckold.

Sir Charles [*Aside*]. Very fine! Can I endure yet more?

Lady Galliard. Perhaps it is your uncle.

Wilding. Hah, my uncle! *Sir Charles makes up to 'em*

Sir Anthony [*Aside*]. Hah! My Charles! Why, well said Charles, he bore up briskly to her.

Sir Charles. Ah, Madam, may I presume to tell you—

Sir Anthony [*Aside*]. Ah, pox, that was stark naught! He begins like a foreman o'th' shop, to his master's daughter.

Wilding [*Aside*]. How, Charles Meriwill acquainted with my widow!

Sir Charles. Why do you wear that scorn upon your face?
I've nought but honest meaning in my passion;

Whilst him you favour so profanes your beauties;
In scorn of marriage and religious rites,
Attempts the ruin of your sacred honour.

Lady Galliard [*Aside*]. Hah, Wilding boast my love!

Sir Anthony [*Aside*]. The Devil take him, my nephew's quite spoiled! Why what a pox has he to do with honour now?

Lady Galliard. Pray leave me, Sir.

Wilding [*Aside*]. Damn it, since he knows all, I'll boldly own my flame. You take a liberty I never gave you, Sir.

Sir Charles. How, this from thee! Nay, then I must take more, and ask you where you borrowed that brutality, t'approach that lady with your saucy passion.

Sir Anthony [*Aside*]. Gad, well done, Charles! Here must be sport anon.

Wilding. I will not answer every idle question.

Sir Charles. Death, you dare not!

Wilding. How, dare not!

Sir Charles. No, dare not: for if you did—

Wilding. What durst you, if I did?

Sir Charles. Death, cut your throat, Sir. *Taking hold on him roughly*

Sir Anthony. Hold, hold, let him have fair play, and then curse him that parts ye. *Taking 'em asunder, they draw.*

Lady Galliard. Hold, I command ye, hold!

Sir Charles. There rest my sword to all eternity.

Lays his sword at her feet

Lady Galliard. Now I conjure ye both, by all your honour,
If you were e'er acquainted with that virtue,
To see my face no more,
Who durst dispute your interest in me thus,
As for a common mistress, in your drink.

She goes out, and all but Wilding, Sir Anthony and Sir Charles who stands sadly looking after her

Sir Anthony. A heavenly girl!—Well, now she's gone, by George, I am for disputing your title to her by dint of sword.

Sir Charles. I wo'not fight.

Wilding. Another time we will decide it, Sir. *Wilding goes out*

Sir Anthony. After your whining prologue, Sir, who the devil would have expected such a farce?—Come, Charles, take up thy sword, Charles and, d'ye hear, forget me this woman.

Sir Charles. Forget her, Sir! There never was a thing so excellent!

Sir Anthony. You lie, Sirrah, you lie, there are a thousand
As fair, as young, and kinder, by this day.
We'll into th' country, Charles, where every grove
Affords us rustic beauties,
That know no pride nor painting,
And that will take it and be thankful, Charles;
Fine wholesome girls that fall like ruddy fruit,
Fit for the gathering, Charles.

Sir Charles. Oh, Sir, I cannot relish the coarse fare. But what's all this, Sir, to my present passion?

Sir Anthony. Passion, Sir! You shall have no passion, Sir.

Sir Charles. No passion, Sir! Shall I have life and breath?

Sir Anthony. It may be not, Sirrah, if it be my will and pleasure.— Why how now! saucy boys be their own carvers?

Sir Charles [*Bowing and sighing*]. Sir, I am all obedience.

Sir Anthony. Obedience! Was ever such a blockhead! Why then, if I command it, you will not love this woman.

Sir Charles. No, Sir.

Sir Anthony. No, Sir! But I say, yes, Sir, love her me; and love her me like a man too, or I'll renounce ye, Sir.

Sir Charles. I've tried all ways to win upon her heart: presented, writ, watched, fought, prayed, kneeled, and wept.

Sir Anthony. Why there's it now; I thought so! Kneeled and wept! A pox upon thee—I took thee for a prettier fellow.—
You should a huffed and blustered at her door;
Been very impudent and saucy, Sir:
Lewd, ruffling, mad; courted at all hours and seasons;
Let her not rest, nor eat, nor sleep, nor visit.
Believe me, Charles, women love importunity.

Watch her close, watch her like a witch, boy,
Till she confess the devil in her,—love.

Sir Charles. I cannot, Sir.
Her eyes strike such an awe into my soul,—

Sir Anthony. Strike such a fiddlestick.—Sirrah, I say, do't; what, you can touse a wench as handsomely—You can be lewd enough upon occasion. I know not the lady, nor her fortune, but I am resolved thou shalt have her, with practising a little courtship of my mode.—Come—
Come, my boy Charles, since you must needs be doing,
I'll show thee how to go a widow-wooing. [*Exeunt*]

ACT II SCENE I

A Room

Enter Charlotte, Fopington and Clacket

Charlotte. Enough, I've heard enough of Wilding's vices, to know I am undone. [*Weeps*]—Galliard his mistress too? I never saw her, but I have heard her famed for beauty, wit, and fortune. That rival may be dangerous.

Fopington. Yes, Madam, the fair, the young, the witty Lady Galliard, even in the height of all his love to you; nay, even whilst his uncle courts her for a wife, he designs himself for a gallant.

Charlotte. Wondrous inconstancy and impudence!

Mrs Clacket. Nay, Madam, you may rely upon Mr Fopington's information; therefore, if you respect your reputation, retreat in time.

Charlotte. Reputation! That I forfeited when I ran away with your friend Mr Wilding.

Mrs Clacket. Ah, that ever I should live to see (*weeps*) the sole daughter and heir of Sir Nicholas Gettall run away with one of the lewdest heathens about town!

Charlotte. How! Your friend Mr Wilding a heathen; and with you too, Mrs Clacket! That friend Mr Wilding, who thought none so worthy as Mrs Clacket to trust with so great a secret as his flight with me; he a heathen!

Mrs Clacket. Aye, and a poor heathen too, Madam. 'Slife,* if you must marry a man to buy him breeches, marry an honest man, a religious man, a man that bears a conscience, and will do a woman some reason. Why here's Mr Fopington, Madam: here's a shape, here's a face, a back as straight as an arrow, I'll warrant.

Charlotte. How! Buy him breeches! Has Wilding then no fortune?

Fopington. Yes, faith, Madam, pretty well; so, so, as the dice run, and now and then he lights upon a squire or so, and between fair and foul play, he makes a shift to pick a pretty livelihood up.

Charlotte. How! does his uncle allow him no present maintenance?

Fopington. No, nor future hopes neither. Therefore, Madam, I hope you will see the difference between him and a man of parts that adores you. [*Smiling and bowing*]

Charlotte. If I find all this true you tell me, I shall know how to value myself and those that love me. [*Aside*.] This may be yet a rascal.

Enter Maid.

Maid. Mistress, Mr Wilding's below. [*Exit*]

Fopington [*In great disorder*]. Below! Oh, Heavens, Madam, do not expose me to his lewd fury for being too zealous in your service.

Charlotte. I will not let him know you told anything, Sir.

Fopington. [*To Clacket*]. Death! To be seen here would expose my life.

Mrs Clacket. Here, here, step out upon the staircase and slip into my chamber.

[*Fopington*] *Going out, returns in fright*

Fopington. 'Owns,* he's here! Lock the door fast; let him not enter.

Mrs Clacket. Oh, Heavens, I have not the key! Hold it, hold it fast, sweet, sweet Mr Foping. Oh, should there be murder done, what a scandal would that be to the house of a true Protestant! *Knocks*

Charlotte. Heavens! What will he say and think, to see me shut in with a man?

Mrs Clacket. Oh, I'll say you're sick, asleep, or out of humour.

Charlotte. I'd give the world to see him. *Knocks*

Wilding (*Without*). Charlotte, Charlotte! Am I denied an entrance? By Heaven, I'll break the door.

Knocks again; Fopington still holding it

Fopington. Oh, I'm a dead man, dear Clacket! *Knocking still*

Mrs Clacket. Oh, hold, Sir, Mrs Charlotte is very sick.

Wilding. How, sick, and I kept from her!

Mrs Clacket. She begs you'll come again an hour hence.

Wilding. Delayed! By Heaven, I will have entrance.

Fopington. Ruined! Undone! For if he do not kill me, he may starve me.

Mrs Clacket. Oh, he will break in upon us! Hold, Sir, hold a little; Mrs Charlotte is just—just—shifting herself,* Sir. You will not be so uncivil as to press in, I hope, at such a time.

Charlotte. I have a fine time on't between ye, to have him think I am stripping myself before Mr Fopington. Let go, or I'll call out and tell him all.

Wilding breaks open the door and rushes in; Fopington stands close up at the entrance till he is past him, then venturing to slip out, finds Wilding has made fast the door, so he is forced to return again and stand close up behind Wilding with signs of fear.

Wilding. How now, Charlotte, what means this new unkindness? What, not a word?

Charlotte. There is so little music in my voice, you do not care to hear it; you have been better entertained, I find, mightily employed, no doubt.

Wilding. Yes faith, and so I have, Charlotte. Damned business, that enemy to love, has made me rude.

Charlotte. Or that other enemy to love, damned wenching.

Wilding. Wenching! How ill hast thou timed thy jealousy! What banker, that tomorrow is to pay a mighty sum, would venture out his stock today in little parcels, and lose his credit by it?

Charlotte [*Angry*]. You would, perfidious as you are, though all your fortune, all your future health, depended on that credit.

Wilding [*Aside, to Clacket*]. Hark ye, Mrs Clacket, you have been prating I find in my absence, giving me a handsome character to Charlotte. You hate any good thing should go by your own nose.

Mrs Clacket. By my nose, Mr Wilding! I defy you; I'd have you to know I scorn any good thing should go by my nose in an uncivil way.

Wilding. I believe so.

Mrs Clacket. Have I been the confident to all your secrets this three years, in sickness and in health, for richer, for poorer; concealed the nature of your wicked diseases under the honest name of surfeits; called your filthy surgeons Mr Doctor,* to keep up your reputation; civilly received your 'tother-end-of-the-town young relations at all hours;—

Wilding. High!

Mrs Clacket. Been up with you and down with you early and late, by night and by day; let you in at all hours, drunk and sober, single and double; and civilly withdrawn, and modestly shut the door after me?

Wilding. Whirr! The storm's up, and the Devil cannot lay it.

Mrs Clacket. And am I thus rewarded for my pain! *Weeps*

Wilding. So tempests are allayed by showers of rain.

Mrs Clacket. That I should be charged with speaking ill of you, so honest, so civil a gentleman—

Charlotte. No, I have better witness of your falsehood.

Fopington [*Aside*]. Hah, 'sdeath, she'll name me!

Wilding. What mean you, my Charlotte? Do you not think I love you?

Charlotte [*Kindly to him*]. Go ask my Lady Galliard, she keeps the best account of all your sighs and vows, and robs me of my dearest softer hours.

Mrs Clacket [*Aside*]. You cannot hold from being kind to him.

Wilding [*Aside*]. Galliard! How came she by that secret of my life? Why aye, 'tis true, I am there sometimes about an arbitration, about a suit in law, about my uncle.

Charlotte. Aye, that uncle too—you swore to me you were your uncle's heir, but you perhaps may chance to get him one, if the lady prove not cruel.

Wilding [*Aside*]. Death and the Devil, what rascal has been prating to her!

Charlotte. Whilst I am reserved for a dead lift,* if fortune prove unkind, or wicked uncles refractory.
[*In a soft tone to him*] Yet I could love you, though you were a slave,
And I were queen of all the universe.

Mrs Clacket [*Aside*]. Aye, there you spoiled all again—you forget yourself.

Charlotte [*Aside*]. And all the world, when he looks kindly on me. But I'll take courage, and be very angry. [*Angry*] Nor do your perjuries rest here; you're equally as false to Galliard, as to me; false for a little mistress of the town, whom you've set up in spite to quality.

Mrs Clacket. So, that was home and handsome.

Wilding [*Aside*]. What damned informer does she keep in pension?

Charlotte [*Angry*]. And can you think my fortune and my youth merits no better treatment?
[*Soft to him*] How could you have the heart to use me so?
[*Aside*] I fall insensibly to love and fondness.

Wilding. Ah, my dear Charlotte! You who know my heart, can you believe me false?

Charlotte. In every syllable, in every look.
Your vows, your sighs, and eyes, all counterfeit;
You said you loved me, where was then your truth?
You swore you were to be your uncle's heir:
Where was your confidence of me the while,
To think my generosity so scanted,
To love you for your Fortune!
[*Aside*] How every look betrays my yielding heart!
No, since men are grown so cunning in their
Trade of love, the necessary vice I'll practise too,
And chaffer* with love-merchants for my heart.
Make it appear you are your uncle's heir,
I'll marry ye tomorrow.

Of all thy cheats, that was the most unkind,
Because you thought to conquer by that lie.
Tonight I'll be resolved.

Wilding. Hum! Tonight!

Charlotte. Tonight, or I will think you love me for my fortune; which if you find elsewhere to more advantage, I may unpitied die—[*Tenderly to him*] and I should die, if you should prove untrue.

Mrs Clacket. There you've dashed all again.

Wilding. [*Aside*] I am resolved to keep my credit with her. Here's my hand:
This night, Charlotte, I'll let you see the writings.*
[*Aside*]—But how, a pox of him that knows for Thomas.

Charlotte. Hah, that hand without the ring!
Nay, never study for a handsome lie.

Wilding. Ring! Oh, aye, I left it in my dressing-room this morning.

Charlotte. See how thou hast inured thy tongue to falsehood!
Did you not send it to a certain creature
They call Diana,
From off that hand that plighted faith to me?

Wilding. By Heaven, 'tis witchcraft all,
Unless this villain Fopington betray me.
Those sort of rascals will do anything
For ready meat and wine.—[*Aside*] I'll kill the Fool [*Turns quick and sees him behind him*]—Hah, here!

Fopington. Here, Lord! Lord!
Where were thy eyes, dear Wilding?

Wilding. Where they have spied a rascal.
Where was this property concealed?

Fopington. Concealed? What dost thou mean, dear Tom? Why I stood as plain as the nose on thy face, mun.*

Wilding. But 'tis the ungrateful quality of all your sort, to make such base returns.
How got this rogue admittance and, when in,
The impudence to tell his treacherous lies?

Fopington. Admittance! Why thou'rt stark mad! Did not I come in with you; that is, followed you?

Wilding. Whither?

Fopington. Why into the house, up stairs, stood behind you when you swore you would come in, and followed you in.

Wilding. All this, and I not see!

Fopington. Oh, love's blind; but this lady saw me; Mrs Clacket saw me.—Admittance quotha!*

Wilding. Why did you not speak?

Fopington. Speak! I was so amazed at what I heard, the villainous scandals laid on you by some pick-thank* rogue or other, I had no power.

Wilding. Aye, thou knowest how I am wronged.

Fopington. Oh, most damnably, Sir!

Wilding. Abuse me to my mistress, too!

Fopington. Oh, villains! Dogs!

Charlotte. Do you think they've wronged him, Sir? For I'll believe you.

Fopington. Do I think, Madam? Aye, I think him a son of a whore that said it, and I'll cut's throat.

Mrs Clacket. Well, this impudence is a heavenly virtue!

Wilding. You see now, Madam, how innocence may suffer.

Charlotte. In spite of all thy villainous dissembling, I must believe, and love thee for my quiet.

Wilding. That's kind, and if before tomorrow I do not show you I deserve your heart, kill me at once by quitting me. Farewell. I know both where my uncle's will and other writings lie, by which he made me heir to his whole estate.
[*Aside*] My craft will be in catching; which if past,
Her love secures me the kind wench at last.

Goes out with Fopington.

Mrs Clacket. What if he should not chance to keep his word now?

Charlotte. How if he should not? By all that's good, if he should not, I am resolved to marry him however. We two may make a pretty shift with three thousand pound a year; yet I would fain be resolved how affairs stand between the old gentleman and him. I would give the world to see that widow too, that Lady Galliard.

Mrs Clacket. If you're bent upon't, I'll tell you what we'll do, Madam. There's every day mighty feasting here at his uncle's hard by, and you shall disguise yourself as well as you can, and go for a niece of mine I have coming out of Scotland. There you will not fail of seeing my Lady Galliard, though I doubt, not Mr Wilding, who is of late discarded.

Charlotte. Enough; I am resolved upon this design. Let's in and practice the Northern dialect.

Exit both.

ACT II SCENE 2

The Street

Enter Wilding and Fopington

Wilding. But then Diana took the ring at last?

Fopington. Greedily; but railed, and swore, and ranted at your late unkindness, and would not be appeased.

Enter Dresswell

Wilding. Dresswell, I was just going to see for thee.

Dresswell. I'm glad, dear Tom, I'm here to serve thee.

Wilding. And now I've found thee, thou must along with me.

Dresswell. Whither? But I'll not ask, but obey.

Wilding. To a kind sinner, Frank.

Dresswell. Pox on 'em all; prithee turn out those petty tyrants of thy heart, and fit it for a monarch: love, dear Wilding, of which thou never knewest the pleasure yet, or not above a day.

Wilding. Not knew the pleasure! Death, the very essence, the first draughts of love:
Ah, how pleasant 'tis to drink when a man's adry!
The rest is all but dully sipping on.

Dresswell. And yet this Diana, for thither thou art going, thou hast been constant to this three or four years.

Wilding. A constant keeper* thou meanest; which is indeed enough to get the scandal of a coxcomb. But I know not, those sort of baggages have a kind of fascination so enticing—and faith, after the fatigues of formal visits to a man's dull relations, or what's as bad, to women of quality; after the busy afflictions of the day, and the debauches of the tedious night, I tell thee, Frank, a man's best retirement is with a soft kind wench. But to say truth, I have a farther design in my visit now. Thou knowest how I stand past hope of grace, excommunicated the kindness of my uncle.

Dresswell. True.

Wilding. My lewd debauches, and being o'th' wrong party,* as he calls it, is now become an irreconcilable quarrel; so that I having many and hopeful intrigues now depending, especially these of my charming widow, and my city-heiress, which can by no means be carried on without that damned necessary called ready money, I have stretched my credit, as all young heirs do, till 'tis quite broke. New liveries, coaches and clothes must be had; they must, my friend.

Dresswell. Why dost thou not in this extremity clap up a match with my Lady Galliard? Or this young heiress you speak of?

Wilding. But marriage, Frank, is such a bug-bear! And this old uncle of mine may one day be gathered together, and sleep with his fathers, and then I shall have six thousand pound a year, and the wide world before me, and who the devil could relish these blessings with the clog of a wife behind him?—But till then, money must be had, I say.

Fopington. Aye, but how, Sir?

Wilding. Why, from the old fountain, Jack, my uncle; he has himself decreed it: he tells me I must live upon my wits, and will, Frank.

Fopington. Gad, I'm impatient to know how.

Wilding. I believe thee, for thou art out at elbows, and when I thrive, you show i'th' pit, behind the scenes, and coffee-houses.* Thy breeches give a better account of my fortune than Lilly with all his schemes and stars.

Fopington. I own I thrive by your influence, Sir.

Dresswell. Well; but to your project, friend, to which I'll set a helping hand, a heart, a sword, and fortune.

Wilding. You make good what my soul conceives of you. Let's to Diana then, and there I'll tell thee all.

Going out, they meet Diana, who enters with her maid Betty, and Boy; looks angrily

—Diana, I was just going to thy lodgings!

Diana. Oh 'las, you are too much taken up with your rich city-heiress.

Wilding. That's no cause of quarrel between you and I, Diana; you were wont to be as impatient for my marrying, as I for the death of my uncle, for your rich wife ever obliges her husband's mistress, and women of your sort, Diana, ever thrive better by adultery than fornication.

Diana. Do, try to appease the easy fool with these fine expectations.—No, I have been too often flattered with the hopes of your marrying a rich wife, and then I was to have a settlement; but instead of that, things go backward with me, my coach is vanished, my servants dwindled into one necessary woman and a boy, which to save charges, is too small for any service; my twenty guineas a week into forty shillings: a hopeful reformation!

Wilding. Patience, Diana, things will mend in time.

Diana. When, I wonder? Summer's come, yet I am still in my embroidered manto,* when I'm dressed, lined with velvet; 'twould give one a fever but to look at me. Yet still I am flammed* off with hopes of a rich wife, whose fortune I am to lavish.—But I see you have neither conscience nor religion in you; I wonder what a devil will become of your soul for thus deluding me! [*Weeps*]

Wilding. By Heaven, I love thee!

Diana. Love me! What if you do? How far will that go at the Exchange for point?* Will the mercer take it for current coin?—But 'tis no matter, I must love a wit, with a pox, when I might have had so many fools of fortune! But the Devil take me, if you deceive me any longer. [*Weeping*]

Wilding. You'll keep your word, no doubt, now you have sworn.

Diana. So I will. I never go abroad, but I gain new conquest. Happy's the man that can approach nearest the side-box where I sit at a play to look at me; but if I deign to smile on him, Lord, how the o're-joyed creature returns it with a bow low as the very benches! Then rising, shakes his ears, looks round with pride to see who took notice how much he was in favour with charming Mrs Di.

Wilding. No more. Come, let's be friends, Diana; for you and I must manage an uncle of mine.

Diana. Damn your projects, I'll have none of 'em.

Wilding. Here, here's the best softener of a woman's heart: 'tis gold: two hundred pieces. Go, lay it on, till you shame quality, into plain silk and fringe.

Diana. Lord, you have the strangest power of persuasion!—Nay, if you buy my peace, I can afford a pennyworth.

Wilding. So thou canst of anything about thee.

Diana. Well, your project, my dear Tommy?

Wilding. Thus then—Thou, dear Frank, shalt to my uncle. Tell him that Sir Nicholas Gettall, as he knows, being dead, and having left, as he knows too, one only daughter his whole executrix, Mrs Charlotte, I have by my civil and modest behaviour so won upon her heart that two nights since she left her father's country-house at Lusum* in Kent, in spite of all her strict guards, and run away with me.

Dresswell. How, wilt thou tell him of it then?

Wilding. Hear me—That I have hitherto secured her at a friend's house here in the city, but diligent search being now made, dare trust her there no longer. And make it my humble request by you, my friend, (who are only privy to this secret) that he would give me leave to bring her home to his house, whose very authority will defend her from being sought for there.

Dresswell. Aye, Sir, but what will come of this, I say?

Wilding. Why a settlement: You know he has already made me heir to all he has, after his decease; but for being a wicked Tory, as he calls me, he has, after the writings were made, signed, and sealed, refused to give 'em in trust. Now when he sees I have made myself master of so vast a fortune, he will immediately surrender; that reconciles all again.

Dresswell. Very likely; but wo't thou trust him with the woman, Thomas?

Wilding. No; here's Diana, who as I shall bedizen,* shall pass for as substantial an alderman's heiress as ever fell into wicked hands. He never knew the right Charlotte, not indeed has anybody ever seen her but an old aunt and nurse, she was so kept up:—And there, Diana, thou shalt have a good opportunity to lie, dissemble, and jilt in abundance, to keep thy hand in ure.* Prithee, dear Dresswell, haste with the news to him.

Dresswell. Faith, I like this well enough; this project may take, and I'll about it. *Goes out*

Wilding. Go, get ye home, and trick and betawder* yourself up like a right city-lady, rich, but ill-fashioned; on with all your jewels, but not a patch, ye gipsy, nor no Spanish paint, d'ye hear.

Diana. I'll warrant you for my part.

Wilding. Then before the old gentleman you must behave yourself very soberly, simple, and demure, and look as prew* as at a conventicle;* and take heed you drink not off your glass at table, nor rant, nor swear; one oath confounds our plot, and betrays thee to be an errant drab.*

Diana. Doubt not my art of dissimulation.

Wilding. Go, haste and dress— *Exeunt Diana, Betty and Boy*

Enter Lady Galliard and Closet above in the balcony; Wilding going out, sees them, stops, and reads a paper.

Wilding. Hah, who's yonder: the widow! A pox upon't, now have not I power to stir: she has a damned hank upon my heart, and nothing but right down lying with her will dissolve the charm. She has forbid me seeing her, and therefore I am sure will the sooner take notice of me. *Reads*

Closet. What will you put on tonight, Madam? You know you are to sup at Sir Timothy Treat-all's.

Lady Galliard. Time enough for that; prithee let's take a turn in this balcony, this city-garden, where we walk to take the fresh air of the sea-coal-smoke.* Did the footman go back, as I ordered him, to see how Wilding and Sir Charles parted?

Closet. He did, Madam; and nothing could provoke Sir Charles to fight after your Ladyship's strict commands. Well, I'll swear he's the sweetest natured gentleman—has all the advantages of nature and fortune: I wonder what exception your Ladyship has to him!

Lady Galliard. Some small exception to his whining humour; but I think my chiefest dislike is, because my relations wish it a match between us. It is not hate to him, but natural contradiction. Hah, is not that Wilding yonder? He's reading of a letter, sure.

Wilding. So, she sees me. Now for an art to make her lure me up, for though I have a greater mind than she, it shall be all her own; the match she told me of this morning with my uncle sticks plaguily upon my stomach; I must break the neck on't, or break the widow's heart, that's certain. If I advance towards the door now, she frowningly retires; if I pass on, 'tis likely she may call me. *Advances.*

Lady Galliard. I think he's passing on, without so much as looking towards the window.

Closet. He's glad of the excuse of being forbidden.

Lady Galliard. But, Closet, knowest thou not he has abused my fame, and does he think to pass thus unupbraided? Is there no art to make him look this way? No trick?—Prithee feign to laugh. *Closet laughs.*

Wilding. So, I shall not answer to that call.

Lady Galliard. He's going! Ah, Closet, my fan!—(*Lets fall her fan just as he passes by; he takes it up, and looks up*) Cry mercy, Sir, I'm sorry I must trouble you to bring it.

Wilding. Faith, so am I; and you may spare my pains, and send your woman for't, I am in haste.

Lady Galliard. Then the quickest way will be to bring it.

Goes out of the balcony with Closet

Wilding. I knew I should be drawn in one way or other. [*Exit*]

Scene changes to a Chamber

Enter Lady Galliard, Closet; to them Wilding, delivers the fan, and is retiring.

Lady Galliard. Stay; I hear you're wondrous free of your tongue, when 'tis let loose on me.

Wilding. Who I, widow? I think of no such trifles.

Lady Galliard. Such railers never think when they're abusive, but something you have said, a lie so infamous!

Wilding. A lie, and infamous of you! Impossible! What was it that I called you, wise, or honest?

Lady Galliard. How, can you accuse me for the want of either?

Wilding. Yes, of both. Had you a grain of honesty, or intended ever to be thought so, would you have the impudence to marry an old coxcomb, a fellow that will not so much as serve you for a cloak, he is so visibly and undeniably impotent?

Lady Galliard. Your uncle you mean.

Wilding. I do: who has not known the joy of fornication this thirty year and now the devil and you have put it into his head to marry, forsooth. Oh the felicity of the wedding-night!

Lady Galliard. Which you, with all your railing rhetoric, shall not have power to hinder.

Wilding. Not if you can help it, for I perceive you are resolved to be a lewd, incorrigible sinner, and marryest this seditious doting fool my uncle only to hang him out for the sign of the cuckold, to give notice where beauty is to be purchased, for fear otherwise we should mistake, and think thee honest.

Lady Galliard. So much for my want of honesty; my wit is the part of the text you are to handle next.

Wilding. Let the world judge of that, by this one action: this marriage undisputably robs you both of your reputation and pleasure. Marry an old fool, because he's rich, when so many handsome, proper younger brothers would be glad of you!

Lady Galliard. Of which hopeful number yourself are one.

Wilding. Who, I! Bear witness, Closet; take notice I'm upon my marriage, widow, and such a scandal on my reputation might ruin me, therefore have a care what you say.

Lady Galliard. Ha, ha, ha, marriage! Yes, I hear you give it out, you are to be married to me, for which defamation, if I be not revenged, hang me.

Wilding. Yes, you are revenged. I had the fame of vanquishing where'ere I laid my siege, till I knew thee, hard-hearted thee; had the honest reputation of lying with the magistrates' wives when their reverend husbands were employed in the necessary affairs of the nation, seditiously petitioning,* and then I was esteemed; but now they look on me as a monstrous thing, that makes honourable love to you. Oh hideous, a husband-lover! So that now I may protest, and swear, and lie my heart out, I find neither credit nor kindness, but when I beg for either, my Lady Galliard's thrown in my dish. Then they laugh aloud, and cry, 'Who would think it of gay, of fine Mr Wilding!' Thus the city she-wits are let loose upon me, and all for you, sweet widow. But I am resolved I will redeem my reputation again, if never seeing you nor writing to you more will do it. And so farewell, faithless and scandalous honest woman.

Lady Galliard. Stay, tyrant!

Wilding. I am engaged.

Lady Galliard. You are not.

Wilding. I am, and am resolved to lose no more time on a peevish woman, who values her honour above her lover. *He goes out*

Lady Galliard. Go; this is the noblest way of losing thee.

Closet. Must not I call him back?

Lady Galliard. No. If any honest lover come, admit him; I will forget this devil. Fetch me some jewels; the company tonight at Sir Timothy's may divert me.

She sits down before her glass.

Enter Boy.

Boy. Madam, one Sir Anthony Meriwill would speak with your Ladyship.

Lady Galliard. Admit him; [*Exit Boy*] sure 'tis Sir Charles, his uncle. If he come to treat a match with me for his nephew, he takes me in the critical minute. Would he but leave his whining, I might love him, if 'twere but in revenge.

Enter Sir Anthony Meriwill and Sir Charles

Sir Anthony [*Aside*]. So, I have tutored the young rogue, I hope he'll learn in time. Good day to your Ladyship; Charles (*putting him forward*) my nephew here, Madam—Sirrah—notwithstanding your Ladyship's commands—[*Aside*] Look how he stands now, being a mad young rascal!—Gad, he would wait on your Ladyship—[*Aside*] A Devil on him, see if he'll budge now—For he's a brisk lover, Madam, when he once begins. [*Aside.*] A pox on him, he'll spoil all yet.

Lady Galliard. Please you sit, Sir.

Sir Charles. Madam, I beg your pardon for my rudeness.

Lady Galliard [*Dressing herself carelessly*]. Still whining?—

Sir Anthony. D'ye hear that, Sirrah? Oh damn it, beg pardon! The rogue's quite out of's part.

Sir Charles. Madam, I fear my visit is unseasonable.

Sir Anthony [*Aside*]. Unseasonable! Damned rogue, unseasonable to a widow!—Quite out.

Lady Galliard. There are indeed some ladies that would be angry at an untimely visit, before they've put on their best faces; but I am none of those that would be fair in spite of nature, Sir.—[*To Closet.*] Put on this jewel here.

Sir Charles. That beauty needs no ornament, Heaven has been too bountiful.

Sir Anthony [*Aside vexed*]. Heaven! Oh Lord, Heaven! A Puritanical rogue, he courts her like her chaplain.

Lady Galliard. You are still so full of university-compliments—

Sir Anthony [*Aside to him*]. D'ye hear that, Sirrah?—Aye so he is, so he is indeed, Madam.—To her like a man, ye knave.

Sir Charles. Ah, Madam, I am come!

Sir Anthony [*Aside*]. To show yourself a coxcomb.

Lady Galliard. To tire me with discourses of your passion.—[*Looking in the glass*] Fie, how this curl sits!

Sir Charles. No, you shall hear no more of that ungrateful subject.

Sir Anthony [*Aside*]. Son of a whore, hear no more of love, damned rogue! Madam, by George he lies; he does come to speak of love, and make love, and to do love, and all for love.—[*Aside to him, he minds it not*] Not come to speak of love, with a pox! 'Owns, Sir, behave yourself like a man; be impudent, be saucy, forward, bold, towzing,* and lewd, d'ye hear, or I'll beat thee before her. Why what a pox!

Sir Charles. Finding my hopes quite lost in your unequal favours to young Wilding, I'm quitting of the town.

Lady Galliard. You will do well to do so.—[*To Closet*] Lay by that necklace; I wear pearl to day.

Sir Anthony [*Aside*]. Confounded blockhead!—By George, he lies again, Madam. [*Aside*] A dog, I'll dis-inherit him. He quit the town, Madam! No, not whilst your Ladyship is in it, to my knowledge. He'll live in the town, nay, in the street where you live; nay, in the house; nay, in the very bed, by George; I've heard him a thousand times swear it. [*Aside*] Swear it now, Sirrah. Look, look, how he stands now! [*Aside to him*] Why dear Charles, good boy, swear a little, ruffle her and swear, damn it, she shall have none but thee. Why you little think, Madam, that this nephew of mine is one of the maddest fellows in all Devonshire.

Lady Galliard. Would I could see't, Sir.

Sir Anthony [*Aside*]. See't! Look ye there, ye rogue.—Why 'tis all his fault, Madam. He's seldom sober; then he has a dozen wenches in pay, that he may with the more authority break their windows. There's never a maid within forty miles of Meriwill Hall to work a miracle on, but all are mothers. He's a hopeful youth, I'll say that for him.

Sir Charles. How I have loved you, my despairs shall witness, for I will die to purchase your content.

She rises

Sir Anthony [*Aside*]. Die, a damned rogue! Aye, aye, I'll disinherit him. A dog, die, with a pox! No, he'll be hanged first, Madam.

Sir Charles. And sure you'll pity me when I am dead.

Sir Anthony [*Aside*]. A curse on him; pity, with a pox! I'll give him ne're a souse.*

Lady Galliard [*To Closet*]. Give me that essence-bottle.

Sir Charles. But for a recompense of all my sufferings—

Lady Galliard. [*To Closet*]. Sprinkle my handkerchief with tuberose.

Sir Charles. I beg a favour you'd afford a stranger.

Lady Galliard. Sooner perhaps. [*To Closet*] What jewel's that?

Closet. One Sir Charles Meriwill—

Lady Galliard. Sent, and you received without my order!
No wonder that he looks so scurvily.
Give him the trifle back to mend his humour

Sir Anthony. I thank you, Madam, for that reprimand. Look in that glass, Sir, and admire that sneaking coxcomb's countenance of yours. [*Aside*] A pox on him, he's past grace, lost, gone, not a souse, not a groat; goodbye to you, Sir. Madam, I beg your pardon; the next time I come a wooing, it shall be for myself, Madam, and I have something that will justify it too; but as for this fellow, if your Ladyship have e'er a small page at leisure, I desire he may have order to kick him down stairs. A damned rogue, to be civil now, when he should have behaved himself handsomely! Not an acre, not a shilling, —bye, Sir Softhead. (*Going out, meets Wilding and returns.*) Hah, who have we here, hum, the fine mad fellow? So, so, he'll swinge* him I hope; I'll stay to have the pleasure of seeing it done.

Enter Wilding, brushes by Sir Charles.

Wilding [*Aside*]. I was sure 'twas Meriwill's coach at door.

Sir Charles [*Aside*]. Hah, Wilding!

Sir Anthony [*To Sir Charles*]. Aye, now Sir, here's one will waken ye, Sir.

Wilding. How now, widow, you are always giving audience to lovers, I see.

Sir Charles. You're very free, Sir.

Wilding. I'm always so in the widow's lodgings, Sir.

Sir Anthony. A rare fellow!

Sir Charles. You will not do't elsewhere?

Wilding. Not with so much authority.

Sir Anthony. An admirable fellow! I must be acquainted with him.

Sir Charles. Is this the respect you pay women of her quality?

Wilding. The widow knows I stand not much on ceremonies.

Sir Anthony [*Aside still*]. Gad, he shall be my heir.

Lady Galliard. Pardon him, Sir, this is his Cambridge-breeding.

Sir Anthony [*Aside*]. Aye so 'tis, so tis; that two years there quite spoiled him.

Lady Galliard. Sir, if you've any farther business with me, speak it; if not, I'm going forth.

Sir Charles. Madam, in short—

Sir Anthony [*Aside*]. In short to a widow, in short! Quite lost.

Sir Charles. I find you treat me ill for my respect;
And when I court you next,
I will forget how very much I love you.

Sir Anthony [*To Wilding*]. Sir, I shall be proud of your farther acquaintance, for I like, love, and honour you.

Wilding. I'll study to deserve it, Sir.

Sir Anthony. Madam, your servant. A damned sneaking dog to be civil and modest, with a pox! *Exeunt Sir Charles and Sir Anthony.*

Lady Galliard. See if my coach be ready. *Exit Closet.*

Wilding. Whither are you jaunting now?

Lady Galliard. Where you dare not wait on me: to your uncle's to supper.

Wilding. That uncle of mine pimps for all the sparks of his Party; there they all meet and bargain without scandal. Fops of all sorts and sizes you may choose. Whig-land affords not such another market.

Enter Closet

Closet. Madam, here's Sir Timothy Treat-All come to wait on your Ladyship to supper.

Wilding. My uncle! Oh, damn him, he was born to be my plague. Not dis-inheriting me had been so great a disappointment, and if he sees me here, I ruin all the plots I've laid for him. Ha, he's here!

Enter Sir Timothy [*Treat-All*]

Sir Timothy. How, my Nephew Thomas here!

Wilding. Madam, I find you can be cruel too, knowing my uncle has abandoned me.

Sir Timothy. How now, Sir, what's your business here?

Wilding. I came to beg a favour of my Lady Galliard, Sir, knowing her power and quality in the city.

Sir Timothy [*Aside*]. How, a favour of my Lady Galliard! The rogue said indeed he would cuckold me. Why, Sir, I thought you had been taken up with your rich heiress?

Wilding. That was my business now, Sir. Having in my possession the daughter and heir of Sir Nicholas Gettall, I would have made use of the authority of my Lady Galliard's house to have secured her, till I got things in order for our marriage; but my Lady, to put me off, cries, I have an uncle.

Lady Galliard [*Aside*]. A well-contrived lie.

Sir Timothy. Well, I have heard of your good fortune, and however a reprobate thou hast been, I'll not show myself so undutiful an uncle, as not to give the gentlewoman a little house-room. I heard indeed she was gone a week ago, and, Sir, my house is at your service.

Wilding. I humbly thank you, Sir. Madam, your servant. [*Aside*] A pox upon him, and all his association.* *Goes out*

Sir Timothy. Come, Madam, my coach waits below.

Exeunt

ACT III SCENE I

A room

Enter Sir Timothy Treat-All and Jervice.

Sir Timothy. Here, take my sword, Jervice. What have you inquired as I directed you concerning the rich heiress, Sir Nicholas Gettall's daughter?

Jervice. Alas, Sir, inquired! Why 'tis all the city news, that she's run away with one of the maddest Tories about town.

Sir Timothy. Good Lord! Aye, aye, 'tis so; the plaguy rogue my nephew has got her. That Heaven should drop such blessings in the mouths of the wicked! Well, Jervice, what company have we in the house, Jervice?

Jervice. Why truly, Sir, a fine deal, considering there's no parliament.

Sir Timothy. What lords have we, Jervice?

Jervice. Lords, Sir! truly none.

Sir Timothy. None! What ne're a lord! Some mishap will befall me, some dire mischance. Ne're a lord! Ominous, ominous! Our Party* dwindles daily. What, nor earl, nor marquess, nor duke, nor ne're a lord? Hum, my wine will lie most villainously upon my hands tonight, Jervice. What, have we store of knights and gentlemen?

Jervice. I know not what gentlemen there be, Sir, but there are knights, citizens, their wives and daughters.

Sir Timothy. Make us thankful for that; our meat will not lie upon our hands then, Jervice. I'll say that for our little Londoners, they are as tall fellows at a well-charged board as any in Christendom.

Jervice. Then, Sir, there's Nonconformist parsons.

Sir Timothy. Nay, then we shall have a clear board, for your true Protestant appetite in a lay-elder, does a man's table credit.

Jervice. Then, Sir, there's country-justices and grand-jury-men.*

Sir Timothy. Well enough, well enough, Jervice.

Enter Mrs Censure

Censure. An't like your worship, Mr Wilding is come in with a lady richly dressed in jewels, masked, in his hand, and will not be denied speaking with your worship.

Sir Timothy. Hah, rich in jewels! This must be she. My sword again, Jervice.—Bring 'em up, Censure. [*Exit Censure*]—Prithee how do I look tonight, Jervice?

Setting himself

Jervice. Oh, most methodically, Sir.

Enter Wilding and Diana and Betty

Wilding. Sir, I have brought into your kind protection the richest jewel all London can afford, fair Mrs Charlotte Gettall.

Sir Timothy. Bless us, she's ravishing fair! Lady, I had the honour of being intimate with your worthy father. I think he has been dead—

Diana [*Aside*]. If he catechise* me much on that point, I shall spoil all. Alas, Sir, name him not, for if you do, (*weeping*) I'm sure I cannot answer you one question.

Wilding [*Aside to him*]. For Heaven sake, Sir, name not her father to her; the bare remembrance of him kills her.

Sir Timothy. Alas, poor soul! Lady, I beg your pardon. [*Aside*] How soft hearted she's! I am in love; I find already a tickling kind of I know not what run frisking through my veins.

Betty [*Weeping*]. Aye, Sir, the good alderman has been dead this twelvemonth just, and has left his daughter here, my mistress, three thousand pound a year.

Sir Timothy. Three thousand pound a year! [*Aside*] Yes, yes, I am in love.

Betty. Besides money, plate, and jewels.

Sir Timothy [*Aside*]. I'll marry her out of hand. Alas, I could even weep too, but 'tis in vain. Well, nephew, you may be gone now, for 'tis not necessary you should be seen here, d'ye see.

Pushing him out

Wilding. You see, Sir, now, what Heaven has done for me; and you have often told me, Sir, when that was kind, you would be so. Those writings, Sir, by which you were so good to make me heir to all your estate, you said you would put into my possession, whene'er I made it appear to you I could live without 'em, or bring you a wife of fortune home.

Sir Timothy. And I will keep my word; tis time enough.

Putting him out

Wilding. I have, 'tis true, been wicked; but I shall now turn from my evil ways, establish myself in the religious city, and enter into the association. There wants but these same writings, Sir, and your good character of me.

Sir Timothy. Thou sha't have both; all in good time, man. Go, go thy ways, and I'll warrant thee for a good character; go.

Wilding. Aye, Sir, but the writings, because I told her, Sir, I was your heir; nay, forced to swear it too, before she would believe me.

Sir Timothy. Alas, alas, how shrewdly thou wert put to't!

Wilding. I told her too, you'd buy a patent* for me, for nothing woos a city-fortune like the hopes of a Ladyship.

Sir Timothy [*Aside*]. I'm glad of that; that I can settle on her presently.

Wilding. You may please to hint something to her of my godly life and conversation, that I frequent conventicles and am drunk nowhere but at your true Protestant consults and clubs, and the like.

Sir Timothy [*Aside*]. Nay, if these will please her, I have her for certain. Go, go, fear not my good word.

Wilding. But the writings, Sir.—

Sir Timothy. Am I a Jew, a Turk? Thou sha't have anything, now I find thee a lad of parts, [*Aside*] and one that can provide so well for thy uncle.

Puts him out, and addresses himself to the lady

Wilding [*Aside*]. Would they were hanged that trust you, that have but the art of legerdemain, and can open the Japan-cabinet in your bed-chamber, where I know those writings are kept. Death, what a disappointment's here! I would a'sworn this sham had passed upon him.—But, Sir, shall I not have the writings now?

Sir Timothy. What not gone yet! For shame, away! Canst thou distrust thy own natural uncle? Fie, away, Tom, away.

Wilding [*Aside*]. A plague upon your damned dissimulation, that never-failing badge of all your party, there's always mischief at the bottom on't; I know ye all and fortune be the word. When next I see you, uncle, it shall cost you dearer. *Exit*

Enter Jervice

Jervice. An't please your worship, supper's almost over, and you are asked for.

Sir Timothy. They know I never sup; I shall come time enough to bid 'em welcome.

Exit Jervice

Diana. I keep you, Sir, from supper and better company.

Sir Timothy. Lady, were I a glutton, I could be satisfied with feeding on those two bright starry eyes.

Diana. You are a courtier, Sir; we city-maids do seldom hear such language, in which you show your kindness to your nephew, more than your thoughts of what my beauty merits.

Sir Timothy [*Aside*]. Lord, Lord, how innocent she is! My nephew, Madam? Yes, yes, I cannot choose but be wondrous kind upon his score.

Diana. Nay, he has often told me you were the best of uncles, and he deserves your goodness, so hopeful a young gentleman.

Sir Timothy [*Aside*]. Would I could see't.

Diana. So modest.

Sir Timothy [*Aside*]. Yes, ask my maids.

Diana. So civil .

Sir Timothy [*Aside*]. Yes, to my neighbours' wives. But so, Madam, I find by this high commendations of my nephew, your Ladyship has a very slender opinion of your devoted servant the while; or else, Madam, with this not disagreeable face and shape of mine, six thousand pound a year, and other virtues and commodities that shall be nameless, I see no reason why I should not beget an heir of my own body, had I the helping hand of a certain victorious person in the world, that shall be nameless.

[*Bowing and smirking.*]

Diana [*Aside*]. Meaning me, I am sure. If I should marry him now, and disappoint my dear inconstant with an heir of his own begetting, 'twould be a most wicked revenge for past kindnesses.

Sir Timothy. I know your Ladyship is studying now who this victorious person should be, whom I dare not name; but let it suffice she is, Madam, within a mile of an oak.

Diana. No, Sir, I was considering, if what you say be true,
How unadvisedly I have loved your nephew,
Who swore to me he was to be your heir.

Sir Timothy. My heir, Madam! Am I so visibly old to be so desperate?
No, I'm in my years of desires and discretion,
And I have thoughts, durst I but utter 'em;
But modestly say, mum—

Diana. I took him for the hopefullest gentleman—

Sir Timothy. Let him hope on, so will I; and yet, Madam, in consideration of your love to him, and because he is my nephew, young, handsome, witty, and so forth, I am content to be so much a parent to him, as, if Heaven please,—to see him fairly hanged.

Diana [*In amaze*]. How, Sir!

Sir Timothy. He has deserved it, Madam; first, for lampooning the reverend city, with its noble government, with the right honourable gown-men; libelling some for feasting, and some for fasting, some for cuckolds, and some for cuckold-makers; charging us with all the seven deadly sins, the sins of our forefathers, adding seven score more to the number; the sins of forty-one* revived again in eighty-one, with additions and amendments, for which, though the writings were drawn by which I made him my whole executor, I will disinherit him. Secondly, Madam, he deserves hanging for seducing and most feloniously bearing away a young city-heiress.

Diana. Undone, undone! Oh with what face can I return again!
What man of wealth or reputation, now
Will think me worth the owning! [*Feigns to weep*]

Sir Timothy [*Bowing and smiling*]. Yes, yes, Madam, there are honest, discreet, religious and true Protestant knights in the city, that would be proud to dignify and distinguish so worthy a gentlewoman.

Betty [*Aside*]. Look to your hits, and take fortune by the forelock, Madam.—Alas, Madam, no knight, and poor too!

Sir Timothy. As a Tory-poet.

Betty. Well, Madam, take comfort; if the worst come to the worst, you have estate enough for both.

Diana [*Weeping*]. Aye, Betty, were he but honest, Betty.

Sir Timothy. Honest! I think he will not steal; but for his body, the Lord have mercy upon't, for he has none.

Diana. 'Tis evident I am betrayed, abused;
H'as looked, and sighed, and talked away my heart;
H'as sworn and vowed, and flattered me to ruin. [*Weeping*]

Sir Timothy. A small fault with him; he has flattered and sworn me out of many a fair thousand. Why, he has no more conscience than a politician, nor no more truth than a narrative (under the rose).*

Diana. Is there no truth nor honesty i'th' world?

Sir Timothy. Troth, very little, and that lies all i'th' city, amongst us sober magistrates.

Diana. Were I a man, how would I be revenged!

Sir Timothy. Your Ladyship might do it better as you are, were I worthy to advise you.

Diana. Name it.

Sir Timothy [*Bowing*]. Why by marrying your Ladyship's most assured friend, and most humble Servant, Timothy Treat-all of London, Alderman.

Betty. Aye, this is something, Mistress; here's reason!

Diana. But I have given my faith and troth to Wilding, Betty.

Sir Timothy. Faith and troth! We stand upon neither faith nor troth in the city, Lady. I have known an heiress married and bedded, and yet with the advice of the wiser magistrates, has been unmarried and consummated anew with another, so it stands with our interest; 'tis law by Magna Carta.* Nay, had you married my ungracious nephew, we might by this our Magna Carta have hanged him for a rape.

Diana. What, though he had my consent?

Sir Timothy. That's nothing, he had not ours.

Diana. Then should I marry you by stealth, the danger would be the same.

Sir Timothy. No, no, Madam, we never accuse one another; 'tis the poor rogues, the Tory rascals, we always hang. Let 'em accuse me if they please, alas, I come off hand-smooth with *Ignoramus*.*

Enter Jervice

Jervice. Sir, there's such calling for your Worship! They are all very merry, the glasses go briskly about.

Sir Timothy. Go, go, I'll come when all the healths are past; I love no healths.*

Jervice. They are all over, Sir, and the ladies are for dancing; so they are all adjourning from the dining-room hither, as more commodious for that exercise. I think they're coming, Sir.

Sir Timothy. Hah, coming! Call Censure to wait on the lady to her apartment.

[*Exit Jervice, enter Censure*]

—And, Madam, I do most heartily recommend my most humble address to your most judicious consideration, hoping you will most vigorously, and with all your might, maintain the rights and privileges of the honourable city, and not suffer the force or persuasion of any arbitrary lover whatsoever, to subvert their ancient and fundamental laws by seducing and forcibly bearing away so rich and so illustrious a lady. And, Madam, we will unanimously stand by you with our lives and fortunes.—This I learnt from a speech at the election of a burgess. [*Leads her to the door, she goes out with Betty and Censure*]

Enter Music playing, Sir Anthony Meriwill dancing with a lady in his hand, Sir Charles with Lady Galliard, several other women and men.

Sir Anthony. [*Singing*].

Philander *was a jolly swain,*
And loved by every lass;
Whom when he met upon the plain,
He laid upon the grass.

And here he kissed, and there he played
With this, and then the t'other,
Till every wanton smiling maid
At last became a mother.

And to her swain, and to her swain,
The nymph begins to yield;
Ruffle, and breathe, then to't again,
Thou'rt master of the field.

[*Sir Anthony*] *Clapping Sir Charles on the back*

Sir Charles. And if I keep it not, say I'm a coward, uncle.

Sir Anthony. More wine there, boys, I'll keep the humour up.

[*Enter Servants* [*with*] *bottles and glasses*]

Sir Timothy. How! young Meriwill so close to the widow!—Madam—

[*Addressing himself to her, Sir Charles puts him by.*]

Sir Charles. Sir Timothy, why what a pox dost thou bring that damned Puritanical, schismatical, fanatical, small-beer-face of thine into good company? Give him a full glass to the widow's health.

Sir Timothy. O lack,* Sir Charles, no healths for me, I pray.

Sir Charles. [*Pulling Sir Timothy to kneel*]. Hark ye, leave that cozening, canting, sanctified sneer of yours, and drink ye me like a sober loyal magistrate, all those healths you are behind, from his sacred Majesty, whom God long preserve, with the rest of the royal family, even down to this wicked widow, whom Heaven soon convert from her lewd designs upon my body.

Sir Anthony. A rare boy! He shall have all my estate.

Sir Timothy [*Aside*]. How, the widow a lewd design upon his body! Nay, then I am jealous.

Lady Galliard. I a lewd design upon your body! For what, I wonder?

Sir Charles. Why, for villainous matrimony.

Lady Galliard. Who, I?

Sir Charles. Who, you? Yes, you.
Why are those eyes dressed in inviting love?
Those soft bewitching smiles, those rising breasts,
And all those charms that make you so adorable,
Is't not to draw fools into matrimony?

Sir Anthony [*Aside*]. How's that, how's that! Charles at his adorables and charms! He must have t'other health, he'll fall to his old dog-trot again else. Come, come, every man his glass. Sir Timothy, you are six behind. Come, Charles, name 'em all.

[*Each take a glass, and force Sir Timothy on his knees.*]

Sir Charles. —Not bate ye an ace, Sir. Come, his Majesty's health, and confusion to his enemies.

They go to force his mouth open to drink

Sir Timothy. Hold, Sir, hold, if I must drink, I must; but this is very arbitrary, methinks. [*Drinks*]

Sir Anthony. And now, Sir, to the Royal Duke of Albany.* Music, play a Scotch jig.

[*Music plays; they drink.*]

Sir Timothy. This is mere tyranny.

Enter Jervice

Jervice. Sir, there is just alighted at the gate a person of quality, as appears by his train, who give him the title of a Lord.

Sir Timothy. How, a strange Lord! Conduct him up with ceremony, Jervice.—'Ods so, he's here!

Enter Wilding in disguise, Dresswell, [*Laboir*] *and footmen and pages.*

Wilding. Sir, by your reverend aspect, you should be the renowned *Mester de Hotel?**

Sir Timothy. Meter de Otell!. I have not the honour to know any of that name; I am called Sir Timothy Treat-all. [*Bowing*]

Wilding. The same, Sir. I have been bred abroad, and thought all persons of quality had spoke French.

Sir Timothy. Not city persons of quality, my Lord .

Wilding. I'm glad on't, Sir, for 'tis a nation I hate, as indeed I do all monarchies.

Sir Timothy. Hum! Hate monarchy! Your Lordship is most welcome. [*Bows*]

Wilding. Unless elective monarchies, which so resemble a commonwealth.

Sir Timothy. Right, my Lord, where every man may hope to take his turn. [*Bows low*]—Your Lordship is most singularly welcome.

Wilding. And though I am a stranger to your person, I am not to your fame. Amongst the sober party of the Amsterdamians, all the French Huguenots throughout Geneva, even to Hungary and Poland, fame's trumpet sounds your praise, making the Pope to fear, the rest admire you.

Sir Timothy. I'm much obliged to the renowned mobily.*

Wilding. So you will say, when you shall hear my embassy. The Polanders* by me salute you, Sir, and have in this next new election, pricked ye down for their succeeding king.

Sir Timothy. How, my Lord, pricked me down for a king! Why, this is wonderful! Pricked me, unworthy me, down for a king! How could I merit this amazing glory!

Wilding. They know, he that can be so great a patriot to his native country, where but a private person, what must he be when power is on his side?

Sir Timothy. Aye, my Lord, my country, my bleeding country! There's the stop to all my rising greatness. Shall I be so ungrateful to disappoint this big expecting nation? Defeat the sober party, and my neighbours, for any Polish crown? But yet, my Lord, I will consider on't. Meantime my house is yours.

Wilding. I've brought you, Sir, the measure of the crown. [*Pulls out a ribbon and measures his head*] Hah, it fits you to a hair. You were by Heaven and nature framed that monarch.

Sir Anthony. Hah, at it again! (*Sir Charles making sober love.*) Come, we grow dull, Charles; where stands the glass? What, baulk my Lady Galliard's Health! *They go to drink*

Wilding [*Aside*]. Hah, Galliard—and so sweet on Meriwill!

Lady Galliard. If it be your business, Sir, to drink, I'll withdraw.

Sir Charles. Gad, and I'll withdraw with you, widow. Hark ye, Lady Galliard, I am damnably afraid you cannot bear your liquor well, you are so forward to leave good company and a bottle.

Sir Timothy. Well, gentlemen, since I have done what I never do, to oblige you, I hope you'll not refuse a health of my denomination.

Sir Anthony. We scorn to be so uncivil. *All take glasses*

Sir Timothy. Why then, here's a concealed health that shall be nameless: to his Grace the King of Poland.

Sir Charles. King of Poland! Lord, Lord, how your thoughts ramble!

Sir Timothy. Not so far as you imagine; I know what I say, Sir.

Sir Charles. Away with it. *Drink all.*

Wilding. I see, Sir, you still keep up that English hospitality that so renowned our ancestors in history. *Looking on Lady Galliard*

Sir Timothy. Aye, my Lord, my noble guests are my wife and children.

Wilding. Are you not married then? [*Aside*] Death, she smiles on him!

Sir Timothy. I had a wife, but, rest her soul, she's dead, and I have no plague left now but an ungracious nephew, perverted with customs, tantivy-opinions,* and court-notions.

Wilding. Cannot your pious examples convert him? [*Aside*] By Heaven, she's fond of him!

Sir Timothy. Alas, I have tried all ways, fair and foul; nay, had settled t'other day my whole estate upon him, and just as I had signed the writings, out comes me a damned libel called *A Warning to All Good Christians Against the City-Magistrates;** and I doubt he had a hand in *Absolon and Achitophel;** a rogue, but some of our sober party have clawed him home, i'faith, and given him rhyme for his reason.

Wilding [*Aside*]. Most visibly in love!—Oh, Sir, nature, laws, and religion, plead for so near a kinsman.

Sir Timothy. Laws and religion! Alas my Lord, he deserves not the name of a patriot, who does not for the public good defy all laws and religion.

Wilding [*Aside*]. Death, I must interrupt 'em!—Sir, pray what lady's that?

Wilding salutes her.

Sir Timothy. I beseech your Lordship, know her; 'tis my Lady Galliard. The rest are all my friends and neighbours, true Protestants all. Well, my Lord, how do you like my method of doing the business of the nation, and carrying on the cause with wine, women, and so forth?

Wilding. High feeding and smart drinking gains more to the Party, than your smart preaching.

Sir Timothy. Your Lordship has hit it right. A rare man this!

Wilding. But come, Sir, leave we serious affairs, and oblige these fair ones.

Addresses himself to Galliard, Sir Charles puts him by.

Enter Charlotte disguised, Clacket, and Fopington.

Charlotte [*Pointing to Wilding and Lady Galliard*]. Heavens, Clacket, yonder's my false one, and that my lovely rival.

Enter Diana and Censure masked, and Betty.

Diana. Dear Mrs Censure, this favour has obliged me.

Censure. I hope you'll not discover it to his worship, Madam.

Wilding. By her mien, this should be handsome.—(*Goes to Diana.*)

Madam, I hope you have not made a resolution to deny me the honour of your hand.

Diana. Hah, Wilding! Love can discover thee through all disguise.

Wilding. Hah, Diana! Would 'twere felony to wear a vizard.* Gad, I'd rather meet it on the King's highway with stand and deliver, than thus encounter it on the face of an old mistress; and the cheat were more excusable—But how— [*Talks aside with her.*]

Sir Charles. Nay, never frown nor chide, for thus do I intend to show my authority, till I have made thee only fit for me.

Wilding [*Aside*]. Is't so, my precious uncle! Are you so great a devil in hypocrisy! Thus had I been served, had I brought him the right woman.

Diana. But do not think, dear Tommy, I would have served thee so: married thy uncle, and have cozened thee of thy birthright.—But see, we're observed! [*Charlotte listening behind him all this while.*]

Charlotte [*Aside*]. By all that's good, 'tis he! That voice is his.

He, going from Diana, turns upon Charlotte and looks.

Wilding. Hah, what pretty creature's this, that has so much of Charlotte in her face? But sure she durst not venture: 'tis not her dress nor mien. Dear pretty stranger, I must dance with you.

Charlotte. Gued deed,* and see ye shall, Sir, gen* you please. Though I's not dance, Sir, I's tell ya that noo.*

Wilding. Nor I: so we're well matched. [*Aside*] By Heaven, she's wondrous like her.

Charlotte. By th' Mass, not so kind, Sir. 'Twere gued that ene of us should dance to guid the other weel.

Wilding. How young, how innocent, and free she is!
And would you, fair one, be guided by me?

Charlotte. In any thing that gued is.

Wilding. I love you extremely, and would teach you to love

Charlotte [*Sighs and smiles*]. Ah, wele aday!

Wilding. A thing I know you do not understand.

Charlotte. Gued faith, and ya're i'th' right, Sir; yet 'tis a thing I's often hear ya gay men talk of.

Wilding. Yes, and no doubt have been told those pretty eyes inspired it.

Charlotte. Gued deed, and so I have. Ya men make sa mickle* ado aboot ens eyes, ways me, I's ene tired with sick-like* compliments.

Wilding. Ah, if you give us wounds, we must complain.

Charlotte. Ya may ene keep out a harm's way then.

Wilding. Oh, we cannot; or if we could, we would not.

Charlotte. Marry and I's have ene a song tol* that tune, Sir.

Wilding. Dear creature, let me beg it.

Charlotte. Gued faith, ya shall not, Sir, I's sing without entreaty.

SONG

Ah, Jenny, *gen your eyes do kill,*
You'll let me tell my pain;
Gued faith, I loved against my will,
But wad not break my chain.*
I ence was called a bonny lad,*
Till that fair face of yours
Betrayed the freedom ence I had,
And ad my bleether howers.*

But noo ways me, like Winter looks,
*My gloomy showering eyne,**
And on the banks of shaded brooks,
I pass my wearied time.
I call the stream that gleedeth on,*
To witness if it see,
On all the flowery brink along,
*A swain so true as iee.**

Wilding. This very swain am I, so true and so forlorn, unless you pity me. [*Aside*] This is an excellency Charlotte wants, at least I never heard her sing.

Sir Anthony. Why Charles, where stands the woman, Charles?

Fopington comes up to Charlotte.

Wilding [*Aside*]. I must speak to Galliard, though all my fortunes depend on the discovery of myself.

Sir Anthony. Come, come, a cooling glass about.

Wilding. Dear Dresswell, entertain Charles Meriwill a little, whilst I speak to Galliard.

The men go all to the drinking-table.

[*Aside*] By Heaven, I die, I languish for a word!
—Madam, I hope you have not made a vow
To speak with none but that young cavalier?
They say, the freedom English ladies use,
Is as their beauty, great.

Lady Galliard. Sir, we are none of those of so nice and delicate a virtue as conversation can corrupt; we live in a cold climate.

Wilding. And think you're not so apt to be in love,
As where the sun shines oftener.
[*Maliciously to her.*] But you too much partake of the inconstancy of this your fickle climate.
One day all sunshine, and th' encouraged lover
Decks himself up in glittering robes of hope;
And in the midst of all their boasted finery
Comes a dark cloud across his mistress' brow,
Dashes the fool, and spoils the gaudy show.

Lady Galliard observing him nearly

Lady Galliard. Hah, do not I know that railing tongue of yours?

Wilding. 'Tis from your guilt, not judgment then.
I was resolved to be tonight a witness
Of that sworn love you flattered me so often with.
By Heaven, I saw you playing with my rival,
Sighed, and looked babies* in his gloating eyes.
When is the assignation? When the hours?
For he's impatient as the raging sea,
Loose as the winds, and amorous as the sun
That kisses all the beauties of the Spring.

Lady Galliard. I take him for a soberer person, Sir.

Wilding. Have I been the companion of his riots
In all the lewd course of our early youth,
Where like unwearied bees we gathered flowers?
But no kind blossom could oblige our stay,
We rifled and were gone.

Lady Galliard. Your virtues I perceive are pretty equal;
Only his love's the honester o'th' two.

Wilding. Honester! That is, he would owe his good fortune to the parson of the parish,
And I would be obliged to you alone.
He would have a license to boast he lies with you,
And I would do't with modesty and silence:
For virtue's but a name kept free from scandal,
Which the most base of women best preserve,
Since gilting and hypocrisy cheat the world best.
[*In a soft tone*]—But we both love, and who shall blab the secret?

Lady Galliard [*Aside*]. Oh, why were all the charms of speaking given to that false tongue that makes no better use of 'em?—I'll hear no more of your enchanting reasons.

Wilding. You must.

Lady Galliard. I will not.

Wilding. Indeed you must.

Lady Galliard. By all the powers above—

Wilding. By all the powers of love, you'll break your oath, unless you swear this night to let me see you.

Lady Galliard. This night?

Wilding. This very night.

Lady Galliard [*First turns away, then sighs and looks on him with joy*]. I'd die first.—At what hour?

Wilding. Oh, name it; and if I fail—

Lady Galliard. I would not for the world—

Wilding. That I should fail!

Lady Galliard. Not name the guilty hour.

Wilding. Then I through eager haste shall come too soon,
And do your honour wrong.

Lady Galliard. My honour! Oh that word!

Wilding [*Aside*]. Which the Devil was in me for naming.—At twelve!

Lady Galliard. My women and my servants then are up.

Wilding. At one, or two.

Lady Galliard. So late! 'Twill be so quickly day!

Wilding. Aye, so it will:
That half our business will be left unfinished.

Lady Galliard. Hah, what do you mean? What business?

Wilding. A thousand tender things I have to say,
A thousand vows of my eternal love;
And now and then we'll kiss and—

Lady Galliard. Be extremely honest.

Wilding. As you can wish.

Lady Galliard. Rather as I command. [*Aside*] For should he know my wish, I were undone.

Wilding. The sign.—

Lady Galliard. Oh, press me not;—yet you may come at midnight under my chamber-window.

Sir Charles sees them so close; comes to them.

Sir Charles. Hold, Sir, hold! Whilst I am listening to the relation of your French fortifications, outworks, and counterscarps, I perceive the enemy in my quarters. [*Puts him by, growing drunk*] My Lord, by your leave.

Charlotte. Persuade me not; I burst with jealousy.

Wilding turns, sees Clacket.

Wilding. Death and the Devil, Clacket! Then *'tis* Charlotte, and I'm discovered to her.

Charlotte [*To Wilding in anger*], Say, are not you a false dissembling thing?

Wilding. What, my little Northern lass translated into English!
This 'tis to practise art in spite of nature.
Alas, thy virtue, youth, and innocence,
Were never made for cunning,
I found ye out through all your forced disguise.

Charlotte. Hah, did you know me then?

Wilding. At the first glance, and found you knew me too,
And talked to yonder lady in revenge,

Whom my uncle would have me marry. But to avoid all discourses of that nature, I came tonight in this disguise you see to be concealed from her, that's all.

Charlotte. And is that all, on honour? Is it, dear?

Wilding. What, no belief, no faith, in villainous women?

Charlotte. Yes, when I see the writings.

Wilding. Go home. I die if you should be discovered,
And credit me, I'll bring you all you ask.
[*Aside to Clacket*] Clacket, you and I must have an odd reckoning about this night's jaunt of yours.

Sir Timothy. Well my Lord, how do you like our English beauties?

Wilding. Extremely, Sir, and was just pressing this young lady to give us a song.

Here is an Italian song in two parts.*

Sir Timothy [*To Clacket*]. I never saw this lady before. Pray who may she be, neighbour?

Mrs Clacket. A niece of mine, newly come out of Scotland, Sir.

Sir Timothy. Nay, then she dances by nature. Gentlemen and ladies, please you to sit, here's a young neighbour of mine will honour us with a dance.

They all sit; Charlotte and Fopington dance.

So, so; very well, very well. Gentlemen and ladies, I am for liberty of conscience and moderation. There's a banquet waits the ladies, and my cellars are open to the men; but for myself, I must retire, first waiting on your Lordship to show you your apartment, then leave you to cher* entire, and tomorrow, my Lord, you and I will settle the nation, and resolve on what return we will make to the noble Polanders.

Exeunt all but Wilding, Dresswell, [*Sir Anthony and Laboir*] *Fopington, Sir Charles leading out Lady Galliard.*

Sir Anthony. Well said, Charles, thou leavest her not, till she's thy own, boy. [*Exit singing*]—And Philander was a jolly Swain, &c.

Wilding. All things succeed above my wish, dear Frank; fortune is kind, and more, Galliard is so. This night crowns all my wishes. [*To his footman.*] Laboir, are all things ready for our purpose?

Laboir. Dark lanterns, pistols, habits and vizards, Sir.

Fopington. I have provided portmantles to carry off the treasure.

Dresswell. I perceive you are resolved to make a through-stitched* robbery on't.

Fopington. Faith, if it lie in our way, Sir, we had as good venture a caper under the triple tree* for one as well as t'other.

Wilding. We will consider on't. 'Tis now just struck eleven; within this hour is the dear assignation with Galliard.

Dresswell. What, whether our affairs be finished or not?

Wilding. 'Tis but at next door; I shall return time enough for that trivial business.

Dresswell. A trivial business of some six thousand pound a year?

Wilding. Trivial to a woman, Frank! No more, do you make as if you went to bed.—Laboir, do you feign to be drunk, and lie on the hall-table; and so when I give the sign, let me softly in.

Dresswell. Death, Sir, will you venture at such a time!

Wilding. My life and future hope—I am resolved,
Let politicians plot, let rogues go on
In the old beaten path of forty one,
Let city-knaves delight in mutiny,
The rabble bow to old Presbytery;
Let petty states be to confusion hurled,
Give me but woman, I'll despise the world.

[*Exeunt*]

ACT IV SCENE I

A dressing-room.

Lady Galliard is discovered in an undress at her table, glass, and toilette, Closet attending. As soon as the scene draws off* she rises from the table as disturbed and out of humour.*

Lady Galliard. Come, leave your everlasting chamber-maid's chat, your dull road of slandering by rote, and lay that paint aside. Thou art fuller of false news than an unlicensed Mercury.

Closet. I have good proof, Madam, of what I say.

Lady Galliard. Proof of a thing impossible! —Away.

Closet. Is it a thing so impossible, Madam, that a man of Mr Wilding's parts and person should get a city-heiress? Such a bonne mien,* and such a pleasant wit!

Lady Galliard. Hold thy fluent tattle, thou hast tongue
Enough to talk an oyster-woman deaf; I say it cannot be.—
[*Aside*] What means the panting of my troubled heart!
Oh my presaging fears! Should what she says prove true,
How wretched and how lost a thing am I!

Closet. Your Honour may say your pleasure, but I hope I have not lived to these years to be impertinent:—No, Madam, I am none of those that run up and down the town a story-hunting, and a lie-catching, and—

Lady Galliard. Eternal rattle, peace!—
Mrs Charlotte Gettall go away with Wilding!
A man of Wilding's extravagant life
Get a fortune in the city!
Thou might'st as well have told me a holder forth* were married to a nun.
There are not two such contraries in nature;
'Tis flam,* 'tis foolery, 'tis most impossible.

Closet. I beg your Ladyship's pardon, if my discourse offend you; but all the world knows Mrs Clacket to be a person—

Lady Galliard. Who is a most devout bawd, a precise procurer;
Saint in the spirit, and whore in the flesh;
A doer of the Devil's work in God's name.
Is she your informer? Nay, then the lie's undoubted.—
I say once more, adone with your idle tittle-tattle,—
And to divert me, bid Betty sing the song which Wilding
Made to his last mistress: we may judge by that
What little haunts and what low game he follows.
This is not like the description of a rich citizen's daughter and heir, but some common hackney* of the suburbs.

Closet. I have heard him often swear she was a gentlewoman, and lived with her friends.

Lady Galliard. Like enough; there are many of these gentlewomen who live with their friends: as rank prostitutes, as errant jilts, as those who make open profession of the trade—almost as mercenary—but come, the song.

Enter Betty

SONG

In Phillis *all vile jilts are met,*
Foolish, uncertain, false, coquette.
Love is her constant welcome guest,
And still the newest pleases best.
Quickly she likes, then leaves as soon;
*Her life on woman's a lampoon.**

Yet for the plague of human race,
This devil has an angel's face;
Such youth, such sweetness in her look,
Who can be man, and not be took?
What former love, what wit, what art,
Can save a poor inclining heart?

In vain, a thousand times an hour,
Reason rebels against her power.
In vain I rail, I curse her charms;
One look my feeble rage disarms.
There is enchantment in her eyes;
Who sees 'em, can no more be wise.

Enter Wilding, who runs to embrace Lady Galliard.

Wilding. 'Twelve was the lucky minute when we met.'*
Most charming of your sex, and wisest of all widows,
My life, my soul, my Heaven to come, and here!
Now I have lived to purpose, since at last—Oh, killing joy!—
Come, let me fold you, press you in my arms,
And kiss you thanks for this dear happy night.

Lady Galliard. You may spare your thanks, Sir, for those that will deserve 'em; I shall give ye no occasion for 'em.

Wilding. Nay, no scruples now, dearest of dears, no more;
'Tis most unseasonable—
I bring a heart full freight with eager hopes,

Oppressed with a vast load of longing love;
Let me unlade me in that soft white bosom,
That store-house of rich joys and lasting pleasures,
And lay me down as on a bed of lilies. *She breaks from him.*

Lady Galliard. You're wondrous full of love and rapture, Sir; but certainly you mistake the person you address 'em to.

Wilding. Why, are you not my Lady Galliard, that very Lady Galliard, who if one may take her word for't, loves Wilding? Am I not come hither by your own appointment; and can I have any other business here at this time of night but love, and rapture, and—

Lady Galliard. Scandalous and vain! By my appointment, and for so lewd a purpose!
Guard me, ye good angels.
If after an affront so gross as this,
I ever suffer you to see me more,
Then think me what your carriage calls me:
An impudent, an open prostitute,
Lost to all sense of virtue, or of honour.

Wilding [*Aside*]. What can this mean?
[*Looking on Closet*]. Oh, now I understand the mystery;
Her woman's here, that troublesome piece of train. I must remove her. Hark ye, Mrs Closet, I had forgot to tell you, as I came up I heard a kinsman of yours very earnest with the servants below, and in great haste to speak with you.

Closet. A kinsman! That's very likely indeed, and at this time of night.

Wilding. Yes, a very near kinsman he said he was: your father's own mother's uncle's sister's son; what d'ye call him?

Closet. Aye, what d'ye call him indeed; I should be glad to hear his name. Alas, Sir, I have no near relation living that I know of, the more's my misfortune, poor helpless orphan that I am. *Weeps.*

Wilding. Nay, but Mrs Closet, pray take me right, this countryman of yours, as I was saying—

Lady Galliard. Changed already from a kinsman to a countryman! A plain contrivance to get my woman out of the room. Closet, as you value my service, stir not from hence.

Wilding. This countryman of yours, I say, being left executor by your father's last will and testament, is come—dull waiting-woman, I would be alone with your lady; know your cue, and retire!

Closet. How, Sir!

Wilding. Learn, I say, to understand reason when you hear it. Leave us a while; love is not a game for three to play at. *Gives her money.*

Closet. I must own to all the world, you have convinced me; I ask a thousand pardons for my dullness. Well, I'll be gone, I'll run; you're a most powerful person, the very spirit of persuasion.—I'll steal out.—You have such a taking way with you—But I forget myself. Well, your most obedient servant. Whenever you've occasion, Sir, be pleased to use me freely.

Wilding. Nay, dear impertinent, no more compliments, you see I'm busy now; prithee be gone, you see I'm busy.

Closet. I'm all obedience to you, Sir—Your most obedient—

Lady Galliard. Whither are you fisking and gigiting* now?

Closet. Madam, I am going down, and will return immediately—immediately. *Exit Closet*

Wilding [*Aside*]. So, she's gone; Heaven and broad gold be praised for the deliverance. And now, dear widow, let's lose no more precious time, we've fooled away too much already.

Lady Galliard. This to me?

Wilding. To you, yes, to whom else should it be? Unless, being sensible you have not discretion enough to manage your own affairs yourself, you resolve, like other widows, with all you're worth to buy a governor, commonly called a husband. I took ye to be wiser; but if that be your design, I shall do my best to serve you,—though to deal freely with you—

Lady Galliard. Trouble not yourself, Sir, to make excuses, I'm not so fond of the offer to take you at your word. Marry you! A rakeshame,* who have not esteem enough for the sex to believe your own mother honest—without money or credit, without land either in present or prospect, and half a dozen hungry vices, like so many bawling brats at your back perpetually craving, and more chargeable to keep than twice the number of children. Besides, I think you are provided for; are you not married to Mrs Charlotte Gettall?

Wilding. Married to her? Do I know her, you should rather ask. What fool has forged this unlikely lie? But suppose 'twere true, could you be jealous of a woman I marry? Do you take me for such an ass, to suspect I shall love my own wife? On the other side, I have a great charge of vices, as you well observe, and I must not be so barbarous to let them starve. Everybody in this age takes care to provide for their vices, though they send their children a begging; I should be worse than an infidel to neglect them. No, I must marry some stiff awkward thing or other with an ugly face and a handsome estate, that's certain. But whoever is ordained to make my fortune, 'tis you only that can make me happy.—Come, do it then.

Lady Galliard. I never will.

Wilding. Unkindly said; you must.

Lady Galliard. Unreasonable man! Because you see
I have unusual regards for you,
Pleasure to hear, and trouble to deny you;
A fatal yielding in my nature toward you,
Love bends my soul that way.—
A weakness I ne'er felt for any other;
And would you be so base? And could you have the heart
To take th' advantage on't to ruin me,
To make me infamous, despised, loathed, pointed at?

Wilding. You reason false—
According to the strictest rules of honour,
Beauty should still be the reward of love,
Not the vile merchandise of fortune
Or the cheap drug of a church-ceremony.
She's only infamous, who to her bed,
For interest, takes some nauseous clown she hates,
And though a jointure or a vow in public
Be her price, that makes her but the dearer whore.

Lady Galliard. I understand not these new morals.

Wilding. Have patience, I say 'tis clear.
All the desires of mutual love are virtuous.

Can Heaven or man be angry that you please
Yourself and me, when it does wrong to none?
Why rave you then on things that ne'er can be?
Besides, are we not alone, and private? Who can know it?

Lady Galliard. Heaven will know't; and I—that, that's enough. But when you're weary of me, first your friend, then his, then all the world.

Wilding. Think not that time will ever come.

Lady Galliard. Oh, it must; it will!

Wilding. Or if it should, could I be such a villain—
Ah cruel! If you loved me as you say,
You would not thus distrust me.

Lady Galliard. You do me wrong; I love you more than ere my tongue,
Or all the actions of my life can tell you—so well —
Your very faults, how gross so e'er, to me
Have something pleasing in 'em. To me you're all
That man can praise, or woman can desire;
All charm without, and all desert within.
But yet my virtue is more lovely still;
That is a price too high to pay for you.
The love of angels may be bought too dear,
If we bestow on them what's kept for Heaven.

Wilding. Hell and the Devil! I'll hear no more
Of this religious stuff, this godly nonsense.
Death, Madam, do you bring me into your chamber to preach virtue to me?

Lady Galliard. I bring you hither! How can you say it?
I suffered you indeed to come, but not
For the base end you fancied, but to take
A last leave of you. Let my heart break with love,
I cannot be that wretched thing you'd have me.
Believe I still shall have a kindness for you,
Always your friend, your mistress now no more.

Wilding [*Aside*]. Cozened, abused, she loves some other man!
Dull blockhead not to find it out before!
—Well, Madam, may I at last believe

This is your fixed and final resolution?
And does your tongue now truly speak your heart,
That has so long belied it?

Lady Galliard. It does.

Wilding. I'm glad on't. Good night. And when I visit you again,
May you again thus fool me. *Offers to go.*

Lady Galliard. Stay but a moment.

Wilding. For what? To praise your night-dress, or make court to your little dog? No, no, Madam, send for Mr Flamfull and Mr Flutterbuz, Mr Lap-fool and Mr Love-all; they'll do it better, and are more at leisure.

Lady Galliard. Hear me a little! You know I both despise and hate those civil coxcombs as much as I esteem and love you. But why will you be gone so soon? And why are you so cruel to urge me thus to part either with your good opinion or your kindness? [*In a soft tone*] I would fain keep 'em both.

Wilding. Then keep your word, Madam.

Lady Galliard. My word! And have I promised then to be
A whore? A whore! Oh let me think of that!
A man's convenience, his leisure hours, his bed of ease,
To loll and tumble on at idle times;
The slave, the hackney of his lawless lust!
A loathed extinguisher of filthy flames;
Made use of, and thrown by.— Oh infamous!

Wilding. Come, come, you love me not, I see it plain;
That makes your scruples; that, that's the reason
You start at words, and run away from shadows.
Already some pert fop, some ribbon-fool,*
Some dancing coxcomb, has supplanted me
In that unsteady treacherous woman's heart of yours.

Lady Galliard. Believe it if you will. Yes, let me be false, unjust, ungrateful, anything but a—whore—

Wilding. Oh, sex on purpose formed to plague mankind!
All that you are, and that you do's a lie.
False are your faces, false your floating hearts;
False are your quarrels, false your reconcilements:

Enemies without reason, and dear without kindness.
Your friendship's false, but much more false your love;
Your damned, deceitful love is all o'er false.

Lady Galliard. False rather are the joys you are so fond of.
Be wise, and cease, Sir, to pursue 'em farther.

Wilding. No, them I can never quit; but you most easily:
A woman changeable, and false as you.

Lady Galliard. Said you 'most easily'? Oh, inhumane!
[*In a soft tone, coming near him*] Your cruel words have waked a dismal thought;
I feel 'em cold and heavy at my heart,
And weakness steals upon my soul apace;
I find I must be miserable.—
I would not be thought false.

Wilding. Nor would I think you so, give me not cause.

Lady Galliard. [*Aside*]. What heart can bear distrust from what it loves?
Or who can always her own wish deny?
My reason's weary of the unequal strife
And love and nature will at last o'ercome.
[*To him in a soft tone*]—Do you not then believe I love you?

Wilding. How can I, while you still remain unkind?

Lady Galliard [*Aside*]. How shall I speak my guilty thoughts?— I have not power to part with you; conceal my shame I doubt I cannot, I fear I would not any more deny you.

Wilding. Oh, heavenly sound! Oh, charming creature! Speak that word again, again, again! Forever let me hear it.

Lady Galliard. But did you not indeed? And will you never, never love Mrs Charlotte—never?

Wilding. Never, never.

Lady Galliard. Turn your face away, and give me leave
To hide my rising blushes. I cannot look on you,

[*As this last speech is speaking she sinks into his arms by degrees.*]

But you must undo me if you will.—
Since I no other way my truth can prove, —

You shall see I love.
Pity my weakness, and admire my love.

Wilding. All Heaven is mine, I have it in my arms,
Nor can ill fortune reach me any more.
Fate, I defy thee, and dull world, adieu.
In love's kind fever let me ever lie,
Drunk with desire, and raving mad with joy.

Exeunt into the bed-chamber, Wilding leading her with his arms about her.

Scene changes

Enter Sir Charles Meriwill and Sir Anthony, Sir Charles drunk

Sir Anthony. A dog, a rogue, to leave her!

Sir Charles. Why look ye, uncle, what would you have a man do? I brought her to her coach.—

Sir Anthony. To her coach! To her coach! Did not I put her into your hand, followed you out, winked, smiled, and nodded; cried 'bye Charles, 'bye rogue; which was as much as to say, 'Go home with her, Charles, home to her chamber, Charles;' ay, as much as to say, 'Home to her bed, Charles;' nay, as much as to say—Hum, hum, a rogue, a dog, and yet to be modest too! That I should bring thee up with no more fear of God before my eyes!

Sir Charles. Nay, dear uncle, don't break my heart now. Why I did proffer, and press, and swear, and lied, and—but a pox on her, she has the damnedest wheedling way with her, as, 'Dear Charles, nay prithee, fie, 'tis late; tomorrow; my honour, which if you loved, you would preserve;' and such obliging reasons.

Sir Anthony. Reasons! Reason! A lover, and talk of reason! You lie, Sirrah, you lie. Leave a woman for reason, when you were so finely drunk too, a rascal!

Sir Charles. Why look ye, d'ye see, uncle, I durst not trust myself alone with her in this pickle, lest I should a fallen foul on her.

Sir Anthony. Why there's it; 'tis that you should adone. I am mistaken if she be not one of those ladies that love to be ravished of a kindness. Why, your willing rape is all the fashion, Charles.

Sir Charles. But hark ye, uncle.

Sir Anthony. Why how now, Jack-sauce,* what, capitulate?

Sir Charles. Why do but hear me, uncle; Lord, you're so hasty! Why look ye, I am as ready, d'ye see, as any man on these occasions.

Sir Anthony. Are you so, Sir? And I'll make you willing, or try toledo* with you, Sir.—Whe, what, I shall have ye whining when you are sober again, traversing your chamber with arms across, railing on love and women, and at last defeated, turn whipping Tom,* to revenge yourself on the whole sex.

Sir Charles. My dear uncle, come kiss me and be friends; I will be ruled. *Kisses him.*

Sir Anthony [*Aside*]. —A most admirable good-natured boy this! Well then, dear Charles, know I have brought thee now hither to the widow's house with a resolution to have thee order matters so as before thou quits her, she shall be thy own, boy.

Sir Charles. Gad, uncle, thou'rt a Cherubim! Introduce me, d'ye see, and if I do not so woo the widow, and so do the widow, that ere morning she shall be content to take me for better for worse—renounce me! Egad, I'll make her know the Lord God from Tom Bell,* before I have done with her. Nay, backed by my noble uncle, I'll venture on her, had she all Cupid's arrows, Venus's beauty, and Messalina's fire,* d'ye see.

Sir Anthony. A sweet boy, a very sweet boy! Hum, thou art damnable handsome tonight, Charles. [*Stands looking on him*]—Aye, thou wilt do't; I see a kind of a resistless lewdness about thee, a most triumphant impudence, loose and wanton.

Enter Closet.

Closet. Heavens, gentlemen, what makes you here at this time of night?

Sir Charles. Where's your Lady?

Closet. Softly, dear Sir.

Sir Charles. Why, is she asleep? Come, come, I'll wake her.

[*Offers to force in as to the bed-chamber.*]

Closet. Hold, hold, Sir. No, no, she's a little busy, Sir.

Sir Charles. I'll have no business done tonight, sweetheart.

Closet. Hold, hold, I beseech you, Sir, her mother's with her. For Heavens sake, Sir, be gone.

Sir Charles. I'll not budge.

Sir Anthony. No not a foot.

Closet. The city, you know, Sir, is so censorious—

Sir Charles. Damn the city.

Sir Anthony. All the Whigs, Charles, all the Whigs.

Sir Charles. In short, I am resolved, d'ye see, to go to the widow's chamber.

Sir Anthony. Hark ye, Mrs Closet, I thought I had entirely engaged you this evening.

Closet. I am perfectly yours, Sir; but now it happens so, her mother being there—Yet if you would withdraw for half an hour into my chamber, till she were gone—

Sir Anthony. This is reason, Charles. Here, here's two pieces to buy thee a gorget.*

Gives her money [and exits].

Sir Charles. And here's my two, because thou art industrious.

Gives her money, and goes out with her.

Enter Lady Galliard in rage, held by Wilding.

Lady Galliard [Weeps]. What have I done? Ah, whither shall I fly?

Wilding. Why all these tears? Ah, why this cruel passion?

Lady Galliard. Undone, undone! Unhand me, false, forsworn;
Be gone, and let me rage till I am dead.
What should I do with guilty life about me?

Wilding. Why, where's the harm of what we two have done?

Lady Galliard. Ah, leave me—
Leave me alone to sigh to flying winds,
That the infection may be born aloft,
And reach no human ear.

Wilding. Cease, lovely charmer, cease to wound me more.

Lady Galliard. Shall I survive this shame! No, if I do,
Eternal blushes dwell upon my cheeks,
To tell the world my crime.
—Mischief and Hell, what devil did possess me?

Wilding. It was no devil, but a deity;

A little gay-winged god, harmless and innocent,
Young as desire, wanton as Summer-breezes,
Soft as thy smiles, resistless as thy eyes.

Lady Galliard. Ah, what malicious god,
Sworn enemy to feeble womankind,
Taught thee the art of conquest with thy tongue?
Thy false deluding eyes were surely made
Of stars that rule our sex's destiny:
And all thy charms were by enchantment wrought,
That first undo the heedless gazers on,
Then show their natural deformity.

Wilding [*In a soft tone*]. Ah, my Galliard, am I grown ugly then?
Has my increase of passion lessened yours?

Lady Galliard. Peace tempter, peace, who artfully betrayest me,
And then upbraidest the wretchedness thou'st made.
—Ah, fool, eternal fool! To know my danger,
Yet venture on so evident a ruin.

Wilding. Say,—what one grace is faded!
Is not thy face as fair, thy eyes as killing?
By Heaven, much more! This charming change of looks
Raises my flame, and makes me wish t'invoke
The harmless god again. [*Embraces her.*]

Lady Galliard. By Heaven, not all thy art
Shall draw me to the tempting sin again.

Wilding. Oh, I must, or die.

Lady Galliard. By all the powers, by—

Wilding. Oh, do not swear, lest love should take it ill
That honour should pretend to give him laws,
And make an oath more powerful than his godhead.
—Say that you will half a long hour hence—

Lady Galliard. Hah?

Wilding. Or say a tedious hour.

Lady Galliard. Death, never—

Wilding. Or if you must—promise me then tomorrow.

Lady Galliard. No, hear my vows.

Wilding. Hold, see me die; if you resolve 'em fatal to my love, by Heaven I'll do't. [*Lays his hand on his sword.*]

Lady Galliard. Ah, what—

Wilding. Revoke that fatal 'never', then.

Lady Galliard. I dare not.

Wilding. Oh, say you will.

Lady Galliard. Alas, I dare not utter it.

Wilding. Let's in, and thou shalt whisper it into my bosom;
Or sighing, look it to me with thy eyes.

Lady Galliard [*Sighs*]. Ah, Wilding—

Wilding. It touched my soul! Repeat that sigh again.

Lady Galliard. Ah, I confess I am but feeble woman. [*Leans on him.*]

Sir Charles [*without*]. Good Mistress Keep-Door, stand by, for I must enter.

Lady Galliard. Hah, young Meriwill's voice!

Closet [*without*]. Pray, Sir Charles, let me go and give my Lady notice.

She enters and goes to Wilding.

—For Heaven's sake, Sir, withdraw, or my Lady's honour's lost.

Wilding [*To Galliard*]. What will you have me do?

Lady Galliard [*In disorder*]. Be gone, or you will ruin me for ever.

Wilding. Nay, then I will obey.

Lady Galliard [*Pulling him*]. Here, down the back-stairs.—As you have honour, go and cherish mine. [*Exit Wilding*]
—He's gone; and now methinks the shivering fit of honour is returned.

Enter Sir Charles, rudely pushing Closet aside, with Sir Anthony.

Sir Charles. Denied an entrance! Nay, then there is a rival in the case, or so; and I'm resolved to discover the hellish plot, d'ye see.

Just as he enters drunk at one door, Wilding returns at the other.

Lady Galliard. Ha, Wilding returned! Shield me, ye shades of night.

Puts out the candles, and goes to Wilding.

Wilding. The back-stairs-door is locked.

Lady Galliard. Oh, I am lost! Curse on this fatal night!
Art thou resolved on my undoing every way?

Closet [*To Wilding*]. Nay, now we're by dark, let me alone to guide you, Sir.

Sir Charles [*Reeling about*]. What, what, all in darkness? Do you make love like cats, by starlight?

Lady Galliard [*Aside*]. Ah, he knows he's here!—Oh, what a pain is guilt!

Wilding. I would not be surprised.

As Closet takes him to lead him out, he takes out his sword, and by dark, pushes by Sir Charles, and almost overthrows Sir Anthony; at which they both draw, whilst he goes out with Closet.

Sir Charles. Hah, Gad 'twas a spark!—What, vanished! hah—

Sir Anthony. Nay, nay, Sir, I am for ye.

Sir Charles. Are you so, Sir? And I am for the widow, Sir, and—

Just as they are passing at each other, Closet enters with a candle.

—Hah, why what have we here,—my nown flesh and blood?

[*Embracing his uncle.*]

Sir Anthony. Cry mercy, Sir! Pray how fell we out?

Sir Charles. Out, Sir! Prithee where's my rival? Where's the spark, the—Gad, I took thee for an errant rival. [*Searching about*] Where, where is he?

Lady Galliard [*Angrily*]. Whom seek ye, Sir? A man, and in my lodgings?

Closet. A man! Merciful, what will this scandalous, lying world come to? Here's no man.

Sir Charles. Away, I say, thou damned, domestic intelligence, that comest out every half hour with some fresh sham.—No man!—What, 'twas an appointment only, hum,—which I shall now make bold to unappoint, render null, void, and of none effect. And if I find him here [*Searches about*] I shall very civilly and accidentally, as it were, being in perfect friendship with him—pray mark that—run him through the lungs.

Lady Galliard [*Aside*]. Oh, what a coward's guilt! What mean you, Sir?

Sir Charles. Mean! why I am obstinately bent to ravish thee, thou hypocritical widow, make thee mine by force, that so I may have no obligation to thee, and consequently use thee scurvily with a good conscience.

Sir Anthony [*Aside*]. A most delicate boy! I'll warrant him as lewd as the best of 'em, God grant him life and health.

Lady Galliard. 'Tis late, and I entreat your absence, Sir. These are my hours of prayer, which this unseasonable visit has disturbed.

Sir Charles. Prayer! No more of that, sweetheart, for let me tell you, your prayers are heard. A widow of your youth and complexion can be praying for nothing so late but a good husband; and see, Heaven has sent him just in the crit—critical minute, to supply your occasions.

Sir Anthony. A wag, an arch wag; he'll learn to make lampoons presently. I'll not give sixpence from him, though to the poor of the parish.

Sir Charles. Come, widow, let's to bed. [*Pulls her, she is angry*]

Lady Galliard. Hold, Sir, you drive the jest too far,
And I am in no humour now for mirth.

Sir Charles. Jest! Gad ye lie, I was never in more earnest in all my life

Sir Anthony [*Getting nearer the door still*]. He's in a heavenly humour, thanks to good wine, good counsel, and good company.

Lady Galliard. What mean you, Sir? What can my woman think, to see me treated thus?

Sir Charles. Well thought on! Nay, we'll do things decently, d'ye see—Therefore, thou sometimes necessary utensil, withdraw.

Gives [*Closet*] *to Sir Anthony.*

Sir Anthony. Aye, aye, let me alone to teach her her duty.

Pushes her out, and goes out.

Lady Galliard. Stay, Closet, I command ye. [*To Sir Charles*]—What have you seen in me should move you to this rudeness?

Sir Charles. No frowning, for by this dear night, 'tis charity, care of your reputation, widow, and therefore I am resolved nobody shall lie with you but myself. You have dangerous wasps buzzing about your hive, widow—mark that—[*She flings from him.*] Nay, no parting but upon terms, which in short, d'ye see, are these: down on your knees, and swear me heartily as Gad shall judge your soul, d'ye see, to marry me tomorrow.

Lady Galliard. Tomorrow! Oh, I have urgent business then.

Sir Charles. So have I. Nay Gad, an you be for the nearest way to wood,* the sober discreet way of loving, I am for you, look ye.

He begins to undress.

Lady Galliard. Hold, Sir, what mean you?

Sir Charles [*Still undressing*]. Only to go to bed, that's all.

Lady Galliard. Hold, hold, or I'll call out.

Sir Charles. Aye do, call up a jury of your female neighbours; they'll be for me, d'ye see, bring in the Bill *Ignoramus*, though I am no very true blue Protestant neither. Therefore dispatch, or—

Lady Galliard. Hold, are you mad? I cannot promise you tonight.

Sir Charles. Well, well, I'll be content with performance then tonight, and trust you for your promise till to morrow.

Sir Anthony [*Peeping*]. Ah, rogue! By George, he out-does my expectations of him.

Lady Galliard. What imposition's this! I'll call for help.

Sir Charles. You need not, you'll do my business better alone.

Pulls her.

Lady Galliard [*Aside*]. What shall I do! How shall I send him hence!

Sir Anthony [*Aside. Peeping unseen*]. He shall ne'er drink small beer more, that's positive; I'll burn all's books too, they have helped to spoil him; and sick or well, sound or unsound, drinking shall be his diet, and whoring his study.

Sir Charles. Come, come, no pausing; your promise, or I'll to bed.

Offers to pull off his breeches, having pulled off almost all the rest of his clothes.

Lady Galliard [*Aside, he fumbling to undo his breeches*]. What shall I do, here is no witness near! And to be rid of him, I'll promise him. He'll have forgot it in his sober passion. Hold, I do swear I will—

Sir Charles. What?

Lady Galliard. Marry you.

Sir Charles. When?

Lady Galliard. Nay, that's too much.—Hold, hold, I will tomorrow.—Now you are satisfied, you will withdraw?

Enter Sir Anthony and Closet.

Sir Anthony. Charles, joy Charles, give ye joy. Here's two substantial witnesses.

Closet. I deny it, Sir; I heard no such thing.

Sir Anthony. What, what, Mrs Closet, a waiting-woman of honour, and flinch from her evidence! Gad, I'll damn thy soul if thou darest swear what thou sayest.

Lady Galliard. How, upon the catch, Sir! Am I betrayed?
Base and unkind, is this your humble love!
Is all your whining come to this, false man! By Heaven, I'll be revenged.

She goes out in rage, with Closet.

Sir Charles [*Looking after her*]. Nay, Gad you're caught, struggle and flounder as you please, sweetheart, you'll but entangle more; let me alone to tickle your gills, i'faith.—Uncle, get ye home about your business. I hope you'll give me the good morrow, as becomes me.—I say no more—A word to the wise—

Sir Anthony. By George, thou'rt a brave fellow; why I did not think it had been in thee, man. [*Going and returning, as not able to leave him.*] Well, adieu. I'll give thee such a good morrow, Charles—the Devil's in him!—'Bye, Charles—a plaguy rogue!—'Night, boy—a divine youth! *Exit*

Sir Charles. Gad, I'll not leave her now, till she is mine;
Then keep her so by constant consummation.
Let man a God do his, I'll do my part,
In spite of all her fickleness and art;
There's one sure way to fix a widow's heart.

[*Exit*]

ACT V SCENE I

Sir Timothy's house.

Enter Dresswell, Fopington, [*Laboir*], *and five or six more disguised with vizards, and dark lanterns.*

Fopington. Not yet! A plague of this damned widow. The Devil owed him an unlucky cast, and has thrown it him tonight.

Enter Wilding in rapture and joy

—Hah, dear Tom, art thou come?

Wilding. I saw how at her length she lay!
I saw her rising bosom bare!*

Fopington. A pox of her rising bosom! My dear, let's dress and about our business.

Wilding. Her loose thin robes, through which appear
A shape designed for love and play!

Dresswell. 'Sheart, Sir, is this a time for rapture? 'Tis almost day.

Wilding. Ah, Frank, such a dear night!

Dresswell. A pox of nights, Sir, think of this and the day to come, which I perceive you were too well employed to remember.

Wilding. The day to come!
Death, who could be so dull in such dear joys,
To think of time to come, or aught beyond 'em!
And had I not been interrupted by Charles Meriwill who, getting drunk, had courage enough to venture on an untimely visit, I'd had no more power of returning than committing treason. But that conjugal lover, who will needs be my cuckold, made me then give him way, that he might give it me another time, and so unseen I got off. But come—my disguise. *Dresses.*

Dresswell. All's still and hush, as if nature meant to favour our design.

Wilding. 'Tis well: And hark ye, my friends, I'll proscribe you no bounds, or moderation, for I have considered if we modestly take nothing but the writings, 'twill be easy to suspect the thief.

Fopington. Right; and since 'tis for the securing our necks, 'tis lawful prize—sirrah leave the portmanteau here.

Exeunt as into the house.

After a small time, enter Jervice undressed, crying out, pursued by some of the thieves.

Jervice. Murder, murder! Thieves, murder!

Enter Wilding with his sword drawn.

Wilding. A plague upon his throat; set a gag in's mouth and bind him, though he be my uncle's chief pimp. [*They bind and gag him*]—So—

Enter Dresswell.

Dresswell. Well, we have bound all within hearing in their beds, ere they could alarm their fellows by crying out.

Wilding. 'Tis well. Come, follow me; like a kind midnight-ghost, I will conduct ye to the rich buried heaps—this door leads to my uncle's apartment; I know each secret nook conscious of treasure.

All go in, leaving Jervice bound on the stage.

Enter Censure, running half undressed as from Sir Timothy's chamber, with his velvet-coat on her shoulders.

Censure. Help, help! Murder! Murder!

Dresswell, Laboir, and others pursue her.

Dresswell [*Holding his lantern to her face*]. What have we here, a female bolted from Mr Alderman's bed?

Censure. Ah mercy, Sir, alas, I am a virgin.

Dresswell. A virgin! Gad and that may be, for any great miracles the old gentleman can do.

Censure. Do! Alas, Sir, I am none of the wicked.

Dresswell. That's well.—The sanctified jilt professes innocence, yet has the badge of her occupation about her neck. *Pulls off the coat.*

Censure. Ah misfortune, I have mistook his Worship's coat for my gown.

A little book drops out of her bosom.

Dresswell. What have we here? *A Sermon Preached* by Richard Baxter, Divine.* Gad a mercy, sweetheart, thou art a hopeful member of the true Protestant cause.

Censure. Alack, how the Saints may be scandalised! I went but to tuck his Worship in.

Dresswell. And comment upon the text a little, which I suppose may be: increase and multiply.—Here, gag and bind her.

Exit Dresswell.

Censure. Hold, hold, I am with child!

Laboir. Then you'll go near to miscarry of a babe of grace.

Enter Wilding, Fopington and others, leading in Sir Timothy in his night-gown and night-cap.

Sir Timothy. Gentlemen, why gentlemen, I beseech you use a conscience in what you do, and have a feeling of what you go about.—Pity my age.

Wilding. Damned beggarly conscience and needless pity—

Sir Timothy. Oh fearful!—But gentlemen, what is't you design? Is it a general massacre, pray, or am I the only person aimed at as a sacrifice for the nation? I know, and all the world knows, how many plots* have been laid against myself, both by men, women, and children, the diabolical emissaries of the Pope.

Wilding [*Fiercely*]. How, Sirrah! [*Sir Timothy*] *starts.*

Sir Timothy. Nay, gentlemen, not but I love and honour his Holiness with all my soul; and if his Grace did but know what I have done for him, d'ye see—

Fopington. You done for the Pope, Sirrah! Why, what have you done for the Pope?

Sir Timothy. Why, Sir, an't like ye, I have done you great service, very great service: for I have been, d'ye see, in a small trial I had, the cause and occasion of invalidating the evidence to that degree, that I suppose no jury in Christendom will ever have the impudence to believe 'em hereafter should they swear against his Holiness himself, and all the conclave of cardinals.

Wilding. And yet you plot on still, cabal, treat, and keep open debauch, for all the renegado-Tories and old Commonwealths-men, to carry on the good cause.*

Sir Timothy. Alas, what signifies that? You know, gentlemen, that I have such a strange and natural agility in turning, —I shall whip about yet, and leave 'em all in the lurch.

Wilding. 'Tis very likely; but at this time we shall not take your word for that.

Sir Timothy. Bloody minded men, are you resolved to assassinate me then?

Wilding. You trifle, Sir, and know our business better than to think we come to take your life, which would not advantage a dog, much less any party or person.—Come, come, your keys, your keys.

Fopington. Aye, aye, discover, discover your money, Sir, your ready—

Sir Timothy. Money, Sir! Good lack, is that all? [*Smiling on 'em*] Why what a beast was I, not knowing of your coming, to put out all my money last week to Alderman Draw-Tooth! Alack, alack, what shift shall I make now to accommodate you?—But if you please to come again to morrow—

Fopington. A shamming rogue; the right sneer and grin of a dissembling Whig. [*Aloud and threatening*] Come, come, deliver, Sir; we are for no rhetoric, but ready money.

Sir Timothy. Hold, I beseech you, gentlemen, not so loud, for there is a Lord, a most considerable person and a stranger, honours my house to night; I would not for the world his Lordship should be disturbed.

Wilding. Take no care for him, he's fast bound, and all his retinue.

Sir Timothy. How, bound! My Lord bound, and all his people! Undone, undone! Disgraced! What will the Polanders say, that I should expose their ambassador to this disrespect and affront?

Wilding. Bind him, and take away his keys.

They bind him hand and foot, and take his keys out of his bosom.
Exeunt all.

Sir Timothy. Aye, aye, what you please, gentlemen, since my Lord's bound—Oh what recompense can I make for so unhospitable usage? I am a most unfortunate magistrate!—Hah, who's there? Jervice? Alas, art thou here too? What, canst not speak? But 'tis no matter and I were dumb too, for what speech or harangue will serve to beg my pardon of my Lord?—And then my heiress, Jervice, aye, my rich heiress: why she'll be ravished, oh Heavens, ravished! The young rogues will have no mercy, Jervice; nay, perhaps as thou sayest, they'll carry her away.—Oh that thought! Gad I'd rather the city-charter were lost.

Enter some [including Fopington] with bags of money.

—Why gentlemen, rob like Christians, gentlemen.

Fopington. What do you mutter, dog?

Sir Timothy. Not in the least, Sir, not in the least; only a conscience, Sir, in all things does well. [*They go out all again.*]—Barbarous rogues! Here's your arbitrary power, Jervice; here's the rule of the sword now for you. These are your Tory rogues, your tantivy roisters; but we shall cry quits with you, rascals, ere long, and if we do come to our old trade of plunder and sequestration, we will so handle ye—we'll spare neither prince, peer, nor prelate. Oh, I long to have a slice at your fat churchmen, your crape-gown-orums.*

Enter Wilding, and the rest, with more bags.

Wilding. A prize, a prize, my lads, in ready guineas! Contribution, my beloved.

Dresswell. Nay then, 'tis lawful prize, in spite of *Ignoramus* and all his tribe.—[*To Fopington who enters with a bagful of papers*] What hast thou there?

Fopington. A whole bag of knavery, damned sedition, libels, treason, successions, rights and privileges, with a new-fashioned oath of abjuration, called the Association.—* Ah rogue, what will you say when these shall be made public?

Sir Timothy. Say, Sir? Why, I'll deny it, Sir, for what jury will believe so wise a magistrate as I, could communicate such secrets to such as you? I'll say you forged 'em, and put 'em in,—or print every one of 'em, and own 'em, as long as they were writ and published in London, Sir. Come, come, the world is not so bad yet, but a man may speak treason within the walls of London, thanks be to God, and honest conscientious jurymen. And as for the money, gentlemen, take notice you rob the Party.

Wilding. Come, come, carry off the booty, and prithee remove that rubbish of the nation out of the way.—Your servant, Sir.—So, away with it to Dresswell's lodgings, his coach is at the door ready to receive it.

[Some] carry off Sir Timothy, and others take up the bags, and go out with 'em.

Dresswell. Well, you are sure you have all you came for?

Wilding. All's safe, my lads, the writings, all—

Fopington. Come, let's away then.

Wilding. Away? What meanest thou? Is there not a Lord to be found bound in his bed, and all his people? Come, come, dispatch, and each man bind his fellow.

Fopington. We had better follow the baggage, Captain.

Wilding. No, we have not done so ill, but we dare show our faces. Come, come, to binding.

Fopington. And who shall bind the last man?

Wilding. Honest Laboir, d'ye hear, Sirrah? You got drunk and lay in your clothes under the hall-table; d'ye conceive me? Look to't, ye rascal, and carry things discreetly, or you'll all be hanged, that's certain. *Exeunt Wilding and Dresswell.*

Fopington. So; now will I i'th' morning to Charlotte, and give her such a character of her lover as, if she have resentment, makes her mine. *Exit Fopington*

Sir Timothy [*Calls within*]. Ho, Jenkin, Roger, Simon! Where are these rogues? None left alive to come to my assistance? So ho, ho, ho! Rascals, sluggards, drones! So ho, ho, ho!

Laboir. So, now's my cue—and stay, I am not yet sober.

Puts himself into a drunken posture.

Sir Timothy [*Within*]. Dogs, rogues, none hear me? Fire, fire, fire!

Laboir. Water, water, I say, for I am damnable dry.

Sir Timothy [*Within*]. Ha, who's there?

Laboir. What doleful voice is that?

Sir Timothy [*Within; in a doleful tone*]. What art thou, friend or foe?

Laboir. Very direful—why what the Devil art thou?

Sir Timothy [*Within*]. If thou'rt a friend, approach, approach the wretched.

Laboir [*Reeling in with a lantern in's hand*]. Wretched! What art thou, ghost, hobgoblin, or walking spirit?

Sir Timothy [*Coming out led by Laboir*]. Oh, neither, neither, but mere mortal Sir Timothy Treat-all, robbed and bound.

Laboir. How, our generous host?

Sir Timothy. How, one of my Lord's servants! Alas, alas, how camest thou to escape?

Laboir. E'en by miracle, Sir, by being drunk and falling asleep under the hall-table with your Worship's dog Tory,* till just now a dream of small beer waked me, and crawling from my kennel to secure the black Jack,* I stumbled upon this lantern, which I took for one, till I found a candle in't, which helps me to serve your Worship. *Goes to unbind his hands.*

Sir Timothy. Hold, hold, I say; for I scorn to be so uncivil to be unbound before his Lordship, therefore run, friend, to his Honour's chamber, for he, alas, is confined too.

Laboir. What, and leave his worthy friend in distress? By no means, Sir.

Sir Timothy. Well then, come, let's to my Lord, whom if I be not ashamed to look in the face, I am an errant Saracen.*

Exeunt Sir Timothy and Laboir.

Scene changes to Wilding's Chamber, he discovered sitting in a chair bound, his valet bound by him; to them Sir Timothy and Laboir.

Wilding. Peace, Sirrah, for such I hear some coming.—Villains, rogues! I care not for myself, but the good pious Alderman.

Sir Timothy [*as listening*]. Wonderful goodness, for me! Alas, my Lord, this sight will break my heart. *Weeps.*

Wilding. Sir Timothy safe! Nay then, I do forgive 'em.

Sir Timothy. Alas my Lord, I've heard of your rigid fate.

Wilding. It is my custom, Sir, to pray an hour or two in my chamber, before I go to bed, and having prayed that drowsy slave asleep, the thieves broke in upon us unawares, I having laid my sword aside.

Sir Timothy. Oh, Heavens, at his prayers! Damned ruffians, and would they not stay till you had said your prayers?

Wilding. By no persuasion.—Can you not guess who they should be, Sir?

Sir Timothy. Oh, some damned Tory-rory rogues, you may be sure, to rob a man at his prayers! Why what will this world come to?

Wilding [*Offering to go*]. Let us not talk, Sir, but pursue 'em.

Sir Timothy. Pursue 'em? Alas, they're past our reach by this time.

Wilding. Oh, Sir, they are nearer than you imagine:
Some that know each corner of your house, I'll warrant.

Sir Timothy. Think ye so, my Lord? Aye, this comes of keeping open house, which makes so many shut up their doors at dinner-time.

Enter Dresswell.

Dresswell. Good morrow, gentlemen! What, was the Devil broke loose tonight?

Sir Timothy. Only some of his imps, Sir, saucy varlets, insupportable rascals.—But well, my Lord, now I have seen your Lordship at liberty, I'll leave you to your rest, and go see what harm this night's work has done.

Wilding. I have a little business, Sir, and will take this time to dispatch it in; my servants shall to bed, though 'tis already day.—I'll wait on you at dinner.

Sir Timothy. Your time, my house and all I have is yours; and so I take my leave of your Lordship. *Exit Sir Timothy.*

Wilding. Now for my angry maid, the young Charlotte;
'Twill be a task to soften her to peace:
She is all new and gay, young as the morn,
Blushing as tender rose-buds on their stalks,
Pregnant with sweets, for the next sun to ravish.
—Come, thou shalt along with me, I'll trust thy friendship.

Exeunt

Scene changes to Diana's chamber; she is discovered dressing, with Betty.

Diana. Methinks I'm up as early as if I had a mind to what I'm going to do: marry this old, rich coxcomb.

Betty. And you do well to lose no time.

Diana. Ah, Betty, and could thy prudence prefer an old husband, because rich, before so young, so handsome, and so soft a lover as Wilding?

Betty. I know not that, Madam, but I verily believe the way to keep your young lover, is to marry this old one, for what youth and beauty cannot purchase, money and quality may.

Diana. Aye, but to be obliged to lie with such a beast; aye, there's the Devil, Betty.
Ah, when I find the difference of their embraces,
The soft dear arms of Wilding round my neck,
From those cold feeble ones of this old dotard;
When I shall meet, instead of Tom's warm kisses,
A hollow pair of thin, blue, withered lips,
Trembling with palsy, stinking with disease,
By age and nature baracadoed up
With a kind nose and chin;*
What fancy or what thought can make my hours supportable?

Betty. What? Why, six thousand pound a year, Mistress. He'll quickly die and leave you rich, and then do what you please.

Diana. Die! No, he's too temperate.—Sure these Whigs, Betty, believe there's no Heaven, they take such care to live so long in this world.—No, he'll out-live me. [*Sighs*]

Betty. In grace a God he may be hanged first, Mistress.—Ha, one knocks, and I believe 'tis he. *She goes to open the door.*

Diana. I cannot bring my heart to like this business;
One sight of my dear Tom would turn the scale.

Betty. Who's there?

Enter Sir Timothy, joyful; Diana walks away.

Sir Timothy. 'Tis I, impatient I, who with the sun have welcomed in the day:
This happy day to be enrolled
In rubric-letters, and in gold.
[*Aside*] —Hum, I am profoundly eloquent this morning.
[*Going towards her*]—Fair excellence, I approach—

Diana [*Aside*]. Like physic in a morning next one's heart;
Which though 'tis necessary, is most filthy loathsome.

Going from him.

Sir Timothy. What, do you turn away, bright sun of beauty?
[*Aside*]—Hum, I'm much upon the suns and days this morning.

Diana [*Turning to him, looks on him, and turns away*]. It will not down.

Sir Timothy [*Heroically*]. Alas, ye gods, am I despised and scorned.
Did I for this, ponder upon the question,
Whether I should be king or alderman?

Diana [*Aside*]. If I must marry him, give him patience to endure the cuckolding, good Heaven.

Sir Timothy. Heaven! Did she name Heaven, Betty?

Betty. I think she did, Sir.

Sir Timothy. I do not like that. What need has she to think of Heaven upon her wedding-day?

Diana. Marriage is a sort of hanging, Sir, and I was only making a short prayer before execution.

Sir Timothy. Oh, is that all? [*Takes her hand*] Come, come, we'll let that alone till we are abed, that we have nothing else to do.

Diana. Not much, I dare swear.

Sir Timothy. And let us, fair one, haste, the parson stays; besides, that heap of scandal may prevent us,—I mean my nephew.

Diana [*Weeps*]. A pox upon him now for naming Wilding.

Sir Timothy. How, weep at naming my ungracious nephew? Nay, then I am provoked—Look on this head, this wise and reverend head; I'd have ye know, it has been taken measure on to fit it to a crown, d'ye see.

Diana [*Aside*]. A halter rather.

Sir Timothy. Aye, and it fits it too, and am I slighted, I that shall receive *billet deux** from infantas?* 'Tis most uncivil and impolitic.

Diana [*Aside*]. I hope he's mad, and then I reign alone.
Pardon me, Sir, that parting tear I shed indeed at naming Wilding,
Of whom my foolish heart has now t'ane leave,
And from this moment is entirely yours.

Gives him her hand, they go out followed by Betty

Scene changes to a street.

Enter Charlotte, led by Fopington, followed by Mrs Clacket

Charlotte. Stay, my heart misgives me I shall be undone. [*Pulls her hand from Fopington*]—Ah, whither was I going?

Fopington. Do stay till the news arrives that he is married to her that had his company tonight: my Lady Galliard.

Charlotte. Oh take heed, lest you sin doubly, Sir.

Fopington. By Heaven 'tis true, he passed the night with her.

Charlotte. All night? What could they find to do?

Mrs Clacket. A very proper question; I'll warrant you they were not idle, Madam.

Charlotte. Oh no; they looked and loved, and vowed and loved, and swore eternal friendship—Haste, haste, and led me to the church, the altar; I'll put it past my power to love him more.

Fopington [*Takes her by the hand*]. Oh, how you charm me!

Charlotte. Yet what art thou? A stranger to my heart. Wherefore, ah why, on what occasion should I?

Mrs Clacket. Acquaintance; 'tis enough I know him, Madam, and I hope my word will be taken for a greater matter i'th' city. In troth you're beholding to the gentleman for marrying you; your reputation's gone.

Charlotte. How, am I not honest then?

Mrs Clacket. Marry, Heaven forbid! But who that knows you have been a single hour in Wilding's hands, that would not swear you'd lost your maidenhead? And back again I'm sure you dare not go unmarried; that would be a fine history to be sung to your eternal fame in a ballad.

Fopington. Right; and you see Wilding has left you for the widow, to whom perhaps you'll shortly hear he's married.

Charlotte. Oh, you trifle, Sir; lead on.

They, going out, meet Sir Anthony with Music; they return.*

Sir Anthony. Come, come, gentlemen, this is the house, and this the window belonging to my Lady's bed-chamber. Come, come, let's have some neat, soft, brisk, languishing, sprightly air now.

Fopington. Old Meriwill—how shall I pass by him? *Stand*[s] *by.*

Sir Anthony. So, here's company too; 'tis very well—Not have the boy? I'll warrant this does the business.—Come, come, screw up your chitterling.* *They play*
—Hold, hold a little.—Good morrow, my Lady Galliard.—Give your Ladyship joy.

Charlotte. What do I hear, my Lady Galliard joyed?

Fopington. How, married her already?

Charlotte. Oh, yes he has. Lovely and false, hast thou deceived my faith?

Mrs Clacket. Oh Heavens, Mr Fopington, she faints—ah me!

They hold her, music plays.

Enter Wilding and Dresswell disguised as before.

Wilding. Ah, music at Galliard's door!

Sir Anthony. Good morrow, Sir Charles Meriwill; give your Worship and your fair lady joy.

Wilding. Hah, Meriwill married the widow?

Dresswell. No matter; prithee advance and mind thy own affairs.

Wilding. Advance, and not inquire the meaning on't!
Bid me not eat, when appetite invites me,
Not draw, when branded with the name of coward,
Nor love, when youth and beauty meet my eyes.

[*Sees Sir Charles come into the balcony undressed*]

—Hah—

Sir Charles. Good morrow, uncle. Gentlemen I thank ye. Here, drink the King's health, with my Royal Master's the Duke.

[*Gives 'em money.*]

Fiddler. Heaven bless your honour, and your virtuous bride.

Fopington. Wilding! Undone!

[*Shelters Charlotte that she may not see Wilding.*]

Wilding. Death and the Devil, Meriwill above?

Sir Anthony. Hah, the boy's rival here! By George, here may be breathing* this morning.—No matter, here's two to two; come, gentlemen, you must in. *Thrusts the music in, and goes in.*

Dresswell. Is't not what you expected? Nay, what you wished?

Wilding. What then? It comes too suddenly upon me,
Ere my last kiss was cold upon her lips,
Before the pantings of her breast were laid,
Raised by her joys with me; oh damned deluding woman!

Dresswell. Be wise, and do not ruin where you love.

Wilding. Nay, if thou comest to reasoning, thou hast lost me.

Breaks from him and runs in.

Charlotte. I say 'twas Wilding's voice, and I will follow it.

Fopington. How, Madam, would you after him?

Charlotte. Nay, force me not. By Heaven I'll cry a rape
Unless you let me go.—Not after him!
Yes to th'infernal shades.—Unhand me, Sir.

Fopington. How, Madam, have you then designed my ruin?

Charlotte. Oh, trust me, Sir, I am a maid of honour.

[*Runs in after Wilding.*]

Mrs Clacket. So; a murrain* of your projects, we're all undone now! For my part I'll e'en after her, and deny to have any hand in the business. *Goes in.*

Fopington. Damn all ill luck, was ever man thus fortune-bit, that he should cross my hopes just in the nick?—But shall I lose her thus? No Gad, I'll after her; and come the worst, I have an impudence shall out-face a Middlesex-jury, and out-swear a discoverer.

Goes in.

Scene changes to a chamber

Enter Lady Galliard pursued by Sir Charles, and Footman [*William*]

Lady Galliard [*To the footman, who is going*]. Sirrah, run to my Lord Mayor's and require some of his officers to assist me instantly; and d'ye hear, rascal, bar up my doors, and let none of his mad crew enter.

Sir Charles. William, you may stay, William.

Lady Galliard. I say, obey me, Sirrah.

Sir Charles. Sirrah, I say—know your lord and master.

William. I shall, Sir. *Goes out*

Lady Galliard. Was ever woman teased thus? Pursue me not.

Sir Charles. You are mistaken; I'm disobedient grown since we became one family, and when I've used you thus a week or two, you will grow weary of this peevish fooling.

Lady Galliard. Malicious thing, I wo' not, I am resolved I'll tire thee out merely in spite to have the better of thee.

Sir Charles. Gad I'm as resolved as you, and do your worst. For I'm resolved never to quit thy house.

Lady Galliard. But, malice, there are officers, magistrates i' th' city, that will not see me used thus, and will be here anon.

Sir Charles. Magistrates! Why they shall be welcome, if they be honest and loyal; if not, they may be hanged in Heaven's good time.

Lady Galliard. Are you resolved to be thus obstinate? Fully resolved to make this way your conquest?

Sir Charles. Most certainly, I'll keep you honest to your word, my dear, I've witness—

Lady Galliard. You will?

Sir Charles. You'll find it so.

Lady Galliard. Then know, if thou darest marry me, I will so plague thee, be so revenged for all those tricks thou'st played me—
—Dost thou not dread the vengeance wives can take?

Sir Charles. Not at all; I'll trust thy stock of beauty with thy wit.

Lady Galliard. Death, I will cuckold thee.

Sir Charles. Why then I shall be free o'th' reverend city.

Lady Galliard. Then I will game without cessation, till I've undone thee.

Sir Charles. Do, that all the fops of empty heads and pockets may know where to be sure of a cully;* and may they rook* ye till ye lose, and fret, and chafe, and rail those youthful eyes to sinking; watch your fair face to pale and withered leanness.

Lady Galliard. Then I will never let thee bed with me, but when I please.

Sir Charles. For that, see who'll petition first, and then I'll change for new ones every night.

Enter William.

William. Madam, here's Mr Wilding at the door, and will not be denied seeing you.

Lady Galliard. Hah, Wilding! Oh my eternal shame! Now thou hast done thy worst.

Sir Charles. Now for a struggle 'twixt your love and honour.
—Yes, here's the bar to all my happiness
You would be left to the wide world and love,
To infamy, to scandal, and to Wilding;
But I have too much honour in my passion
To let you loose to ruin. Consider and be wise.

Lady Galliard [*Aside*]. Ah, he has touched my heart too sensibly.

Sir Anthony (*Within*). As far as good manners goes I'm yours; but when you press indecently to ladies' chambers, civil questions ought to be asked, I take it, Sir.

Lady Galliard [*Aside*]. To find him here, will make him mad with jealousy and in the fit he'll utter all he knows. Oh, guilt, what art thou?

Enter Wilding and Dresswell.

Dresswell. Prithee, dear Wilding, moderate thy passion.

Wilding [*Aside*]. By Heaven, I will; she shall not have the pleasure to see I am concerned.—'Morrow, widow; you are early up, you mean to thrive I see, you're like a mill that grinds with every wind.

Sir Charles. Hah, Wilding this, that passed last night at Sir Timothy's for a man of quality? Oh, give him way; Wilding's my friend, my dear, and now I'm sure I have the advantage of him in thy love, I can forgive a hasty word or two.

Wilding. I thank thee, Charles—What, you are married then?

Lady Galliard [*Scornfully*]. I hope you've no exception to my choice.

Wilding [*To her aside angrily*]. False woman, dost thou glory in thy perfidy?
[*Aloud*]. —Yes, faith, I've many exceptions to him—
Had you loved me, you'd pitched upon a blockhead,
Some spruce gay fool of fortune, and no more,
Who would have taken so much care of his own ill-favoured
Person, he should have had no time to have minded yours,
But left it to the care of some fond longing lover.

Lady Galliard [*Aside*]. Death, he will tell him all! Oh, you are merry, Sir.

Wilding [*In a soft tone aside to her*]. No, but thou art wondrous false,
False as the love and joys you feigned last night.

Lady Galliard [*Softly to him*]. Oh, Sir, be tender of those treacherous minutes. [*Walking away, and speaking loud*]—If this be all you have to say to me—

Wilding [*Aloud*]. Faith, Madam, you have used me scurvily,
To marry and not give me notice.
[*To her softly aside*]—Curse on thee, did I only blow the fire
To warm another lover?

Lady Galliard. Perjured—[*Softly to him aside*] was't not by your advice I married?—Oh where was then your love?

Wilding [*Aside to her in a low tone*]. So soon did I advise,
Didst thou invite me to the feast of love,
To snatch away my joys as soon as tasted;
Ah, where was then your modesty and sense of honour?

Lady Galliard [*Soft*]. Aye, where indeed, when you so quickly vanquished?
[*Aloud*]—But you I find are come prepared to rail.

Wilding. No, 'twas with thee to make my last effort against your scorn. [*Shows her the writings.*]
[*Aloud*] And this I hoped, when all my vows and love,
When all my languishments could nought prevail,
Had made ye mine for ever.

Enter Sir Anthony pulling in Sir Timothy and Diana.

Sir Anthony. 'Morrow, Charles; 'morrow to your Ladyship. Charles, bid Sir Timothy welcome; I met him luckily at the door, and am resolved none of my friends shall pass this joyful day without giving thee joy, Charles, and drinking my Lady's health.

Wilding [*Aside*]. Hah, my uncle here so early?

Sir Timothy. What, has your Ladyship served me so? How finely I had been mumped* now, if I had not took heart of grace and showed your Ladyship trick for trick, for I have been this morning about some such business of life too, gentlemen; I am married to this fair lady, the daughter and heiress of Sir Nicholas Gettall, Knight and Alderman.

Wilding [*Aside*]. Hah, married to Diana!
How fickle is the faith of common women!

Sir Timothy. Hum, who's here, my Lord? What, I see your

Lordship has found the way already to the fair ladies; but I hope your Lordship will do my wedding-dinner the honour to grace it with your presence.

Wilding. I shall not fail, Sir. [*Aside*] A pox on him, he'll discover all.

Lady Galliard. I must own, Sir Timothy, you have made the better choice.

Sir Timothy. I could not help my destiny; marriages are made in Heaven, you know.

Enter Charlotte weeping, and Clacket.

Charlotte. Stand off, and let me loose as are my griefs, which can no more be bounded. Oh let me face the perjured, false, foresworn!

Lady Galliard. Fair creature, who is't that you seek with so much sorrow?

Charlotte. Thou, thou fatally fair enchantress. [*Weeps.*]

Wilding [*Aside*]. Charlotte! Nay, then I am discovered.

Lady Galliard. Alas, what wouldst thou?

Charlotte. That which I cannot have: thy faithless husband.
Be judge, ye everlasting powers of love,
Whether he more belongs to her or me.

Sir Anthony. How, my nephew claimed? Why how now, Sirrah, have you been dabbling here?

Sir Charles. By Heaven, I know her not.—Hark ye, widow, this is some trick of yours, and 'twas well laid, and Gad, she's so pretty, I could find in my heart to take her at her word.

Lady Galliard. Vile man, this will not pass your falsehood off.
[*Aside*] Sure 'tis some art to make me jealous of him,
To find how much I value him.

Sir Charles. Death, I'll have the forgery out.
—Tell me, thou pretty weeping hypocrite, who was it set thee on to lay a claim to me?

Charlotte. To you! Alas, who are you? For till this moment I never saw your face.

Lady Galliard. Mad as the seas when all the winds are raging.

Sir Timothy. Aye, aye, Madam, stark mad! Poor soul—Neighbour, pray let her lie i'th' dark,* d'ye hear.

Sir Charles. How came you, pretty one, to lose your wits thus?

Charlotte. With loving, Sir, strongly; with too much loving.
[*To Lady Galliard*]—Will you not let me see the lovely false one?
For I am told you have his heart in keeping.

Lady Galliard. Who is he? Pray describe him.

Charlotte. A thing just like a man, or rather angel!
He speaks, and looks, and loves, like any God!
All fine and gay, all manly, and all sweet:
And when he swears he loves, you would swear too
That all his oaths were true.

Sir Anthony. Who is she? Someone who knows her and is wiser, speak [*To Clacket*]—you, Mistress.

Mrs Clacket. Since I must speak, there comes the man of mischief.
[*To Wilding*]—'Tis you I mean, for all your leering, Sir.

Wilding. So.

Sir Timothy. What, my Lord?

Mrs Clacket. I never knew your nephew was a Lord. Has his honour made him forget his honesty?

Charlotte runs and catches him in her arms.

Charlotte. I have thee, and I'll die thus grasping thee:
Thou art my own, no power shall take thee from me.

Wilding. Never, thou truest of thy sex, and dearest,
Thou soft, thou kind, thou constant sufferer,
This moment end thy fears, for I am thine.

Charlotte. May I believe thou art not married then?

Wilding. How can I, when I'm yours?
How could I, when I love thee more than life?
[*To Lady Galliard*]—Now, Madam, I'm revenged on all your scorn.
—And, uncle, all your cruelty.

Sir Timothy. Why, what, are you indeed my nephew Thomas?

Wilding. I am Tom Wilding, Sir, that once bore some such title, till you discarded me, and left me to live upon my wits.

Sir Timothy. What, and are you no Polish ambassador then, incognito?

Wilding. No, Sir, nor you no King elect, but must e'en remain as you were ever, Sir, a most seditious, pestilent old knave; one that deludes the rabble with your politics, then leaves 'em to be hanged, as they deserve, for silly mutinous rebels.

Sir Timothy. I'll 'peach* the rogue, and then he'll be hanged in course, because he's a Tory. One comfort is, I have cozened him of his rich heiress, for I am married, Sir, to Mrs Charlotte.

Wilding. Rather Diana, Sir; I wish you joy. See here's Charlotte! I was not such a fool to trust such blessings with the wicked.

Sir Charles. How, Mrs Di ladified! This is an excellent way of disposing an old cast-off mistress.

Sir Timothy. How, have I married a strumpet then?

Diana. You give your nephew's mistress, Sir, too coarse a name. 'Tis true, I loved him, only him, and was true to him.

Sir Timothy. Undone, undone! I shall ne'r make Guildhall-speech more; but he shall hang for't, if there be ere a witness to be had between this and Salamanca* for money.

Wilding. Do your worst, Sir; witnesses are out of fashion now, Sir, thanks to your *Ignoramus* juries.

Sir Timothy. Then I'm resolved to dis-inherit him.

Wilding. See, Sir, that's past your skill too, thanks to my last night's ingenuity. There! (*Shows him the writings*) Signed, sealed, and delivered in the presence of, etc.

Sir Timothy. Bear witness, 'twas he that robbed me last night.

Sir Anthony. We bear witness, Sir, we know of no such matter, we. I thank you for that, Sir, would you make witnesses of gentlemen?

Sir Timothy. No matter for that, I'll have him hanged; nay, drawn and quartered.

Wilding. What, for obeying your commands, and living on my wits?

Sir Anthony. Nay, then 'tis a clear case you can neither hang him nor blame him.

Wilding. I'll propose fairly now, if you'll be generous and pardon all: I'll render your estate back during life, and put the writings in Sir Anthony Meriwill's and Sir Charles his hands.—
I have a fortune here that will maintain me,
Without so much as wishing for your death.

All. This is but reason.

Sir Charles. With this proviso: that he makes not use on't to promote any mischief to the King and government.

All. Good and just.

Sir Timothy pauses.

Sir Timothy [*Aside*]. Hum, I'd as good quietly agree to't as lose my credit by making a noise.—Well, Tom, I pardon all, and will be friends. *Gives him his hand.*

Sir Charles. See, my dear creature, even this hard old man is mollified at last into good nature; yet you'll still be cruel.

Lady Galliard. No, your unwearied love at last has vanquished me. Here, be as happy as a wife can make ye—[*Sighing and looking on Wilding, giving Sir Charles her hand*] One last look more, and then—be gone, fond love.

Sir Charles. Come, Sir, you must receive Diana too; she is a cheerful witty girl, and handsome, one that will be a comfort to your age, and bring no scandal home. Live peaceably, and do not trouble your decrepitage with business of State.

Let all things in their own due order move,
Let Caesar* be the kingdom's care and love:
Let the hot-headed mutineers petition,
And meddle in the rights of just succession;
But may all honest hearts as one agree
To bless the King, and Royal Albany.

[*Exeunt*]

THE END

EPILOGUE

Written by a Person of Quality
SPOKEN by Mrs BOTELER*

My part, I fear, will take with but a few,
A rich young heiress to her first love true!
'Tis damned unnatural, and past enduring,
Against the fundamental laws of whoring.

Marrying's the mask, which modesty assures,
Helps to get new, and covers old amours;
And husband sounds so dull to a town-bride,
You now-a-days condemn him ere he's tried;
Ere in his office he's confirmed possessor,
Like Trincalo's* you choose him a successor,
In the gay Spring of love, when free from doubts,
With early shoots his velvet forehead sprouts.*
Like a poor parson bound to hard indentures,
You make him pay his first-fruits ere he enters.
But for short carnivals of stolen good cheer,
You're after forced to keep Lent all the year;
Till brought at last to a starving nun's condition,
You break into our quarters for provision:
Invade fop-corner with your glaring beauties,
And 'tice our loyal subjects from their duties.
Pray, ladies, leave that province to our care;
A fool is the fee-simple* of a player,
In which we women claim a double share.
In other things the men are rulers made;
But catching woodcocks is our proper trade.
If by stage-fops they a poor living get,
We can grow rich, thanks to our mother wit,
By the more natural blockheads in the pit.
Take then the wits, and all their useless prattles;
But as for fools, they are our goods and chattels.
Return, ingrates, to your first haunt the stage;
We taught your youth, and helped your feeble age.
What is't you see in quality we want?
What can they give you which we cannot grant?
We have their pride, their frolics, and their paint.
We feel the same youth dancing in our blood;
Our dress as gay—all underneath as good.
Most men have found us hitherto more true,
And, if we're not abused by some of you,
We're full as fair—perhaps as wholesome too.
But if at best our hopeful sport and trade is,
And nothing now will serve you but great ladies;
May questioned marriages your fortune be,

And lawyers drain your pockets more than we:
May judges puzzle a clear case with laws,
And musquetoon* at last decide the cause.

FINIS

'Song: Love Armed'*

Love in fantastic triumph sat,
Whilst bleeding hearts around him flowed,
For whom fresh pains he did create,
And strange tyrannic power he showed;
From thy bright eyes he took his fire,
Which round about, in sport he hurled;
But 'twas from mine, he took desire,
Enough to undo the amorous world.

From me he took his sighs and tears,
From thee his pride and cruelty;
From me his languishments and fears,
And every killing dart from thee;
Thus thou and I the God have armed,
And set him up a deity;
But my poor heart alone is harmed,
Whilst thine the victor is, and free.

'The Disappointment'*

I

One day the amorous Lysander,
By an impatient passion swayed,
Surprised fair Cloris, that loved maid,
Who could defend herself no longer.
All things did with his love conspire;
The gilded planet of the day,
In his gay chariot drawn by fire,
Was now descending to the sea,
And left no light to guide the world,
But what from Cloris' brighter eyes was hurled.

II

In a lone thicket made for love,
Silent as yielding maids' consent,
She with a charming languishment,
Permits his force, yet gently strove;
Her hands his bosom softly meet,
But not to put him back designed,
Rather to draw 'em on inclined:
Whilst he lay trembling at her feet,
Resistance 'tis in vain to show;
She wants the power to say—ah! what d'ye do?

III

Her bright eyes sweet, and yet severe,
Where love and shame confusedly strive,
Fresh vigour to Lysander give;
And breathing faintly in his ear,
She cried 'cease, cease your vain desire,
Or I'll call out— —what would you do?
My dearer honour even to you
I cannot, must not give—retire,
Or take this life, whose chiefest part
I gave you with the conquest of my heart.'

IV

But he as much unused to fear,
As he was capable of love,
The blessed minutes to improve,
Kisses her mouth, her neck, her hair;
Each touch her new desire alarms,
His burning trembling hand he pressed
Upon her swelling snowy breast,
While she lay panting in his arms.
All her unguarded beauties lie
The spoils and trophies of the enemy.

V

And now without respect or fear,
He seeks the object of his vows,
(His love no modesty allows)
By swift degrees advancing—where
His daring hand that altar seized,
Where gods of love do sacrifice:
That aweful throne, that paradise
Where rage is calmed, and anger pleased;
That fountain where delight still flows,
And gives the universal world repose.

VI

Her balmy lips encountering his,
Their bodies, as their souls, are joined;
Where both in transports unconfined
Extend themselves upon the moss.
Cloris half dead and breathless lay;
Her soft eyes cast a humid light,
Such as divides the day and night;
Or falling stars, whose fires decay:
And now no signs of life she shows,
But what in short-breathed sighs returns and goes.

VII

He saw how at her length she lay;
He saw her rising bosom bare;
Her loose thin robes, through which appear
A shape designed for love and play;
Abandoned by her pride and shame.
She does her softest joys dispense,
Offering her virgin-innocence
A victim to love's sacred flame;
While the o'er-ravished shepherd lies
Unable to perform the sacrifice.

VIII

Ready to taste a thousand joys,
The too transported hapless swain
Found the vast pleasure turned to pain;
Pleasure which too much love destroys:
The willing garments by he laid,
And Heaven all opened to his view,
Mad to possess, himself he threw
On the defenceless lovely maid.
But Oh what envying God conspires
To snatch his power, yet leave him the desire!

IX

Nature's support, (without whose aid
She can no human being give)
Itself now wants the art to live;
Faintness its slackened nerves invade:
In vain th'enraged youth essayed
To call its fleeting vigour back,
No motion 'twill from motion take;
Excess of love his love betrayed:
In vain he toils, in vain commands;
The insensible fell weeping in his hand.

X

In this so amorous cruel strife,
Where love and fate were too severe,
The poor Lysander in despair
Renounced his reason with his life:
Now all the brisk and active fire
That should the nobler part inflame,
Served to increase his rage and shame,
And left no spark for new desire:
Not all her naked charms could move
Or calm that rage that had debauched his love.

XI

Cloris returning from the trance
Which love and soft desire had bred,
Her timorous hand she gently laid
(Or guided by design or chance)
Upon that fabulous Priapus,*
That potent God, as poets feign;
But never did young shepherdess,
Gathering of fern upon the plain,
More nimbly draw her fingers back,
Finding beneath the verdant leaves a snake:

XII

Than Cloris her fair hand withdrew,
Finding that God of her desires
Disarmed of all his aweful fires,
And cold as flowers bathed in the morning dew.
Who can the nymph's confusion guess?
The blood forsook the hinder place,
And strewed with blushes all her face,
Which both disdain and shame expressed:
And from Lysander's arms she fled,
Leaving him fainting on the gloomy bed.

XIII

Like lightning through the grove she hies
Or Daphne* from the Delphic God,
No print upon the grassy road
She leaves, t'instruct pursuing eyes.
The wind that wantoned in her hair,
And with her ruffled garments played,
Discovered in the flying maid
All that the Gods e'er made, if fair.
So Venus, when her love was slain,
With fear and haste flew o'er the fatal plain.

XIV

The nymph's resentments none but I
Can well imagine or condole:
But none can guess Lysander's soul,
But those who swayed his destiny.
His silent griefs swell up to storms,
And not one God his fury spares;
He cursed his birth, his fate, his stars;
But more the shepherdess's charms,
Whose soft bewitching influence
Had damned him to the Hell of impotence.

'On Desire. A Pindaric'

What art thou, O thou new-found pain?
From what infection dost thou spring?
Tell me—Oh! Tell me thou enchanting thing,
Thy nature, and thy name;
Inform me by what subtle art,
What powerful influence,
You got such vast dominion in a part
Of my unheeded, and unguarded, heart,
That fame and honour cannot drive ye thence.

Oh! Mischievous usurper of my peace;
Oh! Soft intruder on my solitude,
Charming disturber of my ease,
That hast my nobler fate pursued,
And all the glories of my life subdued.
Thou haunt'st my inconvenient hours;
The business of the day, nor silence of the night,
That should to cares and sleep invite,
Can bid defiance to thy conquering powers.

Where hast thou been this live-long age
That from my birth till now,
Thou never couldst one thought engage,
Or charm my soul with the uneasy rage
That made it all its humble feebles* know?

Where wert thou, Oh malicious sprite,
When shining honour did invite?
When interest called, then thou wert shy,
Nor to my aid one kind propension brought,
Nor wouldst inspire one tender thought,
When princes at my feet did lie.

When thou couldst mix ambition with my joy,
Then peevish phantom thou wert nice and coy,
Not beauty could invite thee then
Nor all the arts of lavish men!
Not all the powerful rhetoric of the tongue
Not sacred wit could charm thee on;
Not the soft play that lovers make,
Nor sigh could fan thee to a fire,
Not pleading tears, nor vows could thee awake,
Or warm the unformed something—to desire.
Oft I've conjured thee to appear
By youth, by love, by all the powers,
Have searched and sought thee everywhere,
In silent groves, in lonely bowers:
On flowery beds where lovers wishing lie,
In sheltering woods where sighing maids
To their assigning shepherds hie,
And hide their blushes in the gloom of shades:
Yet there, even there, though youth assailed,
Where beauty prostrate lay and fortune wooed,
My heart insensible to neither bowed
Thy lucky aid was wanting to prevail.

In courts I sought thee then, thy proper sphere
But thou in crowds wert stifled there,
Int'rest did all the loving business do,
Invites the youths and wins the virgins too.
Or if by chance some heart thy empire own
(Ah power ingrate!) the slave must be undone.

Tell me, thou nimble fire that dost dilate
Thy mighty force through every part,
What God, or human power did thee create
In my, till now, unfacile heart?

Art thou some welcome plague sent from above
In this dear form, this kind disguise?
Or the false offspring of mistaken love,
Begot by some soft thought that faintly strove,
With the bright piercing beauties of Lysander's eyes?
Yes, yes, tormentor, I have found thee now;
And found to whom thou dost thy being owe:
'Tis thou the blushes dost impart,
For thee this languishment I wear,
'Tis thou that tremblest in my heart
When the dear shepherd does appear,
I faint, I die with pleasing pain,
My words intruding sighing break
When e'er I touch the charming swain
When e'er I gaze, when e'er I speak.

Thy conscious fire is mingled with my love,
As in the sanctified abodes
Misguided worshippers approve
The mixing idol with their gods.
In vain, alas, in vain I strive
With errors, which my soul do please and vex,
For superstition will survive,
Purer religion to perplex.

Oh! Tell me you, philosophers, in love,
That can its burning feverish fits control,
By what strange arts you cure the soul,
And the fierce calenture* remove?

Tell me, ye fair ones, that exchange desire,
How 'tis you hid the kindling fire.
Oh! Would you but confess the truth,
It is not real virtue makes you nice:
But when you do resist the pressing youth,
'Tis want of dear desire, to thaw the virgin ice.
And while your young adorers lie
All languishing and hopeless at your feet,
Raising new trophies to your chastity,
Oh tell me, how you do remain discreet?

How you suppress the rising sighs,
And the soft yielding soul that wishes in your eyes?
While to th'admiring crowd you nice are found;
Some dear, some secret youth that gives the wound
Informs you, all your virtue's but a cheat
And honour but a false disguise,
Your modesty a necessary bait
To gain the dull repute of being wise.

Deceive the foolish world—deceive it on,
And veil your passions in your pride;
But now I've found your feebles by my own,
For me the needful fraud you cannot hide.
Though 'tis a mighty power must move
The soul to this degree of love
And though with virtue I the world perplex,
Lysander finds the weakness of my sex,
So Helen while from Theseus' arms she fled,
To charming Paris yields her heart and bed.

'To Alexis in Answer to his Poem Against Fruition.'*

Ode

Ah hapless sex! Who bear no charms,
But what like lightning flash and are no more
False fires sent down for baneful harms,
Fires which the fleeting lover feebly warms
And given like past beboches* o'er,
Like songs that please (though bad) when new,
But learned by heart neglected grew.

In vain did Heav'n adore the shape and face
With beauties which by angels' forms it drew:
In vain the mind with brighter glories grace,
While all our joys are stinted to the space
Of one betraying interview,
With one surrender to the eager will
We're short lived nothing or a real ill.

Since man with that inconstancy was born,
To love the absent, and the present scorn.
Why do we deck, why do we dress
For such a short-lived happiness?
Why do we put attraction on,
Since either way 'tis we must be undone?

They fly if honour take our part,
Our virtue drives 'em o'er the field.
We lose 'em by too much desert,
And Oh! They fly us if we yield.
Ye Gods! Is there no charm in all the fair
To fix this wild, this faithless, wanderer.

Man! Our great business and our aim,
For whom we spread out fruitless snares,
No sooner kindles the designing flame,
But to the next bright object bears
The trophies of his conquest and our shame:
In constancy's the good supreme
The rest is airy notion, empty dream!

Then, heedless nymph, be ruled by me
If e'er your swain the bliss desire;
Think like Alexis he may be
Whose wished possession damps his fire;
The roving youth in every shade
Has left some sighing and abandoned maid,
For 'tis a fatal lesson he has learned,
After fruition ne'er to be concerned.

'To The Fair Clarinda, Who Made Love to Me, Imagined More Than Woman'

Fair lovely maid, or if that title be
Too weak, too feminine for nobler thee,
Permit a name that more aproaches truth:
And let me call thee, lovely charming youth.
This last will justify my soft complaint,
While that may serve to lessen my constraint;

And without blushes I the youth pursue,
When so much beauteous woman is in view,
Against thy charms we struggle but in vain
With thy deluding form thou giv'st us pain,
While the bright nymph betrays us to the swain.
In pity to our sex sure thou wert sent,
That we might love, and yet be innocent:
For sure no crime with thee we can commit;
Or if we should—thy form excuses it.
For who, that gathers fairest flowers believes
A snake lies hid beneath the fragrant leaves.

Thou beauteous wonder of a different kind,
Soft Cloris with the dear Alexis joined;
When ere the manly part of thee, would plead
Thou tempts us with the image of the maid,
While we the noblest passions do extend
The love to Hermes, Aphrodite* the friend.

'To Alexis, On His Saying I Loved A Man That Talked Much'

Alexis, since you'll have it so
I grant I am impertinent.
And till this moment did not know
Through all my life what 'twas I meant;
Your kind opinion was th'unflattering glass
In which my mind found how deformed it was.

In your clear sense which knows no art
I saw the error of my soul
And all the feebless of my heart
With one reflection you control
Kind as a god and gently you chastise
By what you hate, you teach me to be wise.

Impertinence, my sex's shame,
(Which has so long my life pursued)
You with such modesty reclaim
As all the woman has subdued.

To so divine a power what must I owe
That renders me so like the perfect—you?

That conversable thing I hate
Already with a just disdain,
Who prides himself upon his prate
And is of word (that nonsense!) vain;
When in your few appears such excellence,
That have reproached and charmed me into sense.

Forever may I listening sit
Though but each hour a word be born:
I would attend the coming wit
And bless what can so well inform.
Let the dull world henceforth to words be damned,
I'm into nobler sense than talking shamed.

'To Lysander, On Some Verses He Writ, And Asking More For His Heart Than 'Twas Worth'

I

Take back that heart, you with such caution give,
Take the fond valued trifle back;
I hate love-merchants that a trade would drive;
And meanly cunning bargains make.

II

I care not how the busy market goes,
And scorn to chaffer* for a price:
Love does one staple rate on all impose,
Nor leaves it to the trader's choice.

III

A heart requires a heart unfeigned and true,
Though subtly you advance the price,
And ask a rate that simple love ne'er knew:
And the free trade monopolise.

IV

An humble slave the buyer must become,
She must not bate a look or glance,
You will have all, or you'll have none;
See how love's market you enhance.

V

Is't not enough, I gave you heart for heart,
But I must add my lips and eyes;
I must no friendly smile or kiss impart;
But you must dun* me with advice.

VI

And every hour still more unjust you grow,
Those freedoms you my life deny,
You to Adraste are obliged to show,
And give her all my rifled joy.

VII

Without control she gazes on that face,
And all the happy envied night,
In the pleased circle of your fond embrace:
She takes away the lover's right.

VIII

From me she ravishes those silent hours,
That are by sacred love my due:
Whilst I in vain accuse the angry powers,
That make me hopeless love pursue.

IX

Adraste's ears with that dear voice are blessed,
That charms my soul at every sound,
And with those love-enchanting touches pressed:
Which I ne'er felt without a wound.

X

She has thee all, whilst I with silent grief,
The fragments of thy softness feel,
Yet dare not blame the happy licensed thief:
That does my dear-bought pleasures steal.

XI

Whilst like a glimmering taper still I burn,
And waste myself in my own flame,
Adraste takes the welcome rich return:
And leaves me all the hopeless pain.

XII

Be just, my lovely swain, and do not take
Freedoms you'll not to me allow;
Or give Aminta so much freedom back:
That she may rove as well as you.

XIII

Let us then love upon the honest square,
Since interest neither have designed,
For the sly gamester, who ne'er plays me fair,
Must trick for trick expect to find.

The Wandering Beauty. A Novel. (1698)

To the Right Honourable Edward Earl of Derwentwater.*

My Lord,
Being to publish these last remains of the celebrated Mrs Behn, I could not lose so proper an occasion of showing the respect and value I have for your Lordship. The humour of novels is so sunk for some years, that it shows an extraordinary desert in Mrs Behn, that they are still in general esteem. Others have sought after extraordinary and scarce possible adventures, she happily consulted nature, which will always prevail, so that I may call her the Otway of this kind of writing, whose natural scenes live and increase every day in

esteem with the ingenious, while the fantastic rants of some of their contemporaries die even before their authors, though so celebrated, and followed in their first representation.

I know 'tis the custom of authors to fill their dedications with fulsome flatteries, but as I am no author so I shall avoid their faults, and only profess a sincere veneration for those many noble qualifications which render you the darling of the witty, and beg leave to subscribe myself,

Your Lordship's most obedient,
Humble Servant,
SAM. BRISCOE*

The Wandering Beauty

I was not above twelve years old, as near as I can remember, when a lady of my acquaintance, who was particularly concerned in many of the passages, very pleasantly entertained me with the relation of the young Lady Arabella's adventures, who was eldest daughter to Sir Francis Fairname, a gentleman of a noble family, and of a very large estate in the West of England, a true Church-man, a great loyalist, and a most discreetly indulgent parent. Nor was his lady any way inferior to him in every circumstance of virtue. They had only two children more, and those were of the soft, unhappy sex too; all very beautiful, especially Arabella, and all very much alike: piously educated, and courtly too, of naturally virtuous principles and inclinations.

'Twas about the sixteenth year of her age that Sir Robert Richland, her father's great friend, and inseparable companion, but superior to him in estate, as well as years, felt the resistless beauty of this young lady raging and burning in his aged veins, which had like to have been as fatal to him as a consumption, or his climacterical year of sixty three, in which he died, as I am told, though he was then hardly sixty. However, the Winter medlar* would fain have been inoculated in the Summer's nectarine. His unseasonable appetite grew so strong and inordinate, that he was obliged to discover it to Sir Francis who, though he loved him very sincerely, had yet a regard to his daughter's youth, and satisfaction in the choice of a husband, especially when he considered the great disproportion in their age, which he rightly imagined would be very disagreeable to Arabella's inclinations. This made him at first use all the most powerful and persuading arguments in his capacity to convince Sir Robert of the inequality of such a match, but all to no purpose, for his passion increasing each day more violently, the more assiduously, and with the greater vehemence he pressed his friend to use his interest and authority with his lady and daughter, to consent to his almost unnatural proposition, offering this as the most weighty and prevailing argument, which undoubtedly it was: that since he was a bachelor, he would settle his whole estate upon her, if she survived him, on the day of marriage, not desiring one penny as a portion with her.

This discourse wrought so powerfully with her mother that she promised the old lover all the assistance he could hope or expect from her, in order to which, the next day she acquainted her fair daughter with the golden advantage she was like to have if she would but consent to lie by the parchment that conveyed 'em to her. The dear, fair creature was so surprised at this overture made by her mother that her roses turned all into lilies, and she had like to have swooned away; but having a greater command of her passions than usually our sex have, and chiefly persons of her age, she, after some little disorder, which by no means she could dissemble, she made as dutiful a return to her mother's proposition as her aversion to it would permit, and for that time got liberty to retreat and lament in private the misfortune which she partly foresaw was impending. But her grief (alas!) was no cure of her malady, for the next day she was again doubly attacked by her father and mother, with all the reasons that interest and duty could urge, which she endeavoured to obviate by all the arguments that nature and inclination could offer. But she found 'em all in vain, since they continued their ungrateful solicitations for several days together, at the end of which they both absolutely commanded her to prepare herself for her nuptials with Sir Robert, so that, finding herself under a necessity of complying, or at least of seeming so, she made 'em hope that her duty had overcome her aversion, upon which she had a whole week's liberty to walk where she would, unattended, or with what company she pleased, and to make visits to whom she had a mind, either of her relations or acquaintance thereabouts; though for three or four days before she was strictly confined to her chamber.

After dinner, on the third day of her enlargement, being Summer-time, she proposed to her mother that she would take a walk to a cousin of hers, who lived about four miles thence, to entreat her to be one of her bride-maids, being then in a careless, plain dress, and having before discoursed very pleasantly and freely of her wedding-day, of what friends she would have invited to that solemnity, and what hospitality Sir Robert should keep when she was married to him. All which was highly agreeable to her parents, who then could not forbear thanking and kissing her for it, which she returned to 'em both with a shower of tears. This did not a little surprise 'em at first, but, asking her what could cause such signs of sorrow after so cheerful a discourse on the late subject, she answered that the thoughts of her going now suddenly to live from so dear and tender a father and mother, were the sole occasion of such expressions of grief.

This affectionate reply did amply satisfy their doubts, and she presently took leave of 'em, after having desired that they would not be uneasy if she should not return till a little before 'twas dark, or if her cousin should oblige her to stay all night with her; which they took for a discreet caution in her, and considering that young maidens love dearly to talk of marriage-affairs, especially when so near at hand. And thus easily parted with her, when they had walked with her about a mile, over a field or two of their own.

Never before that time was the dear creature glad that her father and mother had left her, unless when they had pressed her to a marriage with the old knight. They were therefore no sooner out of sight, ere she took another path that led cross the country, which she pursued till past eight at night, having walked ten miles since two a clock, when Sir Francis and her mother left her; she was just now got to a little cottage, the poor, but cleanly habitation of a husbandman and his wife, who had one only child, a daughter, about the Lady Arabella's age and stature. 'Twas happy for her she got thither before they were a bed, for her soft and beautiful limb[s] began now to be tired, and her tender feet to be galled. To the good woman of the house she applies herself, desiring entertainment for that night, offering her any reasonable satisfaction.

The good wife at first sight of her had compassion of her, and immediately bid her walk in, telling her that she might lie with her daughter if she pleased, who was very cleanly, though not very fine.

The good man of the house came in soon after, who was very well pleased with his new guest; so to supper they went very seasonably for the poor young lady, who was e'en ready to faint with thirst, and not overcharged with what she had eaten the day before. After supper they asked her whence she came, and how she durst venture to travel alone, and a-foot. To which she replied, that she came from a relation who lived at Exeter, with whom she had stayed till she found she was burdensome. That she was of Welsh parents, and of a good family; but her father dying left a cruel mother-in-law, with whom she could by no means continue, especially since she would have her to marry an old man whom it was impossible she should love, though he was very rich; that she was now going to seek her fortune in London, where she hoped, at least, to get her a good service.

They all seemed to pity her very heartily, and in a little time after they went to their two several apartments, in one of which Arabella and the damsel of the house went to bed, where the young lady slept soundly, notwithstanding the hardness of her lodging. In the morning about four, according to her laudable custom, the young, hardy maiden got up to her daily employment, which wakened Arabella, who presently bethought herself of an expedient for her more secure and easy escape from her parents' pursuit and knowledge, proposing to her bedfellow an exchange of their wearing apparel. The heiress and hope of that little family was extremely fond of the proposal, and ran immediately to acquaint her mother with it, who was so well pleased that she could hardly believe it, when the young lady confirmed it; and especially when she understood stood the exchange was to be made on even hands. 'If you be in earnest forsooth,' said the mother, 'you shall e'en have her Sunday clothes.' 'Agreed,' returned Arabella, 'but we must change shifts too; I have now a couple about me, new and clean, I do assure you. For my hoods and head-dress you shall give me two pinners,* and her best straw-hat; and for my shoes, which I have not worn above a week, I will have her holiday-shoes.' 'A match indeed, young mistress,' cried the good wife.

So without more ceremony, the young happy lady was attired in her bedfellow's country-weeds by help of the mother and daughter. Then after she had taken her leave of the good old man too, she put a broad round shilling into his wife's hand, as a reward for her supper and lodging, which she would fain have returned, but t'other would not receive it. 'Nay, then, by th' mackins,'* said her hostess, 'you shall take a breakfast ere you go, and a dinner along with you, for fear you should be sick by the way.' Arabella stayed to eat a mess of warm milk, and took some of their yesterday's provision with her in a little coarse linen bag. Then asking for the direct road to London, and begging a few green walnuts, she took her last farewell of 'em.

Near twelve at noon she came to a pleasant meadow, through which there ran a little rivulet of clear water, about nine miles from her last lodging, but quite out of the way to London. Here she sat down, and after drinking some of the water out of the hollow of her hand, she opened her bag, and made as good a meal as the coarseness of the fare, and the niceness of her appetite, would permit. After which she bruised the outward green shells of a walnut or two, and smeared her lovely face, and part of her arms, with the juice; then looking into the little purling stream that seemed to murmur at the injury she did to so much beauty; she sighed and wept, to think to what base extremities she was now likely to be reduced. That she should be forced to stain that skin which Heaven had made so pure and white! 'But ah! ' cried she to herself, 'if my disobedience to my parents had not stained my conscience worse, this needed not to have been done.'

Here she wept abundantly again; then drying her eyes, she washed her feet to refresh 'em, and thence continued her journey for ten miles more, which she compassed by seven a clock, when she came to a village where she got entertainment for the night, paying for it, and the next morning, before six, as soon as she had filled her little bag with what good cheer that place afforded, she wandered on till twelve again, still crossing the country, and taking her course to the Northern parts of England, which doubtless was the reason her father and his servants missed of her in their pursuit; for he imagined that for certain she had taken her nearest way to London. After she had refreshed herself for an hour's time by the side of a wood, she rose and wandered again near twelve miles by eight a clock, and lodged at a good substantial farmer's.

Thus she continued her errantry for above a fortnight, having no more money than just thirty shillings, half of which brought her to Sir Christian Kindly's house in Lancashire. 'Twas near five a clock in the afternoon when she reached that happy port, when coming to the hall door she inquired for the lady of the house, who happily was just coming into the hall with a little miss in her arms of about four years old, very much troubled with weak and sore eyes. The fair wanderer addressing herself to the lady with all the humility and modesty imaginable, begged to know if her ladyship had any place in her family vacant in which she might do her service. To which the lady returned, by way of question, 'Alas! Poor creature, what canst thou do?' 'Anything, may it please your Ladyship,' replied the disguised beauty, 'anything within my strength and my knowledge, I mean, Madam.' 'Thou sayest well,' said the lady, 'and I'm sorry I have not any vacant for thee.' 'I beseech your Ladyship then,' said Arabella, 'let me lodge in your barn tonight, for I am told it is a great way hence to any town, and I have but little money.' 'In my barn, poor girl!' cried the lady, looking very earnestly on her. 'Aye, God forbid else, unless we can find a better lodging for thee. Art thou hungry or thirsty?' 'Yes, Madam,' replied the wandering fair one, 'I could both eat and drink, if it please your Ladyship.' The lady commanded victuals and drink to be brought, and could not forbear staying in the hall till she had done, when she asked her several questions, as of what country she was. To which she answered, 'Truly of Somersetshire.' What her parents were, and if living. To which she returned, they were good, honest, and religious people, and she hoped they were alive, and in as good health as when she left 'em.

After the lady had done catechising her, Arabella, looking on the little child in her Ladyship's arms, said, 'Pardon me, Madam, I beseech you, if I am too bold in asking your Ladyship how that pretty creature's eyes came to be so bad?' 'By an extreme cold which she took,' replied the lady. 'I had not presumed,' returned t'other, 'to have asked your Ladyship this question, were I not assured that I have an infallible cure for the infirmity. And if, Madam, you will be pleased to let me apply it, I will tell your Ladyship the remedy in private.'

The lady was much surprised to hear a young creature, so meanly habited, talk so genteelly; and after surveying her very strictly, said the lady, 'Have you ever experimented it before?' 'Yes Madam,' replied the fair physician, 'and never without happy success. I dare engage, Madam,' added she, 'that I will make 'em as well as my own, by God's blessing, or else I will be content to lose mine, which Heaven forbid.' 'Amen,' cried the good lady, 'for they are very fine ones, on my word. Stay child, I will desire Sir Christian to hear it with me, and if he approves it, you shall about it, and if it take good effect, we will endeavour to requite the care and pains it shall cost you.'

Saying thus, she immediately left her, and returned very speedily with Sir Christian, who having discoursed Arabella for some time with great satisfaction and pleasure, took her into the parlour with his lady, where she communicated her secret to 'em both; which they found so innocent and reasonable that they desired her to prepare it as soon as possible, and to make her application of it with all convenient speed; which she could not do till the next morning. In the meantime, she was ordered a lodging with the house-maid, who reported to her lady that she found her a very sweet and cleanly bedfellow; adding that she never saw nor felt so white, so smooth, and soft a skin.

Arabella continued her remedy with such good success that in a fortnight's time, little miss's eyes were as lively and strong as ever. This so endeared her to the knight and his lady that they created a new office in their family purposely for her, which was attendant on their eldest daughter Eleanora, a lady much about her years and stature, who was so charmed with her conversation that she could not stir abroad, nor eat, nor sleep, without Peregrina Goodhouse (for those were the names she borrowed). Nor was her modesty, humility, and sweetness of temper less engaging to her fellow-servants, who all strove which should best exprcss their love to her. On festival days, and for the entertainment of strangers, she would lend her helping hand to the cook, and make the sauce for every dish, though her own province was only to attend the young lady, and prepare the quidlings,* and other sweet-meats for the reception of Sir Christian's friends, all which she did to admiration.

In this state of easy servitude she lived there for near three years, very well contented at all times, but when she bethought herself of her father, mother and sisters; courted by all the principal menservants, whom she refused in so obliging a manner, and with such sweet, obliging words, that they could not think themselves injured, though they found their addresses were in vain. Mr Prayfast the chaplain himself could not hold out against her charms, for her skin had long since recovered its native whiteness; nor did she need ornaments of clothes to set her beauty off, if anything could adorn her, since she was dressed altogether as costly, though not so richly (perhaps) as Eleanora. Prayfast therefore found that the spirit was too weak for the flesh, and gave her very broad signs of his kindness in sonnets, anagrams, and acrostics, which she received very obligingly of him, taking a more convenient time to laugh at 'em with her young lady.

Her kind reception of 'em encouraged him to that degree that, within a few days after, supposing himself secure on her side, he applied himself to the good old knight, his patron, for his consent to a marriage with her, who very readily complied with his demands, esteeming it a very advantageous match for Peregrina, and withal told him that he would give him three hundred pounds with her, besides the first benefit that should fall within his gift. 'But,' said he, 'as I doubt not that you are sufficiently acquainted with her virtues, and other excellent qualifications, 'tis necessary that you should know the worst that I can tell you of her, which is, that she came to us a stranger, in a very mean, though cleanly habit; and therefore, as she has owned to us, we may conclude, of very humble, yet honest, parentage. Ah, (possibly) her father might have been, or is, some husbandman, or somewhat inferior to that, for we took her up at the door, begging one night's entertainment in the barn.'

'How, Sir!' cried Prayfast, starting, 'have you no better knowledge of her birth than what you are pleased to discover now?' 'No better, nor more,' replied the knight. 'Alas, Sir, then,' returned the proud, canonical sort of a farmer, 'she is no wife for me! I shall dishonour my family by marrying so basely.' 'Were you never told any thing of this before?' asked the knight. 'You know, Sir,' answered the prelate that would be, 'that I have not had the honour to officiate as your chaplain much more than half a year; in which time, 'tis true, I have heard that she was received as a stranger, but that she came in so low a capacity I never learned till now.' 'I find then, Parson,' said the knight, 'that you do not like the author of your happiness, at least who might be so, because she comes to you in such an humble manner; I tell you the Jews* are answerable for the same reason.' 'She cannot be such perfectly to me,' returned t'other, 'without the advantage of good birth.' 'With that I'm sure she would not,' returned his patron, and left him to go to Peregrina, whom he happily found alone.

'Child,' said he to her, 'have you any obligation to Mr Prayfast?' 'As how, Sir?' she asked. 'Do you love him? Have you made him any promise of marriage? Or, has he in any way engaged himself to you?' 'Neither, Sir,' she answered. ''Tis true, I love him as my fellow-servant, no otherwise. He has indeed been somewhat lavish of his wit and rhymes to me, which served well enough to divert my young lady and me. But of all mankind, perhaps, he should be the last I would choose for a husband.' 'I thought,' said the good humoured old knight, 'that he had already obtained a promise from you, since he came but just now to ask my consent, which I freely gave him at first, upon that thought; but he is doubtful of your birth, and fears it may dishonour his family if he should marry you.' 'On my word, Sir,' returned Peregrina, blushing with disdain, 'no doubt our families are by no means equal.' 'What thy family is I know not,' said Sir Christian, 'but I am sure thou art infinitely superior to him in all the natural embellishments both of body and mind. Be just to thyself, and be not hasty to wed; thou hast more merit than wealth alone can purchase.' 'O dear Sir,' she returned, 'you ruin me with obligations, never to be repaid but in acknowledgment, and that imperfectly too.' Here they were interrupted by the young lady, to whom she repeated the conference betwixt Sir Christian and Prayfast as soon as ever Sir Christian left the room.

About a week after, Sir Lucius Lovewell, a young gentleman of a good presence, wit and learning enough, whose father dying near a twelve-month before had left him upwards of 3000 pounds a year, which too was an excellent accomplishment, though not the best, for he was admirably good humoured, came to visit Sir Christian Kindly, and as some of the family imagined, 'twas with design to make his addresses to the young lady, Sir Christian's daughter. Whatever his thoughts were, his treatment there was very generous and kind. He saw the lady and liked her very well; nay, doubtless would have admitted a passion for her, had not his destiny at the same time shown him Peregrina. She was very beautiful, and he as sensible, and 'tis not to be doubted but that he immediately took fire. However, his application and courtship, free and unaffected as it was, were chiefly directed to Sir Christian's daughter. Some little respects he paid to Peregrina, who could not choose but look on him as a very fine, good-humoured, and well accomplished gentleman.

When the hour came that he thought fit to retreat, Sir Christian asked him when he would make 'em happy again in his conversation, to which he returned that, since he was not above seven or eight miles from him, and that there were charms so attractive at Sir Christian's, he should take the liberty to visit him sooner and oftener than he either expected or desired. T'other replied that was impossible; and so without much more ceremony, he took his leave of that delightful company for two or three days, at the end of which he returned with thoughts much different from those at his first coming thither, being strongly agitated by his passion for Peregrina. He took and made all the opportunities and occasions that chance and his own fancy could offer and present to talk to her, both before, at, and after dinner, and his eyes were so constantly fixed on her, that he seemed to observe nothing else, which was so visible to Sir Christian, his lady and daughter, that they were convinced of their error, in believing that he came to make his court to the young lady. This late discovery of the young knight's inclinations was no way unpleasant to Sir Christian and his lady, and to the young lady it was most agreeable and obliging, since her heart was already pre-engaged elsewhere; and since she did equally desire the good fortune of her beautiful attendant with her own.

The table was no sooner cleared, and a loyal health or two gone round, ere Sir Christian asked his young amorous guest to take a walk with him in the gardens, to which Sir Lucius readily consented, designing to disclose that to him for a secret which was but too apparent to all that were present at table. When, therefore, he thought he had sufficiently admired and commended the neatness of the walks, and beauty of the flowers, he began to this effect:

'Possibly, Sir Christian, I shall surprise you with the discourse I'm going to make you; but 'tis certain no man can avoid the necessity of the fate which he lies under; at least I have now found it so. I came at first, Sir, with the hopes of prevailing on you to honour and make me happy in a marriage with Madam Eleanora, your daughter, but at the same instant I was seized with so irresistible a passion for the charming Peregrina, that I find no empire, fame nor wit, can make me perfectly blessed here below, without the enjoyment of that beautiful creature. Do not mistake me, Sir, I beseech you,' continued he, 'I mean an honourable enjoyment. I will make her my wife, Sir, if you will be generously pleased to use your interest with her on my part.'

To which the good old knight replied, 'What you think, Sir, you have now imparted as a secret has been the general observation of all my family e'er since you gave us the happiness of your company today. Your passion is too great to be disguised, and I am extremely pleased that you can think anything in my house worthy the honour you intend Peregrina. Indeed, had you made any particular and public address to my daughter, I should have believed it want of merit in her, or in us, her parents, that you should after that quit your pretensions to her, without any willing or known offence committed on our side. I therefore, Sir, approve your choice, and promise you my utmost assistance afar.* She is really virtuous in all the latitude of virtue; her beauty is too visible to be disputed, even by envy itself. As for her birth, she less can inform you of it; I must only let you know that, as her name imports, she was utterly a stranger, and entertained by us in pure charity. But the antiquity and honour of your family can receive no diminution by a match with a beautiful and virtuous creature, for whom, you say, and I believe, you have so true a passion. I have now told you the worst, Sir, that I know of her; but your wealth and love may make you both eternally happy on earth.'

'And so they shall, by her dear self,' returned the amorous knight, 'if both of 'em may recommend me to her, with your persuasions added, which still I beg.' 'Say, rather, you command; and with those three hundred pounds which I promised her, if she married with my consent to Sir Lucius.'*

To this, the other smiling, replied, 'Her person and love is all I court or expect, Sir. But since you have thought her worthy of so great an expression of your favour and kindness, I will receive it with all humility as if from a father, which I shall ever esteem you. But see, Sir,' cried he in an ecstasy, 'how she comes, Madam Peregrina, led by your daughter.' The young lady coming to him, began thus. 'I know, Sir, 'tis my father and mother's desire and ambition to show you the heartiest welcome in their power, which can be no means be made appear so particularly and undisputably as by presenting you with what you like best in the family; in assurance therefore that I shall merit their favour by this act, I have brought your dear Peregrina to you, not without advice, and some instructions of mine, that may concern her happiness with you, if discreetly observed, and pursued by her. In short, Sir, I have told her that a gentleman of so good a figure, such excellent parts, and generous education, of so ancient and honourable a family, together with so plentiful an estate as you at present possess, is capable of bringing happiness to any, the fairest lady in this country at least.'

'O Madam,' returned Sir Lucius, 'your obligation is so great that I want sense to receive it as I ought, much more words to return you any proportionable acknowledgment of it. But give me leave to say thus much, Madam: that my thoughts of making my court to your ladyship first invited me to give Sir Christian, your father, the trouble of a visit, since the death of mine. However, the over-ruling powers have thought to divert my purpose, and the offering of my heart, which can never rest, but with this dear, charming creature.'

'Your merits, Madam'—'Are sufficient for the gentleman on whom I entirely fixed my affections, before you did me the honour, and yourself the trouble of your first visit,' interrupted Sir Christian's daughter. 'And now, Sir,' added she to her father, 'if you please, let us leave 'em to make an end of this business between themselves.' 'No, Madam,' cried Sir Lucius, 'your father has promised me to make use of his interest with her for my sake. This I now expect, Sir.' 'Then,' said the old knight, 'thou dear, beautiful and virtuous stranger, if I have any power to persuade thee, take my advice, and this honourable gentleman to thy loving husband; I'm sure he'll prove so to thee. If I could command thee, I would.'

'Ah Sir!' said she, kneeling, with tears falling from her charming eyes, 'I know none living that has greater right and power. But alas Sir, this honourable person knows not the meanness of my birth, at least, he cannot think it any way proportionable or suitable to his.' 'O thou dear creature,' cried her lover, setting one knee to the ground, and taking her up, 'Sir Christian has already discoursed all thy circumstances to me. Rise and bless me with thy consent.' 'I must ask my Lady's, Sir,' she replied. 'See, here my mother comes,' said the young lady, and entreated her good word for Sir Lucius. The good ancient lady began then to use all the arguments to incline her to yield to her happiness; and in fine, she was prevailed on to say, 'I do consent, and will endeavour to deserve the honourable title of your dutiful wife, Sir.'

'Twas with no common joy and transport that he received her hand, and kissed those dear lips that gave him an assurance of his happiness, which he resolved should begin about a month or two afterwards, in which time he might send orders to London for the making their wedding clothes. Into the house then they all went, Sir Lucius leading Peregrina, and the first they met of the family was Prayfast, who was not a little surprised nor discomposed at that sight, and more especially when Sir Christian told him that, though he did not think that beautiful, sweet stranger worthy the title of his wife, yet now he should be obliged to join her to that honourable person. The slave bowed, and looked very pale.

All things were at last got ready for the consummation of their bliss, and Prayfast did their business effectually, though much against his will; however, he received the reward of twenty broad pieces. The wedding was kept for a week at Sir Christian's house, after which they adjourned to the bridegroom's, where it lasted as long as at Sir Christian's; his lady, daughter, and the rest of that family would stay.* As they were leaving him, Sir Lucius disposed of two hundred pounds amongst Sir Christian's servants, and the rest of the three hundred he distributed among the poor of both parishes.

When they were gone, the affectionate, tender bridegroom could by no means be persuaded by any gentlemen his neighbours to hunt with 'em, or to take any divertissement, though but for half a day, esteeming it the highest unkindness imaginable to leave his lady. Not that she could be alone neither in his absence, for she never wanted the visits of all the ladies round about, and those of the best quality; who were equally charmed with her sweetness of temper, as the men were with her outward beauties. But in a month's time, or thereabout, observing that he was continually solicited and courted to some sport or pastime with those gentlemen of his neighbourhood, she was forced to do herself the violence to beg of him that he would divert himself with 'em as before their marriage he used. And she had so good success that he did allow himself two days in the week to hunt. In one of which, coming home about five a clock, and not finding his lady below stairs, he went directly up to her chamber, where he saw her leaning her head on her hand, and her handkerchief all bathed in tears. At this sight he was strangely amazed and concerned.

'Madam,' cried he, in an unusual tone, 'what means such postures as these? Tell me, for I must know the occasion.' Surprised and trembling at this his unwonted manner of saluting her, she started up, and then, falling on her knees, she wept out, 'O thou dear author and lord of all my joys on earth! Look not, I beseech you, so wildly, nor speak terribly to me!' 'Thou centre of all my happiness below,' returned he, 'rise and make me acquainted with the dreadful occasion of this afflicting and tormenting sight!' 'All you shall know,' she replied, 'dearest of human blessings! But sit, and change your looks; then I can speak.' 'Speak then, my life,' said he, 'but tell me all; all I must know.' 'Is there a thought about my soul that you shall not partake?' 'I'm sure there is not,' he replied, 'say on then.'

'You know, Sir,' she returned, 'that I have left my parents now three years, or thereabouts, and know not whether they are living or dead. I was reflecting therefore on the troubles which my undutiful and long absence may have caused 'em. For, poor and mean as they may be, they well instructed me in all good things, and I would once more, by your dear permission, see 'em, and beg their pardon for my fault. For they're my parents still, if living, Sir, though (unhappily) not worth your regard.'

'How!' cried he, 'can that pair, who gave my dearest birth, want my regard? Or ought I can do for 'em! No, thou shalt see 'em, and so will I. But tell me Peregrina, is this the only cause of your discomposure?' 'So may I still be blessed in your dear love,' she replied, 'as this is truth, and all the cause.' 'When shall we see 'em then?' he asked. 'We see 'em!' cried she, 'O your goodness descends too much, and you confound me with your unmerited and unexpected kindness. 'Tis I alone that have offended, and I alone am fit to see 'em.' 'That must not be,' returned her affectionate husband, 'no, we'll both go together; and if they want, either provide for 'em there, or take 'em hither with us. Your education shows their principles, and 'tis no shame to own virtuous relations. Come, dry thy dear, lamenting eyes; the beginning of the next week we'll set forwards.' 'Was ever disobedience so rewarded with such a husband?' said she. 'Those tears have washed that childish guilt away, and there is no reward above thy virtue.'

In a few days, Monday began the date of their journey to the West of England; and in five or six days more, by the help of a coach and six, they got to Cornwall, where, in a little town of little accommodation, they were obliged to take up their lodgings the first night. In the morning, said his lady to him, 'My dear, about a mile and a half hence lives one Sir Francis Fairname and his lady, if yet they be living, who have a very fine house, and worth your seeing; I beg of you therefore, that you will be so kind to yourself as to walk thither, and dine with the old gentleman, for that you must, if you see him, whilst I stay here, and send to my father and mother, if to be found, and prepare 'em to receive you at your return. I must not have no denial,' added she, 'for if you refuse this favour, all my designs are lost. Make haste my life; 'tis now eleven a clock. In your absence, I'll dress, to try if change of clothes can hide me from 'em.'

This was so small a request, that he did not stay to reply to't, but presently left her, and got thither in less than half an hour, attended only by one footman. He was very kindly and respectfully received by the old gentleman, who had certainly been a very beautiful person in his youth; and Sir Lucius, fixing his eyes upon his face, could hardly remove 'em, being very pleasantly and surprisingly entertained with some lines that he observed in it. But immediately recollecting himself, he told him that, having heard how fine a seat that was, his curiosity led him to beg the favour that he might see it. The worthy old knight returned that his house, and all the accommodations in it, were at his service. So inviting him in, he satisfied his pretended curiosity, and after he had shown all that was worthy the sight of a stranger in the house, he led him into his gardens, which furnished Sir Lucius with new matter of admiration; whence the old knight brought him into the parlour, telling him that 'twas his custom to suffer no stranger to return till he had either dined or supped with him, according as the hour of the day or night presented.

'Twas here the affectionate husband was strangely surprised at the sight of a picture which so nearly counterfeited the beauties of his dear lived* lady, that he stood like an image himself, gazing and varying, the colours of his face agitating by the diversity of his thoughts; which Sir Francis perceiving, asked him what it was that so visibly concerned him. To which he replied, that indeed he was concerned, but with great satisfaction and pleasure, since he had never seen anything more beautiful than that picture, unless it were a lady for whom he had the most sincere affection imaginable, and whom it did very nearly represent; and then inquired for whom that was drawn. Sir Francis answered him, ''Twas designed for one who was, I dare not say who is, my daughter, and the other two here drawn for her younger sisters. And see, Sir,' pursued he, 'here they come, following their mother.' At which words Sir Lucius was obliged to divorce his eyes from the charming shadow, and make his compliments to them, which were no sooner over than dinner was served in, where the young knight ate as heartily as he could, considering he sat just opposite to it, and in sight of the two ladies, who were now exactly like his own wife, though not so very beautiful.

The table being uncovered, Sir Lucius desired to know why Sir Francis said he doubted whether the original of that picture were yet his daughter. To which the mother returned, big with sorrow, which was seen in her tears, that her husband had spoken but too rightly. 'For,' added she, ''tis now three years since we have either seen her, or heard from her.' 'How Madam! Three years,' cried Sir Lucius, 'I believe I can show your ladyship a dear acquaintance of mine, so wonderfully like that picture, that I am almost persuaded she is the very original; only (pardon me, Madam) she tells me her parents are of mean birth and fortune.' 'Dear Sir,' cried the tender mother, 'is she in this country?' 'She is not two miles hence,' replied Sir Lucius. 'By all things most dear to you, Sir,' said the lady, 'let us be so happy as to see her, and that with all convenient expedition. For it will be a happiness to see any creature, the only like* my dearest Arabella.' 'Arabella, Madam! Alas. No, Madam, her name is Peregrina.' 'No matter for names, Sir,' cried the lady, 'I want the sight of the dear creature.' 'Sir,' added the worthy old knight, 'I can assure you it will be an eternal obligation to us; or if you please we will attend on you to her.' 'By no means, Sir,' returned Sir Lucius, 'I will repeat my trouble to you with her in an hour at farthest.' 'We shall desire the continuance of such trouble as long as we live,' replied Sir Francis.

So without farther ceremony, Sir Lucius left 'em and returned to his Lady, whom he found ready-dressed, as he wished he might. 'Madam,' said he, 'where are your father and mother?' ' I know not yet, my dear,' she replied. 'Well,' returned he, 'we will expect 'em, or send for 'em hither at night; in the meantime I have engaged to bring you with me to Sir Francis Fairname and his lady with all imaginable expedition.' So immediately as soon as coach and six, and equipage, was ready, he hurried her away with him to Sir Francis, whom they found walking with his lady and two daughters in the outward court, impatiently expecting their coming. The boot of the coach, for that was the fashion in those days, was presently let down, and Sir Lucius led his lady forwards to them; who coming within three or four paces of the good old knight, his lady fell on her knees, and begged their pardon and blessing. Her affectionate father answered 'em with tears from his eyes, but the good, ancient lady was so overcome with joy that she fell into a swoon, and had like to have been accompanied by her daughter, who fell upon her knees by her, and with her shrieks recalled her, when she straight cried out, 'My daughter, my daughter's come again! My Arabella alive!' 'Aye, my dear offended mother, with all the duty and penitence that humanity is capable of,' returned the Lady Lovewell.

Her sisters then expressed their love in tears, embraces and kisses, while her dear husband begged a blessing of her parents, who were very pleasantly surprised to know that their daughter was so happily married, and to a gentleman of such an estate and quality as Sir Lucius seemed to be. 'Twas late that night ere they went to bed at Sir Francis's. The next day, after they had all pretty well eased themselves of their passions, Sir Francis told his son-in-law that, as he had three daughters, so he had 3000 pounds a year, and he would divide it equally among 'em, but for joy of the recovery of his eldest daughter, and her fortunate match with so worthy a gentleman as Sir Lucius, who had given him an account of his estate and quality, he promised him ten thousand pounds in ready money besides, whereas the other young ladies were to have but five thousand apiece, besides their dividend of the estate. 'And now,' said he, 'daughter, the cause of your retreat from us, old Sir Robert Richland, has been dead these three months on such a day.' 'How, Sir,' cried she, 'on such a day! That was the very day on which I was so happy as to be married to my dear Sir Lucius.'

She then gave her father and mother and sisters a relation of all that had happened to her since her absence from her dear parents, who were extremely pleased with the account of Sir Christian and his lady's hospitality and kindness to her; and in less than a fortnight after they took a journey to Sir Lucius's, carrying the two other young Ladies along with 'em, and by the way they called at Sir Christian's, where they arrived time enough to be present the next day at Sir Christian's daughter's wedding, which they kept there for a whole fortnight.

EXPLANATORY NOTES

ISABELLA WHITNEY

3 *Lover*: Whitney's lover has not been identified.

4 *Sinon's trade*: during the Trojan War, the Greek warrior Sinon tricked the Trojans into dragging the Trojan horse into their city, thus breaking a ten-year siege.

Aeneas: during his journey to Italy after the Trojan War, Aeneas abandoned Dido, Queen of Carthage, after a brief love affair. In Virgil's version of the story, Dido commits suicide after Aeneas leaves.

Theseus: in Greek mythology, King Minos of Crete had exacted from Athens an annual sacrifice of fourteen young men and women, who were devoured by the Minotaur. Theseus, having defeated the Minotaur with the assistance of Minos' daughter Ariadne, who was in love with him, sailed away with her, only to abandon her on the island of Naxos.

Jason: in Greek mythology Jason went in quest of the Golden Fleece and was assisted by Medea. Eventually he abandoned Medea in order to marry Glauce, daughter of King Creon. Medea took the terrible revenge of killing their two children.

Aeolus: god of the winds.

5 *Paris*: son of Priam, King of Troy, who began the Trojan War by running off with Helen, wife of Menelaus, King of Sparta, and supposedly the most beautiful woman in the world.

Troilus: in Chaucer and Shakespeare, Troilus, younger son of Priam who was slain in the Trojan War by Achilles, loves Cressida/Criseyde, but she leaves him for Diomedes. Whitney is using him here as a rare example of masculine loyalty to a woman.

6 *Penelope*: wife of Odysseus/Ulysses of Ithaca, who remained faithful to him not just during the ten years of the Trojan War but during the further ten years he took to return home.

Lucrece: in legend, she killed herself after being raped by Sextus, son of Tarquinius Superbus, which led to the expulsion of the Tarquins and the end of monarchy in Rome in 510 BC.

Thisby: Pyramus and Thisby's story (parodied in *A Midsummer Night's Dream*) is a version of the Romeo and Juliet story.

Peto: possibly William Peto, who wrote against the divorce of Henry VIII and in favour of Catherine of Aragon.

Cassandra's: Cassandra was a daughter of Priam. When she resisted the advances of the god Apollo, he undermined his gift of the power to foresee the future by ensuring that her prophecies would never be believed.

King Nestor's: King of Pylos, seen as the wisest of the Greeks in the Trojan War.

Xerxes': Xerxes was King of the Persians and was defeated in his attempt to conquer Greece; he was seen by Herodotus as extravagant.

Cressus' gold: Croesus, King of Lydia, was renowned for his great wealth but lost everything after defeat in war with the Persians.

7 *mould*: earth.

8 *Art of Love*: Ovid (43 BC–AD 17), Roman writer, whose work was extremely popular at the time that Whitney wrote, particularly his erotic poetry: the *Ars Amatoria* [*Art of Love*] was much imitated.

Scilla: Whitney relates in detail the story of Scilla, who was so in love with Minos that she allowed him to defeat and kill her father Nisus.

9 *whom*: i.e. home.

Oenone: the nymph who was loved by Paris, but whom he then abandoned when he saw Helen.

Demophoon's deceit: another of the Greeks, Demophon abandoned his wife Phillis, who committed suicide (but who had her revenge through a gold casket which she gave him before he left her and which, when he opened it, drove him mad).

Hero: Leander swam the Hellespont to reach Hero, but was drowned on his return journey: the story is retold by both Virgil and Ovid and formed the basis for Christopher Marlowe's poem 'Hero and Leander'.

scrat: scratched.

10 *Lynceus' eyes*: in Greek mythology the argonaut Lynceus had such sharp eyes that he could see in the dark or see buried treasure.

sprit: has been emended to sprint, but could mean spirit (i.e. spirit itself away).

11 *mell*: treat with, concern oneself with.

13 *Paul's*: St Paul's cathedral (not the building designed by Wren we see today, but the medieval structure destroyed by the Great Fire of London in 1666).

Watling Street, and Canwick Street: streets just to the south-east of St Paul's; both were inhabited by cloth merchants.

Cheap: Cheapside Street also runs east from St Paul's; it was the site of Cheapside market.

bongraces: broad-brimmed sunhats.

high pearls, gorgets: necklaces; ornaments worn round the throat.

14 *trunks*: short breeches.

Gascoyne guise: a particularly wide pair of breeches.

pantables: slippers.

dags: pistols.

14 *'pothecaries*: apothecaries sold both drugs and spices.

roisters: boasters.

cut it out: show off.

15 *Steelyard*: a hall in Upper Thames Street, where merchants gathered.

drug: drudge.

Counter: debtors' prison.

16 *coggers*: cheats.

hole: a part of the prison where the poorest were housed.

Newgate: a prison located in the area of the present Newgate Street, near the Old Bailey, for those who committed serious criminal offences; it was notoriously insanitary.

Holborn Hill: part of the route, along present-day Holborn, to Tyburn, and located opposite Marble Arch, where prisoners were taken for execution.

The Fleet: a prison near Ludgate Hill for those guilty of Star Chamber or Chancery offences.

Ludgate: just west of St Paul's, a debtors' prison.

17 *Smithfield*: the same site as modern Smithfield in Charterhouse Street, it was famous in the sixteenth century for its cattle market and for being the site of Bartholomew Fair; also a location where heretics were burned at the stake.

18 *neat*: oxen.

'Spital: abbreviation of Hospital of St Bartholomew: a poorhouse.

Bedlam: St Mary of Bethlehem, in Bishopsgate: a 'hospital', where the insane were confined and were visited as an entertaining spectacle.

Bridewell: just along from Ludgate Hill, west of St Paul's, a workhouse for the poor and a prison for women.

Inns of Court: where lawyers trained (e.g. Lincoln's Inn; Gray's Inn).

19 *Ringings*: i.e. ringing of church bells.

20 *Paper, Pen and Standish*: i.e. no people, only her writing tools: standish = inkpot.

AEMILIA LANYER

21 *Salve Deus Rex Judaeorum*: hail God, King of the Jews.

Queen's: James I's consort Queen Anne (1574–1619), who offered patronage to many writers.

Paris: in Greek mythology, Paris was asked to present the golden apple to the most beautiful goddess: Hera, Pallas Athena, or Aphrodite. He awarded it to Aphrodite and she helped him abduct Helen from Menelaus.

22 *Cynthia*: goddess of the moon.

Phoebe: another name for the goddess of the moon.

Apollo's beams: the sun's beams.

23 *sith*: since.

paschal lamb: the Passover lamb (a symbol of Christ's sacrifice); Passover commemorates the Jewish flight from Egypt and the lamb is a symbol of their salvation from the angel of death who slew the firstborn sons of all other inhabitants.

24 *she*: Princess Elizabeth (1596–1662), Anne and James's daughter.

Eliza's: Queen Elizabeth I (1533–1603).

26 *Elizabeth's Grace*: Princess Elizabeth.

her: Elizabeth I (politically at this time, praising Elizabeth usually implied dissatisfaction with James).

bridegroom: i.e. Christ.

Solomon: son of David, he was regarded as both wise and magnificent.

dight: dressed.

27 *Daphne's crown*: in Greek mythology, the nymph Daphne metamorphosed into a laurel while being chased by Apollo.

Minerva's: Roman goddess of wisdom.

Pallas: Pallas Athena, daughter of Zeus, Greek goddess of wisdom.

nine worthies: the Muses.

Aaron's precious oil: Aaron was anointed with oil by Moses (Leviticus 8), thus becoming Israel's first priest.

Titan's shining chariot: i.e. the sun.

Phoebus: Roman god of the sun.

28 *elysium*: Greek place of rest after death.

29 *Lady Arabella*: Arabella Stuart (1575–1615), cousin of King James, had a strong claim to the throne. After secretly marrying in 1610 she was imprisoned until her death in 1615. She was certainly learned.

Lady Susan: Susan Bertie first married the Earl of Kent, then, after his death, married Sir John Wingfield. Her mother, Catherine Bertie, Duchess of Suffolk, a staunch Protestant, had to flee England during the reign of Queen Mary as outlined by Lanyer later in this dedication. The first line of this dedication points to some stay in Lady Susan's household by Lanyer when she was young.

glass: mirror.

30 *your love*: i.e. Christ.

Lady Mary: Mary Sidney, Countess of Pembroke (1561–1621), was an extremely important patron, but she also wrote a series of adaptations of the Psalms. She was a member of a significant literary family, including her famous brother Philip, but her brother Robert wrote poetry and his daughter Mary Wroth, featured in this anthology, was a worthy successor to her uncle, producing works in all the literary genres which he favoured.

30 *Idalian groves*: from Mount Ida, home of the Muses.

Graces: goddesses who traditionally bestowed grace and beauty.

Minerva: goddess of wisdom.

31 *golden chain*: perhaps a reference to the ties of Love in Plato's theory.

nine fair virgins: i.e. the muses.

Titan's: Lanyer means the sun: the Titans originally ruled over all the planets.

Morphy: i.e. Morpheus, Greek god of sleep.

welkin: sky.

currat: armour.

32 *A bid*: = a'bid (direct him).

dight: dressed.

33 *meager elf*: lean sprite: i.e. envy.

anatomy: i.e. subject of a dissection.

Pergusa: Lanyer probably means Pergus, the lake in Sicily near where Pluto abducted Proserpine, as described in Ovid's *Metamorphoses*, Book 5.

34 *rare, sweet songs*: Psalms of David.

Pembroke: Mary Sidney's versions of the Psalms were not printed at this time but circulated widely in manuscript form. Lanyer's tribute points to Mary Sidney's importance as a model for aspiring women writers.

Bellona: goddess of war.

36 *Actaeon's hounds*: in Greek mythology Actaeon the hunter was turned into a stag and killed by his own hounds as punishment for seeing Artemis naked.

sprites: spirits.

many books: given that Mary Sidney did not really write 'many books' Lanyer presumably refers to the large number of translations she produced.

glass: mirror.

37 *Lady Lucy, Countess of Bedford*: Lucy Russell, Countess of Bedford (d. 1627), was a significant patron (well worth cultivation by Lanyer). She also wrote poetry (one elegy, written in reply to a Donne elegy, is extant).

him: i.e. Christ.

38 *Lady Margaret, Countess Dowager of Cumberland*: Margaret Clifford (1560–1616), who, together with her daughter Anne, fought for Anne's right to inherit her father's estate. (See the extract from Anne's diary later in this anthology.) It is clear from this dedication and from 'The Description of Cookham' that Lanyer had some early connection with the Cliffords, though the exact details are unknown.

you: Acts 3: 6.

39 *Lady Katherine Countess of Suffolk*: Katherine Howard, wife of Thomas Howard (1561–1626), a powerful figure at court and member of an influential family at this time.

honourable lord: Thomas Howard became lord high treasurer in 1614; however, he was eventually imprisoned for corruption in 1618, along with his wife.

40 *hind and pleasant roe*: female deer.

42 *Lady Anne*, *Countess of Dorset*: Anne Clifford (1590–1676), who married Richard Sackville, Earl of Dorset in 1609. (For more information, see the Introduction.)

43 *heir apparent*: this passage alludes to Anne Clifford's resistance to demands for her to give up her claim to her father's estate: for further details see the introduction and notes to the selection from Clifford's diary in this volume.

44 *pelf*: money or riches.

46 *Cesarus*: Sisera: Lanyer outlines the narrative from Judges 4, whereby Deborah calls for an attack on Sisera, who is eventually killed by Jael, who hammers a nail through his head while he is asleep.

Haman: Esther 5–7: Queen Esther persuaded King Ahasueras both to rescue the Jews from Haman's persecution and to hang Haman.

Holofernes: Judith 8–13: Judith slew Holofernes.

Susanna: Book of Susanna (Apocrypha): accused of unchastity by two elders who lusted after her, Susanna convinced her judges (with the help of Daniel) of her innocence.

47 *Cynthia*: Queen Elizabeth.

wight: person.

48 *commanded me*: further evidence of Lanyer's connection with the Cliffords: perhaps 'To Cookham' is the poem requested by Margaret Clifford.

waves of woe: presumably a reference to the Clifford women's battle over the rights to their Westmorland estate: for more information see the excerpt from Anne Clifford's diary.

Ne: neither.

49 *vesture*: item of clothing.

52 *that queen's*: Helen, whose abduction by Paris started the Trojan War.

53 *Lucrece*: she committed suicide after being raped by Tarquinius (see note to p. 6).

Antonius: Marcus Antonius (*c.*82–30 BC), Shakespeare's Antony, who abandoned his wife Octavia in favour of Queen Cleopatra.

Rosamund: Henry II's mistress who was supposedly poisoned by Queen Eleanor of Aquitaine.

53 *Matilda*: in a legend discredited by modern historians, but widely recounted when Lanyer wrote, King John (1167–1216) attempted to seduce the chaste Matilda, daughter of Robert FitzWalter, and had her poisoned when she spurned him.

54 *Let*: this extract resumes after 63 stanzas of the poem, during which the passion of Christ is described.

your indiscretion: i.e. men's condemnation of Christ. Lanyer is mounting an argument that the traditional blame associated with women for the introduction of sin into the world is invalid.

56 *Pilate*: his wife dreamt that he condemned an innocent man in a prefiguration of Christ's condemnation.

blood: the extract ends here, while the poem continues for another 125 stanzas: the volume ends with 'The Description of Cookham' given here in its entirety.

Cookham: the residence of William Russell, Margaret Russell's brother; Margaret and Anne lived there at intervals.

57 *Philomela*: nightingale.

Phoenix: mythical bird that immolates and renews itself (i.e. is unique, as is Clifford).

59 *Clifford's race*: Anne Clifford, descended from the Earls of Bedford on her mother's side, married Richard Sackville, Earl of Dorset, in 1609, so Lanyer refers to her as Dorset later in the poem. (For more details see the extract from Anne's diary, below.)

steam: *sic*, either stem, or perhaps a misprint for 'stream'.

Parters in honour: i.e. separated from 'ordinary' people.

conster: construe; converse.

ANNE CLIFFORD

Given the extensive references to Clifford's contemporaries, I have avoided detailed annotation: for further information on individuals mentioned, see the editions of Katherine Acheson and D. J. H. Clifford.

63 *January*: this is the beginning of what survives of Clifford's daily diary, which covers 1616, 1617, and 1619. There are summary diaries for most other years, see the edition by D. J. H. Clifford.

Lady Rich: Frances Hatton, wife of Sir Robert Rich.

sister Sackville: Mary, wife of Clifford's husband Richard's brother, Edward Sackville.

my Lord: i.e. her husband, Richard Sackville (1590–1624), Earl of Dorset.

Sir George Villiers: (1592–1628), the favourite of King James, who eventually became Duke of Buckingham.

my Lady of Effingham: Anne, a relation of Anne Clifford.

my Lady Shrewsbury's: Mary, wife of Gilbert Talbot, Earl of Shrewsbury.

twelfth eve: i.e. the eve of twelfth night following Christmas.

my Lady of Arundel: Acheson suggests this is the 'young' Lady Arundel, i.e. Althea, wife of Thomas Howard, Earl of Arundel, the great collector of continental art.

Lady Raleigh: Elizabeth Throckmorton was imprisoned along with Sir Walter Raleigh; she remained with him in the Tower until his execution in 1618.

Sevenoak: near Knole House, the Sackville country estate, where Anne was to spend so much of her time (see, for example, the next entry).

64 *Mary Neville*: Acheson suggests the daughter of Clifford's sister-in-law.

the composition: this refers to her battle with her uncle Francis Clifford, Earl of Cumberland, for the control of the estate in Westmorland which she claimed she should inherit from her father (for further details, see the Introduction).

Lord Roos: William Cecil, who married Anne Lake, daughter of Thomas Lake, who was secretary of state.

Lady Carr: Frances Howard, wife of Robert Carr, Earl of Somerset, King James's favourite. She was involved in a scandalous divorce from her first husband, the Earl of Essex, and implicated in the even more scandalous murder of Carr's friend Thomas Overbury (who had counselled against the marriage), which took place in 1613, three months before the marriage. The Carrs were tried for the murder in May 1616, convicted and imprisoned, but then later pardoned by James. (See entries below.)

glecko: a card game.

Archbishop of Canterbury: George Abbott (1562–1633), who had been Richard Sackville's grandfather's chaplain, and who therefore gathered together with those who wanted to persuade Anne Clifford to make the settlement over her contested inheritance desired by her husband because it would benefit him financially.

Coz. Russell: her cousin Francis Russell.

prayer of ours: perhaps a family prayer or specifically a prayer Anne shared with her mother, given her need to resist attempts to make her give way.

Lady Wotten: Anne's cousin Margaret, wife of Sir Edward Wotton.

Lord William Howard: Richard Sackville's uncle.

brother Sackville: Richard's younger brother Edward.

Dorset House: the London residence of the Sackvilles.

these agreements: the agreements involved Anne Clifford renouncing all claim to her father's estate (granted by the courts to her uncle Francis), in return for a cash settlement. Anne and her mother argued that a barony like her father's should descend to the nearest heir, whether male or female.

65 *coz. Gorge*: Edward Gorges.

Lord Willoughby: Acheson suggests possibly Robert Bertie.

Acteon: Acheson notes that this is Acton Curvett, Sackville's chief footman.

XX: blank in the text.

Sir Robert Sidney: son of Philip Sidney's brother Robert and brother of Mary Wroth.

judge's award: i.e. the granting of her father's estate to her uncle.

66 *received*: received the sacrament.

Sir Oliver St Johns: brother of Margaret Clifford's mother.

My lady Margaret: Anne's daughter, often referred to in the diary as 'the child'.

67 *impostume*: a kind of abscess.

the standing: Holmes suggests that this is a portion of the Knole garden still known as the Duchess's seat.

Bolebrooke: Bollbroke, a house to which Anne Clifford was entitled under her jointure (the arrangement made upon marriage to ensure that a wife would have some property of her own after her husband's death). See also the references to her 'thirds' below: a jointure was often one-third of a wife's dowry.

sister Beauchamp: Anne's sister-in-law.

Mr Legg: Sackville's steward.

68 *Horsley*: also referred to as West Horsley, an estate in Surrey.

the audit: an assessment of the estate's accounts.

Matthew: Matthew Caldicott, Richard Sackville's 'favourite' and his personal servant. Anne Clifford saw him as her enemy and actually wrote a letter to the Bishop of London complaining about him. Holmes and Lewalski suggest that Matthew and Sackville may have had a homosexual relationship; Matthew certainly seems to have been as jealous of Anne Clifford as she was of him.

my Lord Treasurer and my old Lady: Sackville's paternal grandparents.

wedding ring: Holmes suggests that this gesture of Clifford's may have been inspired by her reading of patient Griselda's story in Chaucer ('Clerk's Tale').

69 *cocking*: cock-fighting.

owl in the desert: this vivid phrase echoes Psalms 102. 6 'I am like an owl of the desert'.

70 *Wat. Raleigh*: son of Sir Walter Raleigh.

71 *Skipton*: i.e. her mother had asked to be buried with her family, not the Cliffords. (In a codicil—see the entry below for the 31st—she gave Anne the choice and Anne chose the key Clifford property of Appleby.)

my Lord of Cumberland: Anne's uncle, whose claim on her mother's jointure went hand in hand with his general claim to the Clifford inheritance.

73 *XX*: blank in the text.

Lady Somerset's little child: Anne, who was born in the Tower and who was to marry Clifford's cousin William Russell.

it: her mother's body.

74 *my Lady Montgomery*: the wife of Philip Herbert (1584–1650), who became Anne's second husband in 1630.

Grey Dick: 'Duck' in Portland MS; a servant.

stuff: linen.

75 *XXX*: blank in the text.

September 1616: there are no entries in either manuscript for this month (Knole has October entries mistakenly placed here).

grogram gown: in Knole MS this entry is for the 21st; grogram is coarse material containing silk.

Netherlands: an example of Clifford's wide reading; it is not clear what this volume was exactly: Clifford suggests *A Tragical History of the Troubles and Civil Wars of the Low Countries*, trans. Thomas Stock (1583).

76 *Prince Henry*: Charles I's elder brother, he died in 1612.

Montaigne's Essays: Michel Montaigne (1533–94), the French essayist whose *Essais* (1580) were translated into English by John Florio in 1603.

Irish stitch: a kind of needlework done in graded shades of colour.

work: i.e. to do needlework.

tables: backgammon.

leads: a kind of terrace on the house roof.

saveguard: a kind of overskirt.

77 *Mr John Tufton*: he married Margaret in 1629.

78 *sweet bag*: a kind of pot-pourri.

the play of the mad lover: playwright John Fletcher's (1579–1625) *The Mad Lover*.

79 *the masque*: Ben Jonson's *The Vision of Delight*. Jonson (1572–1637), poet and playwright, wrote a number of masques, which were a courtly entertainment comprising drama, dancing, and opera.

closet: a private room like a study.

79 *Mr Sandys's book*: George Sandys (1578–1644), a translator, traveller and poet, *A Relation of a Journey* . . . (1615) was published in 1615.

80 *the masque*: *The Vision of Delight*.

my Lord and my Lady: i.e. Edward Somerset, Earl of Worcester (1553–1628) and his wife.

81 *ague*: a fever.

tummel: a kind of woollen cloth.

Fairy Queene: *The Faerie Queene* (1590) by Edmund Spenser (*c.*1522–99).

MARY WROTH

83 *covered*: Cupid is traditionally depicted as blindfolded to emphasize the 'blindness' of love.

harm: when Cupid shot Venus with one of his arrows she fell in love with Mars.

travails: misfortunes.

Philisses: the song that follows echoes Philip Sidney (1554–86), *Certain Sonnets* 18 and is similar to the first sonnet in Wroth's prose romance *Urania* (1621).

mead: meadow.

85 *froward boy*: i.e. Cupid.

Apollo: god of the sun.

86 *chaste Goddess*: Diana.

89 *rue*: repent, regret.

92 *When*: Rustic sings a parodic love song reflecting his rough and rustic nature. This type of song or poem is often found in Renaissance pastoral writing.

94 *sprites*: spirits.

troth: faith or vow.

95 *band*: bond or agreement.

unleek: unlike or untrue.

98 *'chieves*: achieves.

bell: lead the flock.

you'll . . . brook: i.e. you won't like some of the chances that fall.

100 *hap*: chance.

She: i.e. Fortune or blind chance.

solve: MS reads salve, which is perhaps a pun on solve/salve (ameliorate).

103 *'gage*: engage.

106 *my thought*: methought.

108 *bewray*: reveal.

109 *she*: i.e. Musella, her confidant.

110 *Arcadia*: a traditional pastoral realm and perhaps also an acknowledgement of Wroth's uncle Sir Philip Sidney's famous romance of that title.

111 *on cause*: i.e. for good reason.

strangely: coldly.

115 *'pointed*: appointed.

116 *meads*: meadows.

122 *jar*: conflict or quarrel.

129 *all worth lost / For riches*: Cerasano and Wynne-Davies note that the pun on worth/Wroth calls attention to the identification of Musella with Mary Wroth, lamenting her marriage to Robert Wroth (*c*.1576–1614), figured as Rustic, while in love with her first cousin William Herbert (1580–1630), figured as Philisses, although they see this triangle as also reflecting Penelope Rich, Robert Rich, and Philip Sidney.

130 *fatal sisters*: the three fates.

134 *received's*: received is.

Phoebus' light: the sunshine: i.e. as the Indians' black skin shows the marks of the sun, the speaker wishes to 'wear' the mark of Cupid's might in her heart.

hies: goes quickly.

hunt: Wroth's husband (like King James) was a fanatical hunter: the king appointed him to the position of riding forester.

play: play music: the 'rejection' of music in favour of thought is interesting considering that the portrait of Wroth at Penshurst is dominated by an arch-lute.

void of right: as if they were compelled, rather than able to choose.

fond: trivial or foolish.

a lover's fast: the first of a series of ambiguous images in this sonnet, which explores the perils of the multiple gazes directed at women in Wroth's Jacobean aristocratic world: the lover's fast may be both the starvation pangs of love which follow from allowing doubt (i.e. possibility) to the lover, or it may be the process of holding the lover fast. These double meanings continue through the three quatrains, stressed by the image of the hurt (wound) being searched 'in double kind' (i.e. tried to see through her, but also tried/tested her potential weakness).

135 *pride / Of our desires*: in echoing the phrase from the previous sonnet, Wroth emphasizes the dangers of sexual desire. In this sonnet, the image of miscarriage in the first quatrain adds another level to the whole issue of desire and its consequences.

will: Wroth may be punning on the first name of her lover, William Herbert.

prove: this is the last sonnet in the first part of the sequence, and it is signed 'Pamphilia'.

ELEANOR DAVIES

137 *A:lmighty O:mnipotent*: punning on Alpha and Omega (Revelation 1: 8). I have throughout followed Davies's use of italics as they seem an integral part of her style.

Army's General: Oliver Cromwell (1599–1658), whose initials and name are entwined throughout this prophecy, which sees him as linked to Davies's own prophetic purpose.

sun and moon: again a reference to Revelation 12. 1: 'And there appeared a great wonder in heaven; a woman clothed with the sun, and the moon under her feet, and upon her head a crown of twelve stars'.

[symbols]: the symbols are the sun and moon and also, Cope suggests, an eye and a horn.

fifty days: the passage of time from Easter to Pentecost.

A°. Anno (the year, but with another use of the key initials A and O).

138 *the 144 &c.*: i.e. the 144 thousand referred to in this verse of Revelation, who were the only people able to learn the new song (and the only people who would be saved).

she: i.e. Davies, who had her first revelation in the same year that Charles I began his reign; she goes on to describe this first experience of prophecy.

Division's character: John 7. 43.

Anno 44. accomplished: i.e. in the year 1644 William Laud, Archbishop of Canterbury (1573–1644), was executed: he was seen as a symbol of the Catholic tendencies in the English Church, opposed by Davies and many others. Later in her account of Laud's part in having her writings burned and Davies herself imprisoned, Davies points to her prophecy predicting his death.

plague: Parliament left London, driven out by the plague.

age of the world: the number killed by the plague, published each week, equals the age of the world (another sign of approaching revelation).

the term: this refers to the law courts, which also retired from London to escape the plague.

139 *Germany's woeful occurrences*: the Thirty Years' War, which began in 1618 with the acceptance of the Bohemian crown by James I's son-in-law Frederick, setting Protestant against Catholic throughout Europe, and ended with a peace treaty between Spain and the Dutch Provinces in 1648.

Archbishop Abbot's: Davies delivered her prophecy to George Abbot, Archbishop of Canterbury in 1625.

the babe's: i.e. her prophecy, which she takes to Holland to be printed, thereby escaping censorship in England.

innocent blood: in 1621 Abbot accidentally shot a gamekeeper while hunting; while absolved of all blame by the coroner's court, the accident continued to haunt the Archbishop. Laud succeeded Abbot in 1633.

rank: Matthew 13: 57.

140 *apprehended*: Laud called Davies before the Court of High Commission in 1633, where her books were burned and she was imprisoned for two and a half years.

forty eight: Charles I was executed on January 1648 (old calendar, 1649 in our terms).

Scandalum Magnatum: a legal charge (scandal of magnates) against Davies of making public accusations against a person in high office.

Lambeth: the palace in London of the Archbishop of Canterbury (Laud).

prisoner: here Davies recounts the story of her arraignment before Laud and subsequent imprisonment.

23 of October: both the decisive Civil War battle of Edge Hill (1642) and the Irish massacre (1641) occurred on the same date as Davies's imprisonment.

141 *C Stu*: Charles Stuart (King Charles I).

Rachel's : anagram from Charles.

PRISCILLA COTTON AND MARY COLE

142 *babes*: Matthew 11: 25.

143 *Amaziel*: Amaziah: Amos 7: 10.

Haman: Esther 3: 8.

Stephen's persecutors: Acts 11: 19.

144 *light*: a typical Quaker expression of the inner light of God.

Presbytery: Cotton and Cole posit a truth of scripture that transcends sectarian division into, for example, Presbyterians, Independents, supporters of the Church of England, and Baptists.

Apollos: 1 Corinthians 3: 5.

145 *mountain*: Daniel 2: 45.

cry: Isaiah 5: 7.

146 *darkened*: Zechariah 11: 17.

Kore: Korah and his followers were swallowed up by the earth in punishment for challenging Moses' authority.

church: 1 Corinthians 14: 34.

147 *one by one*: 1 Corinthians 14: 31.

her head: 1 Corinthians 11: 5.

Christ: 1 Corinthians 11: 3.

four virgins: Acts 21: 9.

Exeter gaol: like so many Quakers, Cotton and Cole were imprisoned.

HESTER BIDDLE

Biddle's text contains so many biblical quotations and allusions that I have only glossed those that seem particularly important.

148 *royal seed*: cf. 2 Kings 25: 25: the royal seed are the people chosen by God.

Newgate: the prison: like Cotton and Cole, Biddle writes this from prison.

149 *sister*: Ezekiel 23: 32.

Nineveh: see Jonah 3: 2–10.

thee: this section echoes Hosea 2.

150 *sores*: this section echoes Isaiah 1: 6–7.

leopards: if this passage is from Matthew 11: 5, perhaps this should read 'lepers'.

four winds: Matthew 24: 31 and Mark 13: 27.

nasty prisons: a clear reference to the persecution of the Quakers.

151 *harlot*: Ezekiel 15.

152 *Oliver's days*: Oliver Cromwell's rule.

Hammon: Haman: Esther 3: 2.

remnant: i.e. the Quakers, who are true to God.

154 *King*: Charles II.

155 *a people in the North*: the Quakers, whose origins were in the north of England, especially places such as Leicester, Manchester, and Sheffield.

calves in the stall: Malachi 4: 2.

established: Isaiah 54: 14; this important passage stresses the freedom of the Quakers from conventional religious authorities.

156 *Demas*: 2 Timothy 4: 10.

professors: those who make an open profession of their religion.

silver: Ezekiel 22: 18–22.

bucket: Isaiah 40: 15.

moths: Isaiah 50: 9.

157 *long homes*: Ecclesiastes 12: 5.

158 *bishoped*: confirmed.

King's head was taken off: execution of Charles I in 1649.

160 *menstrous cloth*: allusion to Isaiah 64: 6: a polluted (as with menstrual blood) cloth.

162 *asps*: Romans 3: 13.

163 *is*: *sic*: are.

164 *be*: Matthew 18: 20.

166 *is*: *sic*: are.

MARGARET CAVENDISH

167 *Atoms*: this poem is typical of poems (and prose) expressing Cavendish's view of the universe as filled with self-moving matter: a universe without empty space, as every particle (atom) has a place in it.

168 *Lacedemonians*: inhabitants of Laconia/Sparta, renowned for their austerity.

the lie: to accuse someone of lying (the typical challenge preceding a duel).

169 *champain*: open countryside.

172 *Reformation*: the war in *Bell in Campo* has echoes of the English Civil War.

maskered: bewildered.

horses: the general's interest in horses mirrors that of Cavendish's husband, William, Duke of Newcastle (1592–1676), a famous horseman who wrote an influential book on the training of horses.

175 *barricado*: barricade or block.

cuckold: the husband of an unfaithful wife.

178 *Agamemnon's*: Agamemnon, brother of Menelaus and leader of the Greek forces, was murdered by his wife, Clytemnestra, on his return from the Trojan War.

179 *trull*: prostitute.

180 *neats-tongue*: cow's tongue (when eaten).

in years: i.e. getting on in years.

181 *barque*: small boat.

183 *periods*: passages of time.

carpet knights: a stay-at-home soldier (restricted to the carpet instead of the battlefield).

lampoons: satires.

188 *side-taking*: i.e. taking sides in the ensuing quarrel.

190 *ingenioust*: most ingenious.

194 *like Amazons*: presumably dressed in armour (Amazons were mythical female warriors who reputedly amputated their right breasts to make it easier for them to hold a bow in battle).

195 *cerecloth*: the winding-sheet wrapped around a corpse.

198 *curioust*: most curious: those who carve most rarely.

Hymen: Greek god of marriage and fertility.

199 *dress my meat*: to prepare or cook food.

200 *blacks*: the black garments worn for mourning.

201 *Inurn*: literally to place a corpse's ashes in an urn.

202 *almoner*: someone who distributes alms (charity).

202 *lodestone*: guiding principle.

204 *dropsy*: a disease which causes retention of fluid.

caudle: warm gruel.

207 *scutcheons*: shield or heraldic device; this can mean an heiress's arms, used metaphorically here to suggest that the widow is available for remarriage.

209 *deatical*: god-like.

211 *jackalato*: chocolate.

sack: sherry.

muskadine: muscat.

besor: bezoar: usually a kind of antidote to poison, here clearly a restorative.

at the drum's head: at public auction (called together by the beating of a drum).

215 *was*: *sic*, the use of the past tense reinforces a sense that *Bell in Campo* was performed (there is no evidence that this was in fact the case).

powdered ermines: white ermine skins covered with black spots.

Newcastle: Margaret's husband William, Duke of Newcastle, who supported her work in many ways, including the provision of prefaces and, as in certain sections of the second part of *Bell in Campo*, some verses for her plays.

216 *glass*: looking-glass, a mirror.

217 *centric*: concentric: i.e. the fire at the centre of the earth.

220 *black pale complexion*: presumably dark (i.e. weatherbeaten) where it is not pale.

221 *fille*: young girl.

anchoret: hermit.

spoon-meats: food for infants.

223 *rasps*: burps.

pippin: apple.

227 *sons*: *sic*, suns, or perhaps meaning the sad thoughts are like the sons she does not have.

228 *sensitives*: animate creatures.

233 *balled*: bald or round.

234 *squibs*: mean, rough (and perhaps small) people.

235 *buskins*: boots.

240 *micrography*: use of microscope.

241 *dioptrical*: anything that uses a lens: Cavendish's treatise is, in particular, an argument directed against Robert Hooke's *Micrographia*.

245 *Tully*: Marcus Tullius Cicero (106–43 BC), Roman philosopher and political commentator famous in the Renaissance for his prose style.

DOROTHY OSBORNE

247 *this place*: Chicksands, the Osborne family home.

Goring House: in London. Osborne and Temple first met on the Isle of Wight in 1648, where her father was governor at the time that Charles I was prisoner on the island in Carisbrook Castle. The meeting at Goring House was one of the rare occasions when the two met during the exchange of letters.

of his: i.e. his liberty: Osborne is referring to a suitor (unidentified) who presses her to marry him and thus lose her liberty.

248 *the gentleman*: throughout the time of Osborne's correspondence with Temple, her family were endeavouring to arrange a marriage for her with someone of wealth: Temple's comparative poverty was the principal reason for their objections to him.

mother-in-law: stepmother.

widower: this (more serious) suitor was Justinian Isham. Osborne's brother was particularly keen on this match.

Sir Thomas's: Sir Thomas Osborne, her cousin.

commended me: Temple was a friend of Sir Thomas Osborne.

249 *that business*: the attempt to marry her to Sir Thomas.

scurvy spleen: melancholy, though seen in physiological terms at the time.

the waters: Osborne went to Epsom, a famous spa town at the time.

a gentleman: identified by Smith as Dr Charles Scarborough.

hold: Osborne is here writing on the reverse side of her page and beginning to run out of space.

age: Osborne was a year older than Temple: she was born in 1627.

250 *posy*: motto.

Cana of Galilee: John 2: 1: 'And the third day there was a marriage in Cana of Galilee; and the mother of Jesus was there.'

Lilly: William Lilly, a famous astrologer.

strange name: Justinian Isham.

your friend: Sir Thomas Osborne.

niceness: fastidiousness.

251 *quinsy*: throat inflammation.

Holland's: Diana Rich, youngest daughter of Henry Rich, Earl of Holland.

carrier: Osborne sent her letters by a carrier who returned with Temple's letters. (She used two carriers who travelled between Campton and London: Harold and Collins.)

252 *humble*: i.e. humble servant: the signature (as with many letters) is missing.

252 *block*: execution block where one would be beheaded.

the widow: her cousin Elizabeth Thorold.

boy: a servant.

friend: her brother Henry.

infusion of steel: an infusion of a steel powder, presumably intended to cure her scurvy spleen.

253 *Mrs Cl.*: identity not established.

Cleopatra: popular French heroic romance by Gautier de Costes de la Calprenède. Like all works in this genre it was extremely long and published in separate parts (Osborne uses the French word 'tome' for 'volume'). Most were translated into English during this time, but Osborne seems always to have read them in the original.

Artemise: a character in *Cleopatra*, as is Britomart, mentioned below.

the journey: Lord L'Isle's embassy to Sweden.

Fortunatus: Smith and Parker insert 'I' before Fortunatus, which is not entirely necessary, though it makes for a more balanced idea. The invisible ring is perhaps originally from Plato's story of Gyges in *The Republic*, while Fortunatus has a cape which transports him anywhere he wants to be in Thomas Dekker's play *The Pleasant Comedy of Old Fortunatus* (1600).

Harry: Harry Danvers.

254 *fellow servant*: Osborne's companion Jane Wright.

recreation: tennis.

Nan: Nan Stacy, perhaps under Osborne's employ, but her exact relationship is not clear.

255 *moped*: glum and listless.

poor boy: no details of this event are available.

my Lady: Lady Diana Rich.

256 *turning*: turning the paper of the letter around in order to write on the side margin.

too: Osborne writes 'to', which might be a mistake (preceding 'tonight', which she writes as 'to night'), or might mean 'too' (i.e. as well as the other attempts to keep them awake).

Lady Newcastle: Osborne's opinion of Margaret Cavendish's writing is often quoted; in context it is less condemnatory than it seems at first sight.

257 *emperor*: Sir Justinian Isham had renewed his suit.

B.: her brother Henry.

258 *courtesies and legs*: the woman's curtsy is responded to by the man's bow.

Mr Freeman: possibly Ralph Freeman

Mr Fish: Humphrey Fysshe.

259 *Cyrus*: another French heroic romance: Madeleine de Scudéry's *Artamène ou le Grand Cyrus*, one of the largest of the genre.

my Lady: Diana Rich is once again the recipient.

Mr B.: apparently Levinus Bennet, another of Osborne's suitors, whose suit was forwarded by her cousin Henry Molle.

Peyton: Dorothy Peyton, daughter of Osborne's sister Anne.

the Term: the beginning of the Law Term.

youngest brother: Robert Osborne.

coming: Osborne had planned a visit to London (which might have involved a meeting with Temple) but this was cancelled because of the arrival of her niece.

cousin: Jane Rant, who married a physician, William Rant.

Lady Carlisle: Lucy Hay (1599–1660); Temple had told Osborne that he thought she was a better writer than Lady Carlisle. Lady Carlisle's marriage to James Hay in 1617 caused a scandal; during the Civil War she was closely connected to Presbyterian interests which wanted to retain the monarchy but remove Charles I.

Isabella: Isabella Rich married James Thynne, but had a notorious affair with the Duke of Ormond.

260 *my Lord Pembroke*: probably Philip Herbert, Earl of Pembroke (see above note to p. 74), at this stage married to Anne Clifford, who eventually lived apart from him when she succeeded to her Westmorland estates and titles. Smith suggests that the reference is to Herbert's son (also Philip), though this seems on balance less likely (here I agree with Parker).

chimical: chemical: deriving from alchemy, in this case perhaps changeable or weak.

my Lord Liec.: Robert Sidney, Earl of Leicester, married Dorothy Percy in 1616.

Penshurst: the Sidney family seat.

261 *bedstaves*: wooden slats holding up bedding.

tabor: drum.

sister: Martha Temple, who ended up living with Dorothy and William after they were married, following the death of her husband two weeks after her marriage in 1662.

the box: a box which carried quince marmalade made by Jane Wright to Temple.

262 *my B. Peyton*: her brother-in-law Thomas Peyton.

263 *disappoint you*: in not going down to London.

Mr Gibson: Revd Edward Gibson, who possibly resided at Chicksands at this time.

263 *Cyrus*: see above. The story mentioned by Osborne here is in tome 5, book 1.

l'honnest homme: a true or reliable man. Like so many of the discussions in the French heroic romances which Osborne commends to Temple, this centres on issues of love and fidelity which were obviously relevant to their current situation.

Lady Car's letter: Lady Carlisle's letter which led to Temple's praise of Osborne (see above).

264 *methinks*: Osborne writes 'my thinks'.

my picture: two portraits of Osborne by Sir Peter Lely are in existence; one is on the cover of Parker's edition.

Lady Sunderland's: Dorothy Sidney (1617–84); Temple knew her from his childhood, some of which was spent with his uncle, who was rector of Penshurst.

Mr T.: i.e. Temple.

Sir Jus.: Justinian Isham.

266 *itself*: Osborne writes 'its self'.

Lady Anne Blunt: she was involved in a petition to Cromwell over a relationship with William Blunt (not a relative), who insisted that he had her promise to marry him despite the fact that her father would not give his permission.

cousin Fr.: Elizabeth Franklin, married to Richard Franklin of Moor Park.

267 *place 'tis in*: Temple was heading for a post in Ireland.

269 *has*: Osborne writers 'beggar's . . . has', so may mean one or a number.

J.B.: James Beverley, a close friend of Temple.

Lady R.: Lady Grey de Ruthin who was marrying Henry Yelverton.

B.P.: her brother-in-law Thomas Peyton.

KATHERINE PHILIPS

270 *Hector Philips*: as this and the following poem describe, Hector was Philips's first child, born on 23 April 1655. In 1656 Philips had a daughter, Katherine, who lived to adulthood.

St Sith's Church: in London, also called St Benet Sherehog. The church was burnt down in the great fire of London and never rebuilt.

Hermes' seal: a hermetic seal, which an alchemist might try to use: after Hermes Trismegistus, supposed founder of alchemy.

Mr Lawes: the composer Henry Lawes (1596–1662); the setting has not survived.

271 *Mrs Mary Awbrey*: her friendship with Philips dated back to their schooldays at Mrs Salmon's school in Hackney; Philips named her Rosania at school.

273 *lieger*: a permanent resident.

Orinda: Philips's own pastoral name; the source is unknown: she became known as the 'matchless Orinda'.

Ardelia: not able to be identified.

1651: Thomas notes, as a context for this poem (particularly line 5), the defeat of Charles I at the battle of Worcester.

274 *Assured*: this echoes Donne's 'A Valediction: Forbidding Mourning': 'Inter-assured of the mind'.

275 *Lucasia*: Anne Owen, to whom Philips wrote twenty poems, this being the first.

Lawes: Lawes's setting survives in his *Second Book of Airs and Dialogues* (1655).

277 *Red-Cross knight*: in Spenser's *The Faerie Queene*, Book I, he is tricked into believing that Duessa is Fidessa.

278 *schools*: philosophical schools in the universities.

279 *love's excess*: Philips tried, and failed, to arrange a match between Anne Owen and Charles Cotterell at this time; Thomas suggests this as a context for the poem.

APHRA BEHN

283 *Mowbray*: Henry Howard, a member of a famous Catholic family, though he himself was Protestant.

284 *lying, peaching and swearing*: 'peaching' = impeaching. The political context for the play is the Popish Plot, which from 1679 to 1681 produced an atmosphere of suspicion amounting to hysteria, sparked by the allegations that began with Titus Oates's manufactured Catholic conspiracy. This went along with the exclusion crisis, which involved attempts to exclude Charles II's brother James, Duke of York (who was Catholic), from accession to the throne after Charles's death. The Whigs supported exclusion; the Tories opposed it. While one would hesitate to call *The City Heiress* Tory propaganda, Behn's satire directed at the Whigs is abundantly clear.

evaded the snare: i.e. the general attack on noble Catholic families fuelled by the allegations of the Popish Plot.

not guilty!: in the House of Lords, Henry Howard voted against the death sentence passed on William Howard, Viscount Stafford—seven other peers who were members of the Howard family voted for the death sentence.

junta: those responsible for fuelling the Popish Plot prosecutions. By the time Behn wrote *The City Heiress*, the Plot had been largely discredited.

weep: *Hamlet*, III. ii.

well received: first performed in April 1682 and published in the same year.

285 *THE ACTORS' NAMES*: Wilding was played by Thomas Betterton; Sir Timothy by James Nokes; Lady Galliard by Elizabeth Barry (who had played Hellena in *The Rover*); Charlotte by Charlotte Butler (a piece of ironic casting given her scandalous reputation).

Commonwealthsmen: as a Whig, Sir Timothy is considered to be a supporter of the pre-Restoration Commonwealth (and therefore disloyal to the crown).

286 *Otway*: Thomas Otway (1652–85), dramatist, was a friend of Behn; his most famous play, *Venice Preserved*, was also performed in 1682.

convenient: Restoration slang for prostitute.

reverend shape: Behn alludes to the originator of the Plot, Titus Oates, who was treated as a figure of great import at the height of his allegations.

swore: much of the impact Oates' story and those who supported it relied upon their sworn testimony, as physical evidence of a conspiracy was lacking.

doctor: Oates claimed he had a doctorate from the university of Salamanca.

Ananias: Acts 5: 5: a common term for a religious hypocrite.

287 *no feast*: Anthony Ashley Cooper, Earl of Shaftesbury (1621–83), was a leading Whig and supporter of the 'truth' of the Popish Plot and of James' exclusion. He and other Whigs had planned a feast for April 1682 (charging a guinea entry), which was forbidden by the king.

sequestrators' hall: where confiscated estates were administered.

bare: without a hat.

pocky doctors: i.e. doctors who would cure the pox (venereal disease).

exchange-men: money-changers who might also deal in creditors' bills.

sempstresses: they sewed clothing.

long bill: i.e. they were prepared to offer Wilding time to pay on the assumption that he would be bailed out by Sir Timothy.

289 *coffee-houses*: supposedly the venue for Whig political discussions.

French King: Louis XIV, who was, of course, Catholic.

old Oliver: Oliver Cromwell; another example of Sir Timothy as a Commonwealth man.

wholesome act: legislation enacted in 1650 made fornication and adultery punishable by 3 months in jail; bawds could be executed on their second offence.

290 *Forty One*: in 1641 conflict between King and Parliament accelerated: this was the year in which Sir Thomas Wentworth, Earl of Strafford, was executed.

bishops' lands: Church lands sequestered during the interregnum and returned at the Restoration.

guttle: flatter.

293 *Whe!*: this expletive is defined by James Fitzmaurice as 'a man's word', although Behn allows some of her female characters to use it (such as Hellena in *The Rover*). Its exact meaning is unclear but it seems to have coarse sexual overtones, particularly in this case. See James Fitzmaurice, 'The Language of Gender and a Textual Problem in Aphra Behn's *The Rover*', *NM* 96 (1995).

once a month: in order to avoid the penalty for being a dissenter.

porridge: the Book of Common Prayer.

conventicling: dissenters attended religious services outside the established Church, such meetings were known as conventicles.

Prester John: supposedly a Christian king who reigned in somewhere like Ethiopia or Abyssinia: i.e. a marvel.

purty: pure (i.e. prim).

294 *city*: London was the centre of both the emotional response to the Popish Plot and of Whig political sentiment.

scrivener: someone who copies out manuscripts.

295 *draw*: a challenge to draw one's sword.

Tory-rory: a 'roaring' or wild Tory.

302 *'Slife*: truncated oath meaning by God's life.

'Owns: by God's wounds.

303 *shifting herself*: changing her clothes.

304 *filthy surgeons Mr Doctor*: i.e. dignified the surgeons (who were treating him for venereal disease) with the more prestigious title of doctor.

305 *dead lift*: an emergency.

chaffer: bargain.

306 *the writings*: which will prove he is his uncle's heir.

mun: man.

307 *quotha*: says he (used scornfully).

pick-thank: sycophant.

309 *keeper*: of a mistress

wrong party: i.e. a Tory.

pit, behind the scenes, and coffee-houses: all fashionable places for wits to be seen at (the first two being in the theatre).

310 *manto*: mantle.

flammed: fobbed off.

Exchange for point: the Exchange was a centre for shops: point = lace.

311 *Lusum*: Lewisham.

312 *bedizen*: dress gaudily (to make her look wealthy).

312 *in ure*: in practice.

betawder: Todd says this is unique to Behn: it clearly means to adorn oneself in a tawdry fashion.

prew: prudish, proper.

conventicle: dissenting religious meeting.

drab: prostitute.

sea-coal-smoke: coal fires were already polluting London at this time.

315 *seditiously petitioning*: this refers to petitions supporting the Exclusion Bill.

316 *towzing*: worrying (like an animal).

317 *souse*: sou: small coin.

318 *swinge*: beat, strike.

320 *association*: there was rumoured to be a conspiratorial Whig 'Association' which included Shaftesbury.

321 *our Party*: the Whigs certainly lost some momentum at the time the play was written, as the allegations behind the Popish Plot began to unravel.

grand-jury-men: such as those who sat in judgment during the Plot.

catechise: question in detail: emended, following Todd, from 'chastise'.

322 *patent*: for a knighthood.

325 *forty-one*: the year Strafford was executed and the Civil War began in earnest.

narrative (under the rose): a secret, conspiratorial narrative.

326 *law by Magna Carta*: ironical reference to what Tories saw as the abuse of common law by Whigs during the period of the Plot.

Ignoramus: a reference to the grand jury verdict when Shaftesbury was accused of treason, i.e. 'we are ignorant' (a refusal to proceed with an accusation).

I love no healths: because they would be drunk to the King.

328 *lack*: alack.

Duke of Albany: James: Sir Timothy is thus being forced to drink a health to the Catholic heir to the throne, whom the Whigs were attempting to exclude.

329 *Mester de Hotel*: *maître d'hôtel*: in this sense, probably meaning the master of the house, rather than the steward.

mobily: the mob.

Polanders: Poland had an elected monarchy: when the crown was vacant in 1673 there were satirical rumours that Shaftesbury hoped to be a candidate.

330 *tantivy-opinions*: wild opinions.

331 *Magistrates*: no pamphlet with this exact title survives, but there were many Tory publications along these lines.

Absolon and Achitophel: Dryden's satirical poem which criticizes Shaftesbury and Monmouth (Charles's illegitimate son, put forward as a potential heir with the exclusion of James from the accession).

332 *vizard*: mask.

Gued deed: Charlotte has assumed a Scottish accent: meaning indeed.

gen: if.

noo: now.

333 *mickle*: much.

sick-like: such-like.

tol: to.

wad: would.

ence: once.

bleether: more blithe.

eyne: eyes.

gleedeth: glideth.

iee: I.

334 *looked babies*: looked closely enough into each other's eyes for them to see their reflections.

337 *song*: the song does not survive.

cher: this might mean cheer or harmonious company.

338 *through-stitched*: complete or thorough.

caper under the triple tree: a hanging.

glass: looking-glass, mirror.

scene draws off: i.e. the sliding flats draw back to reveal the scene.

339 *bonne mien*: good or attractive appearance.

holder forth: a Protestant preacher.

flam: nonsense.

hackney: prostitute.

340 *lampoon*: harsh satire.

met: this is a line from a song, 'The Happy Night', by Buckingham.

342 *fisking and gigiting*: jumping and scampering about.

rakeshame: dissolute person.

345 *ribbon-fool*: presumably someone tricked out in unnecessary finery.

348 *Jack-sauce*: saucy jack = impudent fellow.

toledo: sword: i.e. he will challenge him.

whipping Tom: whipping boy.

348 *Tom Bell*: an ordinary (low) person: i.e. Sir Charles will make her realize what a special person he is.

Messalina's fire: Messalina, third wife of the Roman Emperor Claudius, was renowned for her debauchery.

349 *gorget*: ornamental collar.

354 *nearest way to wood*: possibly this means 'closest way to make love' (an obscure but current meaning of wood).

356 *bare*: Wilding quotes four lines (here and his next speech) from Behn's poem 'The Disappointment' (ironically about impotence: clearly not a problem for Wilding in this instance); see p. 377.

357 *Richard Baxter, Divine*: Richard Baxter (1615–91) was a popular Presbyterian preacher.

358 *plots*: again the whole exchange is an ironic reference to the Popish Plot.

good cause: the Parliamentarians' rallying cry in the Civil War.

360 *crape-gown-orums*: preachers wore crape gowns.

Association: see note to p. 320: Sir Timothy is revealed here as (in Tory eyes) a Whig conspirator. He goes on to stress that Whig London juries will never convict him of treason.

362 *dog Tory*: there is, of course, a slur intended by the dog's name.

black Jack: a large jug of beer.

errant Saracen: Todd notes that this is a quotation from Behn's source play, Middleton's *A Mad World My Masters* (1608) meaning presumably a wild pagan.

364 *kind nose and chin*: i.e. the chin and nose meet.

365 *billet deux*: love letters.

infantas: princesses (but of Spain or Portugal, not Poland).

366 *Music*: i.e. a group of musicians.

chitterling: gut = the strings of the instruments.

367 *breathing*: i.e. fighting.

368 *murrain*: plague.

369 *cully*: the victim of a trick.

rook: cheat.

371 *mumped*: cheated.

372 *lie i'th' dark*: a common 'cure' for madness was to shut the sufferer up in a dark, confined space (e.g. Malvolio in *Twelfth Night*).

374 *'peach*: impeach: i.e. put on trial.

Salamanca: another sly reference to Titus Oates.

375 *Caesar*: the king.

Mrs Boteler: the actress Charlotte Butler.

376 *Trincalo's*: in the Restoration adaptation of *The Tempest*, Caliban has a sister called Sycorax who is chosen as a bride by Trincalo, but Stephano steals her from him.

sprouts: i.e. with the horns of a cuckold.

fee-simple: absolute property.

377 *musquetoon*: a gun.

'*Song*: *Love Armed*': first printed in *Abdelazar* (1677), where it opens the play.

'*The Disappointment*': Todd notes that the poem is an adaptation of a French original. A number of Restoration poems on impotence exist, but all emphasize the male perspective, in contrast to some passages of Behn's poem. For an interesting anonymous example, see 'One Writing Against His Prick', in Harold Love (ed.), *The Penguin Book of Restoration Verse* (Harmondsworth, 1968).

381 *Priapus*: a term for penis, derived from the classical god of procreation.

Daphne: a nymph pursued by Apollo until she turned into a laurel.

382 *feebles*: feebless = feebleness, infirmity.

384 *calenture*: tropical disease affecting sailors with delirium; fever (literal and metaphorical).

385 Behn's answer is to 'A Poem Against Fruition on the Reading in Mountain's Essay' [i.e. Montaigne, Book 2, essay 15, 'Our Desire is Increased By Difficulty']

Ah wretched man! whom neither fate can please
Nor Heavens indulgent to his wish can bless,
Desire torments him, or fruition cloys,
Fruition which shou'd make his bliss, destroys;
Far from our eyes th'enchanting object's set
Advantage by the friendly distance get.
Fruition shows the cheat, and views 'em near,
Then all their borrow'd splendours plain appears
And we what with much care we gain and skill
An empty nothing find, or real ill.
Thus disappointed, our mistaken thought,
Not finding satisfaction which it sought
Renews its search, and with much toil and pain
Most wisely strives to be deceived again
Hurried by our fantastic wild desire
We loath the present, absent things admire.
Those we adore, and fair ideas frame
And those enjoyed we think wou'd quench the flame,
In vain, the ambitious fever still returns
And with redoubled fire more fiercely burns
Our boundless vast desires can know no rest
But travel forward still and labour to be blest

Philosophers and poets strive in vain
The restless anxious progress to restrain
And to their loss soon found their good supreme
An airy notion and a pleasing dream
For happiness is nowhere to be found
But flies the searcher like enchanted ground.
Are we then masters or the slaves of things?
Poor wretched vassals or terrestrial kings?
Left to our reason, and by that betrayed,
We lose a present bliss to catch a shade.
Unsatisfied with beauteous nature's store,
The universal monarch man is only poor.

385 *beboches*: = deboches = debauches.

387 *Hermes, Aphrodite*: a reference to Hermaphroditus, son of Hermes (Mercury) and Aphrodite (Venus), who grew together with the nymph Salmacis while bathing in her fountain, and thus combined male and female sexual characteristics. (Goreau notes that Aphrodite is also a pun on Behn's first name.) Behn's treatment of lesbian desire in this poem may also be related to her use of 'hermaphroditic' self-conceptions elsewhere; e.g. her sense of 'my masculine part, the poet in me' (preface to *The Lucky Chance*).

388 *chaffer*: haggle.

389 *dun*: make demands (usually for money).

390 *Earl of Derwentwater*: Edward Radclyffe (1655–1705), a Tory.

391 *Sam. Briscoe*: posthumous publisher of a number of Behn's works, particularly her fiction.

medlar: a fruit eaten only when almost rotten (i.e. when Autumn turns to Winter).

394 *pinners*: pinafores.

395 *mackins*: by the Mass.

397 *quidlings*: a kind of sweetmeat.

398 *the Jews*: i.e. they (supposedly) did not recognize Jesus because of his humble origins.

401 *afar*: *sic*: from a distance (i.e. without directly interfering?).

Sir Lucius: i.e. Sir Christian will provide 'Peregrina' with a dowry (albeit a small one).

403 *stay*: the last part of the sentence is in need of some correction: Behn may have meant to write 'as long as Sir Christian, his lady, daughter and the rest would stay'.

405 *lived*: *sic*, may be a misprint for 'loved'.

406 *the only like*: *sic*: the sense is clear but again this suggests the uncorrected state of Behn's posthumous fiction.

TEXTUAL NOTES

ISABELLA WHITNEY

The copy-text of 'I.W. to her Unconstant Lover' and 'The Admonition', from *The Copy of a Letter* (1567) is Bodleian Library copy 8o H44(6) Art. Seld., collated with British Library facsimile WP9350/374.

6 *proof*: emended from 'prof'.

The copy-text of 'Will and Testament' from *A Sweet Nosegay* (1573), is British Library C.39.b.45.

AEMILIA LANYER

Copy-texts of *Salve Deus Rex Judaeorum* (1611) are British Library C.71.h.i.5 and Bodleian Vet.A2f.99, collated with the editions of Woods and Purkiss.

42 *especially*: possibly a misprint for 'especial': emended accordingly by Purkiss.

44 *bleeds*: *sic*.

ANNE CLIFFORD

The copy-text of the diary extract is Portland Papers, vol. 23, fos. 80–117, the MS at Longleat House, collated with the editions of Clifford and Acheson.

64 *up for*: emended from Knole MS from 'for up' in Portland MS.

66 *rid*: Acheson mistranscribes this as 'did rid'.

67 *came down*: Acheson omits 'down'.

75 *betwixt*: Acheson transcribes this as 'between'.

MARY WROTH

Love's Victory: because permission to use the more complete Penshurst MS was refused, the copy-text is Huntington Library MS HM600, collated with the Penshurst MS in the edition of Brennan with reference to the edition of Cerasano and Wynne-Davies. Penshurst MS variants indicated by P.; Huntington Library MS by H. (I list only a tiny proportion of the variants; see Brennan's edition.)

84 *passion*: P = passions

85 *sooner*: P = rather.

87 *hearest*: P, H = dearest.

thus: P = thus ever.

88 *Disburdening*: H = unburdening.

90 *end*: P = ends.

91 *sport*: P, H = mirth.

why: P, H = how.

100 *What*: P = How.

their: P.

105 *rather*: P, H = now have.

106 *would joy more*: P, H = yet joy most.

110 *move*: P = prove; in this case, H seems a clearly superior reading.

113 *distressed*: P = desire.

129 *yielding*: P = humble.

There are two sources for the sonnet sequence 'Pamphilia to Amphilanthus': an autograph MS (Folger V.a.104) and the printed text at the end of her prose romance *Urania* (1621), cited here as F and U. I follow the edition of Roberts in making the *Urania* version the copy-text for the sonnets; the numbers are those given to the sonnets in the sequence as published (a different order to the MS). The copy-text is the Roberts edition collated with the published *Urania* texts British Library 86.h.9 and G.2422 and Bodleian M 5.6 (2) Art.

134 *received's*: F (U has 'receiv'd').

of: F = 'do'.

choose as: F = 'is their'.

sweet: F = dear.

for: F = 'with'.

135 *mine*: F = 'my'.

their: F = 'the'.

a show: F = 'the mask'.

when: F = 'where'.

passions: F = 'longings'.

ELEANOR DAVIES

The copy-text of *The Benediction* (1651) is the three identical Cambridge University Library copies collated with Bodleian 12 Ø 1336 (4), British Library 1389.8.49, and the Cope edition.

137 *bow*: emended from BL 486.f.2; copy-text has 'that general's thundering donative his the Crown'.

The copy-text of *Revelations* (1649) is Bodleian 12 Ø1336 (2) collated with the Cope edition.

Revelations: this is handwritten in copy-text.

139 *then*: emended from 'when'.

140 *of*: hand corrected from 'by' in other versions.

order of the prophets: hand written in the margin.

of: hand corrected from 'this'.

PRISCILLA COTTON AND MARY COLE

The copy-text of *To the Priests and People of England* (1655) is British Library E.854 (13), collated with Bodleian 110.j.241 (13).

HESTER BIDDLE

The copy-text of *The Trumpet of the Lord Sounded Forth* (1662) is British Library 4103.c.6, collated with Bodleian C 117 (32).

159 *woman*: emended from 'women'.

you: emended from 'your'.

MARGARET CAVENDISH

Cavendish made many changes to the texts of her poems, including handwritten corrections in some individual copies, and more substantially between the three main editions of *Poems and Fancies*: 1653, 1664, and 1668. I have only indicated some key variants (the text of 'The Hunting of the Hare' changes quite significantly between 1653 and 1664). In all three poems I take 1664 as my copy-text: the second edition of 1664 Cambridge University Library P*.3.14 (C), collated with Bodleian Library AA 141 Th, Seld. and Douce C subt. 17; Merton College Oxford 37 G. 20; British Library 19054; also collated with 1653 first edition Cambridge University Library P*.3.19 (1) (C) and 9720.a.188; Bodleian Library P1 22 Jus. Sel. and Harding C 3737; British Library 79.h.10 and C.39.h.27 (1); and with 1668 third edition Bodleian Vet. A3c.125 and British Library C.111.g.4.

167 *knit*: 1653 = 'They there remain, lie close, and faste will stick'.

168 *neither superior*: 1653 = 'no superiority'.

palaces: 1653 = 'stately palaces'.

obliquely: 1653 = 'Glaring obliquely with his great grey eyes'.

lies: 1653 = 'Then back returns down in his form he lies'.

169 *there*: 1653 = 'Thinks every shadow still the dogs they were'.

their cry: 1653 = 'the noise'.

touch: 1653 = 'Starting with fear up leaps then doth he run, / And with such speed the ground scarce treads upon'.

170 *spy*: 1653 = 'Thus they so fast came on, with such loud cries, / That he no hopes hath left, nor help espies'.

back: 1653 = 'Thus quick industry, that is not slack, / Is like to witchery, brings lost things back'.

a: 1653 = 'such'.

men did shout: 1653 = 'hunters shout'.

men do: 1653 = 'man doth'.

others': 1653 = 'And appetite, that feeds on'.

say: 1653 = 'To kill poor sheep, straight say'

171 *more*: 1653 = 'them'.

make: 1653 = 'Destroy those lifes that God saw good to make'.

live: 1653 = 'And is so proud, thinks only he shall live'.

The copy-text for *Bel in Campo* is from *Plays* (1662) Cambridge University Library P*3.13 (C), collated with Bodleian Library Harding D 558 and AA.139 Th.Seld, Merton College Oxford Stack 110c2, and British Library G.19053, C.102.k.9 and 17.1.14.

173 *an*: emended from 'a'.

200 *your*: emended from 'you'.

204 *Madam*: emended from 'Lady'.

211 *takes*: emended from 'take'.

215 *her*: emended from 'he'.

223 *digests not well*: Huntington Library copy has a row of asterisks instead of this phrase, which is in the copies in the Bodleian, Cambridge, and British Libraries.

The copy-text for the Preface to *Observations* is the second edition (1668), British Library L.35/61, collated with Bodleian Library C.4.15 and with the first edition of 1666, British Library 31.f.4 Art.

The copy-text of 'The Matrimonial Agreement' is the second edition of *Nature's Pictures* (1671), British Library 8407.h.12 collated with the first edition (1656), British Library 841.m.25 and G.11599 and Bodleian Library fo. BS 159. There are many variants from the first edition (1656) and I have only noted a few of particular interest.

242 *afore*: 1656 = 'as could be'

243 *loss*: 1656 = 'absence'.

kissed: 1656 = 'kissed her'.

244 *was persuaded*: 1656 = 'being persuaded'.

the most of her: 1656 = 'so much of her'.

his and her: 1656 = 'her and his'.

conscience: 1656 = 'confidence' (in both instances).

245 *fair end*: 1656 = 'fair end etc.'.

The copy-text of 'Of a Civil War' from *The World's Olio* (1655) is British Library 90.e.19 collated with 841.m.22, Bodleian Library Douce.c.subt. 16, and the second edition of 1671 British Library 8407.h.11.

DOROTHY OSBORNE

The copy-text of the letters is British Library Add. MS 33975, collated with the Smith and Parker editions.

252 *the*: in MS but omitted by Parker (present in Smith).

not: not in MS, emended following Parker and Smith.

KATHERINE PHILIPS

The copy-texts are the MSS detailed below, collated with the edition of Thomas, the published *Poems* (1664), Bodleian Library 1664: 80 P31 (2) Art. BS, and *Poems* (1667) British Library 83.1.3, and Bodleian K.4.19Art.

The copy-text of 'Epitaph: On Hector Philips' is National Library of Wales MS 776 (Thomas's MS B).

The copy-text of 'On the Death of My First and Dearest Child' follows National Library of Wales MS 775 Thomas's MS A and 1667 *Poems*.

271 *touch*: MS, printed texts read 'pluck'.

The copy-text of 'To Mrs Mary Awbrey at Parting' is University of Texas MS 151 Philips 14,937 (Thomas's MS D).

273 *shall*: Cardiff City Library MS reads 'Our spirits shall united'.

Rosania: Cardiff reads 'Here lies Orinda and Rosania'.

The copy-text of 'A Retired Friendship: To Ardelia' is Thomas's MS A.

The copy-text of 'To My Excellent Lucasia On Our Friendship' is Thomas's MS A.

275 *Friendship*: MS B reads 'on our mutual friendship'.

The copy-text of 'Friendship's Mysteries: To My Dearest Lucasia' is Thomas's MS A.

The copy-text of 'Content: To My Dearest Lucasia' is Thomas's MS A.

278 *far's*: emended from 1664 printed text; MS has 'far'.

either: emended from 'eithers' following Thomas.

The copy-text of 'Orinda to Lucasia: Parting, October 1661, at London' is 1667 *Poems*.

280 *sorrows*: emended, following Saintsbury and Thomas, from 'sorrow'.

The copy-text of 'Orinda to Lucasia' is 1667 *Poems*.

APHRA BEHN

The copy-text of *The City Heiress* is the first edition of 1682, Cambridge University Library, Brett-Smith 55, collated with Cambridge Brett-Smith 56, Sel.2.123 (27), British Library 644.g.13, Bodleian Malone 104 (1), collated with second edition (1698), British Library 644.g.14, Bodleian Holk.d.20 (3) and Malone B 270 (6), and collated with the Todd edition.

298 *Charles*: emended from Sir Anthony, following Todd.

The copy-texts for the poems are *Poems Upon Several Occasions* (1684), referred to as PSO, British Library 1078.18, and *Lycidus* (1688), British Library 11626.66, collated with Bodleian 2799.e.345, and collated with the Todd edition. The text for 'Song: Love Armed' is from PSO; 'The Disappointment' is from PSO (first published in Rochester's *Poems on Several Occasions* (1680), it was misattributed to him); 'On Desire' is from *Lycidus*; 'To Alexis' is from *Lycidus*; 'To The Fair Clarinda' is from *Lycidus*; 'To Alexis, On His Saying . . .' is from *Lycidus*; 'To Lysander on Some Verses He Writ' is from PSO.

The copy-text for *The Wandering Beauty* is *Histories, Novels and Translations* (1700), British Library 1508/432, collated with Huntington Library 345817 on microfilm, and the Todd edition.

392 *friend*: Todd has 'friends'.

401 *if*: emended from 'is'.

daughter: emended from 'led by Madam Peregrina, your daughter'.

403 *do*: not in copy-text.

406 *why*: 'the' in copy-text deleted.

attend: not in copy-text; emended for sense.

A SELECTION OF **OXFORD WORLD'S CLASSICS**

	An Anthology of Elizabethan Prose Fiction
	An Anthology of Seventeenth-Century Fiction
	Early Modern Women's Writing
	Three Early Modern Utopias (Utopia; New Atlantis; The Isle of Pines)
Francis Bacon	Essays
Aphra Behn	Oroonoko and Other Writings The Rover and Other Plays
John Bunyan	Grace Abounding The Pilgrim's Progress
John Donne	The Major Works Selected Poetry
Ben Jonson	The Alchemist and Other Plays The Devil is an Ass and Other Plays Five Plays
John Milton	Selected Poetry
Sir Philip Sidney	The Old Arcadia
Izaak Walton	The Compleat Angler

A SELECTION OF **OXFORD WORLD'S CLASSICS**

	The Anglo-Saxon World
	Beowulf
	Lancelot of the Lake
	The Paston Letters
	Sir Gawain and the Green Knight
	Tales of the Elders of Ireland
	York Mystery Plays
GEOFFREY CHAUCER	**The Canterbury Tales** **Troilus and Criseyde**
HENRY OF HUNTINGDON	**The History of the English People 1000–1154**
JOCELIN OF BRAKELOND	**Chronicle of the Abbey of Bury St Edmunds**
GUILLAUME DE LORRIS and JEAN DE MEUN	**The Romance of the Rose**
WILLIAM LANGLAND	**Piers Plowman**
SIR THOMAS MALORY	**Le Morte Darthur**

A SELECTION OF OXFORD WORLD'S CLASSICS

	Bhagavad Gita
	The Bible Authorized King James Version *With Apocrypha*
	Dhammapada
	Dharmasūtras
	The Koran
	The Pañcatantra
	The Sauptikaparvan (from the Mahabharata)
	The Tale of Sinuhe and Other Ancient Egyptian Poems
	Upaniṣads
ANSELM OF CANTERBURY	**The Major Works**
THOMAS AQUINAS	**Selected Philosophical Writings**
AUGUSTINE	**The Confessions** **On Christian Teaching**
BEDE	**The Ecclesiastical History**
HEMACANDRA	**The Lives of the Jain Elders**
KĀLIDĀSA	**The Recognition of Śakuntalā**
MANJHAN	**Madhumalati**
ŚĀNTIDEVA	**The Bodhicaryāvatāra**

A SELECTION OF **OXFORD WORLD'S CLASSICS**

	Classical Literary Criticism
	The First Philosophers: The Presocratics and the Sophists
	Greek Lyric Poetry
	Myths from Mesopotamia
APOLLODORUS	The Library of Greek Mythology
APOLLONIUS OF RHODES	Jason and the Golden Fleece
APULEIUS	The Golden Ass
ARISTOPHANES	Birds and Other Plays
ARISTOTLE	The Nicomachean Ethics Physics Politics
BOETHIUS	The Consolation of Philosophy
CAESAR	The Civil War The Gallic War
CATULLUS	The Poems of Catullus
CICERO	Defence Speeches The Nature of the Gods On Obligations The Republic and The Laws
EURIPIDES	Bacchae and Other Plays Medea and Other Plays Orestes and Other Plays The Trojan Women and Other Plays
GALEN	Selected Works
HERODOTUS	The Histories
HOMER	The Iliad The Odyssey

A SELECTION OF OXFORD WORLD'S CLASSICS

Thomas Aquinas	**Selected Philosophical Writings**
Francis Bacon	**The Essays**
Walter Bagehot	**The English Constitution**
George Berkeley	**Principles of Human Knowledge and Three Dialogues**
Edmund Burke	**A Philosophical Enquiry into the Origin of Our Ideas of the Sublime and Beautiful** **Reflections on the Revolution in France**
Confucius	**The Analects**
Émile Durkheim	**The Elementary Forms of Religious Life**
Friedrich Engels	**The Condition of the Working Class in England**
James George Frazer	**The Golden Bough**
Sigmund Freud	**The Interpretation of Dreams**
Thomas Hobbes	**Human Nature and De Corpore Politico** **Leviathan**
David Hume	**Selected Essays**
Niccolo Machiavelli	**The Prince**
Thomas Malthus	**An Essay on the Principle of Population**
Karl Marx	**Capital** **The Communist Manifesto**
J. S. Mill	**On Liberty and Other Essays** **Principles of Political Economy and Chapters on Socialism**
Friedrich Nietzsche	**Beyond Good and Evil** **The Birth of Tragedy** **On the Genealogy of Morals** **Twilight of the Idols**

	Six French Poets of the Nineteenth Century
Honoré de Balzac	Cousin Bette Eugénie Grandet Père Goriot
Charles Baudelaire	The Flowers of Evil The Prose Poems and Fanfarlo
Benjamin Constant	Adolphe
Denis Diderot	Jacques the Fatalist
Alexandre Dumas (père)	The Black Tulip The Count of Monte Cristo Louise de la Vallière The Man in the Iron Mask La Reine Margot The Three Musketeers Twenty Years After The Vicomte de Bragelonne
Alexandre Dumas (fils)	La Dame aux Camélias
Gustave Flaubert	Madame Bovary A Sentimental Education Three Tales
Victor Hugo	Notre-Dame de Paris
J.-K. Huysmans	Against Nature
Pierre Choderlos de Laclos	Les Liaisons dangereuses
Mme de Lafayette	The Princesse de Clèves
Guillaume du Lorris and Jean de Meun	The Romance of the Rose

A SELECTION OF **OXFORD WORLD'S CLASSICS**

GUY DE MAUPASSANT	**A Day in the Country and Other Stories** **A Life** **Bel-Ami** **Mademoiselle Fifi and Other Stories** **Pierre et Jean**
PROSPER MÉRIMÉE	**Carmen and Other Stories**
MOLIÈRE	**Don Juan and Other Plays** **The Misanthrope, Tartuffe, and Other Plays**
BLAISE PASCAL	**Pensées and Other Writings**
JEAN RACINE	**Britannicus, Phaedra, and Athaliah**
ARTHUR RIMBAUD	**Collected Poems**
EDMOND ROSTAND	**Cyrano de Bergerac**
MARQUIS DE SADE	**The Misfortunes of Virtue and Other Early Tales**
GEORGE SAND	**Indiana**
MME DE STAËL	**Corinne**
STENDHAL	**The Red and the Black** **The Charterhouse of Parma**
PAUL VERLAINE	**Selected Poems**
JULES VERNE	**Around the World in Eighty Days** **Journey to the Centre of the Earth** **Twenty Thousand Leagues under the Seas**
VOLTAIRE	**Candide and Other Stories** **Letters concerning the English Nation**

A SELECTION OF **OXFORD WORLD'S CLASSICS**

	Eirik the Red and Other Icelandic Sagas
	The German-Jewish Dialogue
	The Kalevala
	The Poetic Edda
LUDOVICO ARIOSTO	**Orlando Furioso**
GIOVANNI BOCCACCIO	**The Decameron**
GEORG BÜCHNER	**Danton's Death, Leonce and Lena, and Woyzeck**
LUIS VAZ DE CAMÕES	**The Lusiads**
MIGUEL DE CERVANTES	**Don Quixote** **Exemplary Stories**
CARLO COLLODI	**The Adventures of Pinocchio**
DANTE ALIGHIERI	**The Divine Comedy** **Vita Nuova**
LOPE DE VEGA	**Three Major Plays**
J. W. VON GOETHE	**Elective Affinities** **Erotic Poems** **Faust: Part One and Part Two** **The Flight to Italy**
E. T. A. HOFFMANN	**The Golden Pot and Other Tales**
HENRIK IBSEN	**An Enemy of the People, The Wild Duck, Rosmersholm** **Four Major Plays** **Peer Gynt**
LEONARDO DA VINCI	**Selections from the Notebooks**
FEDERICO GARCIA LORCA	**Four Major Plays**
MICHELANGELO BUONARROTI	**Life, Letters, and Poetry**